Hough Miller

Tales and sketches

Hough Miller

Tales and sketches

ISBN/EAN: 9783337137540

Printed in Europe, USA, Canada, Australia, Japan

Cover: Foto ©Andreas Hilbeck / pixelio.de

More available books at **www.hansebooks.com**

TALES AND SKETCHES.

TALES AND SKETCHES.

BY

HUGH MILLER,

AUTHOR OF

"THE OLD RED SANDSTONE," "MY SCHOOLS AND SCHOOLMASTERS,"
"THE TESTIMONY OF THE ROCKS," ETC.

EDITED, WITH A PREFACE,

BY

MRS. MILLER.

BOSTON:
GOULD AND LINCOLN,
59 WASHINGTON STREET.
NEW YORK: SHELDON AND COMPANY.
CINCINNATI: GEORGE S. BLANCHARD.
1863.

PREFACE.

THE following "Tales and Sketches" were written at an early period of the author's career, during the first years of his married life, before he had attempted to carry any part of the world on his shoulders in the shape of a public newspaper, and found it by no means a comfortable burden. Yet possibly the period earlier still, when he produced his "Scenes and Legends," had been more favorable for a kind of writing which required in any measure the exercise of the imagination. The change to him was very great, from a life of constant employment in the open air, amid the sights and sounds of nature, to "the teasing monotony of one which tasked his intellectual powers without exercising them." Hence, partly, it may be imagined, the intensity of his sympathy with the poet Ferguson. The greater number of these Tales were composed literally over the midnight lamp, after returning late in the evening from a long day's work over the ledger and the balance-sheet. Tired though he was, his mind could not stagnate — he *must write*. I do not mention these

1*

circumstances at all by way of apology. It has struck me, indeed, that the Tales are nearly all of a pensive or tragical cast, and that in congenial circumstances they might have had a more, joyous and elastic tone, in keeping with a healthier condition of the nervous system. Yet their defects must undoubtedly belong to the mind of their author. I am far from being under the delusion that he was, or was ever destined to be, a Walter Scott or Charles Dickens. The faculties of plot and drama, which find their scope in the story and the novel, were among the weakest, instead of the strongest, of his powers. Yet I am deceived if the lovers and students of Hugh Miller's Works will not find in the "Tales and Sketches" some matter of special interest. In the first three there are, I think, glimpses into his own inner life, such as he, with most men of reserved and dignified character, would choose rather to personify in another than to make a parade of in their own person, when coming forward avowedly to write of themselves. And, then, if he could have held a conversation with Robert Burns, so that all the world might hear, I think there are few who would not have listened with some curiosity. In his " Recollections of Burns " we have his own side of such conversation ; for it seems evident that it is himself that he has set to travelling and talking in the person of Mr. Lindsay.

But of Burns's share in the dialogue the reader is the best judge. Some may hold that he is too like Hugh Miller himself, — too philosophic in idea, and too pure in sentiment. In regard to this, we can only remind such that Burns's prose was not like his poetry, nor his ideal like his actual life.

Unquestionably my husband had a very strong sympathy with many points in the character of Burns. His thorough integrity ; his noble independence, which disdained to place his honest opinions at the mercy of any man or set of men ; his refusal to barter his avowal of the worth and dignity of man for the smiles and patronage of the great, even after he had tasted the sweets of their society, which is a very different matter from such avowal *before* that time, if any one will fairly think of it, — all this, with the acknowledged sovereignty of the greater genius, made an irresistible bond of brotherhood between Miller and Burns. But to the grosser traits of the poet's character my husband's eyes were perfectly open ; and grieved indeed should I be if it could for a moment be supposed that he lent the weight of his own purer moral character to the failings, and worse than failings, of the other. Over these he mourned, he grieved. I believe he would at any time have given the life of his body for the life of his brother's soul. Above all, he deplored that the all-prevailing power of Christian love was never brought to bear on the heart of this greatest of Scotland's sons. If Thomas Chalmers had been in the place of Russell, who knows what might have been ? But, doubtless, God in his providence had wise purposes to serve. It is often by such instruments that he scourges and purifies his church. For let us not forget, that scenes such as are depicted in the " Holy Fair," however painful to our better feelings, were strictly and literally *true*. This I have myself heard from an eye-witness, who could not have been swayed by any leanings towards the anti-puritan side; and, doubtless, many others are aware of testimony on the same side of equal weight.

We may hope that the time is passing away when the more exceptionable parts of Burns's character and writings are capable of working mischief, at least among the higher and middle classes. It is cause of thankfulness that in regard to such, and with him as with others, there is a sort of purifying process going on, which leaves the higher and finer elements of genius to float buoyantly, and fulfil their own destiny in the universal plan, while the grosser are left to sink like lead in the mighty waters. Thus it is in those portions of society already refined and elevated. But there is yet a portion of the lower strata where midnight orgies continue to prevail, and where every idea of pleasure is connected with libertinism and the bottle; and there the worst productions of Burns are no doubt still rife, and working as a deadly poison. Even to a superior class of working-men, who are halting between two opinions, there is danger from the very mixture of good and evil in the character and writings of the poet. They cannot forget that he who wrote

> " The cock may craw, the day may daw,
>
> Yet still we 'll taste the barley bree,"

wrote likewise the immortal song,

> "A man 's a man for a' that";

and they determine, or are in danger of determining, to follow the object of their worship with no halting step. Doubtless political creed and the accidents of birth still color the individual estimate of Burns and his writings. It is but of late that we have seen society torn, on occasion of the centenary of the poet, by conflicting opinion as to the propriety of observing it; and many would fain have it supposed that the religious and anti-religious world were ranged on opposite sides. But it was not so. There were thoroughly good and religious men, self-made, who could not forget that Burns had been the champion of their order, and had helped to win for them respect by the power of his genius; while there were others — religious men of old family — who could remember nothing but his faults. I remember spending one or two evenings about that time in the society of a well-born, earnestly religious, and highly estimable gentleman, who reprobated Burns, and scoffed at the idea that a man *could* be a man for a' that. He might belong to a limited class; for well I know that among peers there are as ardent admirers of Burns as among peasants. All I would say is, that even religious feelings may take edge and bitterness from other causes. But to the other class — those who from loyalty and gratitude are apt to follow Burns too far — well I know that my husband would have said, "Receive all genius as the gift of God, but never let it be to you *as* God. It ought never to supersede the exercise of your own moral sense, nor can it ever take the place of the only infallible guide, the Word of God."

But I beg the reader's pardon for digressing thus, when I ought to be pursuing the proper business of a preface, which is, to state any explanatory circumstances that may be necessary in connection with the work in hand.

The "Recollections of Ferguson" are exquisitely painful — so much so that I would fain have begun with something brighter ; but these two contributions being the most important, and likewise the first in order of a series, they seemed to fall into the beginning as their natural place. I have gone over the Life of Ferguson, which the reader may do for himself, to see whether there is any exaggeration in the " Recollections." I find them all perfectly faithful to the facts. The neglected bard, the stone cell, the straw pallet, the stone paid for by a brother bard out of his own straitened means are not flattering to the " Embro' Gentry"; but amid a great deal of flattery, a little truth is worth remembering. On the other hand it rejoices one to think that Ferguson's death-bed, on the heavenward side, was not dark. The returning reason, the comforts of the Word of Life, are glimpses of God's providence and grace that show gloriously amid the otherwise outer darkness of those depths.

The sort of literature of superstition revived or retained in " The Lykewake," there are a great many good people who think the world would be better without.

It chanced to me some three years ago, when residing in a sea-bathing village, and sitting one day on a green turf-bank overlooking the sea, to hear a conversation in which this point was brought very prominently forward. A party consisting of a number of young people, accompanied by their papa, a young French lady, who was either governess or friend, and a gentleman in the garb of a clergyman, cither friend or tutor, seated themselves very near me; and it was proposed by the elder gentleman that a series of stories should be told for the amusement and edification of the young people. A set of stories and anecdotes were accordingly begun, and very pleasingly told, chiefly by the clergyman, friend or tutor. Among others was a fairy tale entitled " Green Sleeves," to which the name of Hugh Miller was appended, and which evoked great applause from the younger members of the party, but regarding which the verdict of papa, very emphatically delivered, was, " *I approve of faries neither in green sleeves nor white sleeves.* However, "— after a pause, during which he seemed to be revolving in his mind any possible use for the like absurdities, — " they may serve to show us the blessings of the more enlightened times in which we live, when schools for the young, and sciences for all ages, have banished such things from the world." So, with this utilitarian view of the subject let us rest satisfied, unless we are of. those who, feeling that the human mind is a harp of many strings, believe that it is none the worse for having the music of even its minor chords awakened at times by a skilful hand.

I am unable to say whether " Bill Whyte " be a real story, ever narrated by a *bona fide* tinker of the name, or no. I am rather inclined to think that it is not, because I recognize in it several incidents drawn from " Uncle Sandy's " Experiences in Egypt, such as the hovering of the flight of birds, scared and terrified, over the smoke and noise of battle, the encampment in the midst of a host of Turks' bones, etc.

With the " Young Surgeon " I was myself acquainted. It is a sketch strictly true.

" The Story of the Scotch Merchant of the Eighteenth Century," which also is a true story, was written originally at the request of a near relative of Mr. Forsyth, for private circulation among a few friends, and is now for the first time given to the public by the kind consent of the surviving relatives.

CONTENTS.

I.

RECOLLECTIONS OF FERGUSON.

II.

RECOLLECTIONS OF BURNS.

2

III.

THE SALMON-FISHER OF UDOLL.

IV.

THE WIDOW OF DUNSKAITH.

V.

THE LYKEWAKE.

VI.

BILL WHYTE.

VII.

THE YOUNG SURGEON;

VIII.

GEORGE ROSS, THE SCOTCH AGENT;

IX.

M'CULLOCH THE MECHANICIAN;

X.

THE SCOTCH MERCHANT OF THE EIGHTEENTH CENTURY.

TALES AND SKETCHES.

I.

RECOLLECTIONS OF FERGUSON.

CHAPTER I.

Of Ferguson, the bauld and slee.
BURNS.

I HAVE, I believe, as little of the egotist in my composition as most men; nor would I deem the story of my life, though by no means unvaried by incident, of interest enough to repay the trouble of either writing or perusing it were it the story of my one life only; but, though an obscure man myself, I have been singularly fortunate in my friends. The party-colored tissue of my recollections is strangely interwoven, if I may so speak, with pieces of the domestic history of men whose names have become as familiar to our ears as that of our country itself; and I have been induced to struggle with the delicacy which renders one unwilling to speak much of one's self, and to overcome the dread of exertion natural to a period of life greatly advanced, through a desire of preserving to my countrymen a few notices, which would otherwise be lost to them, of two of their greatest favor-

2*

ites. I could once reckon among my dearest and most familiar friends, Robert Burns and Robert Ferguson.

It is now rather more than sixty years since I studied for a few weeks at the University of St. Andrews. I was the son of very poor parents, who resided in a seaport town on the west coast of Scotland. My father was a house-carpenter, — a quiet, serious man, of industrious habits and great simplicity of character, but miserably depressed in his circumstances through a sickly habit of body. My mother was a warm-hearted, excellent woman, endowed with no ordinary share of shrewd good sense and sound feeling, and indefatigable in her exertions for my father and the family. I was taught to read, at a very early age, by an old woman in the neighborhood, — such a person as Shenstone describes in his "Schoolmistress," —and, being naturally of a reflective turn, I had begun, long ere I had attained my tenth year, to derive almost my sole amusement from books. I read incessantly; and, after exhausting the shelves of all the neighbors, and reading every variety of work that fell in my way, — from the "Pilgrim's Progress" of Bunyan, and the "Gospel Sonnets" of Erskine, to a "Treatise on Fortification" by Vauban, and the "History of the Heavens" by the Abbé Pluche, — I would have pined away for lack of my accustomed exercise, had not a benevolent baronet in the neighborhood, for whom my father occasionally wrought, taken a fancy to me, and thrown open to my perusal a large and well-selected library. Nor did his kindness terminate until, after having secured to me all of learning that the parish afforded, he had settled me, now in my seventeenth year, at the University.

Youth is the season of warm friendships and romantic wishes and hopes. We say of the child in its first attempts to totter along the wall, or when it has first learned to rise beside its mother's knee, that it is yet too weak to stand alone; and we may employ the same language in describing a young and ardent mind. It is, like the child, too weak to stand alone, and anxiously seeks out some kindred mind on which to lean. I had had my intimates at school, who, though of no very superior cast, had served me, if I may so speak, as resting-places when wearied with my studies, or when I had exhausted my lighter reading; and now, at St. Andrews, where I knew no one, I began to experience the unhappiness of an unsatisfied sociality. My school-fellows were mostly stiff, illiterate lads, who, with a little bad Latin and worse Greek, plumed themselves mightily on their scholarship, and I had little inducement to form any intimacies among them; for of all men the ignorant scholar is the least amusing. Among the students of the upper classes, however, there was at least one individual with whom I longed to be acquainted. He was apparently much about my own age, rather below than above the middle size, and rather delicately than robustly formed; but I have rarely seen a more elegant figure or more interesting face. His features were small, and there was what might perhaps be deemed a too feminine delicacy in the whole contour; but there was a broad and very high expansion of forehead, which, even in those days, when we were acquainted with only the phrenology taught by Plato, might be regarded as the index of a capacious and powerful mind; and the brilliant light of his large black eyes seemed to give earnest of its activity.

"Who, in the name of wonder, is that?" I inquired of a class-fellow, as this interesting-looking young man passed me for the first time.

"A clever but very unsettled fellow from Edinburgh," replied the lad; "a capital linguist, for he gained our first bursary three years ago; but our Professor says he is certain he will never do any good. He cares nothing for the company of scholars like himself, and employs himself — though he excels, I believe, in English composition — in writing vulgar Scotch rhymes, like Allan Ramsay. His name is Robert Ferguson."

I felt from this moment a strong desire to rank among the friends of one who cared nothing for the company of such men as my class-fellow, and who, though acquainted with the literature of England and Rome, could dwell with interest on the simple poetry of his native country.

There is no place in the neighborhood of St. Andrews where a leisure hour may be spent more agreeably than among the ruins of the cathedral. I was not slow in discovering the eligibilities of the spot, and it soon became one of my favorite haunts. One evening, a few weeks after I had entered on my course at college, I had seated myself among the ruins, in a little ivied nook fronting the setting sun, and was deeply engaged with the melancholy Jaques in the forest of Ardennes, when, on hearing a light footstep, I looked up, and saw the Edinburgh student, whose appearance had so interested me, not four yards away. He was busied with his pencil and his tablets, and muttering, as he went, in a half-audible voice, what, from the inflection of the tones, seemed to be verse. On seeing me, he started, and apologizing in a few hurried but courteous words for what he termed the involuntary intrusion, would have passed, but, on my rising and stepping up to him, he stood.

"I am afraid, Mr. Ferguson," I said, 'tis I who owe *you* an apology; the ruins have long been yours, and I am but an intruder. But you must pardon me; I have often heard of them in the west, where they are hallowed, even more than they are here, from their connection with the history of some of our noblest Reformers; and, besides, I see no place in the neighborhood where Shakspeare can be read to more advantage."

"Ah," said he, taking the volume out of my hand, "a reader of Shakspeare and an admirer of Knox! I question whether the heresiarch and the poet had much in common."

"Nay, now, Mr. Ferguson," I replied, "you are too true a Scot to question that. They had much, very much, in common. Knox was no rude Jack Cade, but a great and powerful-minded man; decidedly as much so as any of the noble conceptions of the dramatist, his Cæsars, Brutuses, or Othellos. Buchanan could have told you that he had even much of the spirit of the poet in him, and wanted only the art. And just remember how Milton speaks of him in his 'Areopagitica.' Had the poet of 'Paradise Lost' thought regarding him as it has become fashionable to think and speak now, he would hardly have apostrophized him as *Knox, the reformer of a nation, — a great man animated by the Spirit of God.*"

"Pardon me," said the young man; "I am little acquainted with the prose writings of Milton, and have, indeed, picked up most of my opinions of Knox at second-hand. But I have read his *merry* account of the murder of Beaton, and found nothing to alter my preconceived notions of him from either the matter or manner of the narrative. Now that I think of it, however, my opinion of Bacon would be no very adequate one were it formed solely from the extract of his history of Henry VII. given by Kames in his late publication. Will you not extend your walk?"

We quitted the ruins together, and went sauntering along the shore. There was a rich sunset glow on the water, and the hills that rise on the opposite side of the Frith stretched their undulating line of azure under a gorgeous canopy of crimson and gold. My companion pointed to the scene. "These glorious clouds," he said, "are but wreaths of vapor, and these lovely hills accumulations of earth and stone. And it is thus with all the past, — with the past of our own little histories, that borrows so much of its golden beauty from the medium through which we survey it; with the past too of all history. There is poetry in the remote; the bleak hill seems a darker firmament, and the chill wreath of vapor a river of fire. And you, Sir, seem to have contemplated the history of our stern Reformers through this poetical medium, till you forget that the poetry was not in them, but in that through which you surveyed them."

"Ah, Mr. Ferguson," I replied, "you must permit me to make a distinction. I acquiesce fully in the justice of your remark: the analogy, too, is nice and striking; but I would fain carry it a little further. Every eye can see the beauty of the remote; but there is beauty in the near, an interest at least, which every eye cannot see. Each of the thousand little plants that spring up at our feet has an interest and beauty to the botanist; the mineralogist would find something to engage him in every little stone. And it is thus with the poetry of life; all have a sense of it in the remote and the distant, but it is only the men who stand high in the art, its men of profound science, that can discover it in the near. The *mediocre* poet shares but the commoner gift, and so he seeks his themes in ages or countries far removed from his own; whilst the man of nobler powers, knowing that all nature is instinct with poetry, seeks and finds it in the men and scenes in his immediate neighborhood. As to our Reformers"—

"Pardon me," said the young poet; "the remark strikes me, and, ere we lose it in something else, I must furnish you with an illustration. There is an acquaintance of mine, a lad much about my own age, greatly addicted to the study of poetry. He has been making verses all his life-long: he began ere he had learned to write them even; and his judgment has been gradually overgrowing his earlier compositions, as you see the advancing tide rising on the beach, and obliterating the prints on the sand. Now, I have observed that in all his earlier compositions he went far from home; he could not attempt a pastoral without first transporting himself to the vales of Arcadia, or an ode to Pity or Hope without losing the warm, living sentiment in the dead, cold personification of the Greek. The Hope and Pity he addressed were, not the undying attendants of human nature, but the shadowy spectres of a remote age. Now, however, I feel that a change has come over me. I seek for poetry among the fields and cottages of my own land. I—a—a—the friend of whom I speak — But I interrupted your remark on the Reformers."

"Nay," I replied, "if you go on so, I would much rather listen than speak. I only meant to say that the Knoxes and Melvilles of our country have been robbed of the admiration and sympathy of many a kindred spirit, by the strangely erroneous notions that have been abroad regarding them for at least the last two ages. Knox, I am convinced, would have been as great as Jeremy Taylor, if not even greater."

We sauntered along the shore till the evening had darkened into night, lost in an agreeable interchange of thought. "Ah!" at length exclaimed my companion, "I had almost forgotten my engagement, Mr. Lindsay; but it must not part us. You are a stranger here, and I must introduce you to some of my acquaintance. There are a few of us — choice spirits, of course — who meet every Saturday evening at John Hogg's; and I must just bring you to see them. There may be much less wit than mirth among us; but you will find us all sober, when at the gayest; and old John will be quite a study for you."

CHAPTER II.

Say, ye red gowns, that aften here
Hae toasted cakes to Katie's beer,
Gin e'er thir days hae had their peer,
  Sae blythe, sae daft!
Ye'll ne'er again in life's career
  Sit half sao saft.
    ELEGY ON JOHN HOGG.

WE returned to town; and, after threading a few of the narrower lanes, entered by a low door into a long dark room, dimly lighted by a fire. A tall thin woman was employed in skinning a bundle of dried fish at a table in a corner.

"Where's the gudeman, Kate?" said my companion, changing the sweet pure English in which he had hitherto spoken for his mother tongue.

"John's ben in the spence," replied the woman. "Little

Andrew, the wratch, has been makin' a totum wi' his faither's a'e razor; an' the puir man's trying to shave himsel' yonder, an' girnan like a sheep's head on the tangs."

"O the wratch! the ill-deedie wratch!" said John, stalking into the room in a towering passion, his face covered with suds and scratches, — "I might as weel shave mysel' wi' a mussel shillet. Rob Ferguson, man, is that you?"

"Wearie warld, John," said the poet, "for a' oor philosophy."

"Philosophy!—it's but a snare, Rab,—just vanity an' vexation o' speerit, as Solomon says. An' isna it clear heterodox besides? Ye study an' study till your brains _gang about like a whirligig; an' then, like bairns in a boat that see the land sailin', ye think it's the solid yearth that's turnin' roun'. An' this ye ca' philosophy; as if David hadna tauld us that the warld sits coshly on the waters, an' canna be moved."

"Hoot, John," rejoined my companion; "it's no me, but Jamie Brown, that differs wi' you on thae matters. I'm a Hoggonian, ye ken. The auld Jews were, doubtless, gran' Christians; an' wherefore no gude philosophers too? But it was cruel o' you to unkennel me this mornin' afore six, an' I up sae lang at my studies the nicht afore."

"Ah, Rob, Rob!" said John, — "studying in *Tam Dun's* kirk. Ye'll be a minister, like a' the lave."

"Mindin' fast, John," rejoined the poet. "I was in your kirk on Sabbath last, hearing worthy Mr. Corkindale. Whatever else he may hae to fear, he's in nae danger a' '*thinking his ain thoughts,*' honest man."

"In oor kirk!" said John; "ye're dune, then, wi' precentin' in yer ain; an' troth, nae wonder. What could

3

hae possessed ye to gie up the puir chield's name i' the prayer, an' him sittin' at yer lug?"

I was unacquainted with the circumstance to which he alluded, and requested an explanation. "Oh, ye see," said John, "Rob, amang a' the ither gifts that he misguides, has the gift o' a sweet voice; an' naething less would ser' some o' oor professors than to hae him for their precentor. They micht as weel hae thocht o' an organ, — it wad be just as devout; but the soun's everything now, laddie, ye ken, an' the heart naething. Weel, Rob, as ye may think, was less than pleased wi' the job, an' tauld them he could whistle better than sing; but it wasna that they wanted, and sae it behoved him to tak' his seat in the box. An' lest the folk should be no pleased wi' a'e key to a'e tune, he gied them, for the first twa or three days, a hale bunch to each; an' there was never sic singing in St. Andrews afore. Weel, but for a' that, it behoved him still to pre-cent, though he has got rid o' it at last; for what did he do twa Sabbaths agane, but put up drunken Tam Moffat's name in the prayer, — the very chield that was sittin' at his elbow, though the minister couldna see him. An' when the puir stibbler was prayin' for the reprobate as weel's he could, a'e half o' the kirk was needcessitated to come oot, that they micht keep decent, an' the ither half to swallow their pocket-napkins. But what think ye" —

"Hoot, John, now leave oot the moral," said the poet. "Here's a' the lads."

Half-a-dozen young students entered as he spoke; and, after a hearty greeting, and when he had introduced me to them one by one, as a choice fellow of immense reading, the door was barred, and we sat down to half-a-dozen of home-brewed, and a huge platter of dried fish. There was much mirth, and no little humor. Ferguson sat at the head of the table, and old John Hogg at the foot. I thought of Eastcheap, and the revels of Prince Henry; but our Falstaff was an old Scotch Seceder, and our Prince a gifted young fellow, who owed all his influence over his fellows to the force of his genius alone.

"Prythee, Hall," I said, "let us drink to Sir John."

"Why, yes," said the poet, "with all my heart. Not quite so fine a fellow, though, 'bating his Scotch honesty. Half Sir John's genius would have served for an epic poet, — half his courage for a hero."

"His courage!" exclaimed one of the lads.

"Yes, Willie, his courage, man. Do you think a coward could have run away with half the coolness? With a tithe of the courage necessary for such a retreat, a man would have stood and fought till he died. Sir John must have been a fine fellow in his youth."

"In mony a droll way may a man fa' on the drap drink," remarked John; "an' meikle ill, dootless, does it do in takin' aff the edge o' the speerit, — the mair if the edge be a fine razor edge, an' no the edge o' a whittle. I mind, about fifty years ago, when I was a slip o' a callant," —

"Losh, John!" exclaimed one of the lads, "hae ye been fechtin wi' the cats? Sic a scrapit face!"

"Wheesht," said Ferguson; "we owe the illustration to that; but dinna interrupt the story."

"Fifty years ago, when I was a slip o' a callant," continued John, "unco curious, an' fond o' kennin everything, as callants will be," —

"Hoot, John," said one of the students, interrupting him, "can ye no cut short, man? Rob promised last

Saturday to gie us, 'Fie, let us a' to the Bridal,' an' ye see the ale an' the nicht's baith wearin' dune."

"The song, Rob, the song!" exclaimed half-a-dozen voices at once; and John's story was lost in the clamor.

"Nay, now," said the good-natured poet, "that's less than kind; the auld man's stories are aye worth the hearing, an' he can relish the auld-warld fisher song wi' the best o' ye. But we maun hae the story yet."

He struck up the old Scotch ditty, "Fie, let us a' to the Bridal," which he sung with great power and brilliancy; for his voice was a richly-modulated one, and there was a fulness of meaning imparted to the words which wonderfully heightened the effect. "How strange it is," he remarked to me when he had finished, "that our English neighbors deny us humor! The songs of no country equal our Scotch ones in that quality. Are you acquainted with 'The Gudewife of Auchtermuchty?'"

"Well," I replied; "but so are not the English. It strikes me that, with the exception of Smollett's novels, all our Scotch humor is locked up in our native tongue. No man can employ in works of humor any language of which he is not a thorough master; and few of our Scotch writers, with all their elegance, have attained the necessary command of that colloquial English which Addison and Swift employed when they were merry."

"A braw redd delivery," said John, addressing me. "Are ye gaun to be a minister too?"

"Not quite sure yet," I replied.

"Ah," rejoined the old man, "'twas better for the Kirk when the minister just made himsel' ready for it, an' then waited till he kent whether it wanted him. There's young Rob Ferguson beside you," —

"Setting oot for the Kirk," said the young poet, interrupting him, "an' yet drinkin' ale on Saturday at e'en wi' old John Hogg."

"Weel, weel, laddie, it's easier for the best o' us to find fault wi' ithers than to mend oorsels. Ye have the head, onyhow; but Jamie Brown tells me it's a doctor ye're gaun to be, after a'."

"Nonsense, John Hogg; I wonder how a man o' your standing "—

"Nonsense, I grant you," said one of the students; "but true enough for a' that, Bob. Ye see, John, Bob an' I were at the King's Muirs last Saturday, and ca'ed at the *pendicle*, in the passing, for a cup o' whey, when the gude-wife tell't us there was ane o' the callants, who had broken into the milk-house twa nichts afore, lying ill o' a surfeit. 'Dangerous case,' said Bob; 'but let me see him. I have studied to small purpose if I know nothing o' med-icine, my good woman.' Weel, the woman was just glad enough to bring him to the bed-side; an' no wonder: ye never saw a wiser phiz in your lives, — Dr. Dumpie's was naething till't; an', after he had sucked the head o' his stick for ten minutes, an' fand the loon's pulse, an' asked mair questions than the gudewife liked to answer, he prescribed. But, losh! sic a prescription! A day's fasting an' twa ladles o' nettle kail was the gist o't; but then there went mair Latin to the tail o' that than oor neebour the doctor ever had to lose."

But I dwell too long on the conversation of this even-ing. I feel, however, a deep interest in recalling it to memory. The education of Ferguson was of a twofold character: he studied in the schools, and among the people; but it was in the latter tract alone that he ac-quired the materials of all his better poetry; and I feel as if, for at least one brief evening, I was admitted to the privileges of a class-fellow, and sat with him on the same form. The company broke up a little after ten; and I did not again hear of John Hogg till I read his elegy, about four years after, among the poems of my friend. It is by no means one of the happiest pieces in the volume, nor, it strikes me, highly characteristic; but I have often perused it with interest very independent of its merits.

CHAPTER III.

But he is weak;— both man and boy
Has been an idler in the land.
WORDSWORTH.

I WAS attempting to listen, on the evening of the following Sunday, to a dull, listless discourse,— one of the discourses so common at this period, in which there was fine writing without genius, and fine religion without Christianity,— when a person who had just taken his place beside me tapped me on the shoulder, and thrust a letter into my hand. It was my newly-acquired friend of the previous evening; and we shook hands heartily under the pew.

"That letter has just been handed me by an acquaintance from your part of the country," he whispered; "I trust it contains nothing unpleasant."

I raised it to the light; and, on ascertaining that it was sealed and edged with black, rose and quitted the church, followed by my friend. It intimated, in two brief lines, that my patron, the baronet, had been killed by a fall from his horse a few evenings before; and that, dying intestate, the allowance which had hitherto enabled me to prosecute my studies necessarily dropped. I crumpled up the paper in my hand.

"You have learned something very unpleasant," said Ferguson. "Pardon me, I have no wish to intrude; but, if at all agreeable, I would fain spend the evening with you."

My heart filled, and, grasping his hand, I briefly intimated the purport of my communication; and we walked out together in the direction of the ruins.

"It is perhaps as hard, Mr. Ferguson," I said, "to fall from one's hopes as from the place to which they pointed. I was ambitious, — too ambitious it may be, — to rise from that level on which man acts the part of a machine, and tasks merely his body, to that higher level on which he performs the part of a rational creature, and employs only his mind. But that ambition need influence me no longer. My poor mother, too, — I had trusted to be of use to her."

"Ah! my friend," said Ferguson, "I can tell you of a case quite as hopeless as your own — perhaps more so. But it will make you deem my sympathy the result of mere selfishness. In scarce any respect do our circumstances differ."

We had reached the ruins. The evening was calm and mild as when I had walked out on the preceding one; but the hour was earlier, and the sun hung higher over the hill. A newly-formed grave occupied the level spot in front of the little ivied corner.

"Let us seat ourselves here," said my companion, "and I will tell you a story, — I am afraid a rather tame one; for there is nothing of adventure in it, and nothing of

incident; but it may at least show you that I am not unfitted to be your friend. It is now nearly two years since
I lost my father. He was no common man,—common neither in intellect nor in sentiment,—but, though he once
fondly hoped it should be otherwise,—for in early youth
he indulged in all the dreams of the poet,—he now fills a
grave as nameless as the one before us. He was a native
of Aberdeenshire, but held lately an inferior situation in
the office of the British Linen Company in Edinburgh,
where I was born. Ever since I remember him, he had
awakened too fully to the realities of life, and they
pressed too hard on his spirits to leave him space for the
indulgence of his earlier fancies; but he could dream for
his children, though not for himself; or, as I should perhaps rather say, his children fell heir to all his more juvenile hopes of fortune and influence and space in the
world's eye; and, for himself, he indulged in hopes of a
later growth and firmer texture, which pointed from the
present scene of things to the future. I have an only
brother, my senior by several years, a lad of much energy, both physical and mental; in brief, one of those
mixtures of reflection and activity which seemed best
formed for rising in the world. My father deemed him
most fitted for commerce, and had influence enough to
get him introduced into the counting-house of a respectable Edinburgh merchant. I was always of a graver
turn,—in part, perhaps, the effect of less robust health,—
and me he intended for the church. I have been a
dreamer, Mr. Lindsay, from my earliest years,—prone to
melancholy, and fond of books and of solitude; and the
peculiarities of this temperament the sanguine old man,
though no mean judge of character, had mistaken for a
serious and reflective disposition. You are acquainted

with literature, and know something, from books at least, of the lives of literary men. Judge, then, of his prospect of usefulness in any profession, who has lived ever since he knew himself among the poets. My hopes from my earliest years have been hopes of celebrity as a writer; not of wealth, or of influence, or of accomplishing any of the thousand aims which furnish the great bulk of mankind with motives. You will laugh at me. There is something so emphatically shadowy and unreal in the object of this ambition, that even the full attainment of it provokes a smile. For who does not know

> How vain that second life in others' breath, —
> The estate which wits inherit after death!

And what can be more fraught with the ludicrous than a union of this shadowy ambition with mediocre parts and attainments? But I digress.

"It is now rather more than three years since I entered the classes here. I competed for a bursary, and was fortunate enough to secure one. Believe me, Mr. Lindsay, I am little ambitious of the fame of mere scholarship, and yet I cannot express to you the triumph of that day. I had seen my poor father laboring far, far beyond his strength, for my brother and myself, — closely engaged during the day with his duties in the bank, and copying at night in a lawyer's office. I had seen, with a throbbing heart, his tall wasted frame becoming tremulous and bent, and the gray hair thinning on his temples; and now I felt that I could ease him of at least part of the burden. In the excitement of the moment, I could hope that I was destined to rise in the world, — to gain a name in it, and something more. You know how a slight success grows in importance when we can deem it the earnest of future good fortune. I met, too, with a kind and influential friend in one of the professors, the late Dr. Wilkie, — alas! good, benevolent man! you may see his tomb yonder beside the wall; and on my return from St. Andrews at the close of the session, I found my father on his death-bed. My brother Henry, who had been unfortunate, and, I am afraid, something worse, had quitted the counting-house, and entered aboard of a man-of-war as a common sailor; and the poor old man, whose heart had been bound up in him, never held up his head after.

"On the evening of my father's funeral I could have lain down and died. I never before felt how thoroughly I am unfitted for the world, how totally I want strength. My father, I have said, had intended me for the church; and in my progress onward from class to class, and from school to college, I had thought but little of each particular step as it engaged me for the time, and nothing of the ultimate objects to which it led. All my more vigorous aspirations were directed to a remote fu-ture and an unsubstantial shadow. But I had witnessed beside my father's bed what had led me seriously to reflect on the ostensible aim for which I lived and stud-ied; and the more carefully I weighed myself in the bal-ance, the more did I find myself wanting. You have heard of Mr. Brown of the Secession, the author of the 'Dictionary of the Bible.' He was an old acquaintance of my father's, and, on hearing of his illness, had come all the way from Haddington to see him. I felt, for the first time, as, kneeling beside his bed, I heard my father's breathings becoming every moment shorter and more difficult, and listened to the prayers of the clergyman, that I had no business in the church. And thus I still continue to feel. 'Twere an easy matter to produce such things as pass for sermons among us, and to go respectably enough through the mere routine of the profession; but I cannot help feeling that, though I might do all this and more, my duty as a clergyman would be still left undone. I want singleness of aim, — I want earnestness of heart. I cannot teach men effectually how to live well; I cannot show them, with aught of confidence, how they may die safe. I cannot enter the church without acting the part of a hypocrite; and the miserable part of a hypocrite it shall never be mine to act. Heaven help me! I am too little of a practical moralist myself to attempt teaching morals to others.

"But I must conclude my story, if story it may be called. I saw my poor mother and my little sister deprived, by my father's death, of their sole stay, and strove to exert myself in their behalf. In the day-time I copied in a lawyer's office; my nights were spent among the poets. You will deem it the very madness of vanity, Mr. Lindsay, but I could not live without my dreams of literary eminence. I felt that life would be a blank waste without them; and I feel so still. Do not laugh at my weakness, when I say I would rather live in the memory of my country than enjoy her fairest lands, — that I dread a nameless grave many times more than the grave itself. But I am afraid the life of the literary aspirant is rarely a happy one; and I, alas! am one of the weakest of the class. It is of importance that the means of living be not disjoined from the end for which we live; and I feel that in my case the disunion is complete. The wants and evils of life are around me; but the energies through which those should be provided for, and these warded off, are otherwise employed. I am like a man pressing onward through a hot and bloody fight, his breast open to every blow, and tremblingly alive to the sense of injury and the feeling of pain, but totally unprepared either to attack or defend. And then those miserable depressions of spirit, to which all men who draw largely on their imagination are so subject, and that wavering irregularity of effort which seems so unavoidably the effect of pursuing a distant and doubtful aim, and which proves so hostile to the formation of every better habit, — alas! to a steady morality itself. But I weary you, Mr. Lindsay; besides, my story is told. I am groping onward, I know not whither; and in a few months hence, when my last session shall have closed, I shall be exactly where you are at present."

He ceased speaking, and there was a pause of several minutes. I felt soothed and gratified. There was a sweet melancholy music in the tones of his voice that sunk to my very heart; and the confidence he reposed in me flattered my pride. "How was it," I at length said, "that you were the gayest in the party of last night?"

"I do not know that I can better answer you," he replied, "than by telling you a singular dream which I had about the time of my father's death. I dreamed that I had suddenly quitted the world, and was journeying, by a long and dreary passage, to the place of final punishment. A blue, dismal light glimmered along the lower wall of the vault, and from the darkness above, where there flickered a thousand undefined shapes, — things without form or outline, — I could hear deeply-drawn sighs, and long hollow groans, and convulsive sobbings, and the prolonged moanings of an unceasing anguish. I was aware, however, though I know not how, that these were but the expressions of a lesser misery, and that the seats of severer torment were still before me. I went on and on, and the vault widened; and the light increased and the sounds changed. There were loud laughters and low mutterings, in the tone of ridicule; and shouts of triumph and exultation; and, in brief, all the thousand mingled tones of a gay and joyous revel. Can these, I exclaimed, be the sounds of misery when at the deepest? 'Bethink thee,' said a shadowy form beside me, — 'bethink thee if it be so on earth.' And as I remembered that it was so, and bethought me of the mad revels of shipwrecked seamen and of plague-stricken cities, I awoke. But on this subject you must spare me."

"Forgive me," I said; "to-morrow I leave college, and not with the less reluctance that I must part from you. But I shall yet find you occupying a place among the *literati* of our country, and shall remember with pride that you were my friend."

He sighed deeply. "My hopes rise and fall with my spirits," he said; "and to-night I am melancholy. Do you ever go to buffets with yourself, Mr. Lindsay? Do you ever mock, in your sadder moods, the hopes which render you happiest when you are gay? Ah! 'tis bitter warfare when a man contends with Hope! — when he sees her, with little aid from the personifying influence, as a thing distinct from himself, — a lying spirit that comes to flatter and deceive him. It is thus I see her to-night.

> See'st thou that grave? — does mortal know
> Aught of the dust that lies below?
> 'Tis foul, 'tis damp, 'tis void of form, —
> A bed where winds the loathsome worm!
> A little heap, mould'ring and brown,
> Like that on flowerless meadow thrown
> By mossy stream, when winter reigns

O'er leafless woods and wasted plains:
And yet, that brown, damp, formless heap
Once glowed with feelings keen and deep;
Once eyed the light, once heard each sound
Of earth, air, wave, that murmurs round.
But now, ah! now, the name it bore —
Sex, age, or form — is known no more.
This, this alone, O Hope! I know,
That once the dust that lies below
Was, like myself, of human race,
And made this world its dwelling-place.
Ah! this, when earth has swept away
The myriads of life's present day,
Though bright the visions raised by thee,
Will all my fame, my history be!

We quitted the ruins, and returned to town.

"Have you yet formed," inquired my companion, "any plan for the future?"

"I quit St. Andrews," I replied, "to-morrow morning. I have an uncle, the master of a West Indiaman now in the Clyde. Some years ago I had a fancy for the life of a sailor, which has evaporated, however, with many of my other boyish fancies and predilections; but I am strong and active, and it strikes me there is less competition on sea at present than on land. A man of tolerable steadiness and intelligence has a better chance of rising as a sailor than as a mechanic. I shall set out therefore with my uncle on his first voyage."

CHAPTER IV.

At first I thought the swankie didna ill, —
Again I glowr'd, to hear him better still;
Bauld, slee, an' sweet, his lines more glorious grew,
Glowed round the heart, an' glanced the soul out through.
ALEXANDER WILSON.

I HAD seen both the Indies and traversed the wide Pacific ere I again set foot on the eastern coast of Scotland. My uncle, the shipmaster, was dead, and I was still a common sailor; but I was light-hearted and skilful in my profession, and as much inclined to hope as ever. Besides, I had begun to doubt — and there cannot be a more consoling doubt when one is unfortunate — whether a man may not enjoy as much happiness in the lower walks of life as in the upper. In one of my later voyages, the vessel in which I sailed had lain for several weeks in Boston in North America, then a scene of those fierce and angry contentions which eventually separated the colonies from the mother country; and when in this place, I had become acquainted, by the merest accident in the world, with the brother of my friend the poet. I was passing through one of the meaner lanes, when I saw my my old friend, as I thought, looking out at me from the window of a crazy-looking building, — a sort of fencing academy, much frequented, I was told, by the Federalists of Boston. I crossed the lane in two huge strides.

"Mr. Ferguson," I said, — "Mr. Ferguson," — for he was withdrawing his head, — "do you not remember me?"

"Not quite sure," he replied; "I have met with many sailors in my time; but I must just see."

He had stepped down to the door ere I had discovered my mistake. He was a taller and stronger-looking man than my friend, and his senior, apparently, by six or eight years; but nothing could be more striking than the resemblance which he bore to him, both in face and figure. I apologized.

"But have you not a brother, a native of Edinburgh," I inquired, "who studied at St. Andrews about four years ago? Never before, certainly, did I see so remarkable a likeness."

"As that which I bear Robert?" he said. "Happy to hear it. Robert is a brother of whom a man may well be proud, and I am glad to resemble him in any way. But you must go in with me, and tell me all you know regarding him. He was a thin, pale slip of a boy when I left Scotland,— a mighty reader, and fond of sauntering into by-holes and corners; I scarcely knew what to make of him; but he has made much of himself. His name has been blown far and wide within the last two years."

He showed me through a large waste apartment, furnished with a few deal seats, and with here and there a fencing foil leaning against the wall, into a sort of closet at the upper end, separated from the main room by a partition of undressed slabs. There was a charcoal stove in one corner, and a truckle-bed in the other. A few shelves laden with books ran along the wall. There was a small chest raised on a stool immediately below the window, to serve as a writing-desk, and another stool standing beside it. A few cooking utensils, scattered round the room, and a corner cupboard, completed the entire furniture of the place.

"There is a certain limited number born to be rich, Jack," said my new companion, "and I just don't happen to be among them; but I have one stool for myself, you see, and, now that I have unshipped my desk, another for a visitor, and so get on well enough."

I related briefly the story of my intimacy with his brother, and we were soon on such terms as to be in a fair way of emptying a bottle of rum together.

"You remind me of old times," said my new acquaintance. "I am weary of these illiterate, boisterous, long-sided Americans, who talk only of politics and dollars. And yet there are first-rate men among them too. I met, some years since, with a Philadelphia printer, whom I cannot help regarding as one of the ablest, best-informed men I ever conversed with. But there is nothing like general knowledge among the average class,—a mighty privilege of conceit, however."

"They are just in that stage," I remarked, "in which it needs all the vigor of an able man to bring his mind into anything like cultivation. There must be many more facilities of improvement ere the mediocritist can develop himself. He is in the egg still in America, and must sleep there till the next age.—But when last heard you of your brother?"

"Why," he replied, "when all the world heard of him, —with the last number of 'Ruddiman's Magazine.' Where can you have been bottled up from literature of late? Why, man, Robert stands first among our Scotch poets."

"Ah! 'tis long since I have anticipated something like that for him," I said; "but for the last two years I have seen only two books,—Shakspeare and the 'Spectator.' Pray, do show me some of the magazines."

4*

The magazines were produced; and I heard for the first time, in a foreign land, and from the recitation of the poet's brother, some of the most national and most highly-finished of his productions. My eyes filled, and my heart wandered to Scotland and her cottage homes, as, shutting the book, he repeated to me, in a voice faltering with emotion, stanza after stanza of the "Farmer's Ingle."

"Do you not see it?—do you not see it all?" exclaimed my companion; "the wide smoky room, with the bright turf-fire, the blackened rafters shining above, the straw-wrought settle below, the farmer and the farmer's wife, and auld grannie and the bairns. Never was there truer painting; and oh, how it works on a Scotch heart! But hear this other piece."

He read "Sandy and Willie."

"Far, far ahead of Ramsay," I exclaimed,—"more imagination, more spirit, more intellect, and as much truth and nature. Robert has gained his end already. Hurrah for poor old Scotland!—these pieces must live for ever. But do repeat to me the 'Farmer's Ingle' once more."

We read, one by one, all the poems in the Magazine, dwelling on each stanza, and expatiating on every recollection of home which the images awakened. My companion was, like his brother, a kind, open-hearted man, of superior intellect; much less prone to despondency, however, and of a more equal temperament. Ere we parted, which was not until next morning, he had communicated to me all his plans for the future, and all his fondly-cherished hopes of returning to Scotland with wealth enough to be of use to his friends. He seemed to be one of those universal geniuses who do a thousand things well, but want steadiness enough to turn any of them to good account. He showed me a treatise on the use of the

sword, which he had just prepared for the press, and a
series of letters on the Stamp Act, which had appeared
from time to time in one of the Boston newspapers, and in
which he had taken part with the Americans.

"I make a good many dollars in these stirring times,"
he said. "All the Yankees seem to be of opinion that
they will be best heard across the water when they have
got arms in their hands, and have learned how to use
them; and I know a little of both the sword and the
musket. But the warlike spirit is frightfully thirsty,
somehow, and consumes a world of rum; and so I have
not yet begun to make rich."

He shared with me his supper and bed for the night;
and, after rising in the morning ere I awoke, and writing
a long letter for Robert, which he gave me in the hope I
might soon meet with him, he accompanied me to the
vessel, then on the eve of sailing, and we parted, as it
proved, for ever. I know nothing of his after-life, or how
or where it terminated; but I have learned that, shortly
before the death of his gifted brother, his circumstances
enabled him to send his mother a small remittance for the
use of the family. He was evidently one of the kind-
hearted, improvident few who can share a very little, and
whose destiny it is to have only a very little to share.

CHAPTER V.

O, Ferguson ! thy glorious parts
Ill suited law's dry, musty arts!
My curse upon your whunstane hearts,
  Ye Embrugh gentry!
The tithe o' what ye waste at cartes
  Wad stowed his pantry!

          BURNS.

I VISITED Edinburgh for the first time in the latter part of the autumn of 1773, about two months after I had sailed from Boston. It was on a fine calm morning, — one of those clear sunshiny mornings of October when the gossamer goes sailing about in long cottony threads, so light and fleecy that they seem the skeleton remains of extinct cloudlets, and when the distant hills, with their covering of gray frost-rime, seem, through the clear close atmosphere, as if chiselled in marble. The sun was rising over the town through a deep blood-colored haze, — the smoke of a thousand fires; and the huge fantastic piles of masonry that stretched along the ridge looked dim and spectral through the cloud, like the ghosts of an army of giants. I felt half a foot taller as I strode on towards the town. It was Edinburgh I was approaching, — the scene of so many proud associations to a lover of Scotland ; and I was going to meet, as an early friend, one of the first of Scottish poets. I entered the town. There was a book-stall in a corner of the street, and I turned aside for half a minute to glance my eye over the books.

"Ferguson's Poems!" I exclaimed, taking up a little

volume. "I was not aware they had appeared in a separate form. How do you sell this?"

"Just like a' the ither booksellers," said the man who kept the stall, — "that's nane o' the buiks that come doun in a hurry, — just for the marked selling price." I threw down the money.

"Could you tell me anything of the writer?" I said. "I have a letter for him from America."

"Oh, that'll be frae his brother Henry, I'll wad; a clever chield too, but ower fond o' the drap drink, maybe, like Rob himsel'. Baith o' them fine humane chields though, without a grain o' pride. Rob takes a stan' wi' me sometimes o' half an hour at a time, an' we clatter ower the buiks; an', if I'm no mista'en, yon's him just yonder, — the thin, pale slip o' a lad wi' the broad brow. Ay, an' he's just comin' this way."

"Anything new to-day, Thomas?" said the young man, coming up to the stall. "I want a cheap second-hand copy of Ramsay's 'Evergreen'; and, like a good man as you are, you must just try and find it for me."

Though considerably altered, — for he was taller and thinner than when at college, and his complexion had assumed a deep sallow hue, — I recognized him at once, and presented him with the letter.

"Ah, from brother Henry," he said, breaking it open, and glancing his eye over the contents. "What! *old college chum, Mr. Lindsay!*" he exclaimed, turning to me. "Yes, sure enough; how happy I am we should have met! Come this way; — let us get out of the streets."

We passed hurriedly through the Canongate and along the front of Holyrood House, and were soon in the

King's Park, which seemed this morning as if left to ourselves.

"Dear me, and this is you yourself! and we have again met, Mr. Lindsay!" said Ferguson : "I thought we were never to meet more. Nothing, for a long time, has made me half so glad. And so you have been a sailor for the last four years. Do let us sit down here in the warm sunshine, beside St. Anthony's Well; and tell me all your story, and how you happened to meet with brother Henry."

We sat down, and I briefly related, at his bidding, all that had befallen me since we had parted at St. Andrews, and how I was still a common sailor; but, in the main, perhaps, not less happy than many who commanded a fleet.

"Ah, you have been a fortunate fellow," he said; "you have seen much and enjoyed much; and I have been rusting in unhappiness at home. Would that I had gone to sea along with you!"

"Nay, now, that won't do," I replied. "But you are merely taking Bacon's method of blunting the edge of envy. You have scarcely yet attained the years of mature manhood, and yet your name has gone abroad over the whole length and breadth of the land, and over many other lands besides. I have cried over your poems three thousand miles away, and felt all the prouder of my country for the sake of my friend. And yet you would fain persuade me that you wish the charm reversed, and that you were just such an obscure salt-water man as myself!"

"You remember," said my companion, "the story of the half-man, half-marble prince of the Arabian tale. One part was a living creature, one part a stone; but the parts were incorporated, and the mixture was misery. I am just such a poor unhappy creature as the enchanted prince of the story."

"You surprise and distress me," I rejoined. "Have you not accomplished all you so fondly purposed, — realized even your warmest wishes? And this, too, in early life. Your most sanguine hopes pointed but to a name, which you yourself perhaps was never to hear, but which was to dwell on men's tongues when the grave had closed over you. And now the name is gained, and you live to enjoy it. I see the *living* part of your lot, and it seems instinct with happiness; but in what does the *dead*, the stony part, consist?"

He shook his head, and looked up mournfully into my face. There was a pause of a few seconds. "You, Mr. Lindsay," he at length replied, — "you, who are of an equable, steady temperament, can know little from experience of the unhappiness of a man who lives only in extremes, who is either madly gay or miserably depressed. Try and realize the feelings of one whose mind is like a broken harp, — all the medium tones gone, and only the higher and lower left; of one, too, whose circumstances seem of a piece with his mind, who can enjoy the exercise of his better powers, and yet can only live by the monotonous drudgery of copying page after page in a clerk's office; of one who is continually either groping his way amid a chill melancholy fog of nervous depression, or carried headlong by a wild gayety to all which his better judgment would instruct him to avoid; of one who, when he indulges most in the pride of superior intellect, cannot away with the thought that that intellect is on the eve of breaking up, and that he must yet rate infinitely lower in the scale of rationality than any of the nameless thousands who carry on the ordinary concerns of life around him."

I was grieved and astonished, and knew not what to answer. "You are in a gloomy mood to-day," I at length said; "you are immersed in one of the fogs you describe, and all the surrounding objects take a tinge of darkness from the medium through which you survey them. Come, now, you must make an exertion, and shake off your melancholy. I have told you all my story as I best could, and you must tell me all yours in return."

"Well," he replied, "I shall, though it mayn't be the best way in the world of dissipating my melancholy. I think I must have told you, when at college, that I had a maternal uncle of considerable wealth, and, as the world goes, respectability, who resided in Aberdeenshire. He was placed on what one may term the table-land of society; and my poor mother, whose recollections of him were limited to a period when there is warmth in the feelings of the most ordinary minds, had hoped that he would willingly exert his influence in my behalf. Much, doubtless, depends on one's setting out in life; and it would have been something to have been enabled to step into it from a level like that occupied by my relative. I paid him a visit shortly after leaving college, and met with apparent kindness. But I can see beyond the surface, Mr. Lindsay, and I soon saw that my uncle was entirely a different man from the brother whom my mother remembered. He had risen, by a course of slow industry, from comparative poverty, and his feelings had worn out by the process. The character was case-hardened all over; and the polish it bore — for I have rarely met a smoother man — seemed no improvement. He was, in brief, one of the class content to dwell for ever in mere decencies, with consciences made up of the conventional moralities, who think by precedent, bow to public opinion as their god, and estimate merit by its weight in guineas."

"And so your visit," I said, "was a very brief one?"

"You distress me," he replied. "It should have been so; but it was not. But what could I do? Ever since my father's death I had been taught to consider this man as my natural guardian, and I was now unwilling to part with my last˙hope. But this is not all. Under much apparent activity, my friend, there is a substratum of apathetical indolence in my disposition: I move rapidly when in motion; but when at rest, there is a dull inertness in the character, which the will, when unassisted by passion, is too feeble to overcome. Poor, weak creature that I am! I had set down by my uncle's fireside, and felt unwilling to rise. Pity me, my friend, — I deserve your pity; but oh! do not despise me!"

"Forgive me, Mr. Ferguson," I said; "I have given you pain, but surely most unwittingly."

"I am ever a fool," he continued. "But my story lags; and, surely, there is little in it on which it were pleasure to dwell. I sat at this man's table for six months, and saw, day after day, his manner towards me becoming more constrained, and his politeness more cold; and yet I staid on, till at last my clothes were worn threadbare, and he began to feel that the shabbiness of the nephew affected the respectability of the uncle. His friend the soap-boiler, and his friend the oil-merchant, and his friend the manager of the hemp manufactory, with their wives and daughters, — all people of high standing in the world, — occasionally honored his table with their presence; and how could he be other than ashamed of mine? It vexes me that I cannot even yet be cool on the subject: it vexes me that a creature so sordid should have so much power to move me; but I cannot, I cannot master my feelings. He — he told me, — and with whom should the blame rest, but with the weak, spiritless thing who lingered on in mean, bitter dependence, to hear what he had to tell? — he told me that all his friends were respectable, and that my appearance was no longer that of a person whom he could wish to see at his table, or introduce to any one as his nephew. And I had staid to hear all this!

"I can hardly tell you how I got home. I travelled, stage after stage, along the rough dusty roads, with a weak and feverish body, and almost despairing mind. On meeting with my mother, I could have laid my head on her bosom and cried like a child. I took to my bed in a high fever, and trusted that all my troubles were soon to terminate; but when the die was cast, it turned up life. I resumed my old miserable employments, — for what could I else? — and, that I might be less unhappy in the prosecution of them, my old amusements too. I copied during the day in a clerk's office that I might live, and wrote during the night that I might be known. And I have in part, perhaps, attained my object. I have pursued and caught hold of the shadow on which my heart had been so long set; and if it prove empty and intangible and unsatisfactory, like every other shadow, the blame surely must rest with the pursuer, not with the thing pursued. I weary you, Mr. Lindsay; but one word more. There are hours when the mind, weakened by exertion or by the teasing monotony of an employment which tasks without exercising it, can no longer exert its powers, and when, feeling that sociality is a law of our nature, we seek the society of our fellow-men. With a creature so much the sport of impulse as I am, it is of these hours of weakness that conscience takes most note. God help me! I have been told that life is short; but it stretches on and on and on before me; and I know not how it is to be passed through."

My spirits had so sunk during this singular conversation that I had no heart to reply.

"You are silent, Mr. Lindsay," said the poet; "I have made you as melancholy as myself; but look around you, and say if ever you have seen a lovelier spot. See how richly the yellow sunshine slants along the green sides of Arthur's Seat; and how the thin blue smoke, that has come floating from the town, fills the bottom of yonder grassy dell as if it were a little lake! Mark, too, how boldly the cliffs stand out along its sides, each with its little patch of shadow. And here, beside us, is St. Anthony's Well, so famous in song, coming gushing out to the sunshine, and then gliding away through the grass like a snake. Had the Deity purposed that man should be miserable, he would surely never have placed him in so fair a world. Perhaps much of our unhappiness originates in our mistaking our proper scope, and thus setting out from the first with a false aim."

"Unquestionably," I replied. "There is no man who has not some part to perform; and if it be a great and uncommon part, and the powers which fit him for it proportionably great and uncommon, nature would be in error could he slight it with impunity. See! there is a wild bee bending the flower beside you. Even that little creature has a capacity of happiness and misery: it derives its sense of pleasure from whatever runs in the line of its instincts, its experience of unhappiness from whatever thwarts and opposes them; and can it be supposed that so wise a law should regulate the instincts of only inferior creatures? No, my friend; it is surely a law of our nature also."

"And have you not something else to infer?" said the poet.

"Yes," I replied; "that you are occupied differently from what the scope and constitution of your mind demand, — differently both in your hours of enjoyment and of relaxation. But do take heart; you will yet find your proper place, and all shall be well."

"Alas! no, my friend," said he, rising from the sward. "I could once entertain such a hope, but I cannot now. My mind is no longer what it was to me in my happier days, a sort of *terra incognita* without bounds or limits. I can see over and beyond it, and have fallen from all my hopes regarding it. It is not so much the gloom of present circumstances that disheartens me as a depressing knowledge of myself, — an abiding conviction that I am a weak dreamer, unfitted for every occupation of life, and not less so for the greater employments of literature than for any of the others. I feel that I am a little man and a little poet, with barely vigor enough to make one half-effort at a time, but wholly devoid of the sustaining will — that highest faculty of the highest order of minds — which can direct a thousand vigorous efforts to the accomplishment of one important object. Would that I could exchange my half-celebrity — and it can never be other than a half-celebrity — for a temper as equable and a fortitude as unshrinking as yours! But I weary you with my complaints: I am a very coward; and you will deem me as selfish as I am weak."

We parted. The poet, sadly and unwillingly, went to copy deeds in the office of the commissary-clerk; and I, almost reconciled to obscurity and hard labor, to assist in unlading a Baltic trader in the harbor of Leith.

CHAPTER VI.

Speech without aim, and without end employ.
CRABBE.

AFTER the lapse of nine months, I again returned to Edinburgh. During that period I had been so shut out from literature and the world, that I had heard nothing of my friend the poet; and it was with a beating heart I left the vessel, on my first leisure evening, to pay him a visit. It was about the middle of July. The day had been close and sultry, and the heavens overcharged with gray ponderous clouds; and as I passed hurriedly along the walk which leads from Leith to Edinburgh, I could hear the newly-awakened thunder, bellowing far in the south, peal after peal, like the artillery of two hostile armies. I reached the door of the poet's humble domicile, and had raised my hand to the knocker, when I heard some one singing from within, in a voice by far the most touchingly mournful I had ever listened to. The tones struck on my heart; and a frightful suspicion crossed my mind, as I set down the knocker, that the singer was no other than my friend. But in what wretched circumstances! what fearful state of mind! I shuddered as I listened, and heard the strain waxing louder and yet more mournful, and could distinguish that the words were those of a simple old ballad, —

O, Marti'mas wind! when wilt thou blaw,
An' shake the green leaves aff the tree?
O, gentle death! when wilt thou come,
An' tak a life that wearies me?

I could listen no longer, but raised the latch and went in. The evening was gloomy, and the apartment ill-lighted; but I could see the singer, a spectral-looking figure, sitting on a bed in the corner, with the bed-clothes wrapped round his shoulders, and a napkin deeply stained with blood on his head. An elderly female, who stood beside him, was striving to soothe him, and busied from time to time in adjusting the clothes, which were ever and anon falling off as he nodded his head in time to the music. A young girl of great beauty sat weeping at the bed-foot.

"O, dearest Robert!" said the woman, "you will destroy your poor head; and Margaret, your sister, whom you used to love so much, will break her heart. Do lie down, dearest, and take a little rest. Your head is fearfully gashed; and if the bandages loose a second time, you will bleed to death. Do, dearest Robert! for your poor old mother, to whom you were always so kind and dutiful a son till now, — for your poor old mother's sake,' do lie down."

The song ceased for a moment, and the tears came bursting from my eyes as the tune changed, and he again sang, —

O, mither dear! make ye my bed,
For my heart it's flichterin' sair;
An' oh! gin I've vex'd ye, mither dear,
I'll never vex ye mair.

I've staid ar'out the lang dark nicht,
I' the sleet and the plashy rain;
But, mither dear, make ye my bed,
An' I'll ne'er gang out again.

"Dearest, dearest Robert!" continued the poor, heart-broken woman, "do lie down, — for your poor old mother's sake, do lie down."

"No, no," he exclaimed, in a hurried voice, "not just now, mother, not just now. Here is my friend Mr. Lindsay come to see me, — my true friend, Mr. Lindsay the sailor, who has sailed all round and round the world; and I have much, much to ask him. A chair, Margaret, for Mr. Lindsay. I must be a preacher like John Knox, you know, — like the great John Knox, the reformer of a nation, — and Mr. Lindsay knows all about him. A chair, Margaret, for Mr. Lindsay."

I am not ashamed to say it was with tears, and in a voice faltering with emotion, that I apologized to the poor woman for my intrusion at such a time. Were it otherwise, I might well conclude my heart grown hard as a piece of the nether millstone.

"I had known Robert at college," I said; "had loved and respected him; and had now come to pay him a visit, after an absence for several months, wholly unprepared for finding him in his present condition." And it would seem that my tears plead for me, and proved to the poor afflicted woman and her daughter by far the most efficient part of my apology.

"All my friends have left me now, Mr. Lindsay," said the unfortunate poet, — "they have all left me now; they love this present world. We were all going down, down, down; there was the roll of a river behind us; it came bursting over the high rocks, roaring, rolling, foaming, down upon us; and, though the fog was thick and dark below, — far below, in the place to which we were going, — I could see the red fire shining through, — the red, hot, unquenchable fire; and we were all going down, down, down. Mother, mother, tell Mr. Lindsay I am going to be put on my trials to-morrow. Careless creature that I am! life is short, and I have lost much time; but I am going to be put on my trials to-morrow, and shall come forth a preacher of the Word."

The thunder, which had hitherto been muttering at a distance, — each peal, however, nearer and louder than the preceding one, — now began to roll overhead, and the lightning, as it passed the window, to illumine every object within. The hapless poet stretched out his thin, wasted arm, as if addressing a congregation from the pulpit.

"There were the flashings of lightning," he said, " and the roll of thunder; and the trumpet waxed louder and louder. And around the summit of the mountain were the foldings of thick clouds, and the shadow fell brown and dark over the wide expanse of the desert. And the wild beasts lay trembling in their dens. But, lo! where the sun breaks through the opening of the cloud, there is the glitter of tents, — the glitter of ten thousand tents, — that rise over the sandy waste thick as waves of the sea. And there, there is the voice of the dance, and of the revel, and the winding of horns, and the clash of cymbals. Oh, sit nearer me, dearest mother, for the room is growing dark, dark; and oh, my poor head!

> The lady sat on the castle wa',
> Looked owre haith dale and down,
> And then she spied Gil-Morice head
> Come steering through the town.

Do, dearest mother, put your cool hand on my brow, and do hold it fast ere it part. How fearfully, oh, how fearfully it aches!—and oh, how it thunders!" He sunk backward on the pillow, apparently exhausted. "Gone, gone, gone," he muttered,—"my mind gone forever. But God's will be done."

I rose to leave the room; for I could restrain my feelings no longer.

"Stay, Mr. Lindsay," said the poet, in a feeble voice. "I hear the rain dashing on the pavement; you must not go till it abates. Would that you could pray beside me! But no; you are not like the dissolute companions who have now all left me, but you are not yet fitted for that; and, alas! I cannot pray for myself. Mother, mother, see that there be prayers at my lykewake; for,—

Her lykewake, it was piously spent
  In social prayer and praise,
Performed by judicious men,
  Who stricken were in days;
And many a heavy, heavy heart,
  Was in that mournful place,
And many a weary, weary thought
  On her who slept in peace.

They will come all to my lykewake, mother, won't they? Yes, all, though they have left me now. Yes, and they will come far to see my grave. I was poor, very poor, you know, and they looked down upon me; and I was no son or cousin of theirs, and so they could do nothing for me. Oh, but they might have looked less coldly! But they will all come to my grave, mother; they will come all to my grave; and they will say, 'Would he were living now, to know how kind we are!' But they will look as coldly as ever on the living poet beside them,—yes, till they have broken his heart; and then they will go to his grave too. O, dearest mother! do lay your cool hand on my brow."

He lay silent and exhausted, and in a few minutes I could hope, from the hardness of his breathing, that he had fallen asleep.

"How long," I inquired of his sister, in a low whisper, "has Mr. Ferguson been so unwell; and what has injured his head?"

"Alas!" said the girl, "my brother has been unsettled in mind for nearly the last six months. We first knew it one evening on his coming home from the country, where he had been for a few days with a friend. He burnt a large heap of papers that he had been employed on for weeks before, — songs and poems that, his friends say, were the finest things he ever wrote; but he burnt them all, for he was going to be a preacher of the Word, he said, and it did not become a preacher of the Word to be a writer of light rhymes. And O, sir! his mind has been carried ever since; but he has been always gentle and affectionate, and his sole delight has lain in reading the Bible. Good Dr. Erskine, of the Gray-friars, often comes to our house, and sits with him for hours together: for there are times when his mind seems stronger than ever; and he sees wonderful things, that seem to hover, the minister says, between the extravagance natural to his present sad condition, and the higher flights of a philosophic genius. And we had hoped that he was getting better; but O, sir! our hopes have had a sad ending. He went out, a few evenings ago, to call on an old acquaintance; and, in descending a stair, missed footing, and fell to the bottom; and his head has been fearfully injured by the stones. He has been just as you have seen

him ever since; and oh! I much fear he cannot now recover. Alas! my poor brother!—never, never was there
a more affectionate heart."

CHAPTER VII.

A lowly muse!
She sings of reptiles yet in song unknown.

I RETURNED to the vessel with a heavy heart; and it
was nearly three months from this time ere I again set
foot in Edinburgh. Alas for my unfortunate friend! He
was now an inmate of the asylum, and on the verge of
dissolution. I was thrown by accident, shortly after my
arrival at this time, into the company of one of his boon
companions. I had gone into a tavern with a brother
sailor,—a shrewd, honest skipper from the north country; and, finding the place occupied by half-a-dozen young
fellows, who were growing noisy over their liquor, I
would have immediately gone out again, had I not
caught, in the passing, a few words regarding my friend.
And so, drawing to a side-table, I sat down.

"Believe me," said one of the topers, a dissolute-looking
young man, " it's all over with Bob Ferguson, — all over;
and I knew it from the moment he grew religious. Had
old Brown tried to convert me, I would have broken his
face."

"What Brown?" inquired one of his companions.

"Is that all you know?" rejoined the other. "Why,
John Brown, of Haddington, the Seceder. Bob was at

Haddington last year at the election; and one morning, when in the horrors, after holding a rum night of it, who should he meet in the churchyard but old John Brown. He writes, you know, a big book on the Bible. Well, he lectured Bob at a pretty rate about election and the call, I suppose; and the poor fellow has been mad ever since. Your health, Jamie. For my own part, I'm a freewill man, and detest all cant and humbug."

"And what has come of Ferguson now?" asked one of the others.

"Oh, mad, sir, mad!" rejoined the toper, — "reading the Bible all day, and cooped up in the asylum yonder. 'Twas I who brought him to it. But, lads, the glass has been standing for the last half-hour. 'Twas I and Jack Robinson who brought him to it, as I say. He was getting wild; and so we got a sedan for him, and trumped a story of an invitation for tea from a lady, and he came with us as quietly as a lamb. But if you could have heard the shriek he gave when the chair stopped, and he saw where we had brought him! I never heard anything half so horrible; it rung in my ears for a week after; and then, how the mad people in the upper rooms howled and gibbered in reply, till the very roof echoed! People say he is getting better; but when I last saw him he was as religious as ever, and spoke so much about heaven that it was uncomfortable to hear him. Great loss to his friends, after all the expense they have been at with his education."

"You seem to have been intimate with Mr. Ferguson," I said.

"Oh, intimate with Bob!" he rejoined; "we were hand and glove, man. I have sat with him in Lucky Middlemass's almost every evening for two years; and I have given him hints for some of the best things in his book. 'Twas I who tumbled down the cage in the Meadows, and began breaking the lamps.

Ye who oft finish care in Lethe's cup, —
Who love to swear and roar, and *keep it up,*—
List to a brother's voice, whose sole delight
Is sleep all day, and riot all the night.

"There's spirit for you! But Bob was never sound at bottom; and I have told him so. ' Bob,' I have said, — ' Bob, you're but a hypocrite after all, man, — without half the spunk you pretend to. Why don't you take a pattern by me, who fear nothing, and believe only the agreeable? But, poor fellow, he had weak nerves, and a church-going propensity that did him no good; and you see the effects. 'Twas all nonsense, Tom, of his throwing the squib into the Glassite meeting-house. Between you and I, that was a cut far beyond him in his best days, poet as he was. 'Twas I who did it, man; and never was there a cleaner row in Auld Reekie."

"Heartless, contemptible puppy!" said my comrade the sailor, as we left the room. "Your poor friend must be ill indeed if he be but half as insane as his quondam companion. But he cannot: there is no madness like that of the heart. What could have induced a man of genius to associate with a thing so thoroughly despicable?"

"The same misery, Miller," I said, "that brings a man *acquainted with strange bed-fellows.*"

6

CHAPTER VIII.

O, thou, my elder brother in misfortune! —
By far my elder brother in the muses, —
With tears I pity thy unhappy fate!

BURNS.

THE asylum in which my unfortunate friend was confined — at this time the only one in Edinburgh — was
situated in an angle of the city wall. It was a dismal-
looking mansion, shut in on every side by the neighboring houses from the view of the surrounding country,
and so effectually covered up from the nearer street by
a large building in front that it seemed possible enough
to pass a lifetime in Edinburgh without coming to the
knowledge of its existence. I shuddered as I looked up
to its blackened walls, thinly sprinkled with miserable-
looking windows barred with iron, and thought of it
as a sort of burial-place of dead minds. But it was a
Golgotha which, with more than the horrors of the grave,
had neither its rest nor its silence. I was startled, as
I entered the cell of the hapless poet, by a shout of
laughter from a neighboring room, which was answered
from a dark recess behind me by a fearfully-prolonged
shriek and the clanking of chains. The mother and
sister of Fergnson were sitting beside his pallet, on a sort
of stone settle, which stood out from the wall; and the
poet himself — weak and exhausted and worn to a
shadow, but apparently in his right mind — lay extended
on the straw. He made an attempt to rise as I entered;

but the effort was above his strength, and, again lying down, he extended his hand.

"This is kind, Mr. Lindsay," he said; "it is ill for me to be alone in these days; and yet I have few visitors save my poor old mother and Margaret. But who cares for the unhappy?"

I sat down on the settle beside him, still retaining his hand. "I have been at sea, and in foreign countries," I said, "since I last saw you, Mr. Ferguson, and it was only this morning I returned; but, believe me, there are many, many of your countrymen who sympathize sincerely in your affliction, and take a warm interest in your recovery."

He sighed deeply. "Ah," he replied, "I know too well the nature of that sympathy. You never find it at the bedside of the sufferer; it evaporates in a few barren expressions of idle pity! and yet, after all, it is but a paying the poet in kind. He calls so often on the world to sympathize over fictitious misfortune that the feeling wears out, and becomes a mere mood of the imagination; and with this light, attenuated pity, of his own weaving, it regards his own real sorrows. Dearest mother, the evening is damp and chill. Do gather the bed-clothes around me, and sit on my feet: they are so very cold, and so dead that they cannot be colder a week hence."

"O, Robert! why do you speak so?" said the poor woman, as she gathered the clothes around him, and sat on his feet. "You know you are coming home to-morrow."

"To-morrow!" he said; "if I see to-morrow, I shall have completed my twenty-fourth year, — a small part, surely, of the threescore and ten; but what matters it when 'tis past?"

"You were ever, my friend, of a melancholy temperament," I said, "and too little disposed to hope. Indulge in brighter views of the future, and all shall yet be well."

"I can now hope that it shall," he said. "Yes, all shall be well with me, and that very soon. But oh, how this nature of ours shrinks from dissolution! — yes, and all the lower natures too. You remember, mother, the poor starling that was killed in the room beside us? Oh, how it struggled with its ruthless enemy, and filled the whole place with its shrieks of terror and agony! And yet, poor little thing, it had been true, all life long, to the laws of its nature, and had no sins to account for and no Judge to meet. There is a shrinking of heart as I look before me; and yet I can hope that all shall yet be well with me, and that very soon. Would that I had been wise in time! Would that I had thought more and earlier of the things which pertain to my eternal peace! — more of a living soul, and less of a dying name! But oh! 'tis a glorious provision, through which a way of return is opened up, even at the eleventh hour."

We sat around him in silence. An indescribable feeling of awe pervaded my whole mind; and his sister was affected to tears.

"Margaret," he said, in a feeble voice, — "Margaret, you will find my Bible in yonder little recess: 'tis all I have to leave you; but keep it, dearest sister, and use it, and in times of sorrow and suffering, that come to all, you will know how to prize the legacy of your poor brother. Many, many books do well enough for life; but there is only one of any value when we come to die.

"You have been a voyager of late, Mr. Lindsay," he continued, "and I have been a voyager too. I have been journeying in darkness and discomfort, amid strange unearthly shapes of dread and horror, with no reason to direct, and no will to govern. Oh, the unspeakable unhappiness of these wanderings! — these dreams of suspicion, and fear, and hatred, in which shadow and substance, the true and the false, were so wrought up and mingled together that they formed but one fantastic and miserable whole. And oh, the unutterable horror of every momentary return to a recollection of what I had been once, and a sense of what I had become! Oh, when I awoke amid the terrors of the night; when I turned me on the rustling straw, and heard the wild wail, and yet wilder laugh; when I heard, and shuddered, and then felt the demon in all his might coming over me, till I laughed and wailed with the others, — oh, the misery! the utter misery! But 'tis over, my friend, — 'tis all over. A few, few tedious days — a few, few weary nights — and all my sufferings shall be over."

I had covered my face with my hands, but the tears came bursting through my fingers. The mother and sister of the poet sobbed aloud.

" Why sorrow for me, sirs ? " he said; " why grieve for me? I am well, quite well, and want for nothing. But 'tis cold, oh, 'tis very cold, and the blood seems freezing at my heart. Ah, but there is neither pain nor cold where I am going, and I trust it will be well with my soul. Dearest, dearest mother, I always told you it would come to this at last."

The keeper had entered, to intimate to us that the hour for locking up the cells was already past; and we now rose to leave the place. I stretched out my hand to my unfortunate friend. He took it in silence; and his thin, attenuated fingers felt cold within my grasp, like those of a corpse. His mother stooped down to embrace him.

6*

"Oh, do not go yet, mother," he said, — "do not go yet, — do not leave me. But it must be so, and I only distress you. Pray for me, dearest mother, and oh, forgive me. I have been a grief and a burden to you all life long; but I ever loved you, mother; and oh, you have been kind, kind and forgiving; and now your task is over. May God bless and reward you! Margaret, dearest Margaret, farewell!"

We parted, and, as it proved, forever. Robert Ferguson expired during the night; and when the keeper entered the cell next morning to prepare him for quitting the asylum, all that remained of this most hapless of the children of genius was a pallid and wasted corpse, that lay stiffening on the straw. I am now a very old man, and the feelings wear out; but I find that my heart is even yet susceptible of emotion, and that the source of tears is not yet dried up.

II.

RECOLLECTIONS OF BURNS.

CHAPTER I.

Wear we not graven on our hearts
The name of Robert Burns?

AMERICAN POET.

THE degrees shorten as we proceed from the lower to the higher latitudes; the years seem to shorten in a much greater ratio as we pass onward through life. We are almost disposed to question whether the brief period of storms and foul weather that floats over us with such dream-like rapidity, and the transient season of flowers and sunshine that seems almost too short for enjoyment, be at all identical with the long summers and still longer winters of our boyhood, when day after day, and week after week, stretched away in dim perspective, till lost in the obscurity of an almost inconceivable distance. Young as I was, I had already passed the period of life when we wonder how it is that the years should be described as short and fleeting; and it seemed as if I had stood but yesterday beside the deathbed of the unfortunate Ferguson, though the flowers of four summers and the snows of four winters had been shed over his grave.

My prospects in life had begun to brighten. I served in the capacity of mate in a large West India trader, the master of which, an elderly man of considerable wealth, was on the eve of quitting the. sea; and the owners had already determined that I should succeed him in the charge. But fate had ordered it otherwise. Our seas were infested at this period by American privateers, — prime sailors and strongly armed; and, when homeward bound from Jamaica with a valuable cargo, we were attacked and captured, when within a day's sailing of Ireland, by one of the most formidable of the class. Vain as resistance might have been deemed, — for the force of the American was altogether overpowering, — and though our master, poor old man! and three of the crew, had fallen by the first broadside, we had yet stood stiffly by our guns, and were only overmastered when, after falling foul of the enemy, we were boarded by a party of thrice our strength and number. The Americans, irritated by our resistance, proved on this occasion no generous enemies: we were stripped and heavily ironed, and, two days after, were set ashore on the wild shore of Connaught, without a single change of dress, or a single sixpence to bear us by the way.

I was sitting, on the following night, beside the turf-fire of a hospitable Irish peasant, when a seafaring man, whom I had sailed with about two years before, entered the cabin. The meeting was equally unexpected on either side. My acquaintance was the master of a smuggling lugger then on the coast; and, on acquainting him with the details of my disaster and the state of destitution to which it had reduced me, he kindly proposed that I should accompany him on his voyage to the west coast of Scotland, for which he was then on the eve of sailing.

"You will run some little risk," he said, "as the companion of a man who has now been thrice outlawed for firing on his Majesty's flag; but I know your proud heart will prefer the danger of bad company, at its worst, to the alternative of begging your way home." He judged rightly. Before daybreak we had lost sight of land, and in four days more we could discern the precipitous shores of Carrick, stretching in a dark line along the horizon, and the hills of the interior rising thin and blue behind, like a volume of clouds. A considerable part of our cargo, which consisted mostly of tea and spirits, was consigned to an Ayr trader, who had several agents in the remote parish of Kirkoswald, which at this period afforded more facilities for carrying on the contraband trade than any other on the western coast of Scotland, and in a rocky bay of the parish we proposed unlading on the following night. It was necessary, however, that the several agents, who were yet ignorant of our arrival, should be prepared to meet with us; and, on volunteering my service for the purpose, I was landed near the ruins of the ancient castle of Turnberry, once the seat of Robert the Bruce.

I had accomplished my object. It was evening, and a party of countrymen were sauntering among the cliffs, waiting for nightfall and the appearance of the lugger. There are splendid caverns on the coast of Kirkoswald ; and, to while away the time, I had descended to the shore by a broken and precipitous path, with a view of exploring what are termed the Caves of Colzean, by far the finest in this part of Scotland. The evening was of great beauty: the sea spread out from the cliffs to the far horizon like the sea of gold and crystal described by the prophet, and its warm orange hues so harmonized with those of the sky that, passing over the dimly-defined line of demarcation, the whole upper and nether expanse seemed but one glorious firmament, with the dark Ailsa, like a thunder-cloud, sleeping in the midst. The sun was hastening to his setting, and threw his strong red light on the wall of rock which, loftier and more imposing than the walls of even the mighty Babylon, stretched onward along the beach, headland after headland, till the last sank abruptly in the far distance, and only the wide ocean stretched beyond. I passed along the insulated piles of cliff that rise thick along the bases of the precipices — now in sunshine, now in shadow — till I reached the opening of one of the largest caves. The roof rose more than fifty feet over my head; a broad stream of light, that seemed redder and more fiery from the surrounding gloom, slanted inwards; and, as I paused in the opening, my shadow, lengthened and dark, fell across the floor — a slim and narrow bar of black — till lost in the gloom of the inner recess. There was a wild and uncommon beauty in the scene that powerfully affected the imagination; and I stood admiring it, in that delicious dreamy mood in which one can forget all but the present enjoyment, when I was roused to a recollection of the business of the evening by the sound of a footfall echoing from within. It seemed approaching by a sort of cross passage in the rock; and, in a moment after, a young man — one of the country people whom I had left among the cliffs above — stood before me. He wore a broad Lowland bonnet, and his plain homely suit of coarse russet seemed to bespeak him a peasant of perhaps the poorest class; but as he emerged from the gloom, and the red light fell full on his countenance, I saw an indescribable something in the expression that in an instant awakened my curiosity. He was rather above the middle size, of a frame the most muscular and compact I have almost ever seen; and there was a blended mixture of elasticity and firmness in his tread that, to one accustomed, as I had been, to estimate the physical capabilities of men, gave evidence of a union of immense personal strength with activity. My first idea regarding the stranger—and I know not how it should have struck me — was that of a very powerful frame, animated by a double portion of vitality. The red light shone full on his face, and gave a ruddy tinge to the complexion, which I afterwards found it wanted, for he was naturally of a darker hue than common; but there was no mistaking the expression of the large flashing eyes, the features that seemed so thoroughly cast in the mould of thought, and the broad, full, perpendicular forehead. Such, at least, was the impression on my mind, that I addressed him with more of the courtesy which my earlier pursuits had rendered familiar to me, than of the bluntness of my adopted profession. "This sweet evening," I said, "is by far too fine for our lugger; I question whether, in these calms, we need expect her before midnight. But 'tis well, since wait we must, that 'tis in a place where the hours may pass so agreeably." The stranger good-humoredly acquiesced in the remark; and we sat down together on the dry, water-worn pebbles, mixed with fragments of broken shells and minute pieces of wreck, that strewed the opening of the cave.

"Was there ever a lovelier evening!" he exclaimed. "The waters above the firmament seem all of a piece with the waters below. And never, surely, was there a scene of wilder beauty. Only look inwards, and see how the stream of red light seems bounded by the extreme darkness, like a river by its banks, and how the reflection of the ripple goes waving in golden curls along the roof!"

"I have been admiring the scene for the last half-hour," I said. "Shakspeare speaks of a music that cannot be heard; and I have not yet seen a place where one might better learn to comment on the passage."

Both the thought and the phrase seemed new to him.

"A music that cannot be heard!" he repeated; and then, after a momentary pause, "You allude to the fact," he continued, "that sweet music, and forms, such as these, of silent beauty and grandeur, awaken in the mind emotions of nearly the same class. There is something truly exquisite in the concert'of to-night."

I muttered a simple assent.

"See!" he continued, "how finely these insulated piles of rock, that rise in so many combinations of form along the beach, break and diversify the red light; and how the glossy leaves of the ivy glisten in the hollows of the precipices above! And then, how the sea spreads away to the far horizon, — a glorious pavement of crimson and gold, — and how the dark Ailsa rises in the midst, like the little cloud seen by the prophet!. The mind seems to enlarge, the heart to expand, in the contemplation of so much of beauty and grandeur. The soul asserts its due supremacy. And oh, 'tis surely well that we can escape from those little cares of life which fetter down our thoughts, our hopes, our wishes to the wants and the enjoyments of our animal existence, and that, amid the grand and the sublime of nature, we may learn from the spirit within us that we are better than the beasts that perish!"

I looked up to the animated countenance and flashing eyes of my companion, and wondered what sort of a peasant it was I had met with. "Wild and beautiful as the scene is," I said, "you will find, even among those who arrogate to themselves the praise of wisdom and learning, men who regard such scenes as mere errors of nature. Burnett would have told you that a Dutch landscape, without hill, rock, or valley, must be the perfection of beauty, seeing that Paradise itself could have furnished nothing better."

"I hold Milton as higher authority on the subject," said my companion, "than all the philosophers who ever wrote. Beauty is a tame, unvaried flat, where a man would know his country only by the milestones! A very Dutch paradise, truly!"

"But would not some of your companions above," I asked, "deem the scene as much an error of nature as Burnet himself? They could pass over these stubborn rocks neither plough nor harrow."

"True," he replied; "there is a species of small wisdom in the world that often constitutes the extremest of its folly, — a wisdom that would change the entire nature of *good*, had it but the power, by vainly endeavoring to render that good universal. It would convert the entire earth into one vast corn-field, and then find that it had ruined the species by its improvement."

"We of Scotland can hardly be ruined in that way for an age to come," I said. "But I am not sure that I understand you. Alter the very nature of good in the attempt to render it universal! How?"

"I dare say you have seen a graduated scale," said my companion, "exhibiting the various powers of the different musical instruments, and observed how some of limited scope cross only a few of the divisions, and how others stretch nearly from side to side. 'Tis but a poor truism, perhaps, to say that similar differences in scope and power obtain among men, — that there are minds who could not join in the concert of to-night, — who could see neither beauty nor grandeur amid these wild cliffs and caverns, or in that glorious expanse of sea and sky; and that, on the other hand, there are minds so finely modulated — minds that sweep so broadly across the scale of nature — that there is no object, however minute, no breath of feeling, however faint, that does not awaken their sweet vibrations: the snow-flake falling in the stream, the daisy of the field, the conies of the rock, the hyssop of the wall. Now, the vast and various frame of nature is adapted, not to the lesser, but to the larger mind. It spreads on and around us in all its rich and magnificent variety, and finds the full portraiture of its Proteus-like beauty in the mirror of genius alone. Evident, however, as this may seem, we find a sort of levelling principle in the inferior order of minds, and which, in fact, constitutes one of their grand characteristics, — a principle that would fain abridge the scale to their own narrow capabilities, that would cut down the vastness of nature to suit the littleness of their own conceptions and desires, and convert it into one tame, uniform *mediocre good*, which would be *good* but to themselves alone, and ultimately not even that."

"I think I can now understand you," I said. "You describe a sort of swinish wisdom, that would convert the world into one vast stye. For my own part, I have travelled far enough to know the value of a blue hill, and would not willingly lose so much as one of these landmarks of our mother land, by which kindly hearts in distant countries love to remember it."

"I dare say we are getting fanciful," rejoined my companion; " but certainly, in man's schemes of improvement, both physical and moral, there is commonly a littleness and want of adaptation to the general good that almost always defeats his aims. He sees and understands but a minute portion; it is always some partial good he would introduce; and thus he but destroys the just proportions of a nicely-regulated system of things, by exaggerating one of the parts. I passed of late through a richly-cultivated district of country, in which the agricultural improver had done his utmost. Never were there finer fields, more convenient steadings, crops of richer promise, a better regulated system of production. Corn and cattle had mightily improved; but what had man, the lord of the soil, become? Is not the body better than food, and life than raiment? If that decline for which all other things exist, it surely matters little that all these other things prosper. And here, though the corn, the cattle, the fields, the steadings had improved, man had sunk. There are but two classes in the district: a few cold-hearted speculators, who united what is worst in the character of the landed proprietor and the merchant, — these were young gentleman farmers; and a class of degraded helots, little superior to the cattle they tended, — these were your farm-servants. And for two such extreme classes — necessary result of such a state of thing — had this unfortunate though highly eulogized district parted with a moral, intelligent, high-minded peasantry, — the true boast and true riches of their country."

"I have, I think, observed something like what you describe," I said.

"I give," he replied, " but one instance of a thousand. But mark how the sun's lower disk has just reached the line of the horizon, and how the long level rule of light stretches to the very innermost recess of the cave. It darkens as the orb sinks. And see how the gauze-like shadows creep on from the sea, film after film; and now they have reached the ivy that mantles round the castle of the Bruce. Are you acquainted with Barbour?"

"Well," I said; — "a spirited, fine old fellow, who loved his country, and did much for it. I could once repeat all his chosen passages. Do you remember how he describes King Robert's rencounter with the English knight?"

My companion sat up erect, and, clenching his fist, began repeating the passage, with a power and animation that seemed to double its inherent energy and force.

"Glorious old Barbour!" ejaculated he, when he had finished the description; "many a heart has beat all the higher, when the bale-fires were blazing, through the tutorage of thy noble verses! Blind Harry, too, — what has not his country owed to him!"

"Ah, they have long since been banished from our popular literature," I said; "and yet Blind Henry's 'Wallace,' as Hailes tells us, was at one time the very Bible of the Scotch. But love of country seems to be old-fashioned among us; and we have become philosophic enough to set up for citizens of the world."

"All cold pretense," rejoined my companion, — "an effect of that small wisdom we have just been decrying. Cosmopolitism, as we are accustomed to define it, can be no virtue of the present age, nor yet of the next, nor perhaps for centuries to come. Even when it shall have attained to its best, and when it may be most safely indulged in, it is according to the nature of man that, instead of running counter to the love of country, it should exist as but a wider diffusion of the feeling, and form, as it were, a wider circle round it. It is absurdity itself to oppose the love of our country to that of our race."

"Do I rightly understand you?" I said. "You look forward to a time when the patriot may safely expand into the citizen of the world; but in the present age he would do well, you think, to confine his energies within the inner circle of the country."

"Decidedly," he rejoined. "Man should love his species at all times; but it is ill with him if, in times like the present, he loves not his country more. The spirit of war and aggression is yet abroad; there are laws to be established, rights to be defended, invaders to be repulsed, tyrants to be deposed. And who but the patriot is equal to these things? We are not yet done with the Bruces, the Wallaces, the Tells, the Washingtons, — yes, the Washingtons, whether they fight for or against us, — we are not yet done with them. The cosmopolite is but a puny abortion, — a birth ere the natural time, — that at once endangers the life and betrays the weakness of the country that bears him. Would that he were sleeping in his elements till his proper time! But we are getting ashamed of our country, of our language, our manners, our music, our literature; nor shall we have enough of the old spirit left us to assert our liberties or fight our battles. Oh for some Barbour or Blind Harry of the present day, to make us once more proud of our country!"

I quoted the famous saying of Fletcher of Salton, — "Allow me to make the songs of a country, and I will allow you to make its laws."

"But here," I said, "is our lugger stealing round Turnberry Head. We shall soon part, perhaps for ever; and I would fain know with whom I have spent an hour so agreeably, and have some name to remember him by. My own name is Matthew Lindsay. I am a native of Irvine."

"And I," said the young man, rising and cordially grasping the proffered hand, "am a native of Ayr. My name is Robert Burns."

CHAPTER· II.

If friendless, low, we meet together,
Then, Sir, your hand, — my friend and brother.
DEDICATION TO G. HAMILTON.

A LIGHT breeze had risen as the sun sank, and our lugger, with all her sails set, came sweeping along the shore. She had nearly gained the little bay in front of the cave, and the countrymen from above, to the number of perhaps twenty, had descended to the beach, when, all of a sudden, after a shrill whistle, and a brief half-minute of commotion among the crew, she wore round and stood out to sea. I turned to the south, and saw a square-rigged vessel shooting out from behind one of the rocky headlands, and then bearing down in a long tack on the smuggler. "The sharks are upon us," said one of the countrymen, whose eyes had turned in the same direction; "we shall have no sport to-night." We stood lining the beach in anxious curiosity. The breeze freshened as the evening fell; and the lugger, as she lessened to our sight, went leaning against the foam in a long bright furrow, that, catching the last light of evening, shone like the milky-way amid the blue. Occasionally we could see the flash and hear the booming of a gun from the other vessel; but the night fell thick and dark ; the waves, too, began to lash against the rocks, drowning every feebler sound in a continuous roaring, and every trace of both the chase and the chaser disappeared. The party broke up, and I was left standing alone on the beach, a little nearer home, but in every other respect in quite the same circumstances as when landed by my American friends on the wild coast of Connaught. "Another of Fortune's freaks!" I ejaculated; "but 'tis well she can no longer surprise me."

A man stepped out in the darkness, as I spoke, from beside one of the rocks. It was the peasant Burns, my acquaintance of the earlier part of the evening.

"I have waited, Mr. Lindsay," he said, "to see whether some of the country folks here, who have homes of their own to invite you to, might not have brought you along with them. But I am afraid you must just be content to pass the night with me. I can give you a share of my bed and my supper; though both, I am aware, need many apologies." I made a suitable acknowledgment, and we ascended the cliff together. "I live, when at home, with my parents," said my companion, "in the inland parish of Tarbolton; but for the last two months I have attended school here, and lodge with an old widow-woman in the village. To-morrow, as harvest is fast approaching, I return to my father."

"And I," I replied, "shall have the pleasure of accompanying you at least the early part of your journey, on my way to Irvine, where my mother still lives."

We reached the village, and entered a little cottage, that presented its gable to the street and its side to one of the narrower lanes.

"I must introduce you to my landlady," said my companion — "an excellent, kind-hearted old woman, with a fund of honest Scotch pride and shrewd good sense in her composition, and with the mother as strong in her heart as ever, though she lost the last of her children more than twenty years ago."

We found the good woman sitting beside a small but very cheerful fire. The hearth was newly swept, and the floor newly sanded; and, directly fronting her, there was an empty chair, which seemed to have been drawn to its place in the expectation of some one to fill it.

"You are going to leave me, Robert, my bairn," said the woman, "an' I kenna how I sall ever get on without you. I have almost forgotten, sin' you came to live with me that I have neither children nor husband." On seeing me she stopped short.

"An acquaintance," said my companion, "whom I have made bold to bring with me for the night; but you must not put yourself to any trouble, mother; he is, I dare say, as much accustomed to plain fare as myself. Only, however, we must get an additional pint of *yill* from the *clachan;* you know this is my last evening with you, and was to be a merry one, at any rate." The woman looked me full in the face.

"Matthew Lindsay!" she exclaimed, "can you have forgotten your poor old aunt Margaret!" I grasped her hand.

"Dearest aunt, this is surely most unexpected! How could I have so much as dreamed you were within a hundred miles of me?" Mutual congratulation ensued.

"This," she said, turning to my companion, "is the nephew I have so often told you about, and so often wished to bring you acquainted with. He is, like yourself, a great reader and a great thinker, and there is no need that your proud, kindly heart should be jealous of him; for he has been ever quite as poor, and maybe the poorer of the two." After still more of greeting and congratulation, the young man rose.

"The night is dark, mother," he said, "and the road to the clachan a rough one. Besides, you and your kinsman will have much to say to one another. I shall just slip out to the clachan for you; and you shall both tell me, on my return, whether I am not a prime judge of ale."

"The kindest heart, Matthew, that ever lived," said my relative, as he left the house. "Ever since he came to Kirkoswald he has been both son and daughter to me, and I shall feel twice a widow when he goes away."

"I am mistaken, aunt," I said, "if he be not the strongest-minded man I ever saw. Be assured he stands high among the aristocracy of nature, whatever may be thought of him in Kirkoswald. There is a robustness of intellect, joined to an overmastering force of character, about him, which I have never yet seen equalled, though I have been intimate with at least one very superior mind, and with hundreds of the class who pass for men of talent. I have been thinking, ever since I met with him, of the William Tells and William Wallaces of history, men who, in those times of trouble which unfix the foundations of society, step out from their obscurity to rule the destiny of nations."

"I was ill about a month ago," said my relative, — "so very ill that I thought I was to have done with the world altogether; and Robert was both nurse and physician to me. He kindled my fire, too, every morning, and sat up beside me sometimes for the greater part of the night. What wonder I should love him as my own child? Had your cousin Henry been spared to me, he would now have been much about Robert's age."

The conversation passed to other matters; and in about half an hour my new friend entered the room, when we sat down to a homely but cheerful repast.

"I have been engaged in argument for the last twenty minutes with our parish schoolmaster," he said, — "a shrewd, sensible man, and a prime scholar, but one of the most determined Calvinists I ever knew. Now, there is something, Mr. Lindsay, in abstract Calvinism that dissatisfies and distresses me; and yet, I must confess, there is so much of good in the working of the system, that I would ill like to see it supplanted by any other. I am convinced, for instance, there is nothing so efficient in teaching the bulk of a people to think as a Calvinistic church."

"Ah, Robert," said my aunt, "it does meikle mair nor that. Look round you, my bairn, an' see if there be a kirk in which puir sinful creatures have mair comfort in their sufferings, or mair hope in their deaths."

"Dear mother," said my companion, "I like well enough to dispute with the schoolmaster, but I must have no dispute with you. I know the heart is everything in these matters, and yours is much wiser than mine."

"There is something in abstract Calvinism," he continued, "that distresses me. In almost all our researches, we arrive at an ultimate barrier which interposes its wall of darkness between us and the last grand truth in the series, which we had trusted was to prove a master-key to the whole. We dwell in a sort of Goshen: there is light in our immediate neighborhood, and a more than Egyptian darkness all around; and as every Hebrew must save known that the hedge of cloud which he saw resting on the landscape was a boundary, not to things themselves, but merely to his view of things, — for beyond there were cities and plains and oceans and continents, — so we in like manner must know that the barriers of which I speak exist only in relation to the faculties which we employ, not to the objects on which we employ them. And yet, notwithstanding this consciousness that we are necessarily and irremediably the bound prisoners of ignorance, and that all the great truths lie outside our prison, we can almost be content that in most cases it should be so; not, however, with regard to those great unattainable truths which lie in the track of Calvinism. They seem too important to be wanted, and yet want them we must; and we beat our very heads against the cruel barrier which separates us from them."

"I am afraid I hardly understand you," I said. "Do assist me by some instance or illustration."

"You are acquainted," he replied, "with the Scripture doctrine of predestination; and, in thinking over it in connection with the destinies of man, it must have struck you that, however much it may interfere with our fixed notions of the goodness of Deity, it is thoroughly in accordance with the actual condition of our race. As far as we can know of ourselves and the things around us, there seems, through the will of Deity, — for to what else can we refer it? — a fixed, invariable connection between what we term cause and effect. Nor do we demand of any class of mere effects, in the inanimate or irrational world, that they should regulate themselves otherwise than the causes which produce them have determined. The roe and the tiger pursue, unquestioned, the instincts of their several natures; the cork rises, and the stone sinks; and no one thinks of calling either to account for movements so opposite. But it is not so with the family of man; and yet our minds, our bodies, our circumstances are but combinations of effects, over the causes of which we have no control. We did not choose a country for ourselves, nor yet a condition in life; nor did we determine our modicum of intellect, or our amount of passion; we did not impart its gravity to the weightier part of our nature, or give expansion to the lighter; nor are our instincts of our own planting. How, then, being thus as much the creatures of necessity as the denizens of the wild and forest,— as thoroughly under the agency of fixed, unalterable causes as the dead matter around us, — why are we yet the subjects of a retributive system, and accountable for all our actions?"

"You quarrel with Calvinism," I said; "and seem one of the most thoroughgoing necessitarians I ever knew."

"Not so," he replied. "Though my judgment cannot disprove these conclusions, my heart cannot acquiesce in them; though I see that I am as certainly the subject of laws that exist and operate independent of my will as the dead matter around me, I feel, with a certainty quite as great, that I am a free, accountable creature. It is according to the scope of my entire reason that I should deem myself bound; it is according to the constitution of my whole nature that I should feel myself free. And in this consists the great, the fearful problem, — a problem which both reason and revelation propound; but the truths which can alone solve it seem to lie beyond the horizon of darkness, and we vex ourselves in vain. 'Tis a sort of moral asymptote; but its lines, instead of approaching through all space without meeting, seem receding through all space and yet meet."

"Robert, my bairn," said my aunt, "I fear you are wasting your strength on these mysteries, to your ain hurt. Did ye no see, in the last storm, when ye staid

out among the caves till cock-crow, that the bigger and
stronger the wave, the mair was it broken against the
rocks? It's just thus wi' the pride o' man's understanding, when he measures it against the dark things o' God.
An' yet, it's sae ordered that the same wonderful truths
which perplex an' cast down the proud reason, should
delight an' comfort the humble heart. I am a lone, puir
woman, Robert. Bairns and husband have gone down to
the grave, one by one; an' now, for twenty weary years,
I have been childless an' a widow. But trow ye that the
puir lone woman wanted a guard, an' a comforter, an' a
provider, through a' the lang mirk nichts and a' the cauld
scarce winters o' these twenty years? No, my bairn; I
kent that Himsel' was wi' me. I kent it by the provision
He made, an' the care He took, an' the joy He gave. An'
how, think you, did He comfort me maist? Just by the
blessed assurance that a' my trials an' a' my sorrows were
nae hasty chance matters, but dispensations for my gude
and the gude o' those He took to Himsel'; that, in the
perfect love and wisdom o' his nature, He had ordained
frae the beginning."

"Ah, mother," said my friend, after a pause, "you understand the doctrine far better than I do. There are, I
find, no contradictions in the Calvinism of the heart."

8

CHAPTER III.

Ayr, gurgling, kissed his pebbled shore,
    O'erhung with wild woods thick'ning green ;
The fragrant birch and hawthorn hoar
    Twined, amorous, round the raptured scene;
The flowers sprang wanton to be prest,
    The birds sang love on every spray,
Till too, too soon, the glowing west
    Proclaimed the speed of wingéd day.
                              To Mary in Heaven.

WE were early on the road together. The day, though somewhat gloomy, was mild and pleasant; and we walked slowly onward, neither of us in the least disposed to hasten our parting by hastening our journey. We had discussed fifty different topics, and were prepared to enter on fifty more, when we reached the ancient burgh of Ayr, where our roads separated.

"I have taken an immense liking to you, Mr. Lindsay," said my companion, as he seated himself on the parapet of the old bridge, "and have just bethought me of a scheme through which I may enjoy your company for at least one night more. The Ayr is a lovely river, and you tell me you have never explored it. We shall explore it together this evening for about ten miles, when we shall find ourselves at the farm-house of Lochlea. You may depend on a hearty welcome from my father, whom, by the way, I wish much to introduce to you, as a man worth your knowing ; and as I have set my heart on the scheme, you are surely too good-natured to disappoint me." Little risk of that, I thought. I had, in fact, become thoroughly enamored of the warm-hearted benevolence and fascinating conversation of my companion, and acquiesced with the best good-will in the world.

We had threaded the course of the river for several miles. It runs through a wild pastoral valley, roughened by thickets of copsewood, and bounded on either hand by a line of swelling, moory hills, with here and there a few irregular patches of corn, and here and there some little nest-like cottage peeping out from among the wood. The clouds, which during the morning had obscured the entire face of the heavens, were breaking up their array, and the sun was looking down in twenty different places through the openings, checkering the landscape with a fantastic though lovely carpeting of light and shadow. Before us there rose a thick wood, on a jutting promontory, that looked blue and dark in the shade, as if it wore mourning; while the sunlit stream beyond shone through the trunks and branches like a river of fire. At length the clouds seemed to have melted in the blue, — for there was not a breath of wind to speed them away, — and the sun, now hastening to the west, shone in unbroken effulgence over the wide extent of the dell, lighting up stream and wood and field and cottage in one continuous blaze of glory. We had walked on in silence for the last half-hour; but I could sometimes hear my companion muttering as he went; and when, in passing through a thicket of hawthorn and honeysuckle, we started from its perch a linnet that had been filling the air with its melody, I could hear him exclaim, in a subdued tone of voice, " Bonny, bonny birdie! why hasten frae me? I wadna skaith a feather o' yer wing." He turned round to me, and I could see that his eyes were swimming in moisture.

"Can he be other," he said, " than a good and benevolent God who gives us moments like these to enjoy? O, my friend! without these sabbaths of the soul, that come to refresh and invigorate it, it would dry up within us! How exquisite," he continued, "how entire, the sympathy which exists between all that is good and fair in external nature and all of good and fair that dwells in our own! And oh, how the heart expands and lightens! The world is as a grave to it, a closely-covered grave; and it shrinks and deadens and contracts all its holier and more joyous feelings under the cold, earth-like pressure. But amid the grand and lovely of nature, — amid these forms and colors of richest beauty, — there is a disinterment, a resurrection, of sentiment; the pressure of our earthly part seems removed; and those senses of the mind, if I may so speak, which serve to connect our spirits with the invisible world around us, recover their proper tone, and perform their proper office."

"Senses of the mind!" I said, repeating the phrase; "the idea is new to me; but I think I can catch your meaning."

"Yes; there are, there must be such," he continued, with growing enthusiasm. "Man is essentially a religious creature, a looker beyond the grave, from the very constitution of his mind; and the sceptic who denies it is untrue not merely to the Being who has made and who preserves him, but to the entire scope and bent of his own nature besides. Wherever man is, — whether he be a wanderer of the wild forest or still wilder desert, — a dweller in some lone isle of the sea, or the tutored and full-minded denizen of some blessed land like our own; —

wherever man is, there is religion ; hopes that look forward and upward ; the belief in an unending existence and a land of separate souls."

I was carried away by the enthusiasm of my companion, and felt for the time as if my mind had become the mirror of his. There seems to obtain among men a species of moral gravitation, analogous in its principles to that which regulates and controls the movements of the planetary system. The larger and more ponderous any body, the greater its attractive force, and the more overpowering its influence over the lesser bodies which surround it. The earth we inhabit carries the moon along with it in its course, and is itself subject to the immensely more powerful influence of the sun. And it is thus with character. It is a law of our nature, as certainly as of the system we inhabit, that the inferior should yield to the superior, and the lesser owe its guidance to the greater. I had hitherto wandered on through life almost unconscious of the existence of this law ; or, if occasionally rendered half aware of it, it was only through a feeling that some secret influence was operating favorably in my behalf on the common minds around me. I now felt, however, for the first time, that I had come in contact with a mind immeasurably more powerful than my own. My thoughts seemed to cast themselves into the very mould, my sentiments to modulate themselves by the very tone, of his. And yet he was but a russet-clad peasant, — my junior by at least eight years, — who was returning from school to assist his father, an humble tacksman, in the labors of the approaching harvest. But the law of circumstance, so arbitrary in ruling the destinies of common men, exerts but feeble control over the children of genius.

8*

The prophet went forth *commissioned by heaven to anoint a king over Israel; and the choice fell on a shepherd-boy, who was tending his father's flocks in the field.

We had reached a lovely bend of the stream. There was a semicircular inflection in the steep bank, which waved over us, from base to summit, with hawthorn and hazel; and while one half looked blue and dark in the shade, the other was lighted up with gorgeous and fiery splendor by the sun, now fast sinking in the west. The effect seemed magical. A little glassy platform, that stretched between the hanging wood and the stream, was whitened over with clothes, that looked like snow-wreaths in the hollow; and a young and beautiful girl watched beside them.

"Mary Campbell!" exclaimed my companion; and in a moment he was at her side, and had grasped both her hands in his. "How fortunate, how very fortunate I am!" he said; "I could not have so much as hoped to have seen you to-night, and yet here you are! This, Mr. Lindsay, is a loved friend of mine, whom I have known and valued for years, — ever, indeed, since we herded our sheep together under the cover of one plaid. Dearest Mary, I have had sad forebodings regarding you for the whole last month I was in Kirkoswald; and yet, after all my foolish fears, here you are, ruddier and bonnier than ever."

She was, in truth, a beautiful, sylph-like young woman, —one whom I would have looked at with complacency in any circumstances; for who that admires the fair and lovely in nature, whether it be the wide-spread beauty of sky and earth, or beauty in its minuter modifications, as we see in the flowers that spring up at our feet, or the butterfly that flutters over them, — who, I say, that admires the fair and lovely in nature, can be indifferent to the fairest and loveliest of all her productions? As the mistress, however, of by far the strongest-minded man I ever knew, there was more of scrutiny in my glance than usual, and I felt a deeper interest in her than mere beauty could have awakened. She was perhaps rather below than above the middle size, but formed in such admirable proportion that it seemed out of place to think of size in reference to her at all. Who, in looking at the Venus de Medicis, asks whether she be tall or short? The bust and neck were so exquisitely moulded that they reminded me of Burke's fanciful remark, viz. that our ideas of beauty originate in our love of the sex, and that we deem every object beautiful which is described by soft waving lines, resembling those of the female neck and bosom. Her feet and arms, which were both bare, had a statue-like symmetry and marble-like whiteness. But it was on her expressive and lovely countenance, now lighted up by the glow of joyous feeling, that nature seemed to have exhausted her utmost skill. There was a fascinating mixture in the expression of superior intelligence and child-like simplicity; a soft, modest light dwelt in the blue eye ; and in the entire contour and general form of the features there was a nearer approach to that union of the straight and the rounded — which is found in its perfection in only the Grecian face — than is at all common, in our northern latitudes, among the descendants of either the Celt or the Saxon. I felt, however, as I gazed, that, when lovers meet, the presence of a third person, however much the friend of either, must always be less than agreeable.

"Mr. Burns," I said, "there is a beautiful eminence a few hundred yards to the right, from which I am desirous to overlook the windings of the stream. Do permit me to leave you for a short half-hour, when I shall return; or, lest I weary you by my stay, 'twere better, perhaps, you should join me there." My companion greeted the proposal with a good-humored smile of intelligence; and, plunging into the wood, I left him with his Mary. The sun had just set as he joined me.

"Have you ever been in love, Mr. Lindsay?" he said.

"No, never seriously," I replied. "I am perhaps not naturally of the coolest temperament imaginable, but the same fortune that has improved my mind in some little degree, and given me high notions of the sex, has hitherto thrown me among only its less superior specimens. I am now in my eight-and-twentieth year, and I have not yet met with a woman whom I could love."

"Then you are yet a stranger," he rejoined, "to the greatest happiness of which our nature is capable. I have enjoyed more heartfelt pleasure in the company of the young woman I have just left, than from every other source that has been opened to me from my childhood till now. Love, my friend, is the fulfilling of the whole law."

"Mary Campbell, did you not call her?" I said. "She is, I think, the loveliest creature I have ever seen; and I am much mistaken in the expression of her beauty if her mind be not as lovely as her person." .

"It is, it is!" he exclaimed, — "the intelligence of an angel, with the simplicity of a child. Oh, the delight of being thoroughly trusted, thoroughly beloved, by one of the loveliest, best, purest-minded of all God's good creatures! to feel that heart beating against my own, and to know that it beats for me only! Never have I passed an evening with my Mary without returning to the world a

better, gentler, wiser man. Love, my friend, is the fulfilling of the whole law. What are we without it?—poor,
vile, selfish animals; our very virtues themselves so exclusively virtues on our own behalf as to be well-nigh as
hateful as our vices. Nothing so opens and improves the
heart; nothing so widens the grasp of the affections;
nothing half so effectually brings us out of our crust of
self, as a happy, well-regulated love for a pure-minded,
affectionate-hearted woman!"

"There is another kind of love of which we sailors see
somewhat," I said, "which is not so easily associated with
good."

"Love!" he replied. "No, Mr. Lindsay, that is not the
name. Kind associates with kind in all nature; and love
—humanizing, heart-softening love—cannot be the companion of whatever is low, mean, worthless, degrading,—
the associate of ruthless dishonor, cunning, treachery, and
violent death. Even independent of its amount of evil as
a crime, or the evils still greater than itself which necessarily accompany it, there is nothing that so petrifies the
feeling as illicit connection."

"Do you seriously think so?" I asked.

"Yes; and I see clearly how it should be so. Neither
sex is complete of itself; each was made for the other,
that, like the two halves of a hinge, they may become an
entire whole when united. Only think of the Scriptural
phrase, "*one flesh*": it is of itself a system of philosophy.
Refinement and tenderness are of the woman; strength
and dignity of the man. Only observe the effects of a
thorough separation, whether originating in accident or
caprice. You will find the stronger sex lost in the rude-
nesses of partial barbarism; the gentler wrapt up in some
pitiful round of trivial and unmeaning occupation,—dry-

nursing puppies, or making pin-cushions for posterity. But how much more pitiful are the effects when they meet amiss; when the humanizing friend and companion of the man is converted into the light, degraded toy of an idle hour, the object of a sordid appetite that lives but for a moment, and then expires in loathing and disgust! The better feelings are iced over at their source, chilled by the freezing and deadening contact, where there is nothing to inspire confidence or solicit esteem; and if these pass not through the first, the inner circle, that circle within which the social affections are formed, and from whence they emanate,—how can they possibly flow through the circles which lie beyond? But here, Mr. Lindsay, is the farm of Lochlea; and yonder brown cottage, beside the three elms, is the dwelling of my parents."

CHAPTER IV.

From scenes like these old Scotia's grandeur springs,
That makes her loved at home, revered abroad.
COTTER's SATURDAY NIGHT.

THERE was a wide and cheerful circle this evening round the hospitable hearth of Lochlea. The father of my friend — a patriarchal-looking old man, with a countenance the most expressive I have almost ever seen — sat beside the wall, on a large oaken settle, which also served to accommodate a young man, an occasional visitor of the family, dressed in rather shabby black, whom I at once set down as a probationer of divinity. I had my own seat beside him. The brother of my friend — a lad cast in nearly the same mould of form and feature, except perhaps that his frame, though muscular and strongly set, seemed in the main less formidably robust, and his countenance, though expressive, less decidedly intellectual — sat at my side. My friend had drawn in his seat beside his mother, — a well-formed, comely brunette, of about thirty-eight, whom I might almost have mistaken for his older sister, — and two or three younger members of the family were grouped behind her. The fire blazed cheerily within the wide and open chimney, and, throwing its strong light on the faces and limbs of the circle, sent our shadows flickering across the rafters and the wall behind. The conversation was animated and rational, and every one contributed his share. But I was chiefly interested in the remarks of the old man, for whom I already felt a growing veneration, and in those of his wonderfully gifted son.

"Unquestionably, Mr. Burns," said the man in black, addressing the farmer, "politeness is but a very shadow, as the poet hath it, if the heart be wanting. I saw to-night, in a strictly polite family, so marked a presumption of the lack of that natural affection of which politeness is but the portraiture and semblance, that, truly, I have been grieved in my heart ever since."

"Ah, Mr. Murdoch," said the farmer, "there is ever more hypocrisy in the world than in the church, and that, too, among the class of fine gentlemen and fine ladies who deny it most. But the instance" —

"You know the family, my worthy friend," continued Mr. Murdoch; "it is a very pretty one, as we say vernacularly, being numerous, and the sons highly genteel young men — the daughters not less so. A neighbor of the same very polite character, coming on a visit when I was among them, asked the father, in the course of the conversation to which I was privy, how he meant to dispose of his sons; when the father replied that he had not yet determined. The visitor said that, were he in his place, seeing they were all well-educated young men, he would send them abroad; to which the father objected the indubitable fact that many young men lost their health in foreign countries, and very many their lives. 'True,' did the visitor rejoin; 'but, as you have a number of sons, it will be strange if some one of them does not live and make a fortune.' Now, Mr. Burns, what will you, who know the feelings of paternity, and the incalculable, and assuredly I may say invaluable value of human souls, think when I add, that the father commended the hint, as showing the wisdom of a shrewd man of the world!"

"Even the chief priests," said the old man, " pronounced it unlawful to cast into the treasury the thirty pieces of silver, seeing it was the price of blood; but the gentility of the present day is less scrupulous. There is a laxity of principle among us, Mr. Murdoch, that, if God restore us not, must end in the ruin of our country. I say laxity of principle; for there have ever been evil manners among us, and waifs in..no inconsiderable number broken loose from the decencies of society, — more, perhaps, in my early days than there are now. But our principles, at least, were sound ; and not only was there thus a restorative and conservative spirit among us, but, what was of not less importance, there was a broad gulf, like that in the parable, between the two grand classes, the good and the evil, — a gulf which, when it secured the better class from contamination, interposed no barrier to the reformation and return of even the most vile and profligate, if repentant. But this gulf has disappeared,

and we are standing unconcernedly over it, on a hollow
and dangerous marsh of neutral ground, which, in the end,
if God open not our eyes, must assuredly give way under
our feet."

"To what, father," inquired my friend, who sat listening with the deepest and most respectful attention, "do
you attribute the change?"

"Undoubtedly," replied the old man, "there have been
many causes at work; and though not impossible, it
would certainly be no easy task to trace them all to their
several effects, and give to each its due place and importance. But there is a deadly evil among us, though you will
hear of it from neither press nor pulpit, which I am disposed to rank first in the number, — the affectation of gentility. It has a threefold influence among us : it confounds
the grand, eternal distinctions of right and wrong, by
erecting into a standard of conduct and opinion that hete-
rogeneous and artificial whole which constitutes the manners and morals of the upper classes; it severs those ties
of affection and good-will which should bind the middle to
the lowers orders, by disposing the one to regard whatever is below them with a too contemptuous indifference,
and by provoking a bitter and indignant, though natural
jealousy in the other, for being so regarded; and, finally,
by leading those who most entertain it into habits of expense, — torturing their means, if I may so speak, on the
rack of false opinion, disposing them to think, in their
blindness, that to be genteel is a first consideration, and
to be honest merely a secondary one, — it has the effect of
so hardening their hearts that, like those Carthagenians of
whom we have been lately reading in the volume Mr.
Murdoch lent us, they offer up their very children, souls

and bodies, to the unreal, phantom-like necessities of their circumstances."

" Have I not heard you remark, father," said Gilbert, " that the change you describe has been very marked among the ministers of our church ? "

" Too marked and too striking," replied the old man ; " and, in affecting the respectability and usefulness of so important a class, it has educed a cause of deterioration distinct from itself, and hardly less formidable. There is an old proverb of our country, ' Better the head of the commonalty than the tail of the gentry.' I have heard you quote it, Robert, oftener than once, and admire its homely wisdom. Now, it bears directly on what I have to remark: the ministers of our church have moved but one step during the last sixty years ; but that step has been an all-important one. It has been from the best place in relation to the people, to the worst in relation to the aristocracy."

" Undoubtedly, worthy Mr. Burns," said Mr. Murdoch. "There is great truth, according to mine own experience, in that which you affirm. I may state, I trust without over-boasting or conceit, my respected friend, that my learning is not inferior to that of our neighbor the clergy-man ; — it is not inferior in Latin, nor in Greek, nor yet in French literature, Mr. Burns, and probable it is he would not much court a competition; and yet, when I last waited at the Manse regarding a necessary and essen-tial certificate, Mr. Burns, he did not as much as ask me to sit down."

" Ah," said Gilbert, who seemed the wit of the family, " he is a highly respectable man, Mr. Murdoch. He has a fine house, fine furniture, fine carpets, — all that consti-tutes respectability, you know ; and his family is on visiting terms with that of the Laird. But his credit is not so respectable, I hear."

"Gilbert," said the old man, with much seriousness, "it is ill with a people when they can speak lightly of their clergymen. There is still much of sterling worth and serious piety in the Church of Scotland; and if the influence of its ministers be unfortunately less than it was once, we must not cast the blame too exclusively on themselves. Other causes have been in operation. The church eighty years ago was the sole guide of opinion, and the only source of thought among us. There was, indeed, but one way in which a man could learn to think. His mind became the subject of some serious impression; he applied to his Bible; and, in the contemplation of the most important of all concerns, his newly-awakened faculties received their first exercise. All of intelligence, all of moral good in him, all that rendered him worthy of the name of man, he owed to the ennobling influence of his church; and is it wonder that that influence should be all-powerful from this circumstance alone? But a thorough change has taken place; — new sources of intelligence have been opened up; we have our newspapers and our magazines, and our volumes of miscellaneous reading; and it is now possible enough for the most cultivated mind in a parish to be the least moral and the least religious; and hence, necessarily, a diminished influence in the church, independent of the character of its ministers."

I have dwelt too long, perhaps, on the conversation of the elder Burns; but I feel much pleasure in thus developing, as it were, my recollections of one whom his powerful-minded son has described — and this after an acquaintance with our Henry M'Kenzies, Adam Smiths, and Dugald Stewarts — as the man most thoroughly acquainted with the world he ever knew. Never, at least, have I met with any one who exerted a more wholesome influence, through the force of moral character, on those around him. We sat down to a plain and homely supper. The slave question had about this time begun to draw the attention of a few of the more excellent and intelligent among the people, and the elder Burns seemed deeply interested in it.

"This is but homely fare, Mr. Lindsay," he said, pointing to the simple viands before us, " and the apologists of slavery among us would tell you how inferior we are to the poor negroes, who fare so much better. But surely 'man does not live by bread alone!' Our fathers who died for Christ on the hill-side and the scaffold were noble men, and never, never shall slavery produce such; and yet they toiled as hard, and fared as meanly, as we their children."

I could feel, in the cottage of such a peasant, and seated beside such men as his two sons, the full force of the remark. And yet I have heard the miserable sophism of unprincipled power against which it is directed — a sophism so insulting to the dignity of honest poverty — a thousand times repeated.

Supper over, the family circle widened round the hearth; and the old man, taking down a large clasped Bible, seated himself beside the iron lamp which now lighted the apartment. There was deep silence among us as he turned over the leaves. Never shall I forget his appearance. He was tall and thin, and, though his frame was still vigorous, considerably bent. His features were high and massy; the complexion still retained much of the freshness of youth, and the eye all its intelligence; but his locks were waxing thin and gray round his high, thoughtful forehead, and the upper part of the head, which was elevated to an unusual height, was bald. There was an expression of the deepest seriousness on the countenance which the strong umbry shadows of the apartment served to heighten ; and when, laying his hand on the page, he half-turned his face to the circle, and said, " Let us worship God," I was impressed by a feeling of awe and reverence to which I had, alas! been a stranger for years. I was affected, too, almost to tears, as I joined in the psalm ; for a thousand half-forgotten associations came rushing upon me; and my heart seemed to swell and expand as, kneeling beside him when he prayed, I listened to his solemn and fervent petition that God might make manifest his power and goodness in the salvation of man. Nor was the poor solitary wanderer of the deep forgotten.

On rising from our devotions, the old man grasped me by the hand. "I am happy," he said, "that we should have met, Mr. Lindsay. I feel an interest in you, and must take the friend and the old man's privilege of giving you an advice. The sailor, of all men, stands most in need of religion. His life is one of continued vicissitude, of unexpected success or unlooked-for misfortune; he is ever passing from danger to safety, and from safety to danger ; his dependence is on the ever-varying winds, his abode on the unstable waters. And the mind takes a peculiar tone from what is peculiar in the circumstances. With nothing stable in the real world around it on which it may rest, it forms a resting-place for itself in some wild code of belief. It peoples the elements with strange occult powers of good and evil, and does them homage, — addressing its prayers to the genius of the winds and the spirits of the waters. And thus it begets a religion for itself ; for what else is the professional superstition of the sailor? Substitute, my friend, for this —shall I call it unavoidable superstition?—this natural religion of the sea, the religion of the Bible. Since you must be a believer in the supernatural, let your belief be true; let your trust be on Him who faileth not, your anchor within the vail; and all shall be well, be your destiny for this world what it may."

We parted for the night, and I saw him no more.

Next morning Robert accompanied me for several miles on my way. I saw, for the last half-hour, that he had something to communicate, and yet knew not how to set about it; and so I made a full stop.

"You have something to tell me, Mr. Burns," I said. "Need I assure you I am one you are in no danger from trusting?" He blushed deeply, and I saw him, for the first time, hesitate and falter in his address.

"Forgive me," he at length said; "believe me, Mr. Lindsay, I would be the last in the world to hurt the feelings of a friend,—a—a—but you have been left among us penniless, and I have a very little money which I have no use for, none in the least. Will you not favor me by accepting it as a loan?"

I felt the full and generous delicacy of the proposal, and, with moistened eyes and a swelling heart, availed myself of his kindness. The sum he tendered did not much exceed a guinea; but the yearly earnings of the peasant Burns fell, at this period of his life, rather below eight pounds.

CHAPTER V.

Corbies an' clergy are a shot right kittle.
BRIGS OF AYR.

THE years passed, and I was again a dweller on the sea; but the ill-fortune which had hitherto tracked me like a bloodhound, seemed at length as if tired in the pursuit, and I was now the master of a West India trader, and had begun to lay the foundation of that competency which has secured to my declining years the quiet and comfort which, for the latter part of my life, it has been my happiness to enjoy. My vessel had arrived at Liverpool in the latter part of the year 1784; and I had taken coach for Irvine, to visit my mother, whom I had not seen for several years. There was a change of passengers at every stage; but I saw little in any of them to interest me till within about a score of miles of my destination, when I met with an old respectable townsman, a friend of my father's. There was but another passenger in the coach, a north-country gentleman from the West Indies. I had many questions to ask my townsman, and many to answer, and the time passed lightly away.

"Can you tell me aught of the Burnses of Lochlea?" I inquired, after learning that my mother and my other relatives were well. "I met with the young man Robert about five years ago, and have often since asked myself what special end Providence could have in view in making such a man."

"I was acquainted with old William Burns," said my companion, "when he was gardener at Denholm, an' got intimate wi' his son Robert when he lived wi' us at Irvine a twalmonth syne. The faither died shortly ago, sairly straitened in his means, I'm fear'd, an' no very square wi' the laird; an' ill wad he hae liked that, for an honester man never breathed. Robert, puir chield, is no very easy either."

"In his circumstances?" I said.

"Ay, an waur. He gat entangled wi' the kirk on an unlucky sculduddery business, an' has been writing bitter wicked ballads on a' the gude ministers in the country ever sinsyne. I'm vexed it's on them he suld hae fallen; an' yet they hae been to blame too."

"Robert Burns so entangled, so occupied!" I exclaimed; "you grieve and astonish me."

"We are puir creatures, Matthew," said the old man; "strength an' weakness are often next-door neighbors in the best o' us; nay, what is our vera strength ta'en on the a'e side, may be our vera weakness ta'en on the ither. Never was there a stancher, firmer fallow than Robert Burns; an', now that he has ta'en a wrang step, puir chield, that vera stanchness seems just a weak want o' ability to yield. He has planted his foot where it lighted by mishanter, and a' the gude an' ill in Scotland wadna budge him frae the spot."

"Dear me! that so powerful a mind should be so frivolously engaged! Making ballads, you say? With what success?"

"Ah, Matthew, lad, when the strong man puts out his strength," said my companion, "there's naething frivolous in the matter, be his object what it may. Robert's ballads are far, far aboon the best things ever seen in Scotland

afore. We auld folk dinna ken whether maist to blame
or praise them; but they keep the young people laughing
frae the a'e nuik o' the shire till the ither."

"But how," I inquired, "have the better clergy rendered themselves obnoxious to Burns? The laws he has
violated, if I rightly understand you, are indeed severe,
and somewhat questionable in their tendencies; and even
good men often press them too far."

"And in the case of Robert," said the old man, "our
clergy have been strict to the very letter. They're gude
men, an' faithfu' ministers; but ane o' them at least, an' he
a leader, has a harsh, ill temper, an' mistakes sometimes
the corruption o' the auld man in him for the proper
zeal o' the new ane. Nor is there ony o' the ithers wha
kent what they had to deal wi' when Robert cam' afore
them. They saw but a proud, thrawart ploughman, that
stood uncow'ring under the glunsh o' a haill session; and
so they opened on him the artillery o' the kirk, to bear
down his pride. Wha could hae tauld them that they
were but frushing their straw an' rotten wood against the
iron scales o' Leviathan? An' now that they hae dune
their maist, the record o' Robert's mishanter is lying in
whity-brown ink yonder in a page o' the session-buik;
while the ballads hae sunk deep, deep intil the very mind
o' the country, and may live there for hunders and
hunders o' years."

"You seem to contrast, in this business," I said, "our
better with what you must deem our inferior clergy.
You mean, do you not, the higher and lower parties in our
church? How are they getting on now?"

"Never worse," replied the old man; "an' oh, it's surely
ill when the ministers o' peace become the very leaders
o' contention! But let the blame rest in the right place.

Peace is surely a blessing frae heaven,— no a gude wark demanded frae man; an' when it grows our duty to be in war, it's an ill thing to be in peace. Our Evangelicals are stan'in', puir folk, whar their faithers stood; an' if they maun either fight or be beaten frae their post, why, it's just their duty to fight. But the Moderates are rinnin' mad a'thegither amang us; signing our auld Confession just that they may get intil the kirk to preach against it; paring the New Testament doun to the vera standard o' heathen Plawto; and sinking a'e doctrine after anither, till they leave ahint naething but Deism that might scunner an infidel. Deed, Matthew, if there comena a change amang them, an' that sune, they'll swamp the puir kirk a'thegither. The cauld morality, that never made ony ane mair moral, tak's nae haud o' the people; an' patronage, as meikle's they roose it, winna keep up either kirk or manse o' itsel'. Sorry I am, sin' Robert has entered on the quarrel at a', it suld hae been on the wrang side."

"One of my chief objections," I said, "to the religion of the Moderate party, is, that it is of no use."

"A gey serious ane," rejoined the old man; "but maybe there's a waur still. I'm unco vexed for Robert, baith on his worthy faither's account and his ain. He's a fearsome fellow when ance angered, but an honest, warm-hearted chield for a' that; an' there's mair sense in yon big head o' his than in ony ither twa in the country."

"Can you tell me aught," said the north-country gentleman, addressing my companion, "of Mr. R——, the chapel minister in K——? I was once one of his pupils in the far north; but I have heard nothing of him since he left Cromarty."

"Why," rejoined the old man, " he's just the man that,

mair nor a' the rest, has borne the brunt o' Robert's fearsome waggery. Did ye ken him in Cromarty, say ye ? "

"He was parish schoolmaster there," said the gentleman, "for twelve years; and for six of these I attended his school. I cannot help respecting him ; but no one ever loved him. Never, surely, was there a man at once ·so unequivocally honest and so thoroughly unamiable."

"You must have found him a rigid disciplinarian," I said.

"He was the most so," he replied, "from the days of Dionysius at least, that ever taught a school. I remember there was a poor fisher-boy among us, named Skinner, who, as is customary in Scottish schools, as you must know, blew the horn for gathering the scholars, and kept the catalogue and the key ; and who, in return, was educated by the master, and received some little gratuity from the scholars besides. On one occasion the key dropped out of his pocket ; and when the school-time came, the irascible dominie had to burst open the door with his foot. He raged at the boy with a fury so insane, and beat him so unmercifully, that the other boys, gathering heart in the extremity of the case, had to rise *en masse* and tear him out of his hands. But the curious part of the story is yet to come. Skinner has been a fisherman for the last twelve years; but never has he been seen disengaged for a moment, from that time to this, without mechanically thrusting his hand into the key-pocket.

Our companion furnished us with two or three other anecdotes of Mr. R ——. He told us of a lady who was so overcome by sudden terror on unexpectedly seeing him, many years after she had quitted his school, in one of the pulpits of the south, that she fainted away ; and of another of his scholars, named M'Glashan, a robust, daring fellow of six feet, who, when returning to Cromarty from some of the colonies, solaced himself by the way with thoughts of the hearty drubbing with which he was to clear off all his old scores with the dominie.

"Ere his return, however," continued the gentleman, "Mr. R—— had quitted the parish; and, had it chanced otherwise, it is questionable whether M'Glashan, with all his strength and courage, would have gained anything in an encounter with one of the boldest and most powerful men in the country."

Such were some of the chance glimpses which I gained at this time of by far the most powerful of the opponents of Burns. He was a good, conscientious man, but unfortunate in a harsh, violent temper, and in sometimes mistaking, as my old townsman remarked, the dictates of that temper for those of duty.

CHAPTER VI.

. It's hardly in a body's pow'r
To keep at times frae being sour,
    To see how things are shared, —
How best 'o chiels are whiles in want,
While coofs on countless thousands rant,
    And kenna how to wair't.
                    Epistle to Davie.

I visited my friend, a few days after my arrival in Irvine, at the farm-house of Mossgiel, to which, on the death of his father, he had removed, with his brother Gilbert and his mother. I could not avoid observing that his manners were considerably changed. My welcome seemed less kind and hearty than I could have anticipated from the warm-hearted peasant of five years ago ; and there was a stern and almost supercilious elevation in his bearing, which at first pained and offended me. I had met with him as he was returning from the fields after the labors of the day. The dusk of twilight had fallen ; and, though I had calculated on passing the evening with him at the farm-house of Mossgiel, so displeased was I that after our first greeting I had more than half changed my mind. The recollection of his former kindness to me, however, suspended the feeling, and I resolved on throwing myself on his hospitality for the night, however cold the welcome.

"I have come all the way from Irvine to see you, Mr. Burns," I said. "For the last five years I have thought more of my mother and you than of any other two persons in the country. May I not calculate, as of old, on my supper and a bed ?"

There was an instantaneous change in his expression.

" Pardon me, my friend," he said, grasping my hand ; "I have, unwittingly, been doing you wrong. One may surely be the master of an Indiaman, and in possession of a heart too honest to be spoiled by prosperity ! "

The remark served to explain the haughty coolness of his manner which had so displeased me, and which was but the unwillingly assumed armor of a defensive pride.

" There, brother," he said, throwing down some plough-irons which he carried ; "send *wee Davoc* with these to the smithy, and bid him tell Rankin I won't be there to-night. The moon is rising, Mr. Lindsay ; shall we not have a stroll together through the coppice ? "

"That of all things," I replied ; and, parting from Gilbert, we struck into the wood.

The evening, considering the lateness of the season, for winter had set in, was mild and pleasant. The moon at full was rising over the Cumnock hills, and casting its faint light on the trees that rose around us, in their winding-sheets of brown and yellow, like so many spectres, or that, in the more exposed glades and openings of the wood, stretched their long naked arms to the sky. A light breeze went rustling through the withered grass; and I could see the faint twinkling of the falling leaves, as they came showering down on every side of us.

"We meet in the midst of death and desolation," said my companion; "we parted when all around us was fresh and beautiful. My father was with me then, and — and Mary Campbell; and now" —

"Mary! your Mary!" I exclaimed, "the young, the beautiful, — alas! is she also gone?"

"She has left me," he said, — "left me. Mary is in her grave!"

I felt my heart swell as the image of that loveliest of creatures came rising to my view in all her beauty, as I had seen her by the river-side, and I knew not what to reply.

"Yes," continued my friend, "she is in her grave. We parted for a few days, to reunite, as we hoped, for ever; and ere those few days had passed she was in her grave. But I was unworthy of her, — unworthy even then; and now — But she is in her grave!"

I grasped his hand. "It is difficult," I said, "to bid the heart submit to these dispensations; and oh, how utterly impossible to bring it to listen! But life — your life, my friend — must not be passed in useless sorrow. I am convinced — and often have I thought of it since our last meeting — that yours is no vulgar destiny, though I know not to what it tends."

"Downwards!" he exclaimed, "it tends downwards! I

see, I feel it. The anchor of my affection is gone, and I drift shoreward on the rocks."

" 'Twere ruin," I exclaimed, "to think so!"

"Not half an hour ere my father died," he continued, "he expressed a wish to rise and sit once more in his chair; and we indulged him. But, alas! the same feeling of uneasiness which had prompted the wish remained with him still, and he sought to return again to his bed. 'It is not by quitting the bed or the chair,' he said, 'that I need seek for ease; it is by quitting the body.' I am oppressed, Mr. Lindsay, by a somewhat similar feeling of uneasiness, and at times would fain cast the blame on the circumstances in which I am placed. But I may be as far mistaken as my poor father. I would fain live at peace with all mankind; nay, more, I would fain love and do good to them all; but the villain and the oppressor come to set their feet on my very neck and crush me into the mire, and must I not resist? And when, in some luckless hour, I yield to my passions, — to those fearful passions that must one day overwhelm me, — when I yield, and my whole mind is darkened by remorse, and I groan under the discipline of conscience, then comes the odious, abominable hypocrite, the devourer of widows' houses and the substance of the orphan, and demands that my repentance be as public as his own detestable prayers! And can I do other than resist and expose him? My heart tells me it was formed to bestow; why else does every misery that I cannot relieve render me wretched? It tells me, too, it was formed not to receive; why else does the proffered assistance of even a friend fill my whole soul with indignation? But ill do my circumstances agree with my feelings. I feel as if I were totally misplaced in some frolic of Nature, and wander onwards, in gloom and unhappiness, for my proper

sphere. But, alas! these efforts of uneasy misery are but
the blind gropings of Homer's Cyclops round the walls of
his cave."

I again began to experience, as on a former occasion,
the o'ermastering power of a mind larger beyond comparison than my own; but I felt it my duty to resist the influence. "Yes, you are misplaced, my friend," I said, —
"perhaps more decidedly so than any other man I ever
knew ; but is not this characteristic, in some measure, of
the whole species? We are all misplaced; and it seems
a part of the scheme of Deity that we should work ourselves up to our proper sphere. In what other respect
does man so differ from the inferior animals as in those aspirations which lead him through all the progressions of
improvement, from the lowest to the highest level of his
nature?"

"That may be philosophy, my friend," he replied, "but a
heart ill at ease finds little of comfort in it. You knew my
father, — need I say he was one of the excellent of the
earth, a man who held directly from God Almighty the
patent of his honors? I saw that father sink broken-
hearted into the grave, the victim of legalized oppression :
yes, saw him overborne in the long contest which his high
spirit and his indomitable love of the right had incited
him to maintain, — overborne by a mean, despicable scoundrel, one of the creeping things of the earth. Heaven
knows I did my utmost to assist in the struggle. In my
fifteenth year, Mr. Lindsay, when a thin, loose-jointed boy,
I did the work of a man, and strained my unknit and
overtoiled sinews as if life and death depended on the issue, till oft, in the middle of the night, I have had to fling
myself from my bed to avoid instant suffocation, — an
effect of exertion so prolonged and so premature. Nor

has the man exerted himself less heartily than the boy.
In the roughest, severest labors of the field I have never
yet met a competitor. But my labors have been all in
vain. I have seen the evil bewailed by Solomon, the
righteous man falling down before the wicked." I could
answer only with a sigh. " You are in the right," he continued, after a pause, and in a more subdued tone : " man
is certainly misplaced ; the present scene of things is below the dignity of both his moral and intellectual nature.
Look around you" (we had reached the summit of a grassy
eminence, which rose over the wood and commanded a
pretty extensive view of the surrounding country) ; " see
yonder scattered cottages, that in the faint light rise dim
and black amid the stubble-fields. My heart warms as I
look on them, for I know how much of honest worth, and
sound, generous feeling shelters under these roof-trees.
But why so much of moral excellence united to a mere
machinery for ministering to the ease and luxury of a few
of perhaps the least worthy of our species — creatures so
spoiled by prosperity that the claim of a common nature
has no force to move them, and who seem as miserably
misplaced as the myriads whom they oppress ?

> If I'm designed yon lordling's slave, —
>   By nature's law designed, —.
> Why was an independent wish
>   E'er planted in my mind ?
> If not, why am I subject to
>   His cruelty and scorn ?
> Or why has man the will and power
>   To make his fellow mourn ?

" I would hardly know what to say in return, my
friend," I rejoined, " did not you yourself furnish me with
the reply. You are groping on in darkness, and, it may

be, unhappiness, for your proper sphere; but it is in obedience to a great though occult law of our nature, — a law general, as it affects the species, in its course of onward progression; particular, and infinitely more irresistible, as it operates on every truly superior intellect. There are men born to wield the destinies of nations; nay, more, to stamp the impression of their thoughts and feelings on the mind of the whole civilized world. And by what means do we often find them roused to accomplish their appointed work? At times hounded on by sorrow and suffering, and this, in the design of Providence, that there may be less of sorrow and suffering in the world ever after; at times roused by cruel and maddening oppression, that the oppressor may perish in his guilt, and a whole country enjoy the blessings of freedom. If Wallace had not suffered from tyranny, Scotland would not have been free."

"But how apply the remark?" said my companion.

"Robert Burns," I replied, again grasping his hand, "yours, I am convinced, is no vulgar destiny. Your griefs, your sufferings, your errors even, the oppressions you have seen and felt, the thoughts which have arisen in your mind, the feelings and sentiments of which it has been the subject, are, I am convinced, of infinitely more importance in their relation to your country than to yourself. You are, wisely and benevolently, placed far below your level, that thousands and ten thousands of your countrymen may be the better enabled to attain to theirs. Assert the dignity of manhood and of genius, and there will be less of wrong and oppression in the world ever after."

I spent the remainder of the evening in the farm-house of Mossgiel, and took the coach next morning for Liverpool.

CHAPTER VII.

His is that language of the heart
  In which the answering heart would speak, —
Thought, word, that bids the warm tear start,
  Or the smile light up the cheek;
And his that music to whose tone
  The common pulse of man keeps time,
In cot or castle's mirth or moan,
  In cold or sunny clime.
                              AMERICAN POET.

THE love of literature, when once thoroughly awakened in a reflective mind, can never after cease to influence it. It first assimilates our intellectual part to those fine intellects which live in the world of books, and then renders our connection with them indispensable by laying hold of that social principle of our nature which ever leads us to the society of our fellows as our proper sphere of enjoyment. My early habits, by heightening my tone of thought and feeling, had tended considerably to narrow my circle of companionship. My profession, too, had led me to be much alone; and now that I had been several years the master of an Indiaman, I was quite as fond of reading, and felt as deep an interest in whatever took place in the literary world, as when a student at St. Andrews. There was much in the literature of the period to gratify my pride as a Scotchman. The despotism, both political and religious, which had overlaid the energies of our country for more than a century, had long been removed; and the national mind had swelled and expanded under a better system of things till its influence had become coëxtensive with civilized man. Hume had produced his inimitable history, and Adam Smith his wonderful work which was to revolutionize and new-model the economy of all the governments of the earth. And there in my little library were the histories of Henry and Robertson, the philosophy of Kames and Reid, the novels of Smollett and M'Kenzie, and the poetry of Beattie and Home. But if there was no lack of Scottish intellect in the literature of the time, there was a decided lack of Scottish manners; and I knew too much of my humble countrymen not to regret it. True, I had before me the writings of Ramsay and my unfortunate friend Ferguson; but there was a radical meanness in the first that lowered the tone of his coloring far beneath the freshness of truth; and the second, whom I had seen perish, — too soon, alas! for literature and his country, — had given us but a few specimens of his power when his hand was arrested for ever.

My vessel, after a profitable though somewhat tedious voyage, had again arrived at Liverpool. It was late in December, 1786; and I was passing the long evening in my cabin, engaged with a whole sheaf of pamphlets and magazines which had been sent me from the shore. "The Lounger" was at this time in course of publication. I had ever been an admirer of the quiet elegance and exquisite tenderness of M'Kenzie; and though I might not be quite disposed to think, with Johnson, that "the chief glory of every people arises from its authors," I certainly felt all the prouder of my country from the circumstance that so accomplished a writer was one of my countrymen. I had read this evening some of the more recent numbers, — half-disposed to regret, however, amid all the pleasure they afforded me, that the Addison of Scotland had not done for the manners of his country what his illustrious prototype had done for those of England, — when my eye fell on the ninety-seventh number. I read the introductory sentences, and admired their truth and elegance. I had felt, in the contemplation of supereminent genius, the pleasure which the writer describes, and my thoughts reverted to my two friends, — the dead and the living. " In the view of highly superior talents, as in that of great and stupendous objects," says the essayist, " there is a sublimity which fills the soul with wonder and delight, — which expands it, as it were, beyond its usual bounds, — and which, investing our nature with extraordinary powers and extraordinary honors, interests our curiosity and flatters our pride."

I read on with increasing interest. It was evident, from the tone of the introduction, that some new luminary had arisen in the literary horizon ; and I felt something like a schoolboy when, at his first play, he waits for the drawing up of the curtain. And the curtain at length rose. " The person," continues the essayist, " to whom I allude" — and he alludes to him as a genius of no ordinary class — " is Robert Burns, an Ayrshire ploughman." The effect on my nerves seemed electrical. I clapped my hands and sprung from my seat. " Was I not certain of it! Did I not foresee it! " I exclaimed. "My nobleminded friend, Robert Burns! " I ran hastily over the warm-hearted and generous critique, — so unlike the cold, timid, equivocal notices with which the professional critic has greeted, on their first appearance, so many works destined to immortality. It was M'Kenzie, the discriminating, the classical, the elegant, who assured me that the productions of this " heaven-taught ploughman were fraught with the high-toned feeling and the power and energy of expression characteristic of the mind and voice of a poet," with the solemn, the tender, the sublime; that they contained images of pastoral beauty which no other writer had ever surpassed, and strains of wild humor which only the higher masters of the lyre had ever equalled; and that the genius displayed in them seemed not less admirable in tracing the manners, than in painting the passions, or in drawing the scenery of nature. I flung down the essay, ascended to the deck in three huge strides, leaped ashore, and reached my bookseller's as he was shutting up for the night.

"Can you furnish me with a copy of 'Burns's Poems,'" I said, "either for love or money?"

"I have but one copy left," replied the man, "and here it is."

I flung down a guinea. "The change," I said, "I shall get when I am less in a hurry."

'Twas late that evening ere I remembered that 'tis customary to spend at least part of the night in bed. I read on and on with a still increasing astonishment and delight, laughing and crying by turns. I was quite in a new world. All was fresh and unsoiled, — the thoughts, the descriptions, the images, — as if the volume I read were the first that had ever been written; and yet all was easy and natural, and appealed with a truth and force irresistible to the recollections I cherished most fondly. Nature and Scotland met me at every turn. I had admired the polished compositions of Pope and Grey and Collins; though I could not sometimes help feeling that, with all the exquisite art they displayed, there was a little additional art wanting still. In most cases the scaffolding seemed incorporated with the structure which it had served to rear; and though certainly no scaffolding could be raised on surer principles, I could have wished that the ingenuity which had been tasked to erect it had been exerted a little further in taking it down. But the work before me was evidently the production of a greater artist. Not a fragment of the scaffolding remained, — not so much as a mark to show how it had been constructed. The whole seemed to have risen like an exhalation, and in this respect reminded me of the structures of Shakspeare alone. I read the inimitable "Twa Dogs." Here, I said, is the full and perfect realization of what Swift and Dryden were hardy enough to attempt, but lacked genius to accomplish. Here are dogs — *bona fide* dogs — endowed, indeed, with more than human sense and observation, but true to character, as the most honest and attached of quadrupeds, in every line. And then those exquisite touches which the poor man, inured to a life of toil and poverty, can alone rightly understand; and those deeply-based remarks on character which only the philosopher can justly appreciate! This is the true catholic poetry, which addresses itself, not to any little circle, walled in from the rest of the species by some peculiarity of thought, prejudice, or condition, but to the whole human family. I read on. "The Holy Fair," "Hallowe'en," "The Vision," the "Address to the Deil," engaged me by turns; and then the strange, uproarious, unequalled "Death and Doctor Hornbook." This, I said, is something new in the literature of the world. Shakspeare possessed above all men the power of instant and yet natural transition, — from the lightly gay to the deeply pathetic, from the wild to the humorous, — but the opposite states of feeling which he induces, however close the neighborhood, are ever distinct and separate: the oil and the water, though contained in the same vessel, remain apart. Here, however, for the first time, they mix and incorporate, and yet each retains its whole nature and full effect. I need hardly remind the reader that the feat has been repeated, and with even more completeness, in the wonderful "Tam o' Shanter." I read on. "The Cotter's Saturday Night" filled my whole soul: my heart throbbed, and my eyes moistened; and never before did I feel half so proud of my country, or know half so well on what score it was I did best in feeling proud. I had perused the entire volume, from beginning to end, ere I remembered I had not taken supper, and that it was more than time to go to bed.

But it is no part of my plan to furnish a critique on the poems of my friend. I merely strive to recall the thoughts and feelings which my first perusal of them awakened, and this only as a piece of mental history. Several months elapsed from this evening ere I could hold them out from me sufficiently at arms' length, as it were, to judge of their more striking characteristics. At times the amazing amount of thought, feeling, and imagery which they contained,— their wonderful continuity of idea, without gap or interstice,—seemed to me most to distinguish them. At times they reminded me, compared with the writings of smoother poets, of a collection of medals, which, unlike the thin polished coin of the kingdom, retained all the significant and pictorial roughnesses of the original die. But when, after the lapse of weeks, months, years, I found them rising up in my heart on every occasion, as naturally as if they had been the original language of all my feelings and emotions; when I felt that, instead of remaining outside my mind, as it were, like the writings of other poets, they had so amalgamated themselves with my passions, my sentiments, my ideas that they seemed to have become portions of my very self, I was led to a final conclusion regarding them. Their grand distinguishing characteristic is their unswerving and perfect truth. The poetry of Shakspeare is the mirror of life; that of Burns the expressive and richly-modulated voice of human nature.

CHAPTER VIII.

Burns was a poor man from his birth, and an exciseman from necessity; but — I *will say* it! — the sterling of his honest worth poverty could not debase; and his independent British spirit oppression might bend, but could not subdue. — LETTER TO Mr. GRAHAM.

I HAVE been listening for the last half-hour to the wild music of an Æolian harp. How exquisitely the tones rise and fall! now sad, now solemn; now near, now distant. The nerves thrill, the heart softens, the imagination awakes as we listen. What if that delightful instrument be animated by a living soul, and these finely-modulated tones be but the expression of its feelings! What if these dying, melancholy cadences, which so melt and sink into the heart, be — what we may so naturally interpret them — the melodious sinkings of a deep-seated and hopeless unhappiness! Nay, the fancy is too wild for even a dream. But are there none of those fine analogies which run through the whole of nature and the whole of art to sublime it into truth? Yes, there have been such living harps among us, — beings the tones of whose sentiments, the melody of whose emotions, the cadences of whose sorrows, remain to thrill and delight and humanize our souls.

They seem born for others, not for themselves. Alas for the hapless companion of my early youth! Alas for him, the pride of his country, the friend of my maturer manhood! But my narrative lags in its progress.

My vessel lay in the Clyde for several weeks during the summer of 1794, and I found time to indulge myself in a brief tour along the western coasts of the kingdom from Glasgow to the borders. I entered Dumfries in a calm, lovely evening, and passed along one of the principal streets. The shadows of the houses on the western side were stretched half-way across the pavement, while on the side opposite the bright sunshine seemed sleeping on the jutting irregular fronts and high antique gables. There seemed a world of well-dressed company this evening in town; and I learned, on inquiry, that all the aristocracy of the adjacent country, for twenty miles round, had come in to attend a country ball. They went fluttering along the sunny side of the street, gay as butterflies, group succeeding group. On the opposite side, in the shade, a solitary individual was passing slowly along the pavement. I knew him at a glance. It was the first poet, perhaps the greatest man, of his age and country. But why so solitary? It had been told me that he ranked among his friends and associates many of the highest names in the kingdom, and yet to-night not one of the hundreds who fluttered past appeared inclined to recognize him. He seemed, too, — but perhaps fancy misled me, — as if care-worn and dejected, — pained, perhaps, that not one among so many of the great should have humility enough to notice a poor exciseman. I stole up to him unobserved, and tapped him on the shoulder. There was a decided fierceness in his manner as he turned abruptly round; but, as he recognized me, his expressive countenance lighted up in a moment, and I shall never forget the heartiness with which he grasped my hand.

We quitted the streets together for the neighboring fields, and, after the natural interchange of mutual congratulations, "How is it," I inquired, "that you do not seem to have a single acquaintance among all the gay and great of the country?"

"I lie under quarantine," he replied, "tainted by the plague of Liberalism. There is not one of the hundreds we passed to-night whom I could not once reckon among my intimates."

The intelligence stunned and irritated me. "How infinitely absurd!" I said. "Do they dream of sinking you into a common man?"

"Even so," he rejoined. "Do they not all know I have been a gauger for the last five years?"

The fact had both grieved and incensed me long before. I knew, too, that Pye enjoyed his salary as poet laureate of the time, and Dibdin, the song writer, his pension of two hundred a year; and I blushed for my country.

"Yes," he continued, — the ill-assumed coolness of his manner giving way before his highly-excited feelings, — "they have assigned me my place among the mean and the degraded, as their best patronage; and only yesterday, after an official threat of instant dismission, I was told that it was my business to act, not to think. God help me! what have I done to provoke such bitter insult? I have ever discharged my miserable duty, — discharged it, Mr. Lindsay, however repugnant to my feelings, as an honest man; and though there awaited me no promotion, I was silent. The wives or sisters of those whom they advanced over me had bastards to some of the —— family, and so their influence was necessarily greater than mine. But now they crush me into the very dust. I take an interest in the struggles of the slave for his freedom; I express my opinions as if I myself were a free man; and they threaten to starve me and my children if I dare so much as speak or think."

I expressed my indignant sympathy in a few broken sentences, and he went on with kindling animation.

"Yes, they would fain crush me into the very dust! They cannot forgive me, that, being born a man, I should walk erect according to my nature. Mean-spirited and despicable themselves, they can tolerate only the mean-spirited and despicable; and were·I not so entirely in their power, Mr. Lindsay, I could regard them with the proper contempt. But the wretches can starve me and my children, and they *know* it; nor does it mend the matter that I *know*, in turn, what pitiful, miserable little creatures they are. What care I for the butterflies of to-night? They passed me without the honor of their notice; and I, in turn, suffered them to pass without the honor of mine, and I am more than quits. Do I not know that they and I are going on to the fulfilment of our several destinies, — they to sleep in the obscurity of their native insignificance, with the pismires and grasshoppers of all the past; and I to be whatever the millions of my unborn countrymen shall yet decide? Pitiful little insects of an hour! What is their notice to me! But I bear a heart, Mr. Lindsay, that can feel the pain of treatment so unworthy; and, I must confess, it moves me. One cannot always live upon the future, divorced from the sympathies of the present. One cannot always solace one's self, under the grinding despotism that would fetter one's very thoughts, with the conviction, however assured, that posterity will do justice both to the oppressor and the oppressed. I am sick at heart; and, were it not for the poor little things that depend so entirely on my exertions, I could as cheerfully lay me down in the grave as I ever did in bed after the fatigues of a long day's labor. Heaven help me! I am miserably unfitted to struggle with even the natural evils of existence; how much more so when these are multiplied and exaggerated by the proud, capricious inhumanity of man!"

"There is a miserable lack of right principle and right feeling," I said, "among our upper classes in the present day; but, alas for poor human nature! it has ever been so, and, I am afraid, ever will. And there is quite as much of it in savage as in civilized life. I have seen the exclusive aristocratic spirit, with its one-sided injustice, as rampant in a wild isle of the Pacific as I ever saw it among ourselves."

"'Tis slight comfort," said my friend, with a melancholy smile, "to be assured, when one's heart bleeds from the cruelty or injustice of our fellows, that man is naturally cruel and unjust, and not less so as a savage than when better taught. I knew you, Mr. Lindsay, when you were younger and less fortunate; but you have now reached that middle term of life when man naturally takes up the Tory, and lays down the Whig; nor has there been aught in your improving circumstances to retard the change; and so you rest in the conclusion that, if the weak among us suffer from the tyranny of the strong, 'tis because human nature is so constituted; and the case therefore cannot be helped."

"Pardon me, Mr. Burns," I said; "I am not quite so finished a Tory as that amounts to."

"I am not one of those fanciful declaimers," he continued, "who set out on the assumption that man is free-born. I am too well assured of the contrary. Man is not free-

11*

born. The earlier period of his existence, whether as a puny child or the miserable denizen of an uninformed and barbarous state, is one of vassalage and subserviency. He is not born free; he is not born rational; he is not born virtuous; he is born to *become* all these. And woe to the sophist who, with arguments drawn from the uncomfirmed constitution of his childhood, would strive to render his imperfect because immature state of pupilage a permanent one! We are yet far below the level of which our nature is capable, and possess, in consequence, but a small portion of the liberty which it is the destiny of our species to enjoy. And 'tis time our masters should be taught so. You will deem me a wild Jacobin, Mr. Lindsay; but persecution has the effect of making a man extreme in these matters. Do help me to curse the scoundrels! My business to act, not to think!"

We were silent for several minutes.

"I have not yet thanked you, Mr. Burns," I at length said, "for the most exquisite pleasure I ever enjoyed. You have been my companion for the last eight years."

His countenance brightened.

"Ah, here I am, boring you with my miseries and my ill-nature," he replied; "but you must come along with me, and see the bairns and Jean, and some of the best songs I ever wrote. It will go hard if we hold not care at the staff's end for at least one evening. You have not yet seen my stone punch-bowl, nor my Tam o' Shanter, nor a hundred other fine things besides. And yet, vile wretch that I am, I am sometimes so unconscionable as to be unhappy with them all. But come along."

We spent this evening together with as much of happiness as it has ever been my lot to enjoy. Never was there a fonder father than Burns, a more attached husband, or a warmer friend. There was an exuberance of love in his large heart that encircled in its flow relatives, friends, associates, his country, the world ; and, in his kindlier moods, the sympathetic influence which he exerted over the hearts of others seemed magical. I laughed and cried this evening by turns. I was conscious of a wider and a warmer expansion of feeling than I had ever experienced before. My very imagination seemed invigorated, by breathing, as it were, in the same atmosphere with his. We parted early next morning ; and when I again visited Dumfries, I went and wept over his grave. Forty years have now passed since his death ; and in that time, many poets have arisen to achieve a rapid and brilliant celebrity ; but they seem the meteors of a lower sky ; the flash passes hastily from the expanse, and we see but one great light looking steadily upon us from above. It is Burns who is exclusively the poet of his country. Other writers inscribe their names on the plaster which covers for the time the outside structure of society ; his is engraved, like that of the Egyptian architect, on the ever-during granite within. The fame of the others rises and falls with the uncertain undulations of the mode on which they have reared it ; his remains fixed and permanent as the human nature on which it is based. Or, to borrow the figure Johnson employs in illustrating the unfluctuating celebrity of a scarcely greater poet, "The sand heaped by one flood is scattered by another, but the rock always continues in its place ; the stream of time which is continually washing the dissoluble fabrics of other poets passes by, without injury, the adamant of Shakspeare."

III.

THE SALMON-FISHER OF UDOLL.

CHAPTER I.

> And the fishers shall mourn and lament;
> All those that cast the hook on the river,
> And those that spread nets on the face of the waters,
>   Shall languish.
> LOWTH'S TRANSLATION OF ISA. xix. 8.

In the autumn of 1759, the Bay of Udoll, an arm of the
sea which intersects the southern shore of the Frith of
Cromarty, was occupied by two large salmon-wears, the
property of one Allan Thomson, a native of the province
of Moray, who had settled in this part of the country a
few months before. He was a thin, athletic, raw-boned
man, of about five feet ten, well-nigh in his thirtieth year,
but apparently younger; erect and clean-limbed, with a
set of handsome features, bright, intelligent eyes, and a
profusion of light brown hair curling around an ample expanse of forehead. For the first twenty years of his life
he had lived about a farm-house, tending cattle when a
boy, and guiding the plough when he had grown up. He
then travelled into England, where he wrought about seven
years as a common laborer. A novelist would scarcely
make choice of such a person for the hero of a tale; but
men are to be estimated rather by the size and color of

their minds than the complexion of their circumstances;
and this ploughman and laborer of the north was by no
means a very common man. For the latter half of his life
he had pursued, in all his undertakings, one main design.
He saw his brother rustics tièd down by circumstance —
that destiny of vulgar minds — to a youth of toil and dependence, and an old age of destitution and wretchedness;
and, with a force of character which, had he been placed
at his outset on what may be termed the table-land of fortune, would have raised him to her higher pinnacles, he
persisted in adding shilling to shilling and pound to pound,
not in the sordid spirit of the miser, but in the hope that
his little hoard might yet serve him as a kind of stepping-
stone in rising to a more comfortable place in society. Nor
were his desires fixed very high; for, convinced that independence and the happiness which springs from situation
in life lie within the reach of the frugal farmer of sixty or
eighty years, he moulded his ambition on the conviction,
and scarcely looked beyond the period at which he anticipated his savings would enable him to take his place among
the humbler tenantry of the country.

Our friths and estuaries at this period abounded with
salmon, one of the earliest exports of the kingdom; but
from the low state into which commerce had sunk in the
northern districts, and the irregularity of the communication kept up between them and the sister kingdom, by far
the greater part caught on our shores were consumed by
the inhabitants. And so little were they deemed a luxury, that it was by no means uncommon, it is said, for servants to stipulate with their masters that they should not
have to diet on salmon oftener than thrice a week. Thomson, however, had seen quite enough, when in England, to
convince him that, meanly as they were esteemed by his

country-folks, they might be rendered the staple of a profitable trade; and, removing to the vicinity of Cromarty, for the facilities it afforded in trading to the capital, he launched boldly into the speculation. He erected his two wears with his own hands; built himself a cottage of sods on the gorge of a little ravine sprinkled over with bushes of alder and hazel; entered into correspondence with a London merchant, whom he engaged as his agent; and began to export his fish by two large sloops which plied at this period between the neighboring port and the capital. His fishings were abundant, and his agent an honest one; and he soon began to realize the sums he had expended in establishing himself in the trade.

Could any one anticipate that a story of fondly-cherished but hapless attachment — of one heart blighted for ever, and another fatally broken — was to follow such an introduction?

The first season of Thomson's speculation had come to a close. Winter set in, and, with scarcely a single acquaintance among the people in the neighborhood, and little to employ him, he had to draw for amusement on his own resources alone. He had formed, when a boy, a taste for reading; and might now be found, in the long evenings, hanging over a book beside the fire. By day he went sauntering among the fields, calculating on the advantages of every agricultural improvement, or attended the fairs and trysts of the country, to speculate on the profits of the drover and cattle-feeder and make himself acquainted with all the little mysteries of bargain-making.

There holds early in November a famous cattle-market in the ancient barony of Ferintosh, and Thomson had set out to attend it. The morning was clear and frosty, and he felt buoyant of heart and limb, as, passing westwards along the shore, he saw the huge Ben Wevis towering darker and more loftily over the Frith as he advanced, or turned aside, from time to time, to explore some ancient burying-ground or Danish encampment. There is not a tract of country of equal extent in the three kingdoms where antiquities of this class lie thicker than in that northern strip of the parish of Resolis which bounds on the Cromarty Frith. The old castle of Craig House, a venerable, time-shattered building, detained him, amid its broken arches, for hours ; and he was only reminded of the ultimate object of his journey when, on surveying the moor from the upper bartizan, he saw that the groups of men and cattle, which since morning had been mottling in succession the track leading to the fair, were all gone out of sight, and that, far as the eye could reach, not a human figure was to be seen. The whole population of the country seemed to have gone to the fair. He quitted the ruins ; and, after walking smartly over the heathy ridge to the west, and through the long birch wood of Kinbeakie, he reached, about mid-day, the little straggling village at which the market holds.

Thomson had never before attended a thoroughly High-land market, and the scene now presented was wholly new to him. The area it occupied was an irregular opening in the middle of the village, broken by ruts and dung-hills and heaps of stone. In front of the little turf-houses, on either side, there was a row of booths, constructed mostly of poles and blankets, in which much whiskey, and a few of the simpler articles of foreign merchandise, were sold. In the middle of the open space there were carts and benches, laden with the rude manufactures of the country : High-land brogues and blankets ; bowls and platters of beech ; a species of horse and cattle harness, formed of the twisted twigs of birch; bundles of split fir, for lath and torches; and hair tackle and nets for fishermen. Nearly seven thousand persons, male and female, thronged the area, bustling and busy, and in continual motion, like the tides and eddies of two rivers at their confluence. There were country-women, with their shaggy little horses laden with cheese and butter; Highlanders from the far hills, with droves of sheep and cattle; shoemakers and weavers from the neighboring villages, with bales of webs and wallets of shoes; farmers and fishermen, engaged, as it chanced, in buying or selling; bevies of bonny lasses, attired in their gayest; ploughmen and mechanics; drovers, butchers, and herd-boys. Whiskey flowed abundantly, whether bargain-makers bought or sold, or friends met or parted; and, as the day wore later, the confusion and bustle of the crowd increased. A Highland tryst, even in the present age, rarely passes without witnessing a fray; and the High-landers seventy years ago were of more combative dispo-sitions than they are now. But Thomson, who had neither friend nor enemy among the thousands around him, neither quarrelled himself, nor interfered in the quarrels of others. He merely stood and looked on, as a European would among the frays of one of the great fairs of Bagdad or Astrakan.

He was passing through the crowd, towards evening, in front of one of the dingier cottages, when a sudden burst of oaths and exclamations rose from within, and the in-mates came pouring out pell-mell at the door, to throttle and pummel one another, in inextricable confusion. A gray-headed old man, of great apparent strength, who seemed by far the most formidable of the combatants, was engaged in desperate battle with two young fellows from the remote Highlands, while all the others were matched man to man. Thomson, whose residence in England had taught him very different notions of fair play and the ring, was on the eve of forgetting his caution and interfering, but the interference proved unnecessary. Ere he had stepped up to the combatants, the old man, with a vigor little lessened by age, had shaken off both his opponents; and, though they stood glaring at him like tiger-cats, neither of them seemed in the least inclined to renew the attack.

"Twa mean, pitiful kerns," exclaimed the old man, "to tak odds against ane auld enough to be their faither; and that, too, after burning my loof wi' the het airn! But I hae noited their twa heads thegither! Sic a trick! — to bid me stir up the fire after they had heated the wrang end o' the poker! Deil, but I hae a guid mind to gie them baith mair o't yet!"

Ere he could make good his threat, however, his daughter, a delicate-looking girl of nineteen, came rushing up to him through the crowd. "Father!" she exclaimed, "dearest father! let us away. For my sake, if not your own, let these wild men alone. They always carry knives; and, besides, you will bring all of their clan upon you that are at the tryst, and you will be murdered."

"No muckle danger frae that, Lillias," said the old man. "I hae little fear frae ony ane o' them; an' if they come by twasome, I hae my friends here too. The ill-deedy wratches, to blister a' my loof wi' the poker! But come awa, lassie; your advice is, I dare say, best after a'."

The old man quitted the place with his daughter, and for the time Thomson saw no more of him. As the night approached, the Highlanders became more noisy and turbulent; they drank, and disputed, and drove their very bargains at the dirk's point; and as the salmon-fisher

12

passed through the village for the last time, he could see the waving of bludgeons, and hear the formidable war-cry of one of the clans, with the equally formidable "Hilloa! help for Cromarty!" echoing on every side of him. He keep coolly on his way, however, without waiting the result; and, while yet several miles from the shores of Udoll, daylight had departed, and the moon at full had risen, red and huge in the frosty atmosphere, over the bleak hill of Nigg.

He had reached the Burn of Newhall, — a small stream which, after winding for several miles between its double row of alders and its thickets of gorse and hazel, falls into the upper part of the bay, — and was cautiously picking his way, by the light of the moon, along a narrow pathway which winds among the bushes. There are few places in the country of worse repute among believers in the supernatural than the Burn of Newhall; and its character seventy years ago was even worse than it is at present. Witch meetings without number have been held on its banks, and dead-lights have been seen hovering over its deeper pools; sportsmen have charged their fowling-pieces with silver when crossing it in the night-time; and I remember an old man who never approached it after dark without fixing a bayonet on the head of his staff. Thomson, however, was but little influenced by the beliefs of the period; and he was passing under the shadow of the alders, with more of this world than of the other in his thoughts, when the silence was suddenly broken by a burst of threats and exclamations, as if several men had fallen a-fighting, scarcely fifty yards away, without any preliminary quarrel; and with the gruffer voices there mingled the shrieks and entreaties of a female. Thomson grasped his stick, and sprang forward. He reached an opening among the bushes,

and saw in the imperfect light the old robust Lowlander
of the previous fray attacked by two men armed with
bludgeons, and defending himself manfully with his staff.
The old man's daughter, who had clung round the knees
of one of the ruffians, was already thrown to the ground,
and trampled under foot. An exclamation of wrath and
horror burst from the high-spirited fisherman, as, rushing
upon the fellow like a tiger from its jungle, he caught the
stroke aimed at him on his stick, and, with a side-long
blow on the temple, felled him to the ground. At the instant he fell, a gigantic Highlander leaped from among the
bushes, and, raising his huge arm, discharged a tremendous
blow at the head of the fisherman, who, though taken un-
awares and at a disadvantage, succeeded, notwithstanding,
in transferring it to his left shoulder, where it fell broken
and weak. A desperate but brief combat ensued. The
ferocity and ponderous strength of the Celt found their
more than match in the cool, vigilant skill and leopard-
like agility of the Lowland Scot; for the latter, after dis-
charging a storm of blows on the head, face, and shoulders
of the giant, until he staggered, at length struck his
bludgeon out of his hand, and prostrated his whole huge
length by dashing his stick end-long against his breast.
At nearly the same moment the burly old farmer, who had
grappled with his antagonist, had succeeded in flinging
him, stunned and senseless, against the gnarled root of an
alder ; and the three ruffians — for the first had not yet
recovered — lay stretched on the grass. Ere they could
secure them, however, a shrill whistle was heard echoing
from among the alders, scarcely a hundred yards away.
" We had better get home," said Thomson to the old man,
" ere these fellows are reinforced by their brother ruffians
in the wood." And, supporting the maiden with his one

hand, and grasping his stick with the other, he plunged among the bushes in the direction of the path, and gaining it, passed onward, lightly and hurriedly, with his charge: the old man followed more heavily behind; and in somewhat less than an hour after they were all seated beside the hearth of the latter, in the farm-house of Meikle Farness.

It is now more than forty years since the last stone of the very foundation has disappeared; but the little grassy eminence on which the house stood may still be seen. There is a deep wooded ravine behind, which, after winding through the table-land of the parish, like a huge crooked furrow, the bed, evidently, of some antediluvian stream, opens far below to the sea; an undulating tract of field and moor, with here and there a thicket of bushes and here and there a heap of stone, spreads in front. When I last looked on the scene, 'twas in the evening of a pleasant day in June. One half the eminence was bathed in the red light of the setting sun; the other lay brown and dark in the shadow. A flock of sheep were scattered over the sunny side. The herd-boy sat on the top, solacing his leisure with a music famous in the pastoral history of Scotland, but well-nigh exploded, that of the *stock* and *horn;* and the air seemed filled with its echoes. I stood picturing to myself the appearance of the place ere all the inmates of this evening, young and old, had gone to the churchyard, and left no successors behind them; and, as I sighed over the vanity of human hopes, I could almost fancy I saw an apparition of the cottage rising on the knoll. I could see the dark turf-walls; the little square windows, barred below and glazed above; the straw roof, embossed with moss and stone-crop; and, high over head, the row of venerable elms, with their gnarled trunks

and twisted branches, that rose out of the garden-wall.
Fancy gives an interest to all her pictures, — yes, even
when the subject is but an humble cottage; and when
we think of human enjoyment, of the pride of strength
and the light of beauty, in connection with a few mouldering and nameless bones hidden deep from the sun,
there is a sad poetry in the contrast which rarely fails to
affect the heart. It is now two thousand years since
Horace sung of the security of the lowly, and the unfluctuating nature of their enjoyments; and every year of the
two thousand has been adding proof to proof that the
poet, when he chose his theme, must have thrown aside
his philosophy. But the inmates of the farm-house thought
little this evening of coming misfortune. Nor would it
have been well if they had; their sorrow was neither
heightened nor hastened by their joy.

Old William Stewart, the farmer, was one of a class
well-nigh worn out in the southern Lowlands, even at
this period, but which still comprised, in the northern districts, no inconsiderable portion of the people, and which
must always obtain in countries only partially civilized
and little amenable to the laws. Man is a fighting animal
from very instinct; and his second nature, custom, mightily
improves the propensity. A person naturally courageous,
who has defended himself successfully in half a dozen different frays, will very probably begin the seventh himself;
and there are few who have fought often and well for
safety and the right who have not at length learned to love
fighting for its own sake. The old farmer had been a man
of war from his youth. He had fought at fairs and trysts
and weddings and funerals; and, without one ill-natured
or malignant element in his composition, had broken more
heads than any two men in the country-side. His late

12*

quarrel at the tryst, and the much more serious affair among the bushes, had arisen out of this disposition; for though well-nigh in his sixtieth year, he was still as warlike in his habits as ever. Thomson sat fronting him beside the fire, admiring his muscular frame, huge limbs, and immense structure of bone. Age had grizzled his hair and furrowed his cheeks and forehead; but all the great strength, and well-nigh all the activity of his youth, it had left him still. His wife, a sharp-featured little woman, seemed little interested in either the details of his adventure or his guest, whom he described as the "brave, hardy chield, wha had beaten twasome at the cudgel, — the vera littlest o' them as big as himsel'."

"Och, gudeman," was her concluding remark, "ye aye stick to the auld trade, bad though it be; an' I'm feared that or ye mend ye maun be aulder yet. I'm sure ye ne'er made your ain money o't."

"Nane o' yer nonsense," rejoined the farmer. "Bring butt the bottle an' your best cheese."

"The gudewife an' I dinna aye agree," continued the old man, turning to Thomson. "She's baith near-gaun an' new-fangled; an' I like aye to hae routh o' a' things, an' to live just as my faithers did afore me. Why sould I bother my head wi' *improvidments*, as they ca' them? The country's gane clean gite wi' pride, Thomson! Naething less sairs folk noo, forsooth, than carts wi' wheels to them; an' it's no a fortnight syne sin' little Sandy Martin, the trifling cat, jeered me for yoking my owson to the plough by the tail. What ither did they get tails for?"

Thomson had not sufficiently studied the grand argument of design, in this special instance, to hazard a reply.

"The times hae gane clean oot o' joint," continued the man. "The law has come a' the length o' Cromarty noo;

an' for breaking the head o' an impudent fallow, ane runs the risk o' being sent aff the plantations. Faith, I wish oor Parliamenters had mair sense. What do they ken aboot us or oor country? Deil haet difference doo they mak' atween the shire o' Cromarty an' the shire o' Lunnon; just as if we could be as quiet beside the red-wud Hielanman here, as they can be beside the queen. Na, na,—naething like a guid cudgel; little wad their law hae dune for me at the Burn o' Newhall the nicht."

Thomson found the character of the old man quite a study in its way; and that of his wife — a very different, and, in the main, inferior sort of person, for she was meanspirited and a niggard — quite a study too. But by far the most interesting inmate of the cottage was the old man's daughter, the child of a former marriage. She was a pale, delicate, blue-eyed girl, who, without possessing much positive beauty of feature, had that expression of mingled thought and tenderness which attracts more powerfully than beauty itself. She spoke but little. That little, however, was expressive of gratitude and kindness to the deliverer of her father; sentiments which, in the breast of a girl so gentle, so timid, so disposed to shrink from the roughnesses of active courage, and yet so conscious of her need of a protector, must have mingled with a feeling of admiration at finding in the powerful champion of the recent fray a modest, sensible young man, of manners nearly as quiet and unobtrusive as her own. She dreamed that night of Thomson; and her first thought, as she awakened next morning, was, whether, as her father had urged, he was to be a frequent visitor at Meikle Farness. But an entire week passed away, and she saw no more of him.

He was sitting one evening in his cottage, poring over a book. A huge fire of brushwood was blazing against the

earthen wall, filling the upper part of the single rude chamber of which the cottage consisted with a dense cloud of
smoke, and glancing brightly on the few rude implements
which occupied the lower, when the door suddenly opened,
and the farmer of Meikle Farness entered, accompanied by
his daughter."

"Ha! Allan, man," he said, extending his large hand,
and grasping that of the fisherman; "if you winna come
an' see us, we maun just come and see you. Lillias an'
mysel' were afraid the gudewife had frichtened you awa,
for she's a near-gaun sort o' body, an' maybe no owre kind-
spoken ; but ye maun just come an' see us whiles, an' no
mind her.   Except at counting-time, I never mind her
mysel'."   Thomson accommodated his visitors with seats.
"Yer life maun be a gay lonely ane here, in this eerie bit o'
a glen," remarked the old man, after they had conversed
for some time on different subjects; "but I see ye dinna
want company a'thegither, such as it is," — his eye glancing, as he spoke, over a set of deal shelves, occupied by
some sixty or seventy volumes.   "Lillias there has a liking
for that kind o' company too, an' spends some days mair
o' her time amang her books than the gudewife or mysel'
would wish."

Lillias blushed at the charge, and hung down her head.
It gave, however, a new turn to the conversation; and
Thomson was gratified to find that the quiet, gentle girl,
who seemed so much interested in him, and whose gratitude to him, expressed in a language less equivocal than
any spoken one, he felt to be so delicious a compliment,
possessed a cultivated mind and a superior understanding.
She had lived under the roof of her father in a little paradise of thoughts and imaginations, the spontaneous growth
of her own mind ; and as she grew up to womanhood, she

had recourse to the companionship of books; for in books only could she find thoughts and imaginations of a kindred character.

It is rarely that the female mind educates itself. The genius of the sex is rather fine than robust; it partakes rather of the delicacy of the myrtle than the strength of the oak; and care and culture seem essential to its full development. Who ever heard of a female Burns or Bloomfield? And yet there have been instances, though rare, of women working their way from the lower levels of intellect to well-nigh the highest,— not wholly unassisted, 'tis true; the age must be a cultivated one, and there must be opportunities of observation; but, if not wholly unassisted, with helps so slender, that the second order of masculine minds would find them wholly inefficient. There is a quickness of perception and facility of adaptation in the better class of female minds — an ability of catching the tone of whatever is good from the sounding of a single note, if I may so express myself— which we almost never meet with in the mind of man. Lillias was a favorable specimen of the better and more intellectual order of women; but she was yet very young, and the process of self-cultivation carrying on in her mind was still incomplete; and Thomson found that the charm of her society arose scarcely more from her partial knowledge than from her partial ignorance. The following night saw him seated by her side in the farm-house of Meikle Farness; and scarcely a week passed during the winter in which he did not spend at least one evening in her company.

Who is it that has not experienced the charm of female conversation, — that poetry of feeling which develops all of tenderness and all of imagination that lies hidden in our nature ? When following the ordinary concerns of life, or engaged in its more active businesses, many of the better faculties of our minds seem overlaid : there is little of feeling, and nothing of fancy; and those sympathies which should bind us to the good and fair of nature lie repressed and inactive. But in the society of an intelligent and virtuous female there is a charm that removes the pressure. Through the force of sympathy, we throw our intellects for the time into the female mould ; our tastes assimilate to the tastes of our companion ; our feelings keep pace with hers ; our sensibilities become nicer and our imaginations more expansive ; and, though the powers of our mind may not much excel, in kind or degree, those of the great bulk of mankind, we are sensible that for the time we experience some of the feelings of genius. How many common men have not female society and the fervor of youthful passion sublimed into poets ? I am convinced the Greeks displayed as much sound philosophy as good taste in representing their muses as beautiful women.

Thomson had formerly been but an admirer of the poets. He now became a poet. And had his fate been a kindlier one, he might perhaps have attained a middle place among at least the minor professors of the incommunicable art. He was walking with Lillias one evening through the wooded ravine. It was early in April, and the day had combined the loveliest smiles of spring with the fiercer blasts of winter. There was snow in the hollows ; but where the sweeping sides of the dell reclined to the south, the violet and the primrose were opening to the sun. The drops of a recent shower were still hanging on the half-expanded buds, and the streamlet was yet red and turbid ; but the sun, nigh at his setting, was streaming in golden glory along the field, and a lark was carolling high in the

air as if its day were but begun. Lillias pointed to the
bird, diminished almost to a speck, but relieved by the red
light against a minute cloudlet.

"Happy little creature!" she exclaimed; "does it not
seem rather a thing of heaven than of earth? Does not its
song frae the clouds mind you of the hymn heard by the
shepherds! The blast is but just owre, an' a few minutes
syne it lay cowering and chittering in its nest; but its sorrows are a' gane, an' its heart rejoices in the bonny blink,
without a'e thought o' the storm that has passed or the
night that comes on. Were you a poet, Allan, like ony o'
your twa namesakes, — he o' 'The Seasons,' or he o'
'The Gentle Shepherd,' — I would ask you for a song on
that bonnie burdie." Next time the friends met, Thomson
produced the following verses :—

TO THE LARK.

Sweet minstrel of the April cloud,
    Dweller the flowers among,
Would that my heart were formed like thine,
    And tuned like thine my song!
Not to the earth, like earth's low gifts,
    Thy soothing strain is given:
It comes a voice from middle sky, —
    A solace breathed from heaven.

Thine is the morn; and when the sun
    Sinks peaceful in the west,
The mild light of departing day
    Purples thy happy breast.
And ah! though all beneath that sun
    Dire pains and sorrows dwell,
Rarely they visit, short they stay,
    Where thou hast built thy cell.

When wild winds rave, and snows descend,
    And dark clouds gather fast,
And on the surf-encircled shore
    The seaman's barque is cast,

> Long human grief survives the storm;
>   But thou, thrice happy bird!
> No sooner has it passed away,
>   Than, lo! thy voice is heard.
>
> When ill is present, grief is thine;
>   It flies, and thou art free;
> But ah! can aught achieve for man
>   What nature does for thee?
> Man grieves amid the bursting storm;
>   When smiles the calm he grieves;
> Nor cease his woes, nor sinks his plaint,
>   Till dust his dust receives.

CHAPTER II.

THE SEQUEL.

As the latter month of spring came on the fisherman again betook himself to his wears, and nearly a fortnight passed in which he saw none of the inmates of the farmhouse. Nothing is so efficient as absence, whether self-imposed or the result of circumstances, in convincing a lover that he is truly such, and in teaching him how to estimate the strength of his attachment. Thomson had sat night after night beside Lillias Stewart, delighted with the delicacy of her taste and the originality and beauty of her ideas; delighted, too, to watch the still partially-developed faculties of her mind shooting forth and expanding into bud and blossom under the fostering influence of his own more matured powers. But the pleasure which arises from the interchange of ideas and the contemplation of mental beauty, or the interest which every thinking mind must feel in marking the aspirations of a superior intellect towards its proper destiny, is not love; and it was only now that Thomson ascertained the true scope and nature of his feelings.

"She is already my friend," thought he. "If my schemes prosper, I shall be in a few years what her father is now; and may then ask her whether she will not be more. Till then, however, she shall be my friend, and my friend only. I find I love her too well to make her the wife of either a poor unsettled speculator, or still poorer laborer."

He renewed his visits to the farm-house, and saw, with a discernment quickened by his feelings, that his mistress had made a discovery with regard to her own affections somewhat similar to his, and at a somewhat earlier period. She herself could have perhaps fixed the date of it by referring to that of their acquaintance. He imparted to her his scheme, and the uncertainties which attended it, with his determination, were he unsuccessful in his designs, to do battle with the evils of penury and dependence without a companion; and, though she felt that she could deem it a happiness to make common cause with him even in such a contest, she knew how to appreciate his motives, and loved him all the more for them. Never, perhaps, in the whole history of the passion, were there two lovers happier in their hopes and each other. But there was a cloud gathering over them.

Thomson had never been an especial favorite with the step-mother of Lillias. She had formed plans of her own for the settlement of her daughter with which the attentions of the salmon-fisher threatened materially to interfere; and there was a total want of sympathy between them besides. Even William, though he still retained a sort of rough regard for him, had begun to look askance on his intimacy with Lillias. His avowed love, too, for the modern, gave no little offence. The farm of Meikle Farness was obsolete enough in its usages and mode of tillage to have formed no uninteresting study to the antiquary. Towards autumn, when the fields vary most in color, it resembled a rudely-executed chart of some large island, — so irregular were the patches which composed it, and so broken on every side by a surrounding sea of moor that here and there went winding into the interior in long river-like strips, or expanded within into friths and lakes. In one corner there stood a heap of stones, in another a thicket of furze ; here a piece of bog, there a broken bank of clay. The implements with which the old man labored in his fields were as primitive in their appearance as the fields themselves : there was the one-stilted plough, the wooden-toothed harrow, and the basket-woven cart with its rollers of wood. With these, too, there was the usual misproportion on the farm, to its extent, of lean, inefficient cattle, — four half-starved animals performing with incredible effort the work of one. Thomson would fain have induced the old man, who was evidently sinking in the world, to have recourse to a better system, but he gained wondrous little by his advice. And there was another cause which operated still more decidedly against him. A wealthy young farmer in the neighborhood had been for the last few months not a little diligent in his attentions to Lillias. He had lent the old man, at the preceding term, a considerable sum of money ; and had ingratiated himself with the step-mother by chiming in on all occasions with her humor, and by a present or two besides. Under the auspices of both parents, therefore, he had paid his addresses to Lillias ; and, on meeting with a repulse, had stirred them both up against Thomson.

The fisherman was engaged one evening in fishing his nets. The ebb was that of a stream tide, and the bottom of almost the entire bay lay exposed to the light of the setting sun, save that a river-like strip of water wound

through the midst. He had brought his gun with him, in
the hope of finding a seal or otter asleep on the outer
banks ; but there were none this evening ; and, laying
down his piece against one of the poles of the wear, he
was employed in capturing a fine salmon, that went darting like a bird from side to side of the inner enclosure,
when he heard some one hailing him by name from outside the nets. He looked up, and saw three men — one of
whom he recognized as the young farmer who was paying
his addresses to Lillias — approaching from the opposite
side of the bay. They were apparently much in liquor, and
came staggering towards him in a zigzag track along the
sands. A suspicion crossed his mind that he might find
them other than friendly ; and, coming out of the enclosure,
where, from the narrowness of the space and the depth
of the water, he would have lain much at their mercy,
he employed himself in picking off the patches of sea-weed
that adhered to the nets, when they came up to him, and
assailed him with a torrent of threats and reproaches. He
pursued his occupation with the utmost coolness, turning
round, from time to time, to repay their abuse by some
cutting repartee. His assailants discovered they were to
gain little in this sort of contest ; and Thomson found, in
turn, that they were much less disguised in liquor than
he at first supposed, or than they seemed desirous to make
it appear. In reply to one of his more cutting sarcasms,
the tallest of the three, a ruffian-looking fellow, leaped
forward and struck him on the face ; and in a moment
he had returned the blow with such hearty good-will
that the fellow was dashed against one of the poles. The
other two rushed in to close with him. He seized his gun,
and, springing out from beside the nets to the open bank,
dealt the farmer, with the butt-end, a tremendous blow on

the face, which prostrated him in an instant; and then, cocking the piece and presenting it, he commanded the other two, on peril of their lives, to stand aloof. Odds of weapons, when there is courage to avail one's self of them, forms a thorough counterbalance to odds of number. After an engagement of a brief half-minute, Thomson's assailants left him in quiet possession of the field; and he found, on his way home, that he could trace their route by the blood of the young farmer. There went abroad an exaggerated and very erroneous edition of the story, highly unfavorable to the salmon-fisher; and he received an intimation shortly after that his visits at the farm-house were no longer expected. But the intimation came not from Lillias.

The second year of his speculation had well-nigh come to a close, and, in calculating on the quantum of his shipments and the state of the markets, he could deem it a more successful one than even the first. But his agent seemed to be assuming a new and worse character. He rather substituted promises and apologies for his usual remittances, or neglected writing altogether; and, as the fisherman was employed one day in dismantling his wears for the season, his worst fears were realized by the astounding intelligence that the embarrassments of the merchant had at length terminated in a final suspension of payments!

"There," said he, with a coolness which partook in its nature in no slight degree of that insensibility of pain and injury which follows a violent blow, — "there go well-nigh all my hard-earned savings of twelve years, and all my hopes of happiness with Lillias!" He gathered up his utensils with an automaton-like carefulness, and, throwing them over his shoulders, struck across the sands in the direction of the cottage. "I must see her," he said, "once more, and bid her farewell." His heart swelled to his throat at the thought; but, as if ashamed of his weakness, he struck his foot firmly against the sand, and, proudly raising himself to his full height, quickened his pace. He reached the door, and, looking wistfully, as he raised the latch, in the direction of the farm-house, his eye caught a female figure coming towards the cottage through the bushes of the ravine. "'Tis poor Lillias!" he exclaimed. "Can she already have heard that I am unfortunate, and that we must part?" He went up to her, and, as he pressed her hand between both his, she burst into tears.

It was a sad meeting. Meetings must ever be such when the parties that compose them bring each a separate grief, which becomes common when imparted.

"I cannot tell you," said Lillias to her lover, " how unhappy I am. My step-mother has not much love to bestow on any one; and so, though it be in her power to deprive me of the quiet I value so much, I care comparatively little for her resentment. Why should I? She is interested in no one but herself. As for Simpson, I can despise without hating him. Wasps sting just because it is their nature; and some people seem born, in the same way, to be mean-spirited and despicable. But my poor father, who has been so kind to me, and who has so much heart about him, his displeasure has the bitterness of death to me. And then he is so wildly and unjustly angry with you. Simpson has got him, by some means, into his power, I know not how. My step-mother annoys him continually; and from the state of irritation in which he is kept, he is saying and doing the most violent things imaginable, and making me so unhappy by his threats." And she again burst into tears.

Thomson had but little of comfort to impart to her. Indeed, he could afterwards wonder at the indifference with which he beheld her tears, and the coolness with which he communicated to her the story of his disaster. But he had not yet recovered his natural tone of feeling. Who has not observed that, while in men of an inferior and weaker cast, any sudden and overwhelming misfortune unsettles their whole minds, and all is storm and uproar, in minds of a superior order, when subjected to the same ordeal, there takes place a kind of freezing, hardening process, under which they maintain at least apparent coolness and self-possession? Grief acts as a powerful solvent to the one class; to the other it is as the waters of a petrifying spring.

"Alas, my Lillias!" said the fisherman, "we have not been born for happiness and each other. We must part, each of us to struggle with our respective evils. Call up all your strength of mind, the much in your character that has as yet lain unemployed, and so despicable a thing as Simpson will not dare to annoy you. You may yet meet with a man worthy of you; some one who will love you as well as — as one who can at least appreciate your value, and who will deserve you better." As he spoke, and his mistress listened in silence and in tears, William Stewart burst in upon then through the bushes; and, with a countenance flushed, and a frame tremulous with passion, assailed the fisherman with a torrent of threats and reproaches. He even raised his hand. The prudence of Thomson gave way under the provocation. Ere the blow had descended, he had locked the farmer in his grasp, and, with an exertion of strength which scarcely a giant would be capable of in a moment of less excitement, he raised him from the earth, and forced him against the grassy side of the ravine, where he held him despite of his efforts. A shriek from Lillias recalled him to the command of himself. " William Stewart," he said, quitting his hold and stepping back, "you are an old man, and the father of Lillias." The farmer rose slowly and collectedly, with a flushed cheek but a quiet eye, as if all his anger had evaporated in the struggle, and, turning to his daughter, —

" Come, Lillias, my lassie," he said, laying hold of her arm, " I have been too hasty; I have been in the wrong." And so they parted.

Winter came on, and Thomson was again left to the solitude of his cottage, with only his books and his own thoughts to employ him. He found little amusement or comfort in either. He could think only of Lillias, that she loved and yet was lost to him.

"Generous and affectionate and confiding," he has said, when thinking of her, "I know she would willingly share with me in my poverty; but ill would I repay her kindness in demanding of her such a sacrifice. Besides, how could I endure to see her subjected to the privations of a destiny so humble as mine? The same heaven that seems to have ordained me to labor, and to be unsuccessful, has given me a mind not to be broken by either toil or disappointment ; but keenly and bitterly would I feel the evils of both were she to be equally exposed. I must strive to forget her, or think of her only as my friend." And, indulging in such thoughts as these, and repeating and re-repeating similar resolutions, — only however to find them unavailing, — winter, with its long, dreary nights, and its days of languor and inactivity, passed heavily away. But it passed.

He was sitting beside his fire, one evening late in February, when a gentle knock was heard at the door. He started up, and, drawing back the bar, William Stewart entered the apartment.

"Allan," said the old man, "I have come to have some conversation with you, and would have come sooner, but pride and shame kept me back. I fear I have been much to blame."

Thomson motioned him to a seat, and sat down beside him.

"Farmer," he said, "since we cannot recall the past, we had perhaps better forget it."

The old man bent forward his head till it rested almost on his knee, and for a few moments remained silent.

"I fear, Allan, I have been much to blame," he at length reiterated. "Ye maun come an' see Lillias. She is ill, very ill, an' I fear no very like to get better. Thomson was stunned by the intelligence, and answered he scarcely knew what. "She has never been richt hersel '," continued the old man, "sin' the unlucky day when you an' I met in the burn here; but for the last month she has been little out o' her bed. Since mornin' there has been a great change on her, an' she wishes to see you. I fear we havena meikle time to spare, an' had better gang." Thomson followed him in silence.

They reached the farm-house of Meikle Farness, and entered the chamber where the maiden lay. A bright fire of brushwood threw a flickering gloom on the floor and rafters; and their shadows, as they advanced, seemed dancing on the walls. Close beside the bed there was a small table, bearing a lighted candle, and with a Bible lying open upon it at that chapter of Corinthians in which the apostle assures us that the dead shall rise, and the mortal put on immortality. Lillias half sat, half reclined, in the upper part of the bed. Her thin and wasted features had already the stiff rigidity of death; her cheeks and lips were color-less; and though the blaze seemed to dance and flicker on her half-closed eyes, they served no longer to intimate to the departing spirit the existence of external things.

"Ah, my Lillias!" exclaimed Thomson, as he bent over her, his heart swelling with an intense agony. "Alas! has it come to this!"

His well-known voice served to recall her as from the precincts of another world. A faint melancholy smile passed over her features, and she held out her hand.

" I was afraid," she said, in a voice sweet and gentle as ever, though scarcely audible, through extreme weakness, — "I was afraid that I was never to see you more. Draw nearer; there is a darkness coming over me, and I hear but imperfectly. I may now say with a propriety which no one will challenge, what I durst not have said before. Need I tell you that you were the dearest of all my friends, the only man I have ever loved, the man whose lot, however low and unprosperous, I would have deemed it a happiness to be invited to share? I do not, however, I cannot reproach you. I depart, and forever; but oh! let not a single thought of me render you unhappy. My few years of life have not been without their pleasures, and I go to a better and brighter world. I am weak, and cannot say more; but let me hear you speak. Read to me the eighth chapter of Romans."

Thomson, with a voice tremulous and faltering through emotion, read the chapter. Ere he had made an end, the maiden had again sunk into the state of apparent insensi-bility out of which she had been so lately awakened; though occasionally a faint pressure of his hand, which she still re-tained, showed him that she was not unconscious of his presence. At length, however, there was a total relaxation of the grasp; the cold damp of the stiffening palm struck a chill to his heart; there was a fluttering of the pulse, a glazing of the eye; the breast ceased to heave, the heart to beat; the silver cord parted in twain, and the golden bowl was broken. Thomson contemplated for a moment the body of his mistress, and, striking his hand against his forehead, rushed out of the apartment.

He attended her funeral; he heard the earth falling heavy and hollow on the coffin-lid; he saw the green sod placed over her grave; he witnessed the irrepressible anguish of her father, and the sad regret of her friends; and all this without shedding a tear. He was turning to depart, when some one thrust a letter into his hand. He opened it almost mechanically. It contained a considerable sum of money, and a few lines from his agent, stating that, in consequence of a favorable change in his circumstances, he had been enabled to satisfy all his creditors. Thomson crumpled up the bills in his hand. He felt as if his heart stood still in his breast; a noise seemed ringing in his ears; a mist-cloud appeared, as if rising out of the earth and darkening around him. He was caught, when falling, by old William Stewart; and, on awakening to consciousness and the memory of the past, found himself in his arms. He lived for about ten years after a laborious and speculative man, ready to oblige, and successful in all his designs; and no one deemed him unhappy. It was observed, however, that his dark brown hair was soon mingled with masses of gray, and that his tread became heavy and his frame bent. It was remarked, too, that when attacked by a lingering epidemic, which passed over wellnigh the whole country, he of all the people was the only one that sunk under it.

IV.

THE WIDOW OF DUNSKAITH.

CHAPTER I.

" Oh, mony a shriek, that waefu' night,
Rose frae the stormy main ;
An' mony a bootless vow was made,
An' mony a prayer vain ;
An' mithers wept, an' widows mourned,
For mony a weary day ;
An' maidens, ance o' blithest mood,
Grew sad, an' pined away."

The northern Sutor of Cromarty is of a bolder character than even the southern one, abrupt and stern and precipitous as that is. It presents a loftier and more unbroken wall of rock ; and, where it bounds on the Moray Frith, there is a savage magnificence in its cliffs and caves, and in the wild solitude of its beach, which we find nowhere equalled on the shores of the other. It is more exposed, too, in the time of tempest. The waves often rise, during the storms of winter, more than a hundred feet against its precipices, festooning them, even at that height, with wreaths of kelp and tangle ; and for miles within the bay we may hear, at such seasons, the savage uproar that maddens amid its cliffs and caverns, coming booming over the lashings of the nearer waves like a roar of artillery. There is a sublimity of desolation on its shores, the effects

of a conflict maintained for ages, and on a scale so gigantic. The isolated spire-like crags that rise along its base
are so drilled and bored by the incessant lashings of the
surf, and are ground down into shapes so fantastic, that
they seem but the wasted skeletons of their former selves;
and we find almost every natural fissure in the solid rock
hollowed into an immense cavern, whose very ceiling,
though the head turns as we look up to it, owes, evidently,
its comparative smoothness to the action of the waves.
One of the most remarkable of these recesses occupies
what we may term the apex of a lofty promontory. The
entrance, unlike most of the others, is narrow and rug-
ged, though of great height; but it widens within into a
shadowy chamber, perplexed, like the nave of a cathedral,
by uncertain cross-lights, that come glimmering into it
through two lesser openings which perforate the opposite
sides of the promontory. It is a strange, ghostly-looking
place. There is a sort of moonlight greenness in the twilight which forms its noon, and the denser shadows which
rest along its sides; a blackness, so profound that it mocks
the eye, hangs over a lofty passage which leads from it,
like a corridor, still deeper into the bowels of the hill; the
light falls on a sprinkling of half-buried bones, the remains
of animals that in the depth of winter have creeped into
it for shelter and to die; and when the winds are up, and
the hoarse roar of the waves comes reverberated from its
inner recesses, or creeps howling along its roof, it needs
no over-active fancy to people its avenues with the shapes
of beings long since departed from every gayer and softer
scene, but which still rise uncalled to the imagination,
in those by-corners of nature which seem dedicated, like
this cavern, to the wild, the desolate, and the solitary.

There is a little rocky bay a few hundred yards to the

west, which has been known for ages to all the seafaring men of the place as the Cova Green. It is such a place as we are sometimes made acquainted with in the narrative of disastrous shipwrecks. First, there is a broad semi-circular strip of beach, with a wilderness of insulated piles of rock in front; and so steep and continuous is the wall of precipices which rises behind, that, though we may see directly over head the grassy slopes of the hill, with here and there a few straggling firs, no human foot ever gained the nearer edge. The bay of the Cova Green is a prison to which the sea presents the only outlet; and the numerous caves which open along its sides, like the arches of an amphitheatre, seem but its darker cells. It is in truth a wild, impressive place, full of beauty and terror, and with none of the squalidness of the mere dungeon about it. There is a puny littleness in our brick and lime receptacles of misery and languor, which speaks as audibly of the feebleness of man as of his crimes or his inhumanity; but here all is great and magnificent, and there is much, too, that is pleasing. Many of the higher cliffs, which rise beyond the influence of the spray, are tapestried with ivy. We may see the heron watching on the ledges beside her bundle of withered twigs, or the blue hawk darting from her cell. There is life on every side of us; life in even the wild tumbling of the waves, and in the stream of pure water which, rushing from the higher edge of the precipice in a long white cord, gradually untwists itself by the way, and spatters ceaselessly among the stones over the entrance of one of the caves. Nor does the scene want its old story to strengthen its hold on the imagination.

I am wretchedly uncertain in my dates; but it must have been some time late in the reign of Queen Anne,

14

that a fishing yawl, after vainly laboring for hours to enter the bay of Cromarty, during a strong gale from the west, was forced at nightfall to relinquish the attempt, and take shelter in the Cova Green. The crew consisted of but two persons, — an old fisherman and his son. Both had been thoroughly drenched by the spray, and chilled by the piercing wind, which, accompanied by thick snow showers, had blown all day through the opening from off the snowy top of Ben Wyvis; and it was with no ordinary satisfaction that, as they opened the little bay on their last tack, they saw the red gleam of a fire flickering from one of the caves, and a boat drawn upon the beach.

"It must be some of the Tarbet fishermen," said the old man, "wind-bound, like ourselves, but wiser than us in having made provision for it. I shall feel willing enough to share their fire with them for the night."

"But see," remarked the younger, "that there be no unwillingness on the other side. I am much mistaken if that be not the boat of my cousins the Macinlas, who would so fain have broken my head last Rhorichie Tryst. But, hap what may, father, the night is getting worse, and we have no choice of quarters. Hard up your helm, or we shall barely clear the skerries. There, now; every nail an anchor." He leaped ashore, carrying with him the small hawser attached to the stern, which he wound securely round a jutting crag, and then stood for a few seconds, until the old man, who moved but heavily along the thwarts, had come up to him. All was comparatively calm under the lee of the precipices; but the wind was roaring fearfully in the woods above, and whistling amid the furze and ivy of the higher cliff; and the two boatmen, as they entered the cave, could see the flakes of a thick snow shower, that had just begun to descend, circling round and round in the eddy.

The place was occupied by three men, who were sitting beside the fire on blocks of stone which had been rolled from the beach. Two of them were young, and comparatively commonplace-looking persons; the third was a gray-headed old man, apparently of great muscular strength, though long past his prime, and of a peculiarly sinister cast of countenance. A keg of spirits, which was placed end up in front of them, served as a table; there were little drinking measures of tin on it; and the mask-like, stolid expressions of the two younger men showed that they had been indulging freely. The elder was apparently sober. They all started to their feet on the entrance of the fisherman, and one of the younger, laying hold of the little cask, pitched it hurriedy into a dark corner of the cave.

"His peace be here!" was the simple greeting of the elder fisherman as he came forward. "Eachen Macinla," he continued, addressing the old man, " we have not met for years before, — not, I believe, since the death o' my puir sister, when we parted such ill friends; but we are short-lived creatures oursels, Eachen ; surely our anger should be short-lived too; and I have come to crave from you a seat by your fire."

"William Beth," replied Eachen, "it was no wish of mine we should ever meet; but to a seat by the fire you are welcome."

Old Macinla and his sons resumed their seats ; the two fishermen took their places fronting them; and for some time neither party exchanged a word.

A fire, composed mostly of fragments of wreck and drift-wood, threw up its broad, cheerful flame towards the roof; but so spacious was the cavern, that, except where here and there a whiter mass of stalactites or bolder projection of cliff stood out from the darkness, the light seemed lost in it. A dense body of smoke, which stretched its blue level surface from side to side, and concealed the roof, went rolling outwards like an inverted river.

"This is but a gousty lodging-place," remarked the old fisherman, as he looked round him; "but I have seen a worse. I wish the folk at hame kent we were half sae snug; and then the fire, too,—I have always felt something companionable in a fire, something consolable, as it were; it appears, somehow, as if it were a creature like ourselves, and had life in it." The remark seemed directed to no one in particular, and there was no reply. In a second attempt at conversation, the fisherman addressed himself to the old man.

"It has vexed me," he said, "that our young folk shouldna, for my sister's sake, be on more friendly terms, Eachen. They hae been quarrelling, an' I wish to see the quarrel made up." The old man, without deigning a reply, knit his gray, shaggy brows, and looked doggedly at the fire.

"Nay, now," continued the fisherman, "we are getting auld men, Eachen, an' wauld better bury our hard thoughts o' ane anither afore we come to be buried ourselves. What if we were sent to the Cova Green the night, just that we might part friends!"

Eachen fixed his keen, scrutinizing glance on the speaker, —it was but for a moment,—there was a tremulous motion of the under lip as he withdrew it, and a setting of the teeth,—the expression of mingled hatred and anger; but the tone of his reply savored more of sullen indifference than of passion.

"William Beth," he said, "ye hae tricked my boys out o' the bit property that suld hae come to them by their mother; it's no lang since they barely escaped being murdered by your son. What more want you? But ye perhaps think it better that the time should be passed in making hollow lip.professions of good-will, than that it suld be employed in clearing off an old score."

" Ay," hickuped out the elder of the two sons; "the · houses might come my way then; an', besides, gin Helen Henry were to lose her a'e jo, the ither might hae a better chance. Rise, brither! rise, man! an' fight for me an' your sweet-heart." The younger lad, who seemed verging towards the last stage of intoxication, struck his clenched fist against his palm, and attempted to rise.

"Look ye, uncle," exclaimed the younger fisherman,— a powerful-looking and very handsome stripling,— as he sprang to his feet; " your threat might be spared. Our little property was my grandfather's, and naturally descended to his only son; and as for the affair at Rhorichie, I dare either of my cousins to say the quarrel was of my seeking. I have no wish to raise my hand against the sons or the husband of my aunt; but if forced to it, you will find that neither my father nor myself are wholly at your mercy."

" Whisht, Earnest," said the old fisherman, laying his hand on the hand of the young man; "sit down; your uncle maun hae ither thoughts. It is now fifteen years, Eachen," he continued, "since I was called to my sister's deathbed. You yoursel' canna forget what passed there. There had been grief an' cauld an' hunger beside that bed. I'll no say you were willingly unkind,— few folk are that, but when they hae some purpose to serve by it, an' you could have.none,— but you laid no restraint on a harsh temper, and none on a craving habit that forgets everything but itsel'; and so my puir sister perished in the middle o' her days, a wasted, heart-broken thing. It's no that I wish to

14*

hurt you.   I mind how we passed our youth thegither among the wild buccaneers. It was a bad school, Eachen; an' I owre often feel I havena unlearned a' my ain lessons, to wonder that you shouldna hae unlearned a' yours. But we're getting old men Eachen, an' we have now, what we hadna in our young days, the advantage o' the light. Dinna let us die fools in the sight o' Him who is so willing to give us wisdom ; dinna let us die enemies. We have been early friends, though maybe no for good, we have fought afore now at the same gun ; we have been united by the luve o' her that's now in the dust ; an' there are our boys, — the nearest o' kin to ane anither that death has spared. But what I feel as strongly as a' the rest, Eachen, we hae done meikle ill thegither. I can hardly think o' a past sin without thinking o' you, an' thinking, too, that if a crea- ture like me may hope he has found pardon, you shouldna despair.   Eachen, we maun be friends."

The features of the stern old man relaxed. "You are perhaps right, William," he at length replied ; " but ye were aye a luckier man than me, — luckier for this world, I'm sure, an' maybe for the next. I had aye to seek, an' aften without finding, the good that came in your gate o' itsel'. Now that age is coming upon us, ye get a snug rental frae the little houses, an' I hae naething ; an' ye hae character an' credit ; but wha would trust me, or cares for me ? Ye hae been made an elder o' the kirk, too, I hear, an' I am still a reprobate ; but we were a' born to be just what we are, an' sae maun submit. An' your son, too, shares in your luck. He has heart an' hand, an' my whelps hae neither ; an' the girl Henry, that scouts that sot there, likes him ; but what wonder o' that ? But you are right, William ; we maun be friends. Pledge me." The little cask was produced ; and, filling the measures, he nodded to Earnest and his father. They pledged him, when, as if seized by a sudden frenzy, he filled his measure thrice in hasty succession, draining it each time to the bottom, and then flung it down with a short, hoarse laugh. His sons, who would fain have joined with him, he repulsed with a firmness of manner which he had not before exhibited. "No, whelps," he said; "get sober as fast as ye can."

" We had better," whispered Earnest to his father, " not sleep in the cave to-night."

"Let me hear now o' your quarrel, Earnest," said Eachan; "your father was a more prudent man than you; and, however much he wronged me, did it without quarrelling."

" The quarrel was none of my seeking," replied Earnest. " I was insulted by your sons, and would have borne it for the sake of what they seemed to forget; but there was another whom they also insulted, and that I could not bear."

" The girl Henry.   And what then ? "

" Why, my cousins may tell the rest. They were mean enough to take odds against me, and I just beat the two spiritless fellows that did so."

But why record the quarrels of this unfortunate evening? An hour or two passed away in disagreeable bickerings, during which the patience of even the old fisherman was worn out, and that of Earnest had failed him altogether. They both quitted the cave, boisterous as the night was, — and it was now stormier than ever, — and, heaving off their boat till she rode at the full length of her swing from the shore, sheltered themselves under the sail. The Macinlas returned next evening to Tarbet; but, though the wind moderated during the day, the yawl of William Beth did not enter the Bay of Cromarty. Weeks passed away, during which the clergyman of the place corresponded regarding the missing fisherman with all the lower parts of the Frith, but they had disappeared, as it seemed, for ever.

CHAPTER II.

HELEN'S VISION.

WHERE the northern Sutor sinks into the low sandy tract that nearly fronts the town of Cromarty, there is a narrow grassy terrace raised but a few yards over the level of the beach. It is sheltered behind by a steep, undulating bank; for, though the rock here and there juts out, it is too rich in vegetation to be termed a precipice. It is a sweet little spot, with its grassy slopes, that recline towards the sun, partially covered with thickets of wild rose and honeysuckle, and studded in their season with violets and daisies and the delicate rock geranium. Towards its eastern extremity, with the bank rising immediately behind, and an open space in front, which seemed to have been cultivated at one time as a garden, there stood a picturesque little cottage. It was that of the widow of William Beth. Five years had now elapsed since the disappearance of her son and husband, and the cottage bore the marks of neglect and decay. The door and window, bleached white by the sea-winds, shook loosely to every breeze; clusters of chickweed luxuriated in the hollows of the thatch, or mantled over the eaves; and a honeysuckle, that had twisted itself round the chimney, lay withering in a tangled mass at the foot of the wall.

But the progress of decay was more marked in the widow

herself than in her dwelling. She had had to contend with grief and penury; a grief not the less undermining in its effects from the circumstance of its being sometimes suspended by hope; a penury so extreme that every succeeding day seemed as if won by some providential interference from absolute want. And she was now, to all appearance, fast sinking in the struggle. The autumn was well-nigh over. She had been weak and ailing for months before, and had now become so feeble as to be confined for days together to her bed. But, happily, the poor solitary woman had at least one attached friend in the daughter of a farmer of the parish, a young and beautiful girl, who, though naturally of no melancholy temperament, seemed to derive almost all she enjoyed of pleasure from the society of the widow. Helen Henry was in her twenty-first year, but she seemed older in spirit than in years. She was thin and pale, though exquisitely formed. There was a drooping heaviness in her fine eyes, and a cast of pensive thought on her forehead, that spoke of a longer experience of grief than so brief a portion of life might be supposed to have furnished. She had once lovers, but they had gradually dropped away in the despair of moving her, and awed by a deep and settled pensiveness, which, in the gayest season of youth, her character had suddenly but permanently assumed. Besides, they all knew her affections were already engaged, and had come to learn, though late and unwillingly, that there are cases in which no rival can be more formidable than a dead one.

Autumn, I have said, was near its close. The weather had given indications of an early and severe winter; and the widow, whose worn-out and delicate frame was affected by every change of atmosphere, had for a few days been more than usually indisposed. It was now long past noon, and she had but just risen. The apartment, however, bore witness that her young friend had paid her the accustomed morning visit; the fire was blazing on a clean, comfortable-looking hearth, and every little piece of furniture it contained was arranged with the most scrupulous care. Her devotions were hardly over when the well-known tap was again heard at the door.

"Come in, my lassie," said the widow; and then lowering her voice, as the light foot of her friend was heard on the threshold, "God," she said, "has been ever kind to me; far, very far, aboon my best deservings; and oh, may he bless and reward her who has done so meikle, meikle for me!" The young girl entered and took her seat beside her.

"You told me, mother," she said, "that to-morrow is Earnest's birthday. I have been thinking of it all last night, and feel as if my heart were turning into stone. But when I am alone it is always so. There is a cold, death-like weight at my breast, that makes me unhappy; though, when I come to you, and we speak together, the feeling passes away, and I become cheerful."

"Ah, my bairn," replied the old woman, "I fear I'm no your friend, meikle as I love you. We speak owre, owre often o' the lost, for our foolish hearts find mair pleasure in that than in anything else; but ill does it fit us for being alone. Weel do I ken your feeling, — a stone deadness o' the heart, — a feeling there are no words to express, but that seems as it were insensibility itself turning into pain; and I ken, too, my lassie, that it is nursed by the very means ye tak to flee from it. Ye maun learn to think mair o' the living, and less o' the dead. Little, little does it matter how a puir worn-out creature like me passes the few broken days o' life that remains to her; but ye are

young, my Helen, an' the world is a' before you; and ye
maun just try an' live for it."

"To-morrow," rejoined Helen, "is Earnest's birthday.
Is it no strange that, when our minds make pictures o' the
dead, it is always as they looked best an' kindest an' maist
life-like; I have been seeing Earnest all night long, as
when I saw him on his last birthday; an' oh, the sharp-
ness o' the pang, when, every now an' then, the back o' the
picture is turned to me, an' I see him as he is, — dust!"

The widow grasped her young friend by the hand.
"Helen," she said, "you will get better when I am taken
from you; but so long as we continue to meet, our thoughts
will aye be running the one way. I had a strange dream
last night, an' must tell it to you. You see yon rock to
the east, in the middle o' the little bay, that now rises
through the back draught o' the sea, like the hull o' a ship,
an' is now buried in a mountain o' foam? I dreamed I
was sitting on that rock, in what seemed a bonny summer's
morning. The sun was glancin' on the water, an' I could
see the white sand far down at the bottom, wi' the reflection o' the little wavies running o'er it in long curls o'
goud. But there was no way o' leaving the rock, for the
deep waters were round an' round me; an' I saw the tide
covering one wee bittie after another, till at last the whole
was covered. An' yet I had but little fear; for I remembered that baith Earnest an' William were in the sea afore
me; an' I had the feeling that I could hae rest nowhere
but wi' them. The water at last closed o'er me, an' I
sank frae aff the rock to the sand at the bottom. But
death seemed to have no power given him to hurt me;
an' I walked as light as ever I hae done on a gowany brae,
through the green depths o' the sea. I saw the silvery
glitter o' the trout an' the salmon shining to the sun, far,

far aboon me, like white pigeons in the lift; an' around me there were crimson star-fish an' sea-flowers an' long trailing plants, that waved in the tide like streamers; an' at length I came to a steep rock, wi' a little cave like a tomb in it. 'Here,' I said, 'is the end o' my journey. William is here, an' Earnest.' An', as I looked into the cave, I saw there were bones in it, an' I prepared to take my place beside them. But, as I stooped to enter, some one called me, an', on looking up, there was William. 'Lillias,' he said, 'it is not night yet, nor is that your bed; you are to sleep, not with me, but with Earnest. Haste you home, for he is waiting you.' 'Oh, take me to him!' I said; an' then all at once I found myself on the shore, dizzied an' blinded wi' the bright sunshine; for at the cave there was a darkness like that o' a simmer's gloamin'; an' when I looked up for William, it was Earnest that stood before me, life-like an' handsome as ever; an' you were beside him."

The day had been gloomy and lowering, and, though there was little wind, a tremendous sea, that, as the evening advanced, rose higher and higher against the neighboring precipice, had been rolling ashore since morning. The wind now began to blow in long hollow gusts among the cliffs, and the rain to patter against the widow's casement.

"It will be a storm from the sea," she said; "the scarts an' gulls hae been flying landward sin' daybreak, an' I hae never seen the ground-swell come home heavier against the rocks. Wae's me for the puir sailors!"

"In the lang stormy nights," said Helen, "I canna sleep for thinking o' them, though I have no one to bind me to them now. Only look how the sea rages among the rocks, as if it were a thing o' life an' passion! That last wave rose to the crane's nest. An' look, yonder is a boat round-

ing the rock wi' only a'e man in it. It dances on the surf
as if it were a cork; an' the wee bittie o' sail, sae black an'
weet, seems scarcely bigger than a napkin. Is it no bearing in for the boat-haven below? "

"My poor old eyes," replied the widow, "are growing
dim, an' surely no wonder ; but yet I think I should ken
that boatman. Is it no Eachen Macinla o' Tarbet ? "

"Hard-hearted, cruel old man ! " exclaimed the maiden;
" what can be takin' him here ? Look how his skiff shoots
in like an arrow on the long roll o' the surf! an' now she is
high on the beach. How unfeeling it was o' him to rob
you o' your little property in the very first o' your grief!
But see, he is so worn out that he can hardly walk over
the rough stones. Ah me! he is down ; wretched old man,
I must run to his assistance. But no; he has risen again.
See, he is coming straight to the house ; an' now he is at the
door." In a moment after, Eachen entered the cottage.

"I am perishing, Lillias," he said, "with cold an' hunger,
an' can gang nae further ; surely ye'll no shut your door on
me in a night like this."

The poor widow had been taught in a far different school.
She relinquished to the worn-out fisherman her seat by the
fire, now hurriedly heaped with fresh fuel, and hastened
to set before him the simple viands which her cottage
afforded.

As the night darkened, the storm increased. The wind
roared among the rocks like the rattling of a thousand car-
riages over a paved street; and there were times when,
after a sudden pause, the blast struck the cottage as if it
were a huge missile flung against it, and pressed on its roof
and walls till the very floor rocked, and the rafters strained
and shivered like the beams of a stranded vessel. There
was a ceaseless patter of mingled rain and snow, now

15

lower, now louder; and the fearful thunderings of the waves, as they raged among the pointed crags, were mingled with the hoarse roll of the storm along the beach. The old man sat beside the fire, fronting the widow and her companion, with his head reclined nearly as low as his kneé, and his hands covering his face. There was no attempt at conversation. He seemed to shudder every time the blast yelled along the roof; and, as a fiercer gust burst open the door, there was a half-muttered ejaculation.

"Heaven itsel' hae mercy on them! for what can man do in a night like this?"

"It is black as pitch," exclaimed Helen, who had risen to draw the bolt; "an' the drift flies sae thick, that it feels to the hand like a solid snaw wreath. An' oh, how it lightens!"

"Heaven itsel' hae mercy on them!" again ejaculated the old man. "My two boys," said he, addressing the widow, "are at the far Frith; an' how can an open boat live in a night like this?"

There seemed something magical in the communication, —something that awakened all the sympathies of the poor bereaved woman; and she felt she could forgive him every unkindness.

"Wae's me!" she exclaimed; "it was in such a night as this, an' scarcely sae wild, that my Earnest perished."

The old man groaned and wrung his hands.

In one of the pauses of the hurricane there was a gun heard from the sea, and shortly after a second. "Some puir vessel in distress," said the widow; "but, alas! where can succor come frae in sae terrible a night? There is help only in Ane. Wae's me! would we no better light up a blaze on the floor, an', dearest Helen, draw off the cover frae the window? My puir Earnest has told me that my

light has aften showed him his bearing frae the deadly bed
o' Dunskaith. That last gun," — for a third was now heard
booming over the mingled roar of the sea and the wind, —
" that last gun cam' frae the very rock-edge. Wae's me,
wae's me! maun they perish, an' sae near ! " Helen hastily lighted a bundle of more fir, that threw up its red ſput-
tering blaze half way to the roof, and, dropping the covering, continued to wave it opposite the window. Guns were
still heard at measured intervals, but apparently from a
safer offing; and at last, as it sounded faintly against the
wind, came evidently from the interior of the bay.

"She has escaped," said the old man. "It's a feeble
hand that canna do good when the heart is willing. But
what has mine been doin' a' life lang?" He looked at
the window, and shuddered.

Towards morning 'the wind fell, and the moon, in her
last quarter, rose red and glaring out of the Frith, lighting
the melancholy roll of the waves, that still rose like moun-
tains, and the broad white belt of surf that skirted the
shores. The old fisherman left the cottage, and sauntered
along the beach. It was heaped with huge wreaths of kelp
and tangle, uprooted by the storm; and in the hollow of the
rocky bay lay the scattered fragments of a boat. Eachen
stooped to pick up a piece of the wreck, in the fearful expectation of finding some known mark by which to recognize it, when the light fell full on the swollen face of a
corpse that seemed staring at him from out a wreath of
weed. It was that of his eldest son. The body of the
younger, fearfully gashed and mangled by the rocks, lay a
few yards further to the east.

The morning was as .pleasant as the night had been
boisterous; and except that the distant hills were covered
with snow, and that a swell still continued to roll in from

the sea, there remained scarce any trace of the recent tempest. Every hollow of the neighboring hill had its little runnel, formed by the rains of the previous night, that now splashed and glistened to the sun. The bushes round the cottage were well-nigh divested of their leaves; but their red berries, hips and haws, and the juicy fruit of the honeysuckle, gleamed cheerfully to the light; and a warm steam of vapor, like that of a May morning, rose from the roof and the little mossy platform in front. But the scene seemed to have something more than merely its beauty to recommend it to a young man, drawn apparently to the spot, with many others, by the fate of the two unfortunate fishermen, and who now stood gazing on the rocks and the hills and the cottage, as a lover on the features of his mistress. The bodies had been carried to an old store-house, which may still be seen a short mile to the west; and the crowds that, during the early part of the morning, had been perambulating the beach, gazing at the wreck, and discussing the various probabilities of the accident, had gradually dispersed. But this solitary individual, whom no one knew, remained behind. He was a tall and swarthy, though very handsome man, of about five-and-twenty, with a slight scar on his left cheek. His dress, which was plain and neat, was distinguished from that of the common seaman by three narrow stripes of gold-lace on the upper part of one of the sleeves. He had twice stepped towards the cottage-door, and twice drawn back, as if influenced by some unaccountable feeling, — timidity, perhaps, or bashfulness; and yet the bearing of the man gave little indication of either. But at length, as if he had gathered heart, he raised the latch and went in.

The widow, who had had many visitors that morning, seemed to be scarcely aware of his entrance. She was sitting on a low seat beside the fire, her face covered with her hands; while the tremulous rocking motion of her body showed that she was still brooding over the distresses of the previous night. Her companion, who had thrown herself across the bed, was fast asleep. The stranger seated himself beside the fire, which seemed dying amid its ashes; and, turning sedulously from the light of the window, laid his hand gently on the widow's shoulder. She started, and looked up.

"I have strange news for you," he said. "You have long mourned for your husband and your son; but, though the old man has been dead for years, your son Earnest is still alive, and is now in the harbor of Cromarty. He is lieutenant of the vessel whose guns you must have heard during the night."

The poor woman seemed to have lost all power of reply.

"I am a friend of Earnest's," continued the stranger, "and have come to prepare you for meeting with him. It is now five years since his father and he were blown off to sea by a strong gale from the land. They drove before it for four days, when they were picked up by an armed vessel then cruising in the North Sea, and which soon after sailed for the coast of Spanish America. The poor old man sank under the fatigues he had undergone; though Earnest, better able, from his youth, to endure hardship, was little affected by them. He accompanied us on our Spanish expedition; indeed, he had no choice, for we touched at no British port after meeting with him; and, through good fortune, and what his companions call merit, he has risen to be the second man aboard, and has now brought home with him gold enough from the Spaniards to make his old mother comfortable. He saw your light yester-evening, and steered by it to the roadstead, blessing you all the way.

15*

Tell me, for he anxiously wished me to inquire of you, whether Helen Henry is yet unmarried."

"It is Earnest! it is Earnest himself!" exclaimed the maiden, as she started from the widow's bed. In a moment after, she was locked in his arms. But why dwell on a scene which I feel myself unfitted to describe?

It was ill before evening with old Eachen Macinla. The fatigues of the present day, and the grief and horror of the previous night, had prostrated his energies, bodily and mental; and he now lay tossing, in a waste apartment of the storehouse, in the delirium of a fever. The bodies of his two sons occupied the floor below. He muttered unceasingly, in his ravings, of William and Earnest Beth. They were standing beside him, he said; and every time he attempted to pray for his poor boys and himself the stern old man laid his cold swollen hand on his lips.

"Why trouble me?" he exclaimed. "Why stare with your white dead eyes on me? Away, old man; the little black shells are sticking in your gray hairs; away to your place! Was it I who raised the wind on the sea? — was it I? — was it I? Uh, u! — no — no; you were asleep, — you were fast asleep, — and could not see me cut the *swing;* and, besides, it was only a piece of rope. Keep away; touch me not; I am a free man, and will plead for my life. Please your honor, I did not murder these two men; I only cut the rope that fastened their boat to the land. Ha! ha! ha! he has ordered them away, and they have both left me unskaithed." At this moment Earnest Beth entered the apartment, and approached the bed. The miserable old man raised himself on his elbow, and, regarding him with a horrid stare, shrieked out, " Here is Earnest Beth, come for me a second time!" and, sinking back on the pillow, instantly expired.

V.

THE LYKEWAKE.

CHAPTER I.

Why start at Death?   Where is he?
Death arrived, is past; not come or gone, he's never here.
                                        YOUNG.

I KNOW no place where one may be brought acquainted
with the more credulous beliefs of our forefathers at a
less expense of inquiry and exertion than in a country
lykewake.   The house of mourning is naturally a place
of sombre thoughts and ghostly associations.   There is
something, too, in the very presence and appearance of
death that leads one to think of the place and state of the
dead.   Cowper has finely said that the man and the beast
who stand together side by side on the same hill-top, are,
notwithstanding their proximity, the denizens of very different worlds.   And I have felt the remark to apply still
more strongly when sitting beside the dead.   The world
of intellect and feeling in which we ourselves are, and of
which the lower propensities of our nature form a province,
may be regarded as including, in part at least, that world
of passion and instinct in which the brute lives ; and we
have but to analyze and abstract a little, to form for ourselves ideas of this latter world from even our own experi-

ence. But by what process of thought can we bring experience to bear on the world of the dead ? It lies entirely beyond us, a *terra incognita* of cloud and darkness; and yet the thing at our side — the thing over which we can stretch our hand, the thing dead to us but living to it — has entered upon it; and, however uninformed or ignorant before, knows more of its dark, and to us inscrutable mysteries, than all our philosophers and all our divines. Is it wonder that we would fain put it to the question; that we would fain catechise it, if we could, regarding its newly-acquired experience; that we should fill up the gaps in the dialogue, which its silence leaves to us, by imparting to one another the little we know regarding its state and its place ; or that we should send our thoughts roaming in long excursions, to glean from the experience of the past all that it tells us of the occasional visits of the dead, and all that in their less taciturn and more social moments they have communicated to the living? And hence, from feelings so natural and a train of associations so obvious, the character of a country lykewake, and the cast of its stories. I say a *country* lykewake; for in at least all our larger towns, where a cold and barren scepticism has chilled the feelings and imaginations of the people, without, I fear, much improving their judgments, the conversation on such occasions takes a lower and less interesting range.

I once spent a night with a friend from the south — a man of an inquiring and highly philosophic cast of mind — at a lykewake in the upper part of the parish of Cromarty. I had excited his curiosity by an incidental remark or two of the kind I have just been dropping; and, on his expressing a wish that I should introduce him, by way of illustration, to some such scene as I had been describing, we had set out together to the wake of an elderly female who had died that morning. Her cottage, an humble erection of stone and lime, was situated beside a thick fir-wood, on the edge of the solitary Mullbuoy, one of the dreariest and most extensive commons in Scotland. We had to pass in our journey over several miles of desolate moor, sprinkled with cairns and tumuli — the memorials of some forgotten conflict of the past; we had to pass, too, through a thick, dark wood, with here and there an intervening marsh, whitened over with moss and lichens, and which, from this circumstance, are known to the people of the country as the white bogs. Nor was the more distant landscape of a less gloomy character. On the one hand there opened an interminable expanse of moor, that went stretching onwards mile beyond mile — bleak, dreary, uninhabited and uninhabitable — till it merged into the far horizon. On the other there rose a range of blue, solitary hills, towering, as they receded, into loftier peaks and bolder acclivities, till they terminated on the snow-streaked Ben Weavis. The season, too, was in keeping with the scene. It was drawing towards the close of autumn ; and, as we passed through the wood, the falling leaves were eddying round us with every wind, or lay in rustling heaps at our feet.

"I do not wonder," said my companion, "that the superstitions of so wild a district as this should bear in their character some marks of a corresponding wildness. Night itself, in a populous and cultivated country, is attended with less of the stern and the solemn than mid-day amid solitudes like these. Is the custom of watching beside the dead of remote antiquity in this part of the country ? "

"Far beyond the reach of history or tradition," I said. "But it has gradually been changing its character, as the people have been changing theirs, and is now a very dif-

ferent thing from what it was a century ago. It is not yet
ninety years since lykewakes in the neighboring Highlands
used to be celebrated with music and dancing; and even
here, on the borders of the low country, they used invariably, like the funerals, to be the scenes of wild games and
amusements never introduced on any other occasion. You
remember how Sir Walter describes the funeral of Athel-
stane ? The Saxon ideas of condolence were the most
natural imaginable. If grief was hungry, they supplied it
with food ; if thirsty, they gave it drink. Our simple ancestors here seem to have reasoned by a similar process.
They made their seasons of deepest grief their times of
greatest merriment; and the more they regretted the deceased, the gayer were they at his wake and his funeral.
A friend of mine, now dead, a very old man, has told me
that he once danced at a lykewake in the Highlands of
Sutherland. It was that of an active and a very robust
man, taken away from his wife and family in the prime of
life ; and the poor widow, for the greater part of the evening, sat disconsolate beside the fire, refusing every invitation to join the dancers. She was at length, however,
brought out by the father of the deceased. 'Little, little
did he think,' he said, ' that we should be the last to dance
at poor Rory's lykewake.' "

We reached the cottage and went in. The apartment
in which the dead lay was occupied by two men and three
women.   Every little piece of furniture ·it contained was
hung in white, and the floor had recently been swept and
sanded ; but it was on the bed where the body lay, and on
the body itself, that the greatest care had been lavished.
The curtains had been taken down, and their places supplied by linen white as snow ; and on the sheet that served
as a counterpane the body was laid out in a dress of white,

fantastically crossed and re-crossed in·every direction by scalloped fringes, and fretted into a species of open work, at least intended to represent alternate rows of roses and tulips. A plate containing a little salt was placed over the breast of the corpse. As we entered one of the women rose, and, filling two glasses with spirits, presented them to us on a salver. We tasted the liquor, and sat down on chairs placed for us beside the fire. The conversation, which had been interrupted by our entrance, began to flow apace; and an elderly female, who had lived under the same roof with the deceased, began to relate, in answer to the queries of one of the others, some of the particulars of her last illness and death.

CHAPTER II.

THE STORY OF ELSPAT M'CULLOCH.

"Elspat was aye," she said, "a retired body, wi' a cast o' decent pride aboot her ; an', though bare and puirly aff sometimes in her auld days, she had never been chargeable to onybody. She had come o' decent, 'sponsible people, though they were a' low enough the day; ay, an' they were God-fearing people too, wha had gien plenty in their time, an' had aye plenty to gie. An' though they had been a' langsyne laid in the kirkyard, — a' except hersel', puir body, — she wouldna disgrace their gude name, she said, by takin' an alms frae ony ane. Her sma means fell oot o' her hands afore her last illness. Little had aye dune her turn, but the little failed at last; an' sair thocht did it gie her for a while what was to come o' her. I could hear her, in the butt end o' the hoose, a'e mornin' mair earnest an' langer in her prayers than usual, though she never neglected them, puir body ; an' a' the early part o' that day she seemed to be no weel. She was aye up and down; an' I could ance or twice hear her gaunting at the fireside ; but when I went ben to her, an' asked what was the matter wi' her, she said she was just in her ordinar'. She went oot for a wee ; an' what did I do, but gang to her amry, for I jaloused a' wasna right there ; an' oh! it was a sair sicht to see, neebors ; for there was neither a bit o' bread nor a grain of meal within its four corners, — naething but the sealed up graybeard wi' the whiskey that for twenty years an' mair she had been keepin' for her lyke-wake ; an', ye ken, it was oot o' the question to think that she would meddle wi' it. Weel did I scold her, when she cam' in, for being sae close-minded. I asked her what harm I had ever done to her, that she wad rather hae died than hae trusted her wants to me ? But though she said naething, I could see the tears in her e'e; an' sae I stopped, an' we took a late breakfast thegither at my fireside.

"She tauld me that mornin' that she weel kent she wouldna lang be a trouble to onybody. The day afore had been Sabbath; an' every Sabbath morning, for the last ten years, her worthy neeboor the elder, whom they had buried only four years afore, used to call on her, in the passing on his way to the kirk. 'Come awa, Elspat,' he would say ; an' she used to be aye decent an' ready, for she liked his conversation ; an' they aye gaed thegither to the kirk. She had been contracted, when a young lass, to a brither o' the elder's, a stout, handsome lad ; but he had been ca'ed suddenly awa atween the contract an' the marriage, an' Elspat, though she had afterwards mony a gude offer, had lived single for his sake. Weel, on the very mornin' afore, just sax days after the elder's death, an' four after his burial, when Elspat was sitting dowie aside the fire, thinkin' o' her gude auld neebor, the cry cam' to the door just as it used to do ; but, though the voice was the same, the words were a wee different. 'Elspat,' it said, 'mak' ready, an' come awa.' She rose hastily to the window, an' there, sure enough, was the elder, turning the corner, in his Sunday's bonnet an' his Sunday's coat. An' weel did she ken, she said, the meaning o' his call, an' kindly did she tak' it. An' if it was but God's will that she suld hae enough to put her decently under the ground, without going into any debt to any one, she would be weel content. She had already the linen for the dead-dress, she said ; for she had spun it for the purpose afore her contract wi' William ; an' she had the whiskey, too, for the wake ; but she had naething anent the coffin an' the bedral.

"Weel, we took our breakfast, an' I did my best to comfort the puir body ; but she looked very down-hearted for a' that. About the middle o' the day, in cam' the minister's boy wi' a letter. It was directed to his master, he said ; but it was a' for Elspat ; an' there was a five-pound note in it. It was frae a man who had left the country mony, mony a year afore, a good deal in her faither's debt. You would hae thought the puir thing wad hae grat her een out when she saw the money ; but never was money mair thankfully received, or ta'en mair directly frae heaven. It sent her aboon the warld, she said ; an' coming at the time it did, an estate o' a thousand a year wadna be o' mair use to her. Next morning she didna rise, for her strength had failed her at once, though she felt nae meikle pain ; an' . she sent me to get the note changed, an' to leave twenty

shillings o't wi' the wright for a decent coffin like her mither's, an' five shillings mair wi' the bedral, an' to tak' in
necessaries for a sick-bed wi' some o' the lave. Weel, I
did that; an' there's still twa pounds o' the note yonder in
the little cupboard.

"On the fifth morning after she had been taken sae ill, I
cam' in till ask after her; for my neebor here had relieved
me o' that night's watchin', an' I had gotten to my bed.
The moment I opened the door I saw that the haill room
was hung in white, just as ye see it now; an' I'm sure it
staid that way a minute or sae; but when I winked it went
awa'. I kent there was a change no far off; and when I
went up to the bed, Elspat didna ken me. She was wirkin'
wi' her han' at the blankets, as if she were picking off the
little motes; an' I could hear the beginning o' the dead-
rattle in her throat. I sat at her bedside for a while wi' my
neebor here; an' when she spoke to us, it was to say that
the bed had grown hard an' uneasy, an' that she wished to
be brought out to the chair. Weel, we indulged her, though
we baith kent that it wasna in the bed the uneasiness
lay. Her mind, puir body, was carried at the time. She
just kent that there was to be a death an' a lykewake, but
no that the death and the lykewake were to be her ain;
an' when she looked at the bed, she bade us tak' down the
black curtains an' put up the white; an' tauld us where
the white were to be found.

"'But where is the corp?' she said; 'it's no there.
Where is the corp?'

"'O, Elspat! it will be there vera soon,' said my neebor;
an' that satisfied her.

"She cam' to hersel' an hour afore she departed. God
had been very gude to her, she said, a' her life lang, an' he
hadna forsaken her at the last. He had been gude to her

when he had gien her friens, an' gude to her when he took them to himsel'; an' she kent she was now going to baith him an' them. There wasna such a difference, she said, atween life an' death as folk were ready to think. She was sure that, though William had been ca'ed awa suddenly, he hadna been ca'ed without being prepared; an' now that her turn had come, an' that she was goin' to meet wi' him, it was maybe as weel that he had left her early; for, till she had lost him, she had been owre licht an' thochtless; an' had it been her lot to hae lived in happiness wi' him, she micht hae remained light an' thochtless still. She bade us baith fareweel, an' thanked an' blessed us; an' her last breath went awa' in a prayer no half an hour after. Puir, decent body! But she's no puir now."

"A pretty portrait," whispered my companion, "of one of a class fast wearing away. Nothing more interests me in the story than the woman's undoubting faith in the supernatural. She does not even seem to know that what she believes so firmly herself is so much as doubted by others. Try whether you can't bring up, by some means, a few other stories furnished with a similar machinery, — a story of the second sight, for instance."

"The only way of accomplishing that," I replied, "is by contributing a story of the kind myself."

"The vision of the room hung in white," I said, "reminds me of a story related, about a hundred and fifty years ago, by a very learned and very ingenious countryman of ours, George, first Earl of Cromarty. His lordship, a steady Royalist, was engaged, shortly before the Restoration (he was then, by the way, only Sir George Mackenzie), in raising troops for the king on his lands on the western coast of Ross-shire. There came on one of those days of rain and tempest so common in the district, and Sir George, with some of his friends, were storm-bound, in a solitary cottage, somewhere on the shores of Loch-broom. Towards evening one of the party went out to look after their horses. He had been sitting beside Sir George, and the chair he had occupied remained empty. On Sir George's servant, an elderly Highlander, coming in, he went up to his master, apparently much appalled, and, tapping him on the shoulder, urged him to rise. 'Rise!' he said, 'rise! There's a dead man sitting on the chair beside you.' The whole party immediately started to their feet; but they saw only the empty chair. The dead man was visible to the Highlander alone. His head was bound up, he said, and his face streaked with blood, and one of his arms hung broken by his side. Next day, as a party of horsemen were passing along the steep side of a hill in the neighborhood, one of the horses stumbled and threw its rider; and the man, grievously injured by the fall, was carried in a state of insensibility to the cottage. His head was deeply gashed and one of his arms was broken, — though he ultimately recovered, — and, on being brought to the cottage, he was placed, in a death-like swoon, in the identical chair which the Highlander had seen occupied by the spectre. Sir George relates the story, with many a similar story besides, in a letter to the celebrated Robert Boyle."

" I have perused it with much interest," said my friend, " and wonder our booksellers should have suffered it to become so scarce. Do you not remember the somewhat similar story his lordship relates of the Highlander, who saw the apparition of a troop of horse ride over the brow of a hill and enter a field of oats, which, though it had been sown only a few days before, the horsemen seemed to cut down with their swords? He states that, a few

months after, a troop of cavalry actually entered the same
field, and carried away the produce for fodder to their
horses. He tells, too, if I remember aright, that on the
same expedition to which your story belongs, one of his
Highlanders, on entering a cottage, started back with horror. He had met in the passage, he said, a dead man in
his shroud, and saw people gathering for a funeral. And,
as his lordship relates, one of the inmates of the cottage,
who was in perfect health at the time of the vision, died
suddenly only two days after."

CHAPTER III.

THE STORY OF DONALD GAIR.

" THE second sight," said an elderly man who sat beside me, and whose countenance had struck me as highly
expressive of serious thought, " is fast wearing out of this
part of the country. Nor should we much regret it perhaps. It seemed, if I may so speak, as something outside
the ordinary dispositions of Providence, and, with all the
horror and unhappiness that attended it, served no apparent good end. I have been a traveller in my youth,
masters. About thirty years ago, I served for some time
in the navy. I entered on the first breaking out of the
Revolutionary war, and was discharged during the short
peace of 1801. One of my chief companions on shipboard,
for the first few years, was a young man, a native of Sutherland, named Donald Gair. Donald, like most of his
16*

countrymen, was a staid, decent lad, of a rather melancholy cast; and yet there were occasions when he could be gay enough too. We sailed together in the Bedford, under Sir Thomas Baird; and, after witnessing the mutiny at the Nore, — neither of us did much more than witness it, for in our case it merely transferred the command of the vessel from a very excellent captain to a set of low Irish doctor's-list men, — we joined Admiral Duncan, then on the Dutch station. We were barely in time to take part in the great action. Donald had been unusually gay all the previous evening. We knew the Dutch had come out, and that there was to be an engagement on the morrow; and, though I felt no fear, the thought that I might have to stand in a few brief hours before my Maker and my Judge had the effect of rendering me serious. But my companion seemed to have lost all command of himself. He sung and leaped and shouted, not like one intoxicated, — there was nothing of intoxication about him, — but under the influence of a wild, irrepressible flow of spirits. I took him seriously to task, and reminded him that we might both at that moment be standing on the verge of death and judgment. But he seemed more impressed by my remarking that, were his mother to see him, she would say he was *fey*.

"We had never been in action before with our captain Sir Thomas. He was a grave, and, I believe, God-fearing man, and much a favorite with at least all the better seamen. But we had not yet made up our minds on his character, — indeed, no sailor ever does with regard to his officers till he knows how they fight, — and we were all curious to see how the parson, as we used to call him, would behave himself among the shot. But truly we might have had little fear for him. I have sailed with

Nelson, and not Nelson himself ever showed more courage or conduct than Sir Thomas in that action. He made us all lie down beside our guns, and steered us, without firing a shot, into the very thickest of the fight; and when we did open, masters, every broadside told with fearful effect. I never saw a man issue his commands with more coolness or self-possession.

"There are none of our continental neighbors who make better seamen, or who fight more doggedly, than the Dutch. We were in a blaze of flame for four hours. Our rigging was slashed to pieces, and two of our ports were actually knocked into one. There was one fierce, ill-natured Dutchman, in particular, — a fellow as black as night, without so much as a speck of paint or gilding about him, save that he had a red lion on the prow, — that fought us as long as he had a spar standing; and when he struck at last, fully one half the crew lay either dead or wounded on the decks, and all his scupper-holes were running blood as freely as ever they had done water at a deck-washing. The Bedford suffered nearly as severely. It is not in the heat of action that we can reckon on the loss we sustain. I saw my comrades falling around me, — falling by the terrible cannon-shot as they came crashing in through our sides; I felt, too, that our gun wrought more heavily as our numbers were .thinning around it; and at times, when some sweeping chain-shot or fatal splinter laid open before me those horrible mysteries of the inner man which nature so sedulously conceals, I was conscious of a momentary feeling of dread and horror. But in the prevailing mood, an unthinking anger, a dire thirsting after revenge, a dogged, unyielding firmness, were the chief ingredients. I strained every muscle and sinew; and, amid the smoke and the thunder and the frightful carnage, fired and loaded, and fired and loaded, and, with every discharge, sent out, as it were, the bitterness of my whole soul against the enemy. But very different were my feelings when victory declared in our favor, and, exhausted and unstrung, I looked abroad among the dead. As I crossed the deck my feet literally splashed in blood; and I saw the mangled fragments of human bodies sticking in horrid patches to the sides and the beams above. There was a fine little boy aboard with whom I was an especial favorite. He had been engaged, before the action, in the construction of a toy ship, which he intended sending to his mother; and I used sometimes to assist him, and to lend him a few simple tools; and, just as we were bearing down on the enemy, he had come running up to me with a knife which he had borrowed from me a short time before.

"'Alick, Alick,' he said, 'I have brought you your knife; we are going into action, you know, and I may be killed, and then you would lose it.'

"Poor little fellow! The first body I recognized was his. Both his arms had been fearfully shattered by a cannon-shot, and the surgeon's tourniquets, which had been fastened below the shoulders, were still there; but he had expired ere the amputating knife had been applied. As I stood beside the body, little in love with war, masters, a comrade came up to me to say that my friend and countryman, Donald Gair, lay mortally wounded in the cockpit. I went instantly down to him. But never shall I forget, though never may I attempt to describe, what I witnessed that day in that frightful scene of death and suffering. Donald lay in a low hammock, raised not a foot over the deck; and there was no one beside him, for the surgeons had seen at a glance the hopelessness of his case, and were busied about others of whom they had hope. He lay on his back, breathing very hard, but perfectly insensible; and in the middle of his forehead there was a round little hole without so much as a speck of blood about it, where a musket-bullet had passed through his brain. He continued to breathe for about two hours; and when he expired I wrapped the body decently up in a hammock, and saw it committed to the deep. The years passed; and, after looking death in the face in many a storm and many a battle, peace was proclaimed, and I returned to my friends and my country.

. "A few weeks after my arrival, an elderly Highland woman, who had travelled all the way from the further side of Loch Shin to see me, came to our door. She was the mother of Donald Gair, and had taken her melancholy journey to hear from me all she might regarding the last moments and death of her son. She had no English, and I had not Gaelic enough to converse with her; but my mother, who had received her with a sympathy all the deeper from the thought that her own son might have, been now in Donald's place, served as our interpreter. She was strangely inquisitive, though the little she heard served only to increase her grief; and you may believe it was not much I could find heart to tell her; for what was there in the circumstances of my comrade's death to afford pleasure to his mother? And so I waived her questions regarding his wound and his burial as best I could.

" ' Ah,' said the poor woman to my mother, 'he need not be afraid to tell me all. I know too, too well that my Donald's body was thrown into the sea; I knew of it long ere it happened; and I have long tried to reconcile my mind to it, tried when he was a boy even; and so you need not be afraid to tell me now.'

"'And how,' asked my mother, whose curiosity was excited, 'could you have thought of it so early?'

"'I lived,' rejoined the woman, 'at the time of Donald's birth, in a lonely shieling among the Sutherland hills, — a full day's journey from the nearest church. It was a long, weary road, over moors and mosses. It was in the winter season, too, when the days are short; and so, in bringing Donald to be baptized, we had to remain a night by the way in the house of a friend. We there found an old woman of so peculiar an appearance that, when she asked me for the child, I at first declined giving it, fearing she was mad and might do it harm. The people of the house, however, assured me she was incapable of hurting it, and so I placed it on her lap. She took it up in her arms, and began to sing to it; but it was such a song as none of us had ever heard before.

"'Poor little stranger!' she said, 'thou hast come into the world in an evil time. The mists are on the hills, gloomy and dark, and the rain lies chill on the heather; and thou, poor little thing, hast a long journey through the sharp, biting winds, and thou art helpless and cold. Oh, but thy long after-journey is as dreary and dark! A wanderer shalt thou be, over the land and the ocean; and in the ocean shalt thou lie at last. Poor little thing, I have waited for thee long. I saw thee in thy wanderings, and in thy shroud, ere thy mother brought thee to the door; and the sounds of the sea and of the deadly guns are still ringing in my ears. Go, poor little thing, to thy mother. Bitterly shall she yet weep for thee, and no wonder; but no one shall ever weep over thy grave, or mark where thou liest amid the deep green, with the shark and the seal.'

"'From that evening,' continued the mother of my friend, 'I have tried to reconcile my mind to what was to happen Donald. But oh, the fond, foolish heart! I loved him more than any of his brothers, because I was to lose him soon ; and though when he left me I took farewell of him for ever, — for I knew I was never, never to see him more, — I felt, till the news reached me of his fall in battle, as if he were living in his coffin. But oh! do tell me all you know of his death. I am old and weak, but I have travelled far, far to see you, that I might hear all; and surely, for the regard you bore to Donald, you will not suffer me to return as I came.'

"But I need not dwell longer on the story. I imparted to the poor woman all the circumstances of her son's death as I have done to you ; and, shocking as they may seem, I found that she felt rather relieved than otherwise."

"This is not quite the country of the second sight," said my friend ; "it is too much on the borders of the Lowlands. The gift seems restricted to the Highlands alone, and it is now fast wearing out even there."

"And weel it is," said one of the men, "that it should be sae. It is surely a miserable thing to ken o' coming evil, if we just merely ken that it is coming, an' that come it must, do what we may. Hae ye ever heard the story o' the kelpie that wons in the Conon?"

My friend replied in the negative.

CHAPTER IV.

THE STORY OF THE DOOMED RIDER.

"The Conon," continued the man, "is as bonny a river as we hae in a' the north country. There's mony a sweet

sunny spot on its banks; an' mony a time an' aft hae I
waded through its shallows, when a boy, to set my little
scantling-line for the trouts an' the eels, or to gather the
big pearl-mussels that lie sae thick in the fords. But its
bonny wooded banks are places for enjoying the day in,
no for passing the nicht. I kenna how it is: it's nane o'
your wild streams, that wander desolate through desert
country, like the Avon, or that come rushing down in
foam and thunder, owre broken rocks, like the Foyers, or
that wallow in darkness, deep, deep in the bowels o' the
earth, like the fearfu' Auldgraunt; an' yet no ane o' these
rivers has mair or frightfuler stories connected wi' it than
the Conon. Ane can hardly saunter owre half a mile in its
course frae where it leaves Contin till where it enters the
sea, without passing owre the scene o' some frightful auld
legend o' the kelpie or the water-wraith. And ane o' the
maist frightful-looking o' these places is to be found among
the woods o' Conon House. Ye enter a swampy meadow,
that waves wi' flags an' rushes like a cornfield in harvest,
an' see a hillock covered wi' willows rising like an island in
the midst. There are thick mirk woods on ilka side: the
river, dark an' awesome, an' whirling round and round in
mossy eddies, sweeps away behind it; an' there is an auld
burying-ground, wi' the broken ruins o' an auld Papist kirk
on the tap. Ane can still see among the rougher stanes
the rose-wrought mullions of an arched window an' the
trough that ance held the holy water. About twa hunder
years ago, — a wee mair, maybe, or a wee less, for ane
canna be very sure o' the date o' thae auld stories, — the
building was entire; an' a spot near it, where the wood
now grows thickest, was laid out in a cornfield. The
marks o' the furrows may still be seen amang the trees.
A party o' Highlanders were busily engaged a'e day in

harvest in cutting down the corn o' that field; an' just aboot noon, when the sun shone brightest, an' they were busiest in the work, they heard a voice frae the river exclaim, 'The hour, but not the man, has come.' Sure enough, on looking round, there was the kelpie standin' in what they ca' a fause ford, just fornent the auld kirk. There is a deep, black pool baith aboon an' below, but i' the ford there's a bonny ripple, that shows, as ane might think, but little depth o' water; an, just i' the middle o' that, in a place where a horse might swim, stood the kelpie. An' it again repeated its words, ' The hour, but not the man, has come'; an' then, flashing through the water like a drake, it disappeared in the lower pool. When the folk stood wondering what the creature might mean, they saw a man on horseback come spurring down the hill in hot haste, making straight for the fause ford. They could then understand her words at ance; an' four o' the stoutest o' them sprang oot frae amang the corn, to warn him o' his danger an' keep him back. An' sae they tauld him what they had seen an heard, an' urged him either to turn back an' tak' anither road or stay for an hour or sae where he was. But he just wadna hear them, for he was baith unbelieving an' in haste, an' would hae ta'en the ford for a' they could say hadna the Highlanders, determined on saving him whether he would or no, gathered round him an' pulled him frae his horse, an' then, to make sure o' him, locked him up in the auld kirk. Weel, when the hour had gone by, — the fatal hour o' the kelpie, — they flung open the door, an' cried to him that he might noo gang on his journey. Ah! but there was nae answer, though; an' sae they cried a second time, an' there was nae answer still; an' then they went in, and found him lying stiff an' cauld on the floor, wi' his face buried in the water o' the very stane trough

17

that we may still see amang the ruins. His hour had come, an' he had fallen in a fit, as 'twould seem, head foremost amang the water o' the trough, where he had been smothered; an' sae, ye see, the prophecy o' the kelpie availed nothing."

"The very story," exclaimed my friend, "to which Sir Walter alludes, in one of the notes to 'The Heart of Mid-Lothian.' The kelpie, you may remember, furnishes him with a motto to the chapter in which he describes the gathering of all Edinburgh to witness the execution of Porteous, and their irrepressible wrath on ascertaining that there was to be no execution, — 'The hour, but not the man, is come.'"

"I remember making quite the same discovery," I replied, "about twelve years ago, when I resided for several months on the banks of the Conon, not half a mile from the scene of the story. One might fill a little book with legends of the Conon. The fords of the river are dangerous, especially in the winter season; and about thirty years ago, before the erection of the fine stone bridge below Conon House, scarcely a winter passed in which fatal accidents did not occur; and these were almost invariably traced to the murderous malice of the water-wraith."

"But who or what is the water-wraith?" said my friend. "We heard just now of the kelpie, and it is the kelpie that Sir Walter quotes."

"Ah," I replied, "but we must not confound the kelpie and the water-wraith, as has become the custom in these days of incredulity. No two spirits, though they were both spirits of the lake and the river, could be more different. The kelpie invariably appeared in the form of a young horse; the water-wraith in that of a very tall woman, dressed in green, with a withered, meagre countenance ever distorted by a malignant scowl. It is the water-wraith, not the kelpie, whom Sir Walter should have quoted ; and yet I could tell you curious stories of the kelpie too."

"We must have them all," said my friend, "ere we part. Meanwhile, I should like to hear some of your stories of the Conon.

"As related by me," I replied, "you will find them rather meagre in their details. In my evening walks along the river, I have passed the ford a hundred times out of which, only a twelvemonth before, as a traveller was entering it on a moonlight night, the water-wraith started up, not four yards in front of him, and pointed at him with her long skinny fingers, as if in mockery. I have leaned against the identical tree to which a poor Highlander clung when, on fording the river by night, he was seized by the goblin. A lad who accompanied him, and who had succeeded in gaining the bank, strove to assist him, but in vain. The poor man was dragged from his hold into the current, where he perished. The spot has been pointed out to me, too, in the opening of the river, where one of our Cromarty fishermen, who had anchored his yawl for the night, was laid hold of by the spectre when lying asleep on the beams, and almost dragged over the gunwale into the water. Our seafaring men still avoid dropping anchor, if they possibly can, after the sun has set, in what they term the *fresh ;* that is, in those upper parts of the frith where the waters of the river predominate over those of the sea.

"The scene of what is deemed one of the best authenticated stories of the water-wraith lies a few miles higher up the river. It is a deep, broad ford, through which horsemen coming from the south pass to Brahan Castle. A thick wood hangs over it on the one side ; on the other it is skirted by a straggling line of alders and a bleak moor. On a winter night, about twenty-five years ago, a servant of the late Lord Seaforth had been drinking with some companions till a late hour, in a small house in the upper part of the moor ; and when the party broke up, he was accompanied by two of them to the ford. The moon was at full, and the river, though pretty deep in flood, seemed noway formidable to the servant. He was a young, vigorous man, and mounted on a powerful horse ; and he had forded it, when half a yard higher on the bank, twenty times before. As he entered the ford, a thick cloud obscured the moon ; but his companions could see him guiding the animal. He rode in a slanting direction across the stream until he had reached nearly the middle, when a dark, tall figure seemed to start out of the water and lay hold of him. There was a loud cry of distress and terror, and a frightful snorting and plunging of the horse. A moment passed, and the terrified animal was seen straining towards the opposite bank, and the ill-fated rider struggling in the stream. In a moment more he had disappeared."

CHAPTER V.

THE STORY OF FAIRBURN'S GHOST.

"I suld weel keen the Conon," said one of the women, who had not yet joined in the conversation. " I was born no a stane's-cast frae the side o't. My mither lived in her last days beside the auld Tower o' Fairburn, that stands sae like a ghaist aboon the river, an' looks down on a' its turns and windings frae Contin to the sea. My faither, too, for a twelvemonth or sae afore his death, had a boat on ane o' its ferries, for the crossing, on weekdays, o' passengers, an' o' the kirkgoing folks on Sunday. He had a little bit farm beside the Conon, an' just got the boat by way o' eiking out his means; for we had aye eneugh to do at rent-time, an' had maybe less than plenty through a' the rest o' the year besides. Weel, for the first ten months or sae the boat did brawly. The Castle o' Brahan is no half a mile frae the ferry, an' there were aye a hantle o' gran' folk comin' and gangin' frae the Mackenzie, an' my faither had the crossin' o' them a'. An' besides, at Marti'mas, the kirk-going people used to send him firlots o' bear an' pecks o' oatmeal; an' he soon began to find that the bit boat was to do mair towards paying the rent o' the farm than the farm itsel'.

"The Tower o' Fairburn is aboot a mile and a half aboon the ferry. It stands by itsel' on the tap o' a heathery hill, an' there are twa higher hills behind it. Beyond there spreads a black, dreary desert, where ane micht wander a lang simmer's day withoot seeing the face o' a human creature, or the kindly smoke o' a lum. I dare say nane o' you hae heard hoo the Mackenzies o' Fairburn an' the Chisholms o' Strathglass parted that bit o' kintra atween them. Nane o' them could tell where the lauds o' the ane ended or the ither began, an' they were that way for generations, till they at last thocht them o' a plan o' division. Each o' them gat an auld wife o' seventy-five, an' they set them aff a'e Monday at the same time, the ane frae Erchless Castle an' the ither frae the Tower, warning them aforehand that the braidness o' their maisters' lands depended on their speed; for where the twa would meet amang the hills, there would be the boundary.

17*

"You may be sure that neither o' them lingered by the way that morning. They kent there was mony an e'e on them, an' that their names would be spoken o' in the kintra-side lang after themsels were dead an' gane; but it sae happened that Fairburn's carline, wha had been his nurse, was ane o' the slampest women in a' the north of Scotland, young or auld; an', though the ither did weel, she did sae meikle better that she had got owre twenty lang Highland miles or the ither had got owre fifteen. They say it was a droll sicht to see them at the meeting, — they were baith tired almost to fainting; but no sooner did they come in sicht o' ane anither, at the distance o' a mile or sae, than they began to run. An' they ran, an' better ran, till they met at a little burnie; an' there wad they hae focht, though they had ne'er seen ane anither atween the een afore, had they had strength eneugh left them; but they had neither pith for fechtin' nor breath for scoldin', an' sae they just sat down an' girned at ane anither across the stripe. The Tower o' Fairburn is naething noo but a dismal ruin o' five broken stories, the ane aboon the ither, an' the lands hae gane oot o' the auld family; but the story o' the twa auld wives is a weel-kent story still.

"The laird o' Fairburn, in my faither's time, was as fine an open-hearted gentleman as was in the haill country. He was just particular gude to the puir; but the family had ever been that; ay, in their roughest days, even whan the Tower had neither door nor window in the lower story, an' only a wheen shot-holes in the story aboon. There wasna a puir thing in the kintra but had reason to bless the laird; an' at a'e time he had nae fewer than twelve puir orphans living about his house at ance. Nor was he in the least a proud, haughty man. He wad chat for hours thegither wi' ane o' his puirest tenants; an' ilka time he crossed the ferry, he wad tak' my faither wi' him, for company just, maybe half a mile on his way out or hame. Weel, it was a'e nicht about the end o' May, — a bonny nicht, an hour or sae after sundown, — an' my faither was mooring his boat, afore going to bed, to an auld oak tree, whan wha does he see but the laird o' Fairburn coming down the bank? Od, thocht he, what can be takin' the laird frae hame sae late as this? I thocht he had been no weel. The laird cam' steppin' into the boat, but, instead o' speakin' frankly, as he used to do, he just waved his hand, as the proudest gentleman in the kintra micht, an' pointed to the ither side. My faither rowed him across; but, oh! the boat felt unco dead an' heavy, an' the water stuck around the oars as gin it had been tar; an' he had just eneugh ado, though there was but little tide in the river, to mak' oot the ither side. The laird stepped oot, an' then stood, as he used to do, on the bank, to gie my faither time to fasten his boat, an' come alang wi' him; an' were it no for that, the puir man wadna hae thocht o' going wi' him that nicht; but as it was, he just moored his boat an' went. At first he thocht the laird must hae got some bad news that made him sae dull, an' sae he spoke on to amuse him, aboot the weather an' the markets; but he found he could get very little to say, an' he felt as arc an' eerie in passin' through the woods as gin he had been passin' alane through a kirkyard. He noticed, too, that there was a fearsome flichtering an' shriekin' amang the birds that lodged in the tree-taps aboon them; an' that, as they passed the *Talisoe*, there was a collie on the tap o' a hillock, that set up the awfulest yowling he had ever heard. He stood for a while in sheer consternation, but the laird beckoned him on, just as he had done at the riverside, an' sae he gaed a bittie further alang the wild, rocky glen that opens into the deer-park. But oh, the fright that was amang the deer! They had been lyin' asleep on the knolls, by sixes an' sevens; an' up they a' started at ance, and gaed driving aff to the far end o' the park as if they couldna be far eneugh frae my faither an' the laird. Weel, my faither stood again, an' the laird beckoned an' beckoned as afore ; but, Gude tak' us a' in keeping! whan my faither looked up in his face, he saw it was the face o' a corp: it was white . an' stiff, an' the nose was thin an' sharp, an' there was nae winking wi' the wide-open een. Gude preserve us! my faither didna ken where he was stan'in, — didna ken what he was doin'; an', though he kept his feet, he was just in a kind o' swarf like. The laird spoke twa or three words to him, — something about the orphans, he thocht; but he was in such a state that he couldna tell what ; an' when he cam' to himsel' the apparition was awa'. It was a bonny clear nicht when they had crossed the Conon; but there had been a gatherin' o' black cluds i' the lift as they gaed, an' there noo cam' on, in the clap o' a han', ane o' the fearsomest storms o' thunder an' lightning that was ever seen in the country. There was a thick gurly aik smashed to shivers owre my faither's head, though nane o' the splinters steered him; an' whan he reached the river, it was roaring frae bank to brae like a little ocean ; for a water-spout had broken amang the hills, an' the trees it had torn doun wi' it were darting alang the current like arrows. He crossed in nae little danger, an' took to his bed ; an', though he raise an' went aboot his wark for twa or three months after, he was never, never his ain man again. It was found that the laird had departed no five minutes afore his apparition had come to the ferry ; an' the very last words he had spoken — but his mind was carried at the time — was something aboot my faither."

CHAPTER VI.

THE STORY OF THE LAND FACTOR.

"There maun hae been something that weighed on his mind," remarked one of the women, "though your faither had nae power to get it frae him. I mind that, when I was a lassie, there happened something o' the same kind. My faither had been a tacksman on the estate o' Blackhall; an' as the land was sour an' wat, an' the seasons for a while backward, he aye contrived — for he was a hard-working, carefu' man — to keep us a' in meat and claith, and to meet wi' the factor. But, waes me! he was sune ta'en frae us. In the middle o' the seed-time there cam' a bad fever intil the country; an' the very first that died o't was my puir faither. My mither did her best to keep the farm, an' haud us a' thegither. She got a carefu', decent lad to manage for her, an' her ain e'e was on everything; an' had it no been for the cruel, cruel factor, she micht hae dune gey weel. But never had the puir tenant a waur friend than Ranald Keilly. He was a toun writer, an' had made a sort o' living, afore he got the factorship, just as toun writers do in ordinar'. He used to be gettin' the haud o' auld wives' posies when they died; an' there were aye some litigeous, troublesome folk in the place, too, that kept him doing a little in the way o' troublin' their neebors; an' sometimes, when some daft, gowked man, o' mair means than sense, couldna mismanage his ain affairs eneugh, he got Keilly to mismanage them for him. An' sae he had picked up a bare livin' in this way; but the factorship made him just a gentleman. 'But, oh, an ill use did he mak' o' the power that it gied him owre puir, honest folk! Ye maun ken that, gin they were puir, he liked them a' the waur for being honest; but, I dare say, that was natural eneugh for the like o' him. He contrived to be baith writer an' factor, ye see; an' it wad just seem that his chief aim in a'e the capacity was to find employment for himsel' in the ither. If a puir tenant was but a day behind-hand wi' his rent, he had creatures o' his ain that used to gang half-an'-half wi' him in their fees · an' them he wad send aff to poind him; an' then, if the expenses o' the poinding werena forthcoming, as weel as what was owing to the master, he wad hae a roup o' the stocking twa or three days after, an' anither account, as a man o' business, for that. An' when things were going dog-cheap, — as he took care that they should sometimes gang, — he used to buy them in for himsel,' an' part wi' them again for maybe twice the money. The laird was a quiet, silly, good-na-tured man; an', though he was tauld weel o' the factor at times, ay, an' believed it too, he just used to say: 'Oh, puir Keilly, what wad he do gin I were to part wi' him? He wad just starve.' An' oh, sirs, his pity for him was bitter cruelty to mony, mony a puir tenant, an' to my mither amang the lave.

"The year after my faither's death was cauld an' wat, an' oor stuff remained sae lang green that we just thocht we wouldna get it cut ava. An' when we did get it cut, the stacks, for the first whilie, were aye heatin' wi' us; an' when Marti'mas came, the grain was still saft an' milky, an' no fit for the market. The term cam' round, an' there was little to gie the factor in the shape o' money, though there was baith corn and cattle; an' a' that we wanted was just a little time. Ah, but we had fa'en into the hands o' ane that never kent pity. My mither hadna the money gin, as it were, the day, an' on the morn the messengers came to poind. The roup was no a week after; an' oh, it was a grievous sicht to see how the crop an' the cattle went for just naething. The farmers were a' puirly aff with the late ha'rst, an' had nae money to spare; an' sae the factor knocked in ilka thing to himsel', wi' hardly a bid against him. He was a rough-faced little man, wi' a red, hooked nose, a gude deal gi'en to whiskey, an' very wild an' desperate when he had ta'en a glass or twa aboon ordinar'; an' on the day o' the roup he raged like a perfect madman. My mither spoke to him again an' again, wi' the tear in her e'e, an' implored him, for the sake o' the orphan an' the widow, no to hurry hersel' an' her bairns; but he just cursed an' swore a' the mair, an' knocked down the stacks an' the kye a' the faster; an' whan she spoke to him o' the Ane aboon a', he said that Providence gied lang credit an' reckoned on a lang day, an' that he wald tak' him intil his ain hands. Weel, the roup cam' to an end, an' the sum o' the whole didna come to meikle mair nor the rent an' clear the factor's lang, lang account for expenses; an' at nicht my mither was a ruined woman. The factor staid up late an' lang, drinkin' wi' some creatures o' his ain; an' the last words he said on going to his bed was, that he hadna made a better day's wark for a twelvemonth. But, Gude tak' us a' in keeping! in the morning he was a corp, — a cauld lifeless corp, wi' a face as black as my bonnet.

"Weel, he was buried, an' there was a grand character o' him putten in the newspapers, an' we a' thocht we were to hear nae mair about him. My mither got a wee bittie o' a house on the farm o' a neebor, and there we lived dowie eneugh; but she was aye an eident, workin' woman au' she now span late an' early for some o' her auld friends, the farmers' wives; an' her sair-won penny, wi' what we got frae kindly folk wha minded us in better times, kept us a' alive. Meanwhile, strange stories o' the dead factor began to gang aboot the kintra. First, his servants, it was said, were hearing arc, curious noises in his counting-office. The door was baith locked an' sealed, waiting till his friends would cast up, for there were some doots aboot them; but, locked an' sealed as it was, they could hear it opening an' shutting every nicht, an' hear a rustlin' among the papers, as gin there had been half a dozen writers scribblin' amang them at ance. An' then, Gude preserve us a'! they could hear Keilly himsel', as if he were dictating to his clerk. An', last o' a', they could see him in the gloamin', nicht an mornin', ganging aboot his house wringing his hands, an' aye, aye muttering to himsel' aboot roups and poindings. The servant girls left the place to himsel'; an' the twa lads that wrought his farm an' slept in a hayloft, were sae disturbed nicht after nicht, that they had just to leave it to himsel' too.

"My mither was a'e nicht wi' some a' her spinnin' at a neeborin' farmer's, — a worthy, God-fearing man, an' an elder o' the kirk. It was in the simmer time, an' the nicht was bricht an' bonny; but, in her backcoming, she had to pass the empty house o' the dead factor, an' the elder said that he would take a step hame wi' her, for fear she michtna be that easy in her mind. An' the honest man did sae. Naething happened them in the passin', except that a dun cow, ance a great favorite o' my mither's, cam' lowing up to them, puir beast, as gin she would hae better liked to be gaun hame wi' my mother than stay where she was. But the elder didna get aff sae easy in the backcoming. He was passin' beside a thick hedge, whan what does he see, but a man inside the hedge, takin' step for step wi' him as he gaed! The man wore a dun coat, an had a hunting-whip under his arm, an' walked, as the elder thocht, very like what the dead factor used to do when he had gotten a glass or twa aboon ordinar. Weel, they cam' to a slap in the hedge, an' out cam' the man at the slap; an' Gude tak' us a' in keeping! it was sure enough the dead factor himsel'. There were his hook nose, an' his rough, red face, — though it was maybe bluer noo than red, — an' there were the boots an' the dun coat he had worn at my mither's roup, an' the very whip he had lashed a puir gangrel woman wi' no a week before his death. He was mutterin' something to himsel'; but the elder could only hear a wordie noo an' then. 'Poind an' roup,' he would say, — 'poind an' roup'; an' then there would come out a blatter o' curses. — 'Hell, hell! an' damn, damn! The elder was a wee fear-stricken at first, — as wha wadna? — but then the ill words an' the way they were said made him angry, — for he could never bear ill words without checking them, — an' sae he turned round wi' a stern brow, an' asked the appearance what it wanted, an' why it should hae come to disturb the peace o' the kintra, and to disturb him? It stood still at that, an' said, wi' an awsome grane, that it couldna be quiet in the grave till there was some justice done to Widow Stuart. It then tauld him that there were forty gowd guineas in a secret drawer in his desk, that hadna been found, an' tauld him where to get them, an' that he wad need gang wi' the laird an' the minister to the drawer, an' gie them a' to the widow. It couldna hae rest till then, it said, nor wad the kintra hae rest either. It willed that the lave o' the gear should be gien to the poor o' the parish; for nane o' the twa folk that laid claim to it had the shadow o' a right. An' wi'

18

that the appearance left him. It just went back through the slap in the hedge; an' as it stepped owre the ditch, vanished in a puff o' smoke.

" Weel, — but to cut short a lang story, — the laird and the minister were at first gay slow o' belief; no that they misdoubted the elder, but they thocht that he must hae been deceived by a sort o' wakin' dream. But they soon changed their minds, for, sure enough, they found the forty guineas in a secret drawer. An' the news they got frae the south about Keilly was just as the appearance had said; no ane mair nor anither had a richt to his gear, for he had been a foundlin', an' had nae friends. An' sae my mither got the guineas, an' the parish got the rest, an' there was nae mair heard o' the apparition. We didna get back oor auld farm; but the laird gae us a bittie that served oor turn as weel; an' or my mither was ca'ed awa frae us, we were a' settled in the warld, an' doin' for oorsels."

CHAPTER VII.

THE STORY OF THE MEALMONGER.

" It is wonderful," remarked the decent-looking, elderly man who had contributed the story of Donald Gair, — " it is wonderful how long a recollection of that kind may live in the memory without one's knowing it is there. There is no possibility of one taking an inventory of one's recollections. They live unnoted and asleep, till roused by some likeness of themselves, and then up they start, and answer to it, as ' face answereth to face in a glass.' There comes a story into my mind, much like the last, that has lain there all unknown to me for the last thirty years, nor have I heard any one mention. it since; and yet when I was a boy no story could be better known. You have all heard of the dear years that followed the harvest of '40, and how fearfully they bore on the poor. The scarcity, doubtless, came mainly from the hand of Providence, and yet man had his share in it too. There were forestallers of the market, who gathered their miserable gains by heightening the already enormous price of victuals, thus adding starvation to hunger; and among the best known and most execrated of these was one M'Kechan, a residenter in the neighboring parish. He was a hard-hearted foul-spoken man; and often what he *said* exasperated the people as much against him as what he *did*. When, on one occasion, he bought up all the victuals in a market, there was a wringing of hands among the women, and they cursed him to his face; but when he added insult to injury, and told them, in his pride, that he had not left them an ounce to foul their teeth, they would that instant have taken his life, had not his horse carried him through. He was a mean, too, as well as a hard-hearted man, and used small measures and light weights. But he made money, and deemed himself in a fair way of gaining a character on the strength of that alone, when he was seized by a fever, and died after a few days' illness. Solomon tells us, that when the wicked perish there is shouting; there was little grief in the sheriffdom when M'Kechan died; but his relatives buried him decently; and, in the course of the next fortnight, the meal fell twopence the peck. You know the burying-ground of St. Bennet's : the chapel has long since been ruinous, and a row of wasted elms, with white skeleton-looking tops, run around the enclosure and look over the fields that surround it on every side. It lies out of the way of any thoroughfare, and months may sometimes pass, when burials are unfrequent, in which no one goes near it. It was in St. Bennet's that M'Kechan was buried; and the people about the farm-house that lies nearest it were surprised, for the first month after his death, to see the figure of a man, evening and morning, just a few minutes before the sun had risen and a few after it had set, walking round the yard under the elms three times, and always disappearing when it had taken the last turn beside an old tomb near the gate. It was of course always clear daylight when they saw the figure; and the month passed ere they could bring themselves to suppose that it was other than a thing of flesh and blood, like themselves. The strange regularity of its visits, however, at length bred suspicion; and the farmer himself, a plain, decent man, of more true courage than men of twice the pretence, determined one evening on watching it. He took his place outside the wall a little before sunset; and no sooner had the red light died away on the elm-tops, than up started the figure from among the ruins on the opposite side of the burying-ground, and came onward in its round, muttering incessantly as it came, 'Oh, for mercy sake, for mercy sake, a handful of meal! I am starving, I am starving: a handful of meal!' And then, changing its tone into one still more doleful, 'Oh,' it exclaimed, ' alas for the little lippie and the little peck! alas for the little lippie and the little peck!' As it passed, the farmer started up from his seat; and there, sure enough, was M'Kechan, the corn-factor, in his ordinary dress, and, except that he was thinner and paler than usual, like a man suffering from hunger, presenting nearly his ordinary appearance. The figure passed with a slow, gliding sort of motion ; and, turning the further corner of the burying-ground, came onward in its second round ; but the farmer, though he had felt rather curious than afraid as it went by, found his heart fail him as it approached the second time, and, without waiting its coming up, set off homeward through the corn. The apparition continued to take its rounds evening and morning for about two months after, and then disappeared for ever. Mealmongers had to forget the story, and to grow a little less afraid, ere they could cheat with their accustomed coolness. Believe me, such beliefs, whatever may be thought of them in the present day, have not been without their use in the past."

As the old man concluded his story, one of the women rose to a table in the little room and replenished our glasses. We all drank in silence.

" It is within an hour of midnight," said one of the men, looking at his watch. " We had better recruit the fire, and draw in our chairs. The air aye feels chill at a lykewake or a burial. At this time to-morrow we will be lifting the corpse."

There was no reply. We all drew in our chairs nearer the fire, and for several minutes there was a pause in the conversation ; but there were more stories to be told, and before the morning many a spirit was evoked from the grave, the vast deep, and the Highland stream.

18*

VI.

BILL WHYTE.

CHAPTER I.

Sʜᴀᴋsᴘᴇᴀʀᴇ.

I ʜᴀᴅ occasion, about three years ago, to visit the ancient burgh of Fortrose. It was early in winter; the days were brief, though pleasant, and the nights long and dark; and, as there is much in Fortrose which the curious traveller deems interesting, I had lingered amid its burying-grounds and its broken and mouldering tenements till the twilight had fairly set in. I had explored the dilapidated ruins of the Chanonry of Ross; seen the tomb of old Abbot Boniface and the bell blessed by the Pope; run over the complicated tracery of the Runic obelisk, which had been dug up, about sixteen years before, from under the foundations of the old parish church; and visited the low, long house, with its upper windows buried in the thatch, in which the far-famed Sir James Mackintosh had received the first rudiments of his education. And in all this I had been accompanied by a benevolent old man of the place, a mighty chronicler of the past, who, when a boy, had sat

on the same form with Sir James, and who on this occasion
had seemed quite as delighted in meeting with a patient
and interested listener as I had been in finding so intelligent and enthusiastic a storyist. There was little wonder,
then, that twilight should have overtaken me in such a
place, and in such company.

There are two roads which run between Cromarty and
Fortrose, — the one the king's highway, the other a narrow footpath that goes winding for several miles under the
immense wall of cliffs which overhangs the northern shores
of the Moray Frith, and then ascends to the top by narrow
and doubtful traverses along the face of an immense precipice termed the Scarf's Crag. The latter route is by far
the more direct and more pleasant of the two to the day-
traveller; but the man should think twice who proposes
taking it by night. The Scarf's Crag has been a scene of
frightful accidents for the last two centuries. It is not yet
more than twelve years since a young and very active man
was precipitated from one of its higher ledges to the very
beach, — a sheer descent of nearly two hundred feet; and
a multitude of little cairns which mottle the sandy platform
below bear witness to the not unfrequent occurrence of
such casualties in the remote past. With the knowledge
of all this, however, I had determined on taking the more
perilous road. It is fully two miles shorter than the other;
and, besides, in a life of undisturbed security a slight ad-
mixture of that feeling which the sense of danger awakens
is a luxury which I have always deemed worth one's while
running some little risk to procure. The night fell thick
and dark while I was yet hurrying along the footway
which leads under the cliffs; and, on reaching the Scarf's
Crag, I could no longer distinguish the path, nor even
catch the huge outline of the precipice between me and

the sky. I knew that the moon rose a little after nine, but it was still early in the evening; and, deeming it too long to wait its rising, I set myself to grope for the path, when, on turning an abrupt angle, I was dazzled by a sudden blaze of light from an opening in the rock. A large fire of furze and brushwood blazed merrily from the interior of a low-browed but spacious cave, bronzing with dusky yellow the huge volume of smoke which went rolling outwards along the roof, and falling red and strong on the face and hands of a thick-set, determined-looking man, well-nigh in his sixtieth year, who was seated before it on a block of stone. I knew him at once, as an intelligent, and, in the main, rather respectable gipsy, whom I had once met with about ten years before, and who had seen some service as a soldier, it was said, in the first British expedition to Egypt. The sight of his fire determined me at once. I resolved on passing the evening with him till the rising of the moon; and, after a brief explanation, and a blunt, though by no means unkind invitation to a place beside his fire, I took my seat, fronting him, on a block of granite which had been rolled from the neighboring beach. In less than half an hour we were on as easy terms as if we had been comrades for years; and, after beating over fifty different topics, he told me the story of his life, and found an attentive and interested auditor.

Who of all my readers is unacquainted with Goldsmith's admirable stories of the sailor with the wooden leg and the poor half-starved merry-andrew? Independently of the exquisite humor of the writer, they are suited to interest us from the sort of cross vistas which they open into scenes of life where every thought and aim and incident has at once all the freshness of novelty and all the truth of nature to recommend it. And I felt nearly the same kind of interest in listening to the narrative of the gipsy. It was much longer than either of Goldsmith's stories, and perhaps less characteristic; but it presented a rather curious picture of a superior nature rising to its proper level through circumstances the most adverse; and, in the main, pleased me so well, that I think I cannot do better than present it to the reader.

"I was born, master," said the gipsy, "in this very cave, some sixty years ago, and so am a Scotchman like yourself. My mother, however, belonged to the Debatable-land; my father was an Englishman; and of my five sisters, one first saw the light in Jersey, another in Guernsey, a third in Wales, a fourth in Ireland, and the fifth in the Isle of Man. But this is a trifle, master, to what occurs in some families. It can't be much less than fifty years since my mother left us, one bright sunny day, on the English side of Kelso, and staid away about a week. We thought we had lost her altogether; but back she came at last; and when she did come, she brought with her a small sprig of a lad of about three summers or thereby. Father grumbled a little. We had got small fry enough already, he said, and bare enough and hungry enough they were at times; but mother showed him a pouch of yellow pieces, and there was no more grumbling. And so we called the little fellow Bill Whyte, as if he had been one of ourselves; and he grew up among us, as pretty a fellow as e'er the sun looked upon. I was a few years his senior; but he soon contrived to get half a foot ahead of me; and when we quarrelled, as boys will at times, master, I always came off second best. I never knew a fellow of a higher spirit. He would rather starve than beg, a hundred times over, and never stole in his life; but then for gin-setting, and deer-stalking, and black-fishing, not a poacher in the country

got beyond him; and when there was a smuggler in the
Solway, who more active than Bill? He was barely nineteen, poor fellow, when he made the country too hot to
hold him. I remember the night as well as if it were yesterday. The Cat-maran lugger was in the Frith, d'ye see,
a little below Caerlaverock; and father and Bill, and some
half-dozen more of our men, were busy in bumping the
kegs ashore, and hiding them in the sand. It was a thick,
smuggy night: we could hardly see fifty yards around us;
and on our last trip, master, when we were down in the
water to the gunwale, who should come upon us, in the
turning of a handspike, but the revenue lads from Kirkcudbright! They hailed us to strike, in the devil's name.
Bill swore he wouldn't. Flash went a musket, and the
ball whistled through his bonnet. Well, he called on them
to row up, and up they came; but no sooner were they
within half-oar's length, than, taking up a keg, and raising
it just as he used to do the putting-stone, he made it spin
through their bottom as if the planks were of window
glass, and down went their cutter in half a jiffy. They
had wet powder that night, and fired no more bullets.
Well, when they were gathering themselves up as they
best could, — and, goodness be praised! there were no
drownings amongst them, — we bumped our kegs ashore,
hiding them with the others, and then fled up the country.
We knew there would be news of our night's work; and
so there was; for before next evening there were adver-
tisements on every post for the apprehension of Bill, with
an offered reward of twenty pounds.

"Bill was a bit of a scholar, — so am I, for that matter,
— and the papers stared him on every side.

"'Jack,' he said to me, — 'Jack Whyte, this will never
do: the law's too strong for us now; and if I don't make

away with myself, they'll either have me tucked up or sent over the seas to slave for life. I'll tell you what I'll do. I stand six feet in my stocking-soles, and good men were never more wanted than at present. I'll cross the country this very night, and away to Edinburgh, where there are troops raising for foreign service. Better a musket than the gallows!'

" ' Well, Bill,' I said, 'I don't care though I go with you. I'm a good enough man for my inches, though I ain't so tall as you, and I'm woundily tired of spoon-making.'

" And so off we set across the country that very minute, travelling by night only, and passing our days in any hiding hole we could find, till we reached Edinburgh, and there we took the bounty. Bill made as pretty a soldier as one could have seen in a regiment; and, men being scarce, I wasn't rejected neither; and after just three weeks' drilling, — and plaguey weeks they were, — we were shipped off, fully finished, for the south. Bonaparte had gone to Egypt, and we were sent after him to ferret him out; though we weren't told so at the time. And it was our good luck, master, to be put aboard of the same transport.

" Nothing like seeing the world for making a man smart. We had all sorts of people in our regiment, from the broken-down gentleman to the broken-down lamplighter; and Bill was catching from the best of them all he could. He knew he wasn't a gipsy, and had always an eye to getting on in the world; and as the voyage was a woundy long one, and we had the regimental schoolmaster aboard, Bill was a smarter fellow at the end of it than he had been at the beginning. Well, we reached Aboukir Bay at last. You have never been in Egypt, master; but just look across the Moray Frith here, on a sunshiny day, and you will see a picture of it, if you but strike off the blue Highland hills, that rise behind, from the long range of low sandy hillocks that stretches away along the coast between Findhorn and Nairn. ·I don't think it was worth all the trouble it cost us; but the king surely knew best. Bill and I were in the first detachment, and we had to clear the way for the rest. The French were drawn up on the shore, as thick as flies on a dead snake, and the bullets rattled round us like a shower of May hail. It was a glorious sight, master, for a bold heart. The entire line of sandy coast seemed one unbroken streak of fire and smoke; and we could see the old tower of Aboukir rising like a fiery dragon at the one end, and the straggling village of Rosetta, half-cloud half-flame, stretching away on the other. There was a line of launches and gunboats behind us, that kept up an incessant fire on the enemy, and shot and shell went booming over our heads. We rowed shorewards, under a canopy of smoke and flame : the water was broken by ten thousand oars; and never, master, have you heard such cheering; it drowned the roar of the very cannon. Bill and I pulled at the same oar; but he bade me cheer, and leave the pulling to him.

"'Cheer, Jack,' he said, 'cheer! I am strong enough to pull ten oars, and your cheering does my heart good.'

"I could see, in the smoke and the confusion, that there was a boat stove by a shell just beside us, and the man immediately behind me was shot through the head. But we just cheered and pulled all the harder; and the moment our keel touched the shore we leaped out into the water, middle deep, and, after one well-directed volley, charged up the beach with our bayonets fixed. I missed footing in the hurry, just as we closed, and a big-whiskered fellow in blue would have pinned me to the sand had not

Bill struck him through the wind-pipe, and down he fell above me; but when I strove to rise from under him, he grappled with me in his death agony, and the blood and breath came rushing through his wound in my face. Ere I had thrown him off my comrades had broken the enemy and were charging up the side of a sand-hill, where there were two field-pieces stationed that had sadly annoyed us in the landing. There came a shower of grape-shot whistling round me, that carried away my canteen and turned me half round; and when I looked up, I saw, through the smoke, that half my comrades were swept away by the discharge, and that the survivors were fighting desperately over the two guns, hand-to-hand with the enemy. Ere I got up to them, however, — and, trust me, master, I didn't linger, — the guns were our own. Bill stood beside one of them, all grim and bloody, with his bayonet dripping like an eaves-spout in a shower. He had struck down five of the French, besides the one he had levelled over me; and now, all of his own accord, — for our sergeant had been killed, — he had shotted the two pieces and turned them on the enemy. They all scampered down the hill, master, on the first discharge, — all save one brave, obstinate fellow, who stood firing upon us, not fifty yards away, half under cover of a sand-bank. I saw him load thrice ere I could hit him, and one of his balls whisked through my hat; but I catched him at last, and down he fell. My bullet went right through his forehead. We had no more fighting that day. The French fell back on Alexandria, and our troops advanced about three miles into the country, over a dreary waste of sand, and then lay for the night on their arms.

"In the morning, when we were engaged in cooking our breakfasts, master, making what fires we could with the withered leaves of the date-tree, our colonel and two officers came up to us. The colonel was an Englishman, as brave a gentleman as ever lived, aye, and as kind an officer too. He was a fine-looking old man, as tall as Bill, and as well built too; but his health was much broken. It was said he had entered the army out of break-heart on losing his wife. Well, he came up to us, I say, and shook Bill by the hand as cordially as if he had been a colonel like himself. He was a brave, good soldier, he said, and, to show him how much he valued good men, he had come to make him a sergeant, in room of the one he had lost. He had heard he was a scholar, he said, and he trusted his conduct would not disgrace the halberd. Bill, you may be sure, thanked the colonel, and thanked him, master, very like a gentleman; and that very day he swaggered scarlet and a sword, as pretty a sergeant as the army could boast of; aye, and for that matter, though his experience was little, as fit for his place.

"For the first fortnight we didn't eat the king's biscuit for nothing. We had terrible hard fighting on the 13th; and, had not our ammunition failed us, we would have beaten the enemy all to rags; but for the last two hours we hadn't a shot, and stood just like so many targets set up to be fired at. I was never more fixed in my life than when I saw my comrades falling around me, and all for nothing. Not only could I see them falling, but, in the absence of every other noise, — for we had ceased to cheer, and stood as silent and as hard as foxes, — I could hear the dull, hollow sound of the shot as it pierced them through. Sometimes the bullets struck the sand, and then rose and went rolling over the level, raising clouds of dust at every skip. At times we could see them coming through the air like little clouds, and singing all the way as they came. But it was the frightful smoking shot that annoyed us most — these horrid shells. Sometimes they broke over our heads in the air as if a cannon charged with grape had been fired at us from out the clouds. At times they sank into the sand at our feet, and then burst up like so many Vesuviuses, giving at once death and burial to hundreds. But we stood our ground, and the day passed. I remember we got, towards evening, into a snug hollow between two sand-hills, where the shot skimmed over us, not two feet above our heads; but two feet is just as good as twenty, master; and I began to think, for the first time, that I hadn't got a smoke all day. I snapped my musket and lighted my pipe; and Bill, whom I hadn't seen since the day after the landing, came up to share with me.

"'Bad day's work, Jack,' he said; 'but we have at least taught the enemy what British soldiers can endure, and ere long we shall teach them something more. But here comes a shell! Nay, do not move,' he said; 'it will fall just ten yards short.' And down it came, roaring like a tempest, sure enough, about ten yards away, and sank into the sand. 'There now, fairly lodged,' said Bill; 'lie down, lads, lie down.' We threw ourselves flat on our faces; the earth heaved under us like a wave of the sea; and in a moment Bill and I were covered with half a ton of sand. But the pieces whizzed over us; and, save that the man who was across me had an ammunition-bag carried away, not one of us more than heard them. On getting ourselves disinterred, and our pipes re-lighted, Bill, with a twitch on the elbow — so — said he wished to speak with me a little apart; and we went out together into a hollow in front.

"'You will think it strange, Jack,' he said, 'that all this day, when the enemy's bullets were hopping around us like hail, there was but just one idea that filled my mind, and I could find room for no other. Ever since I saw Colonel Westhope, it has been forced upon me, through a newly-awakened, dream-like recollection, that he is the gentleman with whom I lived ere I was taken away by your people; for taken away I must have been. Your mother used to tell me that my father was a Cumberland gipsy, who met with some bad accident from the law; but I am now convinced she must have deceived me, and that my father was no such sort of man. You will think it strange, but when putting on my coat this morning, my eye caught the silver bar on the sleeve, and there leaped into my mind a vivid recollection of having worn a scarlet dress before, — scarlet bound with silver, — and that it was in the house of a gentleman and lady whom I had just learned to call papa and mamma. And every time I see the colonel, as I say, I am reminded of the gentleman. Now, for heaven's sake, Jack, tell me all you know about me. You are a few years my senior, and must remember better than I can myself under what circumstances I joined your tribe.'

"'Why, Bill,' I said, 'I know little of the matter, and 'twere no great wonder though these bullets should confuse me somewhat in recalling what I do know. Most certainly we never thought you a gipsy like ourselves; but then I am sure mother never stole you; she had family enough of her own; and, besides, she brought with her for your board, she said, a purse with more gold in it than I have seen at one time before or since. I remember it kept us all comfortably in the *creature* for a whole twelvemonth; and it wasn't a trifle, Bill, that could do that. You were at first like to die among us. You hadn't been accustomed to sleeping out, or to food such as ours. And, dear me! how the rags you were dressed in used to annoy you; but you soon got over all, Bill, and became the hardiest little fellow among us. I once heard my mother say that you were a *love-begot*, and that your father, who was an English gentleman, had to part from both you and your mother on taking a wife. And no more can I tell you, Bill, for the life of me.'

"We slept that night on the sand, master, and found in the morning that the enemy had fallen back some miles nearer Alexandria. Next evening there was a party of us despatched on some secret service across the desert. Bill was with us; but the officer under whose special charge we were placed was a Captain Turpie, a nephew of Colonel Westhope, and his heir. But he heired few of his good qualities. He was the son of a pettifogging lawyer, and was as heartily hated by the soldiers as the colonel was beloved. Towards sunset the party reached a hollow valley in the waste, and there rested, preparatory, as we all intended, for passing the night. Some of us were engaged in erecting temporary huts of branches, some in providing the necessary materials; and we had just formed a snug little camp, and were preparing to light our fires for supper, when we heard a shot not two furlongs away. Bill, who was by far the most active among us, sprang up one of the tallest date trees to reconnoitre. But he soon came down again.

"'We have lost our pains this time,' he said; 'there is a party of French, of fully five times our number, not half a mile away.' The captain, on the news, wasn't slow, as you may think, in ordering us off; and, hastily gathering up our blankets and the contents of our knapsacks, we struck across the sand just as the sun was setting. There is scarce any twilight in Egypt, master; it is pitch dark twenty minutes after sunset. The first part of the evening,

19*

too, is infinitely disagreeable. The days are burning hot, and not a cloud can be seen in the sky; but no sooner has the sun gone down than there comes on a thick white fog that covers the whole country, so that one can't see fifty yards around; and so icy cold is it, that it strikes a chill to the very heart. It is with these fogs that the dews descend; and deadly things they are. Well, the mist and the darkness came upon us at once; we lost all reckoning, and, after floundering on for an hour or so among the sand-hills, our captain called a halt, and bade us burrow as we best might among the hollows. Hungry as we were we were fain to leave our supper to begin the morning with, and huddled all together into what seemed a deep, dry ditch. We were at first surprised, master, to find an immense heap of stone under us, — we couldn't have lain harder had we lain on a Scotch cairn, — and that, d'ye see, is unusual in Egypt, where all the sand has been blown by the hot winds from the desert, hundreds of miles away, and where, in the course of a few days' journey, one mayn't see a pebble larger than a pigeon's egg. There were hard, round, bullet-like masses under us, and others of a more oblong shape, like pieces of wood that had been cut for fuel; and, tired as we were, their sharp points, protruding through the sand, kept most of us from sleep. But that was little, master, to what we felt afterwards. As we began to take heat together, there broke out among us a most disagreeable stench, — bad at first, but unlike anything I had felt before, but at last altogether overpowering. Some of us became dead sick, and some, to show how much bolder they were than the rest, began to sing. One half the party stole away, one by one, and lay down outside. For my own part, master, I thought it was the plague that was breaking out upon us from below, and lay still in despair of escaping it. I was wretchedly tired too; and, despite of my fears and the stench, I fell asleep, and slept till daylight. But never before, master, did I see such a sight as when I awoke. We had been sleeping on the carcasses of ten thousand Turks, whom Bonaparte had massacred about a twelvemonth before. There were eyeless skulls, grinning at us by hundreds from the side of the ditch, and black, withered hands and feet sticking out, with the white bones glittering between the shrunken sinews. The very sand, for roods around, had a brown ferruginous tinge, and seemed baked into a half-solid mass resembling clay. It was no place to loiter in, and you may trust me, master, we breakfasted elsewhere. Bill kept close to our captain all that morning. He didn't much like him, even so early in their acquaintance as this, — no one did, in fact, — but he was anxious to learn from him all he could regarding the colonel. He told him, too, something about his own early recollections; but he would better have kept them to himself. From that hour, master, Captain Turpie never gave him a pleasant look, and sought every means to ruin him.

"We joined the army again on the evening of the 20th March. You know, master, what awaited us next morning. I had been marching, on the day of our arrival, for twelve hours under a very hot sun, and was fatigued enough to sleep soundly. But the dead might have awakened next morning. The enemy broke in upon us about three o'clock. It was pitch dark. I had been dreaming, at the moment, that I was busily engaged in the landing, fighting in the front rank beside Bill; and I awoke to hear the enemy outside the tent struggling in fierce conflict with such of my comrades as, half-naked and half-armed, had been roused by the first alarm, and had rushed out to oppose them. You will not think that I was long in joining them, master, when I tell you that Bill himself was hardly two steps ahead of me. Colonel Westhope was everywhere at once that morning, bringing his men, in the darkness and the confusion, into something like order, — threatening, encouraging, applauding, issuing orders, all in a breath. Just as we got out, the French broke through beside our tent, and we saw him struck down in the throng. Bill gave a tremendous cry of 'Our colonel! our colonel!' and struck his pike up to the cross into the breast of the fellow who had given the blow. And hardly had that one fallen than he sent it crashing through the face of the next foremost, till it lay buried in the brain. The enemy gave back for a moment; and as he was striking down a third the colonel got up, badly wounded in the shoulder; but he kept the field all day. He knew Bill the moment he rose, and leant on him till he had somewhat recovered. 'I shall not forget, Bill,' he said, 'that you have saved your colonel's life.' We had a fierce struggle, master, ere we beat out the French; but, broken and half-naked as we were, we did beat them out, and the battle became general.

"At first the flare of the artillery, as the batteries blazed out in the darkness, dazzled and blinded me; but I loaded and fired incessantly; and the thicker the bullets went whistling past me, the faster I loaded and fired. A spent shot, that had struck through a sand-bank, came rolling on like a bowl, and, leaping up from a hillock in front, struck me on the breast. It was such a blow, master, as a man might have given with his fist; but it knocked me down, and ere I got up, the company was a few paces in advance. The bonnet of the soldier who had taken my place came rolling to my feet ere I could join them. But alas! it was

full of blood and brains; and I found that the spent shot
had come just in time to save my life. Meanwhile, the
battle raged with redoubled fury on the left, and we in the
centre had a short respite. And some of us needed it.
For my own part, I had fired about a hundred rounds; and
my right shoulder was as blue as your waistcoat.

"You will wonder, master, how I should notice such a
thing in the heat of an engagement; but I remember
nothing better than that there was a flock of little birds
shrieking and fluttering over our heads for the greater
part of the morning. The poor little things seemed as if
robbed of their very instinct by the incessant discharges
on every side of them; and, instead of pursuing a direct
course, which would soon have carried them clear of us,
they kept fluttering in helpless terror in one little spot.
About mid-day, an aide-de-camp went riding by us to the
right.

"'How goes it? how goes it?' asked one of our officers.

"'It is just who will,' replied the aide-de-camp, and
passed by like lightning. Another followed hard after.

"'How goes it now?' inquired the officer.

"'Never better, boy!' said the second rider. 'The forty-
second have cut Bonaparte's invincibles to pieces, and all
the rest of the enemy are falling back!'

"We came more into action a little after. The enemy
opened a heavy fire upon us, and seemed advancing to the
charge. I had felt so fatigued, master, during the previous
pause, that I could scarcely raise my hand to my head;
but, now that we were to be engaged again, all my fatigue
left me, and I found myself grown fresh as ever. There
were two field pieces to our left that had done noble execution during the day; and Captain Turpic's company, including Bill and me, were ordered to stand by them in the

expected charge. They were wrought mostly by seamen from the vessels, — brave, tight fellows who, like Nelson, never saw fear; but they had been so busy that they had shot away most of their ammunition; and, as we came up to them, they were about despatching a party to the rear for more.

" 'Right,' said Captain Turpic; 'I don't care though I lend you a hand, and go with you.'

" 'On your peril, sir!' said Bill Whyte. 'What! leave your company in the moment of the expected charge! I shall assuredly report you for cowardice and desertion of quarters if you do.'

" 'And I shall have you broke for mutiny,' said the captain. 'How can these fellows know how to choose their ammunition without some one to direct them ?'

" And so off he went to the rear with the sailors; but, though they returned, poor fellows, in ten minutes or so, we saw no more of the captain till evening. On came the French in their last charge. Ere they could close with us the sailors had fired their field-pieces thrice, and we could see wide avenues opened among them with each discharge. But on they came. Our bayonets crossed and clashed with theirs for one half-minute, and in the next they were hurled headlong down the declivity, and we were fighting among them pell-mell. There are few troops superior to the French, master, in a first attack; but they want the bottom of the British; and, now that we had broken them in the moment of their onset, they had no chance with us, and we pitched our bayonets into them as if they had been so many sheaves in harvest. They lay in some places three and four tiers deep; for our blood was up, master; just as they advanced on us we had heard of the death of our general, and they neither asked for quarter nor got it. Ah, the good and gallant Sir Ralph! We all felt as if we had lost a father; but he died as the brave best love to die. The field was all our own; and not a Frenchman remained who was not dead or dying. That action, master, fairly broke the neck of their power in Egypt.

"Our colonel was severely wounded, as I have told you, early in the morning; but, though often enough urged to retire, he had held out all day, and had issued his orders with all the coolness and decision for which he was so remarkable; but now that the excitement of the fight was over his strength failed him at once, and he had to becarried to his tent. He called for Bill to assist in bearing him off. I believe it was merely that he might have the opportunity of speaking to him. He told him that, whether he died or lived, he would take care that he should be provided for. He gave Captain Turpic charge, too, that he should keep a warm side to Bill. I overheard our major say to the captain, as we left the tent, 'Good heavens! did you ever see two men liker one another than the colonel and our new sergeant?' But the captain carelessly remarked that the resemblance didn't strike him.

"We met outside with a comrade. He had had a cousin in the forty-second, he said, who had been killed that morning, and he was anxious to see the body decently buried, and wished us to go along with him. And so we both went. It is nothing, master, to see men struck down in warm blood, and when one's own blood is up; but oh, 'tis a grievous thing, after one has cooled down to one's ordinary mood, to go out among the dead and the dying! We passed through what had been the thick of the battle. The slain lay in hundreds and thousands, — like the ware and tangle on the shore below us, — horribly broken, some of them, by the shot; and blood and brains lay spattered on the sand. But it was a worse sight to see, when some poor wretch, who had no chance of living an hour longer, opened his eyes as we passed and cried out for water. We soon emptied our canteens, and then had to pass on. In no place did the dead lie thicker than where the forty-second had engaged the invincibles; and never were there finer fellows. They lay piled in heaps, — the best men of Scotland over the best men of France, — and their wounds and their number and the postures in which they lay showed how tremendous the struggle had been. I saw one gigantic corpse with the head and neck cloven through the steel cap to the very brisket. It was that of a Frenchman; but the hand that had drawn the blow lay cold and stiff not a yard away, with the broadsword still firm in its grasp. A little further on we found the body we sought. It was that of a fair young man. The features were as composed as if he were asleep; there was even a smile on the lips; but a cruel cannon-shot had torn the very heart out of the breast. Evening was falling. There was a little dog whining and whimpering over the body, aware, it would seem, that some great ill had befallen its master, but yet tugging from time to time at his clothes, that he might rise and come away.

"'Ochon, ochon! poor Evan M'Donald!' exclaimed our comrade; 'what would Christy Ross or your good old mother say to see you lying here!'

"Bill burst out a-crying as if he had been a child; and I couldn't keep dry-eyed neither, master. But grief and pity are weaknesses of the bravest natures. We scooped out a hole in the sand with our bayonets and our hands, and burying the body, came away.

"The battle of the 21st broke — as I have said — the

strength of the French in Egypt; for though they didn't
surrender to us until about five months after, they kept
snug behind their walls, and we saw little more of them.
Our colonel had gone aboard of the frigate desperately ill
of his wounds; so ill that it was several times reported he
was dead; and most of our men were suffering sadly from
sore eyes ashore. But such of us as escaped had little to
do, and we contrived to while away the time agreeably
enough. Strange country, Egypt, master. You know our
people have come from there; but, trust me, I could find
none of my cousins among either the Turks or the Arabs.
The Arabs, master, are quite the gipsies of Egypt; and
Bill and I — but he paid dearly for them afterwards, poor
fellow — used frequently to visit such of their straggling
tribes as came to the neighborhood of our camp. You and
the like of you, master, are curious to see *our* people, and
how we get on; and no wonder; and we were just as curious to see the Arabs. Towards evening they used to
come in from the shore or the desert in parties of ten or
twelve. And wild-looking fellows they were; tall, but
not very tall, thin and skinny and dark, and an amazing proportion of them blind of an eye, — an effect, I suppose, of the disease from which our comrades were suffering
so much. In a party of ten or twelve — and their parties
rarely exceeded a dozen — we found that every one of
them had some special office to perform. One carried a
fishing-net, like a herring have; one, perhaps, a basket of
fish, newly caught; one a sheaf of wheat; one a large copper basin, or rather platter; one a bundle of the dead
boughs and leaves of the date-tree; one the implements
for lighting a fire; and so on. The first thing they always
did, after squatting down in a circle, was to strike a light;
the next to dig a round pot-like hole in the sand, in

which they kindle their fire. When the sand had become sufficiently hot, they threw out the embers, and placing the fish, just as they had caught them, in the bottom of the hole, heaped the hot sand over them, and the fire over that. The sheaf of wheat was next untied, and each taking a handful, held it over the flame till it was sufficiently scorched, and then rubbed out the grain between their hands into the copper plate. The fire was then drawn off a second time, and the fish dug out; and, after rubbing off the sand and taking out the bowels, they sat down to supper. And such, master, was the ordinary economy of the poorer tribes, that seemed drawn to the camp merely by curiosity. Some of the others brought fruit and vegetables to our market, and were much encouraged by our officers. But a set of greater rascals never breathed. At first several of our men got flogged through them. They had a trick of raising a hideous outcry in the market-place for every trifle, certain, d'ye see, of attracting the notice of some of our officers, who were all sure to take part with them. The market, master, had to be encouraged at all events; and it was some time ere the tricks of the rascals were understood in the proper quarter. But, to make short, Bill and I went out one morning to our walk. We had just heard — and heavy news it was to the whole regiment — that our colonel was despaired of, and had no chance of seeing out the day. Bill was in miserably low spirits. Captain Turpie had insulted him most grossly that morning. So long as the colonel had been expected to recover, he had shown him some degree of civility; but he now took every opportunity of picking a quarrel with him. There was no comparison in battle, master, between Bill and the captain, for the captain, I suspect, was little better than a coward; but then there was just as little on parade the other way;

for Bill, you know, couldn't know a great deal, and the captain was a perfect martinet. He had called him vagrant and beggar, master, for omitting some little piece of duty. Now he couldn't help having been with *us*, you know; and as for beggary, he had never begged in his life. Well, we had walked out towards the market, as I say.

"'It's all nonsense, Jack,' says he, 'to be so dull on the matter; I'll e'en treat you to some fruit. I have a Sicilian dollar here. See that lazy fellow with the spade lying in front, and the burning mountain smoking behind him. We must see if he can't dig out for us a few *prans'* worth of dates.'

"Well, master, up he went to a tall, thin, rascally-looking Arab, with one eye, and bought as much fruit from him as might come to one tenth of the dollar which he gave him, and then held out his hand for the change. But there was no change forthcoming. Bill wasn't a man to be done out of his cash in that silly way, and so he stormed at the rascal; but he, in turn, stormed as furiously, in his own lingo, at him, till at last Bill's blood got up, and, seizing him by the breast, he twisted him over his knee as one might a boy of ten years or so. The fellow raised a hideous outcry, as if Bill were robbing and murdering him. Two officers, who chanced to be in the market at the time, came running up at the noise. One of them was the scoundrel Turpic; and Bill was laid hold of, and sent off under guard to the camp. Poor fellow, he got scant justice there. Turpic had procured a man-of-war's-man, who swore, as well he might, indeed, that Bill was the smuggler who had swamped the Kirkcudbright custom-house boat. There was another brought forward who swore that both of us were gipsies, and told a blasted rigmarole story, without one word of truth in it, about the stealing of a silver spoon.

The Arab had his story, too, in his own lingo; and they received every word; for my evidence went for nothing. I was of a race who never spoke the truth, they said, as if I weren't as good as a Mohammedan Arab. To crown all, in came Turpie's story about what he called Bill's mutinous spirit in the action of the 21st. You may guess the rest, master. The poor fellow was broke that morning, and told that, were it not in consideration of his bravery, he would have got a flogging into the bargain.

"I spent the evening of that day with Bill outside the camp, and we ate the dates together that in the morning had cost him so dear. The report had gone abroad, — luckily a false one, — that our colonel was dead; and that put an end to all hope with the poor fellow of having his case righted. We spoke together for I am sure two hours; spoke of Bill's early recollections, and of the hardship of his fate all along. And it was now worse with him, he said, than it had ever been before. He spoke of the strange, unaccountable hostility of Turpie; and I saw his brow grow dark, and the veins of his neck swell almost to bursting. He trusted they might yet meet, he said, where there would be none to note who was the officer and who the private soldier. I did my best, master, to console the poor fellow, and we parted. The first thing I saw, as I opened the tent-door next morning, was Captain Turpie, brought into the camp by the soldier whose cousin Bill and I had assisted to bury. The captain was leaning on his shoulder, somewhat less than half alive, as it seemed, with four of his front teeth struck out, and a stream of blood all along his vest and small clothes. He had been met with by Bill, who had attacked him, he said, and, after breaking his sword, would have killed him, had not the soldier come up and interfered. But that, master, was the captain's story. The soldier told me afterwards that he saw the captain draw his sword ere Bill lifted hand at all; and that, when the poor fellow did strike, he gave him only one knock-down blow on the mouth, that laid him insensible at his feet; and that, when down, though he might have killed him twenty times over, he didn't so much as crook a finger on him. Nay, more, Bill offered to deliver himself up to the soldier, had not the latter assured him that he would to a certainty be shot, and advised him to make off. There was a party despatched in quest of him, master, the moment Turpie had told his story; but he was lucky enough, poor fellow, to elude them; and they returned in the evening just as they had gone out. And I saw no more of Bill in Egypt, master.

CHAPTER II.

THE DENOUEMENT.

" After all our fears and regrets, master, our colonel recovered, and one morning about four months after the action, came ashore to see us. We were sadly pestered with flies, master. They buzzed all night by millions round our noses, and many a plan did we think of to get rid of them; but after destroying hosts on hosts, they still seemed as thick as before. I had fallen on a new scheme this morning. I placed some sugar on a board, and surrounded it with gunpowder; and when the flies had settled by thousands on the sugar, I fired the gunpowder by means of a train, and the whole fell dead on the floor of the tent. I had just got a capital shot, when up came the colonel and sat down beside me.

20*

"'I wish to know,' he said, 'all you can tell me about Bill Whyte. You were his chief friend and companion, I have heard, and are acquainted with his early history. Can you tell me aught of his parentage?'

"'Nothing of that, Colonel,' I said; 'and yet I have known Bill almost ever since he knew himself.'

"And so, master, I told him all that I knew: how Bill had been first taken to us by my mother; of the purse of gold she had brought with her, which had kept us all so merry; and of the noble spirit he had shown among us when he grew up. I told him, too, of some of Bill's early recollections; of the scarlet dress trimmed with silver, which had been brought to his mind by the sergeant's coat the first day he wore it; of the gentleman and lady, too, whom he remembered to have lived with; and of the supposed resemblance he had found between the former and the colonel. The colonel, as I went on, was strangely agitated, master. He held an open letter in his hand, and seemed every now and then to be comparing particulars; and when I mentioned Bill's supposed recognition of him, he actually started from off his seat.

"'Good heavens!' he exclaimed, 'why was I not brought acquainted with this before?'

"I explained the why, master, and told him all about Captain Turpic; and he left me with, you may be sure, no very favorable opinion of the captain. But I must now tell you, master, a part of my story, which I had but from hearsay.

"The colonel had been getting over the worse effects of his wound, when he received a letter from a friend in England informing him that his brother-in-law, the father of Captain Turpic, had died suddenly, and that his sister, who to all appearance was fast following, had been making strange discoveries regarding an only son of the colonel's, who was supposed to have been drowned about seventeen years before. The colonel had lost both his lady and child by a frightful accident. His estate lay near Olney, on the banks of the Ouse ; and the lady one day, during the absence of the colonel, who was in London, was taking an airing in the carriage with her son, a boy of three years or so, when the horses took fright, and, throwing the coachman, who was killed on the spot, rushed into the river. The Ouse is a deep, sluggish stream, dark and muddy in some of the more dangerous pools, and mantled over with weeds. It was into one of these the carriage was overturned. Assistance came late, and the unfortunate lady was brought out a corpse ; but the body of the child was nowhere to be found. It now came out, however, from the letter, that the child had been picked up unhurt by the colonel's brother-in-law, who, after concealing it for nearly a week during the very frenzy of the colonel's distress, had then given it to a gipsy. The rascal's only motive — he was a lawyer, master — was, that his own son, the captain, who was then a boy of twelve years or so, and not wholly ignorant of the circumstance, might succeed to the colonel's estate. The writer of the letter added that, on coming to the knowledge of this singular confession, he had made instant search after the gipsy to whom the child had been given, and had been fortunate enough to find her, after tracing her over half the kingdom, in a cave near Fortrose, in the north of Scotland. She had confessed all ; stating, however, that the lad, who had borne among the tribe the name of Bill Whyte, and had turned out a fine fellow, had been outlawed for some smuggling feat, about eighteen months before, and had enlisted with a young man, her son, into a regiment bound for Egypt.

You see, master, there couldn't be a shadow of doubt that my comrade Bill Whyte was just Henry Westhope, the colonel's son and heir. But the grand matter was where to find him. Search as we might, all search was in vain. We could trace him no further than outside the camp to where he had met with Captain Turpie. I should tell you, by the way, that the captain was now sent to Coventry by every one, and that not an officer in the regiment would return his salute.

" Well, master, the months passed, and at length the French surrendered; and, having no more to do in Egypt, we all re-embarked, and sailed for England. The short peace had been ratified before our arrival; and I, who had become heartily tired of the life of a soldier now that I had no one to associate with, was fortunate enough to obtain my discharge. The colonel retired from the service at the same time. He was as kind to me as if he had been my father, and offered to make me his forester if I would but come and live beside him. But I was too fond of a wandering life for that. He was corresponding, he told me, with every British consul within fifteen hundred miles of the Nile; but he had heard nothing of Bill, master. Well, after seeing the colonel's estate, I parted from him, and came north to find out my people, which I soon did; and, for a year or so, I lived with them just as I have been doing since. I was led in the course of my wanderings to Leith, and was standing one morning on the pier among a crowd of people, who had gathered round to see a fine vessel from the Levant that was coming in at the time, when my eye caught among the sailors a man exceedingly like Bill. He was as tall, and even more robust, and he wrought with all Bill's activity; but for some time I could not catch a glimpse of his face. At length, however, he

turned round, and there, sure enough, was Bill himself. I
was afraid to hail him, master, not knowing who among
the crowd might also know him, and know him also as a
deserter or an outlaw; but you may be sure I wasn't long
in leaping aboard and making up to him. And we were
soon as happy, master, in one of the cellars of the Coal
Hill, as we had been all our lives before.

"Bill told me his history since our parting. He had left
the captain lying at his feet, and struck across the sand in
the direction of the Nile, one of the mouths of which he
reached next day. He there found some Greek sailors,
who were employed in watering; and, assisting them in
their work, he was brought aboard their vessel, and engaged
as a seaman by the master, who had lost some of his crew
by the plague. As you may think, master, he soon became
a prime sailor, and continued with the Greeks, trading
among the islands of the Archipelago for about eighteen
months, when, growing tired of the service, and meeting
with an English vessel, he had taken a passage home. I
told him how much ado we had all had about him after he
had left us, and how we were to call him Bill Whyte no
longer. And so, in short, master, we set out together for
Colonel Westhope's.

"In our journey we met with some of our people on a
wild moor of Cumberland, and were invited to pass the
night with them. They were of the Curlit family; but
you will hardly know them by that. Two of them had
been with us when Bill swamped the custom-house boat.
They were fierce, desperate fellows, and not much to be
trusted by their friends even; and I was afraid that
they might have somehow come to guess that Bill had
brought some clinkers home with him. And so, master, I
would fain have dissuaded him from making any stay with

them in the night-time ; for I did not know, you see, in what case we might find our *weasands* in the morning. But Bill had no fears of any kind, and was, beside, desirous to spend one last night with the gipsies ; and so he staid. The party had taken up their quarters in a waste house on the moor, with no other human dwelling within four miles of it. There was a low, stunted wood on the one side, master, and a rough, sweeping stream on the other. The night, too, was wild and boisterous ; and, what between suspicion and discomfort, I felt well-nigh as drearily as I did when lying among the dead men in Egypt. We were nobly treated, however, and the whiskey flowed like water. But we drank no more than was good for us. Indeed, Bill was never a great drinker ; and I kept on my guard, and refused the liquor on the plea of a bad head. I should have told you that there were but three of the Curlits — all of them raw-boned fellows, however, and all of them of such stamp that the three have since been hung. I saw they were sounding Bill; but he seemed aware of them.

" ' Aye, aye,' says he, ' I have made something by my voyaging, lads, though, mayhap, not a great deal. What think you of that there now, for instance ? ' — drawing, as he spoke, a silver-mounted pistol out of each pocket. ' These are pretty pops, and as good as they are pretty. The worst of them sends a bullet through an inch-board at twenty yards.'

" ' Are they loaded, Bill ? ' asked Tom Curlit.

" ' To be sure,' said Bill, returning them again each to its own pouch. ' What is the use of an empty pistol ? '

" ' Ah,' replied Tom, ' I smell a rat, Bill. You have given over making war on the king's account, and have taken the road to make war on your own. Bold enough, to be sure.'

" From the moment they saw the pistols, the brothers seemed to have changed their plan regarding us; for some plan I am certain they had. They would now fain have taken us into partnership with them; but their trade was a woundy bad one, master, with a world more of risk than profit.

" 'Why, lads,' said Tom Curlit to Bill and me, 'hadn't you better stay with us altogether? The road won't do in these days at all. No, no; the law is a vast deal over-strong for that, and you will be tucked up like dogs for your very first affair. But if you stay with us, you will get on in a much quieter way on this wild moor here. Plenty of game, Bill; and sometimes, when the nights are long, we contrive to take a purse with as little trouble as may be. We had an old peddler only three weeks ago that brought us sixty good pounds. By the way, brothers, we must throw a few more sods over him, for I nosed him this morning as I went by. And, lads, we have something in hand just now, that, with, to be sure, a little more risk, will pay better still. Two hundred yellow boys in hand, and five hundred more when our work is done. Better that, Bill, than standing to be shot at for a shilling per day.'

" 'Two hundred in hand and five hundred more when you have done your work!' exclaimed Bill. 'Why, that is sure enough princely pay, unless the work be very bad indeed. But come, tell us what you propose. You can't expect us to make it a leap-in-the-dark matter.'

" 'The work is certainly a little dangerous,' said Tom, 'and we of ourselves are rather few; but if you both join with us there would be a vast deal less of danger indeed. The matter is just this. A young fellow, like ourselves, has a rich old uncle, who has made his will in his favor; but then he threatens to make another will that won't be so favorable to him by half; and you see the drawing across of a knife — so — would keep the first one in force. And that is all we have to do before pocketing the blunt. But then the old fellow is as brave as a lion, and there are two servants with him, worn-out soldiers like himself, that would, I am sure, be rough customers. With your help, however, we shall get on primely. The old boy's house stands much alone, and we shall be five to three.'

" ' Well, well,' said Bill; ' we shall give your proposal a night's thought, and tell you what we think of it in the morning. But remember, no tricks, Tom! If we engage in the work, we must go share and share alike in the booty.'

" ' To be sure,' said Tom ; and so the conversation closed.

" About eight o'clock or so, master, I stepped out to the door. The night was dark and boisterous as ever, and there had come on a heavy rain. But I could see that, dark and boisterous as it was, some one was approaching the house with a dark lantern. I lost no time in telling the Curlits so.

" ' It must be the captain,' said they, ' though it seems strange that he should come here to-night. You must away, Jack and Bill, to the loft, for it mayn't do for the captain to find you here; but you can lend us a hand afterwards, should need require it.'

" There was no time for asking explanations, master, and so up we climbed to the loft, and had got snugly concealed among some old hay, when in came the captain. But what captain, think you? Why, just our old acquaintance Captain Turpie !

" ' Lads,' he said to the Curlits, ' make yourselves ready; get your pistols. Our old scheme is blown, for the colonel has left his house at Olney on a journey to Scotland ; but he passes here to-night, and you must find means to stop him, — now or never !'

" ' What force and what arms has he with him, captain?' asked Tom.

" ' The coachman, his body servant, and himself,' said the captain ; ' but only the servant and himself are armed. The stream outside is high to-night; you must take them just as they are crossing it, and thinking of only the water; and whatever else you may mind, make sure of the colonel.'

" ' Sure as I live,' said Bill to me, in a low whisper, ' 'tis a plan to murder Colonel Westhope ! And, good heavens !' he continued, pointing through an opening in the gable, ' yonder is his carriage not a mile away. You may see the lantern, like two fiery eyes, coming sweeping along the moor. We have no time to lose. Let us slide down through the opening and meet with it.'

" As soon done as said, master. We slid down along the turf gable; crossed the stream, which had risen high on its banks, by a plank bridge for foot-passengers ; and then dashed along the broken road in the direction of the carriage. We came up to it as it was slowly crossing an open drain.

" ' Colonel Westhope !' I cried, ' Colonel Westhope ! — stop ! — stop ! — turn back ! You are waylaid by a party of ruffians, who will murder you if you go on.'

The door opened, and the colonel stepped out, with his sword under his left arm, and a cocked pistol in his hand.

" ' Is not that Jack Whyte?' he asked.

" ' The same, noble colonel,' I said ; ' and here is Henry, your son.'

" It was no place or time, master, for long explanations; there was one hearty congratulation, and one hurried embrace; and the colonel, after learning from Bill the number of the assailants and the plan of the attack, ordered the carriage to drive on slowly before, and followed, with us and his servant, on foot, behind.

"'The rascals,' he said, 'will be so dazzled with the flare of the lanterns in front, that we will escape notice till they have fired, and then we shall have them for the picking down.'

"And so it was, master. Just as the carriage was entering the stream, the coachman was pulled down by Tom Curlit; at the same instant, three bullets went whizzing through the glasses, and two fellows came leaping out from behind some furze to the carriage door. A third, whom I knew to be the captain, lagged behind. I marked him, however; and when the colonel and Bill were disposing of the other two, — and they took them so sadly by surprise, master, that they had but little difficulty in throwing them down and binding them, — I was lucky enough to send a piece of lead through the captain. He ran about twenty yards, and then dropped down stone dead. Tom escaped us; but he cut a throat some months after, and suffered for it at Carlisle. And his two brothers, after making a clean breast, and confessing all, were transported for life. But they found means to return in a few years after, and were both hung on the gallows on which Tom had suffered before them.

"I have not a great deal more to tell you, master. The colonel has been dead for the last twelve years, and his son has succeeded him in his estate. There is not a completer gentleman in England than Henry Westhope, master, nor a finer fellow. I call on him every time I go round, and never miss a hearty welcome; though, by the by, I am quite as sure of a hearty scold. He still keeps a snug little house empty for me, and offers to settle on me fifty pounds a year, whenever I choose to give up my wandering life and go and live with him. But what's bred in the bone won't come out of the flesh, master, and I have not yet closed with his offer. And really, to tell you my mind, I don't think it quite respectable. Here I am, at present, a free, independent tinker, — no man more respectable than a tinker, master, all allow that, — whereas, if I go and live with Bill, on an unwrought-for fifty pounds a year, I will be hardly better than a mere master-tailor or shoemaker. No, no, that would never do! Nothing like respectability, master, let a man fare as hard as he may."

I thanked the gipsy for his story, and told him I thought it almost worth while putting into print. He thanked me, in turn, for liking it so well, and assured me I was quite at liberty to put it in print as soon as I chose. And so I took him at his word.

"But yonder," said he, "is the moon rising, red and huge, over the three tops of Belrinnes, and throwing, as it brightens, its long strip of fire across the frith. Take care of your footing just as you reach the top of the crag; there is an awkward gap there, on the rock edge, that reminds me of an Indian trap; but as for the rest of the path, you will find it quite as safe as by day. Good-bye."

I left him, and made the best of my way home, where, while the facts were fresh in my mind, I committed to paper the gipsy's story.

VII.

THE YOUNG SURGEON.

CHAPTER I.

It's no' in books, it's no' in lear,
To make us truly blest,
If Happiness has not her seat
And centre in the breast.
BURNS.

THERE is a little runnel in the neighborhood of the town of——, which, rising amid the swamps of a mossy hollow, pursues its downward way along the bottom of a deep-wooded ravine; and so winding and circuitous is the course which, in the lapse of ages, it has worn for itself through a subsoil of stiff diluvial clay, that, ere a late proprietor lined its sides with garden-flowers and pathways covered with gravel, and then willed that it should be named the "Ladies' Walk," it was known to the townspeople as the Crook Burn. It is a place of abrupt angles and sudden turns. We see that when the little stream first leaped from its urn it must have had many a difficulty to encounter, and many an obstacle to overcome; but they have all been long since surmounted; and when in the heat of summer we hear it tinkling through the pebbles, with a sound so feeble that it hardly provokes the chirp of the robin, and see that, even where it spreads widest to the light, it presents a too narrow space for the gambols of the water-spider, we marvel how it could ever have scooped out for itself so capacious a bed. But what will not centuries of perseverance accomplish! The tallest trees that rise beside it — and there are few taller in the country — scarcely overtop its banks; and, as it approaches the parish burying-ground, — for it passes close beside the wall,— we may look down from the fields above on the topmost branches, and see the magpie sitting on her nest. This little stream, so attenuated and thread-like during the droughts of July and August, and which after every heavier shower comes brawling from its recesses, reddened by a few handfuls of clay, has swept to the sea, in the long unreckoned succession of ages, a mass mighty enough to have furnished the materials of an Egyptian pyramid.

In even the loneliest windings of the Crook Burn we find something to remind us of the world. Every smoother trunk bears its inscription of dates and initials; and to one who has resided in the neighboring town, and mingled freely with the inhabitants, there is scarcely a little cluster of characters he meets with that has not its story. Human nature is a wonderful thing, and interesting in even its humblest appearances to the creatures who partake of it; nor can the point from which one observes it be too near, or the observations themselves too minute. It is perhaps best, however, when we have collected our materials, to combine and arrange them at some little distance. We are always something more than mere observers, — we possess that which we contemplate, with all its predilections and all its antipathies, — and there is dimness or distortion in the mirror on which we catch the features of our neighbors, if the breath of passion has passed over it. Do we not see that the little stream beside us gives us a faithful picture of what surrounds it only when it is at rest? And it is well, if we desire to think correctly, and in the spirit of charity, of our brother men, that we should be at rest too. For our own part, we love best to think of the dead when their graves are at our feet, and our feelings are chastened by the conviction that we ourselves are very soon to take our place beside them.   We love to think of the living, not amid the hum and bustle of the world, when the thoughts are hurried, and perhaps the sterner passions aroused, but in the solitude of some green retreat, by the side of some unfrequented stream, when drinking largely of the beauty and splendor of external things, and feeling that we our- selves are man, — in nature and destiny the being whom we contemplate.   There is nought of contempt in the smile to which we are provoked by the eccentricities of a creature so strange and wilful, nor of bitterness in the sorrow with which we regard his crimes.

In passing one of the trees, a smooth-rinded ash, we see a few characters engraved on it, which at the first glance we deem Hebrew, but which we find, on examination, to belong to some less known alphabet of the East. There hangs a story of these obscure characters, which, though little checkered by incident, has something very interesting in it. It is of no distant date ; — the characters, in all their minuter strokes, are still unfilled ; but the hand that traced them, and the eye that softened in expression as it marked the progress of the work, — for they record the name of a lady-love, — are now mingled with the clods of the valley.

Early in an autumn of the present century, — and we need not be more explicit, for names and dates are no way essential to what we have to relate, — a small tender entered the bay of ——, and cast anchor in the roadstead,

where she remained for nearly two months. Our country
had been at peace with all the world for years before, and
the arts which accompany peace had extended their softening influence to our seamen, a class of men not much
marked in the past, as a body at least, — though it had produced a Dampier and a Falconer, — for aught approaching
to literary acquirement, or the refinement of their manners.
And the officers of this little vessel were no unfavorable
specimens of the more cultivated class. They were in general well read ; and possessing, with the attainments, the
manners of gentlemen, were soon on terms of intimacy
with some of the more intelligent inhabitants of the place.
There was one among them, however, whose society was
little courted. He was a young and strikingly handsome
man, with bright, speaking eyes, and a fine development of
forehead ; but the higher parts of his nature seemed more
than balanced by the lower ; and, though proud-spirited and
honorable, he was evidently sinking into a hopeless degradation, — the slave of habits which strengthen with indulgence, and which already seemed too strong to be overcome.

He accompanied, on two or three occasions, some of his
brother officers when engaged in calling on their several
acquaintances of the place. The grosser traits of his character had become pretty generally known, and report had,
as usual, rather aggravated than lessened them. There
was something whispered of a low intrigue in which he was
said to have been engaged ; something, too, of those disreputable habits of solitary indulgence in which the stimu-
lating agent is recklessly and despairingly employed to
satisfy for the moment the ever-recurring cravings of a
depraved appetite, and which are regarded as precluding
the hope of reform ; and he seemed as if shunned by every
one. His high spirit, however, though it felt neglect, could

support him under it. He was a keen satirist, too, like
almost all men of talent, who, thinking and feeling more
correctly than they live, wreak on their neighbors the unhappiness of their own remorse; and he could thus neu-
tralize the bitterness of his feelings by the bitterness of his
thoughts. But with every such help one cannot wholly
dispense with the respect of others, unless one be possessed
of one's own; and when a lady of the place, who on one
occasion saw and pitied his chagrin, invited him to pass
an evening at her house with a small party of friends, the
feeling awakened by her kindness served to convince him
that he was less indifferent than he could have wished to
the coldness of the others. His spirits rose in the company
to which he was thus introduced; he exerted his powers of
pleasing, — and they were of no ordinary description, for,
to an imagination of much liveliness, he added warm feelings and an exquisite taste, — and, on rising to take his
leave for the evening, his hostess, whose interest in him was
heightened by pity, and whose years and character secured
her from the fear of having her motives misconstrued,
kindly urged him to repeat his visit every time he thought
he could not better employ himself, or when he found it
irksome or dangerous to be alone. And her invitation was
accepted in the spirit in which it was given.

She soon became acquainted with his story. He had
lost his mother when very young, and had been bred up
under the care of an elder brother, with an eye to the
church; but his inclinations interfering as he grew up, the
destination was altered, and he applied himself to the
study of medicine. He had passed through college in a
way creditable to his talents, and on quitting it he seemed
admirably fitted to rise in the profession which he had
made choice of; for, to very superior acquirements, and

much readiness of resource, he added a pleasing address and a soft, winning manner. There seemed, however, to be something of a neutralizing quality in the moral constitution of the man. He was honest, and high-spirited, and ready to oblige ; but there was a morbid restlessness in his feelings which, languishing after excitement as its proper element, rendered him too indifferent to those ordinary concerns of life which seem so tame and little when regarded singly, but which prove of such mighty importance in the aggregate. There was, besides, an unhappy egotism in the character, which led him to regard himself as *extraordinary*, the circumstances in which he was placed as *common*, and therefore unsuited, and which, instead of exciting him to the course of legitimate exertion through which men of talent rise to their proper sphere, spent itself in making out ingenious cases of sorrow and apologies for unhappiness, from very ordinary events, and a condition of life in which thousands attain to contentment. One might almost suppose that that sense of the ludicrous — bestowed on the species undoubtedly for wise ends — which finds its proper vocation in detecting and exposing incongruities of this kind, could not be better employed than in setting such a man right. It would have failed in its object, however ; and certain it is, that geniuses of the very first order, who could have rendered us back our ridicule with fearful interest, have been of nearly the same disposition with the poor surgeon, — creatures made up of idiosyncrasies and eccentricities. A similar turn was attended with unhappiness in Byron and Rousseau ; and such is the power of true genius over the public mind, however fantastic its vagaries, that they had all Europe to sympathize with them.

The poor surgeon experienced no such sympathy. The

circumstances, too, in which he had been reared were well-nigh as unfavorable as his disposition ; nor had they at all improved as he grew up. The love of a mother might have nursed the feelings of so delicate a mind, and fitted them for the world; for, as in dispositions of a romantic cast the affections are apt to wander after the unreal and the illusive, and to become chilled and crippled in the pursuit, it is well that they should be prepared for resting on real objects by the thousand kindlinesses of this first felt and tenderest relation. But his mother he had lost in infancy. His brother, though substantially kind, had a way of saying bitter things, — not unprovoked, perhaps, — which, once heard, were never forgotten. He was now living among strangers, — who, to a man of his temper, were likely to remain such, — without friends or patron, and apparently out of the reach of promotion. And, to sum up the whole, he was a tender and elegant poet, for he had become skilful in the uncommunicable art, and had learned to give body to his emotions and color to his thoughts ; but, though exquisitely alive to the sweets of fame, he was of all poets the most obscure and nameless. With a disposition so unfortunate in its peculiarities, with a groundwork, too, of strong animal passion in the character, he strove to escape from himself by means revolting to his better nature, and which ultimately more than doubled his unhappiness. To a too active dislike of his brother men, — for he was infinitely more successful in finding enemies than friends, — there was now added a sickening disgust of himself. Habit produced its usual effects ; and he found he had raised to his assistance a demon which he could not lay, and which threatened to destroy him.

We insert a finished little poem, the composition of this stage, in which he portrays his feelings, and which may serve to show, were any such proof needed, that gross habits and an elegant taste are by no means incompatible.

Fain would I seek in scenes more gay
  That pleasure others find,
And strive to drown in revelry
  The anguish of the mind.

But still, where'er I go, I bear
  The marks of inward pain;
The lines of misery and care
  Are written in my brain.

I cannot raise the cheerful song,
  Nor frolic with the free,
Nor mingle in the dance among
  The sons of mirth and glee.

For there's a spell upon my soul,
  A secret anguish there,
A grief which I cannot control,
  A deep, corroding care.

And do not ask me why I sigh, —
  Draw not the veil aside;
Though dark, 'tis fairer to the eye
  Than that which it would hide.

The downward progress of the young surgeon, ere it re-. ceived the ultimate check which restored him to more than the vantage-ground of his earliest years, was partially arrested by a circumstance more efficient in suspending the influence of the grosser habits than any other which occurs in the ordinary course of things. When in some of the southern ports of England, he had formed an attachment for a young and beautiful lady, of great delicacy of sentiment and a highly cultivated mind, and succeeded in inspiring her with a corresponding regard. Who is not acquainted with Dryden's story of Cymon? It may be a harder matter, indeed, to unfix deeply-rooted habits than merely to polish the manners; but we are the creatures of motive; and there is no appetite, however unconquerable it may appear when opposed by only the dictates of judgment or conscience, but what yields to the influence of a passion more powerful than itself. To the young surgeon his attachment for this lady proved for a time the guiding motive and the governing passion; the effect was a temporary reform, a kind of minor conversion, which, though the work of no undying spirit, seemed to renovate his whole moral nature; and had he resided in the neighborhood of his lady-love, it is probable that, during 'at least the term of his courtship, all his grosser appetites would have slept. But absence, though it rather strengthens than diminishes a true attachment, frequently lessons its moral efficiency, by forming, as it were, a craving void in the heart which old habits are usually called 'upon to fill. The philospher of Rosseau solaced himself with his bottle when absent from his mistress; the poor fellow whose story I attempt to relate returned in a similar way to most of his earlier indulgences when separated from his. And yet never was there lover more thoroughly attached, or whose affection had less of earth in it. His love seemed rather an abstraction of the poet than based on the passions of the man; and, colored by the taste and delicacy of his intellectual nature, it might be conceived of as a sort of religion exquisitely fervent in its worship, and abounding in gorgeous visions, the phantoms of a vigorous fancy, conjured up by a too credulous hope. Nor did it lack its dedicatory inscriptions or its hymns. Almost the only cheerful verses he ever wrote were his love ones; the others were filled with a kind of metaphysical grief — shall we call it? — common to our literature since the days of Byron and

Shelley, but which seems to have been unknown to either Burns or Shakspeare. The surgeon, however, was no mere imitator — no mere copyist of unfelt and impossible sorrow. His pieces, like all the productions of the school to which they belonged, included nearly the usual amount of false thought and sentiment; but the feeling which had dictated them was not a false one. Had he lived better, he would have written more cheerfully. It is with the mind often as with the body. It is not always in the main seat of disease that the symptoms proper to the disease are exhibited; nor does it need any very extensive acquaintance with our nature to know that real remorse often forms the groundwork of an apparently fictitious sorrow.

Another poem, of somewhat the same stamp as the former, we may insert here. It is in the handwriting of the young surgeon, among a collection of his pieces, but is marked "Anonymous." We have never met with it elsewhere; and as it bears upon it the impress of this singular young man's mind, and is powerfully expressive of the gloom in which he loved to enshroud himself, and of the deep bitterness which is the only legitimate fruit of a life of sinful pleasure, we may shrewdly guess that it can be the production of no one else. It is entitled

THE MOURNER.

I do not sigh
That I catch not the glance of woman's eye:
I am weary of woman. I know too well
How the pleasant smiles of the love-merchant sell
To waste one serious thought on her,
Though I've been, like others, a worshipper.
I do not sigh for the silken creature;
The tinge of good in her milky blood
Marks not her worth, but her feebler nature.

22

.   I do not pine   ,
That the treasures of India are not mine:
I have feasted on all that gold could buy,
I have drained the fount men call pleasure dry,
And I feel the after scorch of pain
On a lip that would not drink again.
Oh! wealth on me were only wasted;
I am far above the usurer's love.
And all other love on earth I've tasted.

I do not weep
That apart from the noble my walk I keep;
That the name I bear shall never be set
'Mid the gems of Fame's sparkling coronet;
That I shall slink, with the meanest clay,
To a hasty grave as mean as they.
Oh! the choice of a sepulchre does not grieve me:
I have that within a name might win
And a tomb, if such things could deceive me.

I do not groan
That I life's poison-plant have known;
That in my spirit's drunkenness
I ate of its fruit of bitterness,
Nor knew, until it was too late,
The ills that on such banquet wait.
'Tis not for this I cherish sadness:
I've taught my heart to endure the smart
Produced by my youth's madness.

But I do sigh,
And deeply, darkly pine, weep, groan, — and why?
Because with unclouded eye I see
Each turn in human destiny,
The knowledge of which will not depart,
But lingers and rankles in my heart;
Because it is my chance to know
That good and ill, that weal and woe,
Are words that NOTHING mean below;
Because all earth can't buy a morrow,
Or draw from breath, or the vital breath,
Aught but uncertainty and sorrow.

This strange poem he read to his elderly friend, with the evident purpose of eliciting some criticism. While admitting its power, she protested against its false philosophy, — the result of a distorted vision, in its turn the result of a perverted life. By way of attempting to strike out a healthier vein of sentiment, she begged him to furnish her with an answer. With this request he complied; but the production, although with glimpses of true poetry, and with the same power over rhythm, has, as might be expected, the air of something made to order. It is as follows : —

ANSWER TO THE MOURNER.

I daily sigh
That I meet not the glance of my lady's eye.
I am weary of absence: I know too well
How lonely and tiresome the dull hours tell
Not to wish every moment to be with her
Of whom I have long been the worshipper.
Oh, how I long for the lovely creature!
The olive-bud, at the general Flood,
To the patriarch sailor was not sweeter.

I often pine
That the gifts of fortune are not mine,
Yet covet not wealth from the wish to taste
The enervating sweets of thoughtless waste.
The slave of pleasure I scorn to be,
And the usurer's love has no charms for me.
I wish but an easy competence,
With a pound to lend to an needy friend,
But I care not for splendid affluence.

I sometimes weep
That I with the lowly my walk must keep:
I would that my humble name were set
In the centre of Fame's bright coronet;
That my tomb might be decked with a gorgeous stone,

And the tears of the virtuous shed thereon.
Oh! the thoughts of death should never grieve me,
Could I stamp my name with a spotless fame,
And a garland of deathless roses weave me.

I deeply groan
When I think on the follies my youth has known, —
When the still small voice of conscience brings
Before me the memory of bygone things,
And its softest whisper appalls me more
Than the earthquake's crash or the thunder's roar;
And my sorrow is deeper, because I know
That neither from chance nor from ignorance,
But with open eyes, I have wandered so.

I murmur not
That the volume of fate to man is shut, —
That he is forbidden with daring eye
Into its mysteries to pry.
Content with the knowledge God has given,
I seek not to fathom the plans of heaven;
I believe that *good* may be found below,
And that evil is tasted, alas! I know;
Yet I trust there's a balm for every woe, —
That the saddest night will have a morrow;
And I hope through faith to live after death,
In a world that knows nor sin nor sorrow.

The truest answer to the mourner was, however, yet to come.

It is not the least faulty among men that are most successful in interesting us in their welfare. A ruin often awakens deeper emotions than the edifice, however noble, could have elicited when entire; and there is something in a broken and ruined character, if we can trace in it the lineaments of original beauty and power, that inspires us with similar feelings. The friend of the young surgeon felt thus. He was in truth a goodly ruin, in which she saw much to admire and much to regret; and, impressed by a serious and long-cherished belief in the restorative efficacy of religion, her pity for him was not unmixed with hope. She had treated him on every occasion with the kindness of a mother; and now, with the affection and freedom proper to the character, she pressed on his consideration the important truths which she knew concerned him most deeply. He listened with a submissive and respectful attention, — the effect, doubtless, of those feelings with which he must have regarded one so disinterestedly his friend; for the subject could not have been introduced to his notice under circumstances more favorable. The sense of obligation had softened his heart; the respectful deference which he naturally paid to the sex and character of his friend prepared him rather to receive than to challenge the truths which she urged on his acceptance; the conviction that a heartfelt interest in his welfare furnished her only motive, checked that noiseless though fatal under-current of objection which can defeat in so many cases an end incontrovertibly good, by fixing on it the imputation of sinister design; and, above all, there was a plain earnestness in her manner, the result of a deep-seated belief, which, disdaining the niceties of metaphysical speculation, spoke more powerfully to his conscience than it could have done had it armed itself with half the arguments of the schools. Rarely does mere argument bring conviction to an ingenious mind, fertile in doubts and objections. Conscience sleeps when the rationative faculty contends for victory, — a thing it is seldom indifferent to; and a few perhaps ingenious sophisms prove the only fruits of the contest.

The little vessel lay in ——, as I have said, for about two months, when she received orders to sail for the south of England. A storm arose, and she was forced by stress of weather into Aberdeen. From this place the surgeon first wrote to his friend. His epistolary style, like his poetry, was characterized by an easy elegance; and there was no incident which he related, however trifling in itself, which did not borrow some degree of interest from his pen. He relates, in one of his earlier letters, that, in a solitary ramble in the neighborhood of Aberdeen, he came to a picturesque little bridge on the river Don. He had rarely seen a prettier spot. There were rocks and trees, and a deep, dark stream; and he stood admiring it till there passed a poor old beggar, of whom he inquired the name of the bridge. "It is called," said the mendicant, "the brig of Don; but in my young days it was better known as the brig of Balgownie; and if you be a Scotchman perhaps you have heard of it, for there are many prophecies about it by Thomas the Rhymer." "Ah," exclaimed the surgeon, "'Balgownie brig's black wa!' And so I have been admiring, for its own sake, the far-famed scene of Byron's boyhood. I cannot tell you," he adds, "what I felt on the occasion. It was perhaps lucky for me that I had not much money in my pocket, but the little that I had made the old man happy."

Our story hastens abruptly to its conclusion. During the following winter and the early part of spring, the little tender was employed in cruising in the English Channel and the neighborhood of Jersey; and from the latter place most of the surgeon's letters to his friends were addressed. They relate the progress of an interesting and highly-important change in a mind of no ordinary character. There was an alteration effected in the very tone of his intellect; it seemed, if I may so express myself, as if strung less sharply than before, and more in accordance with the realities of life. Even his love appeared as if changed into a less romantic but tenderer passion, that sought the welfare of its object even more than the object itself. But it was in his moral nature — in those sentiments of the man which look forward and upward — that the metamorphosis seemed most complete. When a powerful mind first becomes the subject of serious impressions, there is something in Christianity suited to take it by surprise. When viewed at a distance, and with that slight degree of attention which the great bulk of mankind are contented to bestow on that religion which God revealed, there seems a complex obscurity in its peculiar doctrines which contrasts strongly with the simplicity of its morals. It seems to lie as *unconformably* (if we may employ the metaphor) as some of the deductions of the higher sciences to what is termed the common sense of mankind. It seems at first sight, for instance, no very rational inference that the whiteness of light is the effect of a harmonious mixture of color, or that the earth is confined to its orbit by the operations of the same law which impels a falling pebble towards the ground. And to the careless, because uninterested observer, such doctrines as the doctrine of the fall and the atonement appear rational in as slight a degree. But when Deity himself interposes, when the heart is seriously affected, when the divine law holds up its mirror to the conscience, and we begin to examine the peculiar doctrines in a clearer light and from a nearer point of observation, they at once seem to change their character, — to assume so stupendous a massiveness of aspect, to discover a profundity so far beyond every depth of a merely human philosophy, to appear so wonderfully fitted to the nature and to the wants of man, that we are at once convinced their author can be no other than the adorable Being who gave light and gravitation to the universe which he willed to exist. The young surgeon had a mind capacious enough to be impressed by this feeling of surprise. He began to see, and to wonder he had missed seeing it before, that Christianity is in keeping, if we may so speak, with the other productions of its Author; that to a creature solely influenced by motive, no moral code, however perfect, can be efficient in directing or restraining, except through its connection with some heart-influencing belief; that it is essential to his nature as man that he meet with a corresponding nature in Deity, a human nature like his own, and that he must be conscious of owing to Him more than either his first origin or his subsequent support, or any of the minor gifts which he shares in common with the inferior animals, and which cost the Giver a less price than was paid on Calvary. It is unnecessary to expatiate on the new or altered feelings which accompanied the change, or to record the process of a state of mind described by so many. The surgeon, in his last letter to his friend, dwelt on these with an earnest, yet half-bashful delight, that, while it showed how much they engrossed him, showed also how new it was to him either to experience or describe them.

The next she received regarding him recorded his death. It was written at his dying request by a clergyman of Jersey. He had passed a day, early in April, in the cabin of the little vessel, engaged with his books and his pen; towards evening he went on deck; and, stepping on the quay, missed his footing and fell backwards. The spine sustained a mortal injury in the fall. He was carried by the unskilful hands of sailors to lodgings in the town of St. Helier's, a distance of five miles. During this long and painful transport, he was, as he afterwards said, conscious although speechless, and aware that, if he had been placed in an easier position, with his head better supported, he might have a chance of recovery. Yet he never gave expression to a single murmur. Besides the clergyman, he was fortunate enough to be assiduously attended by some excellent friends whom he had made on occasion of a former visit of his vessel to the same port. These he kept employed in reading the Scriptures aloud by night and by day. As he had formerly drunk deeply of the fount men call pleasure, he now drank insatiably at the pure Fount of Inspiration. "It is necessary to stop," one of his kind attendants would say; "your fever is rising." "It is only," he would reply with a smile, "the loss of a little blood after you leave." He lingered thus for about four weeks in hopeless suffering, but in the full possession of all his mental faculties, till death came to his relief, and he departed full of the hope of a happy immortality. The last tie that bound him to the world was his attachment to the lady whose name, so obscurely recorded, has introduced his story to the reader. But as death neared, and the world receded, he became reconciled to the necessity of parting from even her. His last request to the clergyman who attended him was, that, after his decease, he should write to his friend in ——, and say, " that if, as he trusted, he entered, a sinner saved, into glory, he would have to bless her, as being, under God, the honored instrument of mercy."

VIII.

GEORGE ROSS, THE SCOTCH AGENT.

CHAPTER I.

Men resemble the gods in nothing so much as in doing good to their fellow-creatures. — CICERO.

IN the letter in which Junius accuses the Duke of Grafton of having sold a patent-place in the collection of customs to one Mr. Hine, he informs the reader that the person employed by his grace in negotiating the business "was George Ross, the Scotch Agent, and worthy confidant of Lord Mansfield. And no sale by the candle," he adds, " was ever conducted with greater formality." Now, slight as this notice is, there is something in it sufficiently tangible for the imagination to lay hold of. If the reader thinks of the Scotch Agent at all, he probably thinks of him as one of those convenient creatures so necessary to the practical statesman, whose merit does not consist more in their being ingenious in a great degree, than in their being honest in a very small one. So mixed a thing is poor human nature, however, that, though the statement of Junius has never yet been fairly controverted, no possible estimate of character could be more unjust. The Scotch

Agent, whatever the nature of his services to the Duke of Grafton, was in reality a high-minded, and, what is more, a truly patriotic man; so good a person, indeed, that, in a period of political heats and animosities, his story, fairly told, might teach us a lesson of charity and moderation. I wish I could transport the reader to where his portrait hangs, side by side with that of his friend the Lord Chief Justice, in the drawing-room of Cromarty House. The air of dignified benevolence impressed on the features of the handsome old man, with his gray hair curling round his temples, would secure a fair hearing for him from even the sturdiest of the class who hate their neighbors for the good of their country. Besides, the very presence of the noble-looking lawyer, so much more like the Murray eulogized by Pope and Lyttleton than the Mansfield denounced by Junius, would of itself serve as a sort of guarantee for the honor of his friend.

George Ross was the son of a petty proprietor of Easter-Ross, and succeeded, on the death of his father, to the few barren acres on which, for a century or two before, the family had been ingenious enough to live. But he possessed, besides, what was more valuable than twenty such patrimonies, an untiring energy of disposition, based on a substratum of the soundest good sense; and, what was scarcely less important than either, ambition enough to turn his capacity of employment to the best account. Ross-shire a century ago was no place for such a man; and as the only road to preferment at this period was the road that led south, George Ross, when very young, left his mother's cottage for England, where he spent nearly fifty years amongst statesmen and courtiers, and in the enjoyment of the friendship of such men as President Forbes and Lord Mansfield. At length he returned, when an old,

gray-headed man, to rank among the greatest capitalists
and proprietors of the county, and purchased, with other
lesser properties in the neighborhood, the whole estate of
Cromarty. Perhaps he had come to rest him ere he died.
But there seems to be no such thing as changing one's natural bent, when confirmed by the habits of half a lifetime;
and the energies of the Scotch Agent, now that they had
gained him fortune and influence, were as little disposed to
fall asleep as they had been forty years before. As it was
no longer necessary, however, that they should be employed on his own account, he gave them full scope in
behalf of his poorer neighbors. The country around him
lay dead. There were no manufactories, no trade, no
knowledge of agriculture, no consciousness that matters
were ill, and, consequently, no desire of making them better; and the herculean task imposed upon himself by the
Scotch Agent, now considerably turned of sixty, was to
animate and revolutionize the whole. And such was his
statesman-like sagacity in developing the hitherto undis-
covered resources of the country, joined to a high-minded
zeal that could sow liberally in the hope of a late harvest
for others to reap, that he fully succeeded.

He first established in the town an extensive manufactory of hempen cloth, which has ever since employed about
two hundred persons within its walls, and fully twice that
number without. He next built an ale brewery, which, at
the time of its erection, was by far the largest in the north
of Scotland. He then furnished the town, at a great expense, with an excellent harbor, and set on foot a trade
in pork which for the last thirty years has been carried
on by the people of the place to an extent of from about
fifteen to twenty thousand pounds annually. He set himself, too, to initiate his tenantry in the art of rearing wheat;

and finding them wofully unwilling to become wiser on the subject, he tried the force of example, by taking an extensive farm under his own management and conducting . it on the most approved principles of modern agriculture. He established a nail and spade manufactory ; brought women from England to instruct the young girls in the art of working lace; provided houses for the poor; presented the town with a neat, substantial building, the upper part of which serves for a council-room and the lower as a prison ; and built for the accommodation of the poor Highlanders, who came thronging into the town to work on his land and in his manufactories, a handsome Gaelic chapel. He built for his own residence an elegant house of hewn stone ; surrounded it with pleasure-grounds, designed in the best style of the art; planted many hundred acres of the less improvable parts of his property; and laid open the hitherto scarcely accessible beauties of the hill of Cromarty by crossing and re-crossing it with well-nigh as many walks as there are veins in the human body. He was proud of his exquisite landscapes, and of his own skill in heightening their beauty, and fully determined, he said, if he but lived long enough, to make Cromarty worth an Englishman's while coming all the way from London to see it.

When Oscar fell asleep, says the old Irish bard, it was impossible to awaken him before his time except by cutting off one of his fingers or flinging a rock at his head ; and woe to the poor man who disturbed him ! The Agent found it every whit as difficult to awaken a sleeping country, and in some respects almost as unsafe. I am afraid human nature is nearly the same thing in the people that it is in their rulers, and that both are alike disposed to prefer the man who flatters them to the man who merely

23

does them good.   George Ross was by no means the most
popular of proprietors.   He disturbed old prejudices, and
unfixed old habits.   The farmers thought it hard that they
should have to break up their irregular map-like patches
of land, divided from each other by little strips and corners not yet reclaimed from the waste, into awkward-
looking rectangular fields, and that they durst no longer
fasten their horses to the plough by the tail, — a piece of
natural harness evidently formed for the express purpose.
The townspeople deemed the hempen manufactory un-
wholesome; and found that the English lace-women, who
to a certainty were tea-drinkers, and even not very hostile,
it was said, to gin, were in a fair way of teaching their
pupils something more than the mere weaving of lace.
What could be more heathenish, too, than the little temple
covered with cockle-shell which the laird had just reared
on a solitary corner of the hill, but which they soon sent
spinning over the cliff into the sea, a downward journey
of a hundred yards?   And then his odious pork trade!
There was no prevailing on the people to rear pigs for
him; and so he had to build a range of offices, in an out-
of-the-way nook of his lands, which he stocked with hordes
of these animals, that he might rear them for himself.
The herds increased in size and number, and, voracious
beyond calculation, almost occasioned a famine.   Even the
great wealth of the speculatist proved insufficient to supply them with food, and the very keepers were in danger
of being eaten alive.   The poor animals seemed departing
from their very nature; for they became long and lank,
and bony as the griffins of heraldry, until they looked more
like race-horses than pigs; and as they descended with
every ebb in huge droves to browse on the sea-weed, or
delve for shell-fish among the pebbles, there was no lack

of music befitting their condition when the large rock-crab revenged with his nippers on their lips the injuries inflicted on him with their teeth. Now, all this formed a fine subject for joking to people who indulged in a half-Jewish dislike of the pig, and who could not guess that the pork trade was one day to pay the rents of half the widows' cottages in the country. But no one could lie more open than George Ross to that species of ridicule which the men who see further than their neighbors, and look more to the advantage of others than to their own, cannot fail to encounter. He was a worker in the dark, and at no slight expense; for, though all his many projects were ultimately found to be benefits conferred on his country, not one of them proved remunerative to himself. But he seems to have known mankind too well to have expected a great deal from their gratitude, though on one occasion at least his patience gave way.

The town in the course of years had so entirely marched to the west, that the town's cross came at length to be fairly left behind, with a hawthorn hedge on the one side and a garden fence on the other; and when the Agent had completed the house which was to serve as council-room and prison to the place, the cross was taken down from its stand of more than two centuries, and placed in front of the new building. That people might the better remember the circumstance, there was a showy procession got up; healths were drunk beside the cross in the Agent's best wine, and not a little of his best crystal broken against it; and the evening terminated in a ball. It so happened, however, through some cross chance, that, though all the gentility of the place were to be invited, three young men, who deemed themselves quite as genteel as the best of their neighbors, were passed over. The dignified manager

of the hemp manufactory had received no invitation, nor
the clever superintendent of the nail-work, nor yet the
spruce clerk of the brewery; and as they were all men of
spirit, it so happened that during the very next night the
cross was taken down from its new pedestal, broken into
three pieces, and carried still further to the west, to an
open space where four lanes met; and there it was found
in the morning, the pieces piled over each other, and surrounded by a profusion of broken ale bottles. The Agent
was amazingly angry, — angrier, indeed, than his acquaintance had deemed him capable of becoming; and in the
course of the day the town's crier went through the streets
proclaiming a reward of ten pounds in hand, and a free
room in Mr. Ross's new buildings for life, to any one who
would give such information as might lead to the conviction of the offenders.

In one of his walks a few days after, the Agent met with
a poor, miserable-looking Highland woman, who had been
picking a few withered sticks out of one of his hedges,
and whose hands and clothes seemed torn by the thorns.
"Poor old creature," he said, as she dropped her courtesy in
passing, "you must go to my manager, and tell him I have
ordered you a barrel of coals. And stay, — you are hungry: call at my house, in passing, and the servants will find
you something to bring home with you." The poor woman blessed him, and looked up hesitatingly in his face.
She had never betrayed any one, she said; but his honor
was so good a gentleman, — so very good a gentleman ;
and so she thought she had best tell him all she knew
about the breaking of the cross. She lived in a little gar-
ret over the room of Jamie Banks, the nailer; and having
slept scarcely any all the night in which the cross was
taken down, — for the weather was bitterly cold, and her

bed-clothes very thin, — she could hear weighty footsteps traversing the streets till near morning, when the house-door opened, and in came Jamie, with a tottering, unequal step, and disturbed the whole family by stumbling over a stool into his wife's washing-tub. Besides, she had next day overheard his wife rating him for staying out to so *untimeous* an hour, and his remark, in reply, that she would do well to keep quiet, unless she wished to see him hanged. This was the sort of clue the affair required; and, in following it up, the unlucky nailer was apprehended and examined; but it was found that, through a singular lapse of memory, he had forgotten every circumstance connected with the night in question, except that he had been in the very best company, and one of the happiest men in the world.

Jamie Banks was decidedly the most eccentric man of his day, in at least one parish, — full of small wit and small roguery, and famous for a faculty of invention fertile enough to have served a poet. On one occasion, when the gill of whiskey had risen to three halfpence in Cromarty, and could still be bought for a penny in Avoch, he had prevailed on a party of his acquaintance to accompany him to the latter place, that they might drink themselves rich on the strength of the old proverb; and as they actually effected a saving of two shillings in spending six, it was clear, he said, that, had not their money failed them, they would have made fortunes apiece. Alas for the littleness of that great passion, the love of fame! I have observed that the tradespeople among whom one meets with most instances of eccentricity, are those whose shops, being places of general resort, furnish them with space enough on which to achieve a humble notoriety, by rendering themselves unlike everybody else. To secure to Jamie

23*

Banks due leisure for recollection, he was committed to jail.

He was sitting one evening beside the prison fire, with one of his neighbors and the jailer, and had risen to exclude the chill night air by drawing a curtain over the open-barred window of the apartment, when a man suddenly started from behind the wall outside, and discharged a large stone with tremendous force at his head. The missile almost brushed his ear as it sung past, and, rebounding from the opposite wall, rolled along the floor. "That maun be Rob Williamson," exclaimed Jamie, "wanting to keep me quiet. Out, neebor Jonathan, an' after him." Neebor Jonathan, an active young fellow, sprung to the door, caught the sounds of retreating footsteps as he turned the gate, and, dashing after like a greyhound, succeeded in laying hold of the coat-skirts of Rob Williamson, as he strained onwards through the gate of the hemp manufactory. He was immediately secured, and lodged in another apartment of the prison; and in the morning Jamie Banks was found to have recovered his memory.

He had finished working, he said, on the evening after the ball, and was just putting on his coat preparatory to leaving the shop, when the superintendent called him into his writing-room, where he found three persons sitting at a table half covered with bottles. Rob Williamson, the weaver, was one of these; the other two were the clerk of the brewery and the manager of the hemp manufactory; and they were all arguing together on some point of divinity. The manager cleared a seat for him beside himself, and filled his glass thrice in succession, by way of making up for the time he had lost. Nothing could be more untrue than that the manager was proud. They then all began to speak about morals and Mr. Ross. The clerk was certain that, with his harbor, and his piggery, and his heathen temples, and his lace-women, he would not leave a ray of morality in the place; and Rob was quite as sure he was no friend to the gospel. He a builder of Gaelic kirks, forsooth! Had he not yesterday put up a popish dagon of a cross, and made the silly mason bodies worship it for the sake o' a dram? And then, how common ale-drinking had become in the place!—in his young days they drank nothing but gin,—and what would their grandfathers have said to a *whigmaleerie* o' a ball! "I sipped and listened," continued Jamie, "and thought that the time could not have been better spent at an elders' meeting in the kirk; and as the night wore later the conversation became still more edifying, until at length all the bottles were emptied, when we sallied out in a body, to imitate the old Reformers by breaking the cross. 'We may suffer, Jamie, for what we have done,' said Rob to me as we parted for the night; 'but, remember, it was duty, Jamie, it was duty; we have been testifying wi' our hands, an' when the hour o' trial comes we mauna be slow in testifying wi' our tongues too.' He wasna slack, the deceitfu' body!" concluded Jamie, "in trying to stop mine." And thus closed the evidence. The Agent was no vindictive man. He dismissed his two managers and the clerk, to find for themselves a more indulgent master; but the services of Jamie Banks he still retained; and the first employment which he found for him after his release was the fashioning of four iron bars for the repair of the cross.

The Agent, in the closing scene of his life, was destined to experience the unhappiness of blighted hope. He had an only son, a weak and very obstinate young man, who, without intellect enough to appreciate his well-calculated schemes, and yet conceit enough to sit in judgment on them, was ever showing his spirit by opposing a sort of selfish nonsense, that aped the semblance of common sense, to the expansive and benevolent philosophy of his father. But the old man bore patiently with his conceit and folly. Like the great bulk of the class who attain to wealth and influence through their own exertions, he was anxiously ambitious to live in his posterity, and be the founder of a family; and he knew it was quite as much according to the nature of things that a fool might be the father, as that he should be the son, of a wise man. He secured, therefore, his lands to his posterity by the law of entail; did all that education and example could do for the young man; and succeeded in getting him married to a sweet, amiable English woman, the daughter of a bishop. But, alas! his precautions, and the hopes in which he indulged, proved equally vain. The young man, only a few months after his marriage, was piqued, when at table, by some remark of his father regarding his mode of carving, — some slight allusion, it is said, to the maxim that little men cannot afford to neglect little matters,— and rising, with much apparent coolness, from beside his wife, he stepped into an adjoining room, and there blew out his brains with a pistol. The stain of his blood may still be seen in two large brownish-colored blotches on the floor.

George Ross survived his son for several years; and he continued, though a sadder and a graver man, to busy himself with all his various speculations as before. It was observed, however, that he seemed to care less than formerly for whatever was exclusively his own, for his fine house and his beautiful lands, and that he chiefly employed himself in maturing his several projects for the good of his country-folks. Time at length began to set its seal on his labors, by discovering their value; though not until death had first affixed *his* to the character of the wise and benevolent projector. He died full of years and honor, mourned by the poor, and regretted by every one; and even those who had opposed his innovations with the warmest zeal were content to remember him, with all the others, as "the good laird."

IX.

M'CULLOCH THE MECHANICIAN.

CHAPTER I.

Anything may become nature to man; the rare thing is to find
a nature that is truly natural. — ANON.

IN the "Scots Magazine" for May 1789, there is a report
by Captain Philip d'Auvergne, of the Narcissus frigate, on
the practical utility of Kenneth M'Culloch's sea-compasses.
The captain, after an eighteen months' trial of their merits,
compared with those of all the other kinds in use at the
time, describes them as immensely superior, and earnestly
recommends to the admiralty their general introduction
into the navy. In passing, on one occasion, through the
Race of Alderney in the winter of 1787, there broke out a
frightful storm; and so violent was the opposition of the
wind and tide, that while his vessel was sailing at the rate
of eleven miles on the surface, she was making scarce any
headway by the land. The sea rose tremendously, at
once short, high, and irregular; and the motions of the
vessel were so fearfully abrupt and violent that scarce a
seaman aboard could stand on deck. At a time so critical,
when none of the compasses supplied from his majesty's

stores *would stand*, but vacillated more than three points on each side of the pole, " it commanded," says the captain, " the admiration of the whole crew, winning the confidence of even the most timorous, to see how quickly and readily M'Culloch's steering compass recovered the vacillations communicated to it by the motion of the ship and the shocks of the sea, and how truly, in every brief interval of rest, it pointed to the pole." It is further added, that on the captain's recommendation these compasses were tried on board the Andromeda, commanded at the time by Prince William Henry, our late king; and so satisfied was the prince of the utility of the invention, that he, too, became a strenuous advocate for their general introduction, and testified his regard for the ingenious inventor by appointing him his compass-maker. M'Culloch, however, did not long survive the honor, dying a few years after; and we have been unable to trace with any degree of certainty the further history of his improved compass. But, though only imperfectly informed regarding his various inventions, — and they are said to have been many, and singularly practical,—we are tolerably well acquainted with the story of his early life; and, as it furnishes a striking illustration of that instinct of genius, if we may so express ourselves, which leads the possessor to exactly the place in which his services may be of most value to the community, by rendering him useless and unhappy in every other, we think we cannot do better than communicate it to the reader.

There stood, about forty years ago, on the northern side of the parish of Cromarty, an old farm-house,—one of those low, long, dark-looking erections of turf and stone which still survive in the remoter districts of Scotland, as if to show how little man may sometimes improve, in even a civilized country, on the first rude shelter which his necessities owed to his ingenuity. A worn-out barrel, fixed slantwise in the ridge, served as a chimney for the better apartment, — the spare room of the domicile, — which was furnished also with a glazed window; but the smoke was suffered to escape from the others, and the light to enter them, as chance or accident might direct. The eaves, over-hung by stonecrop and bunches of the houseleek, drooped heavily over the small blind windows and low door; and a row of ancient elms, which rose from out the fence of a neglected garden, spread their gnarled and ponderous arms over the roof. Such was the farm-house of Wood-side, in which Kenneth M‘Culloch, the son of the farmer, was born, some time in the early half of the last century. The family from which he sprang — a race of honest, plodding tacksmen — had held the place from the proprietor of Cromarty for more than a hundred years; and it was deemed quite a matter of course that Kenneth, the eldest son, should succeed his father in the farm. Never was there a time, in at least this part of the country, in which agriculture stood more in need of the services of original and inventive minds. There was not a wheeled cart in the parish, nor a plough constructed on the modern principle. There was no changing of seed to suit the varieties of soil, no green cropping, no rotatory system of production; and it seemed as if the main object of the farmer had been to raise the least possible amount of grain at the greatest possible expense of labor. The farm of Woodside was prim-itive enough in its usages and modes of tillage to have formed a study to the antiquary. Towards autumn, when the fields vary most in color, it resembled a rudely-executed chart of some large island, so irregular were the patches which composed it, and so broken on every side by a sur-rounding sea of brown, sterile moor, that here and there

went winding into the interior in long river-like strips,
or expanded within into friths and lakes. In one corner
there stood a heap of stones, in another a thicket of furze,
here a piece of bog, there a broken bank of clay. The
implements, too, with which the fields were labored were
quite as uncouth in their appearance as the fields themselves. There was the single-stilted plough, that did little
more than scratch the surface; the wooden-toothed harrow, that did hardly so much; the cumbrous sledge, — no
inconsiderable load of itself, — for carrying home the corn
in harvest; and the basket-woven conical cart, with its
rollers of wood, for bearing out the manure in spring.
With these, too, there was the usual misproportion to the
extent and produce of the farm of lean, inefficient cattle, —
four half-starved animals performing with incredible labor
the work of one. And yet, now that a singularly inventive mind had come into existence on this very farm, and
though its attentions had been directed, as far as external
influence could direct them, on the various employments
of the farmer, the interests of husbandry were to be in no
degree improved by the circumstance. Nature, in the midst
of her wisdom, seems to cherish a dash of the eccentric.
The ingenuity of the farmer's son was to be employed, not
in facilitating the labors of the farmer, but in inventing
binnacle-lamps which would yield an undiminished light
amid the agitations of a tempest, and in constructing mar-
iners' compasses on a new principle. There are instances
of a similar character furnished by the experience of almost
every one. In passing some years since over a dreary
moor in the interior of the country, our curiosity was excited by a miniature mast, furnished, like that of a ship,
with shrouds and yards, bearing a-top a gaudy pinnet,
which we saw beside a little Highland cottage; and on

inquiring regarding it at the door, we were informed that it was the work of the cottager's son, a lad who, though he had scarcely ever seen the sea, had taken a strange fancy to the life of a sailor, and who had left his father only a few weeks before to serve aboard a man-of-war.

Kenneth's first employment was the tending of a flock of sheep, the property of his father; and wretchedly did he acquit himself of the charge. The farm is bounded on the eastern side by a deep, bosky ravine, through the bottom of which a scanty runnel rather trickles than flows; and when it was discovered on any occasion that Kenneth's flock had been left to take care of themselves, and of his father's corn to boot, — and such occasions were wofully frequent, — Kenneth himself was almost invariably to be found in this ravine. He would sit for hours among the bushes, engaged with his knife in carving uncouth faces on the heads of walking-sticks, or in constructing little water-mills, or in making Lilliputian pumps of the dried stalks of the larger hemlock, and in raising the waters of the runnel to basins dug in the sides of the hollow. Some-times he quitted his charge altogether, and set out for a meal-mill about a quarter of a mile from the farm, where he would linger for half a day at a time watching the mo-tion of the wheels. His father complained that he could make nothing of him; " the boy," he said, " seemed to have nearly as much sense as other boys of his years, and yet for any one useful purpose he was nothing better than an idiot." His mother, as is common with mothers, and who was naturally an easy, kind-hearted woman, had bet-ter hopes of him. Kenneth, she affirmed, was only a little peculiar, and would turn out well after all. He was grow-ing up, however, without improving in the slightest; and when he became tall enough for the plough, he made a dead stand. He would go and be a tradesman, he said, a mason or smith or house-carpenter, — anything his friends chose to make him, — but a farmer he would not be. His father, after a fruitless struggle to overcome his obstinacy, carried him with him to an acquaintance in Cromarty, an ingenious cabinet-maker, named Donald Sandison ; and, after candidly confessing that he was of no manner of use at home, and would, he was afraid, be of little use any-where, he bound him by indenture to the mechanic for four years.

Kenneth's new master — a shrewd, sagacious man, who had been actively engaged, it was said, in the Porteous mob about twenty years before — was one of the best work-men in his profession in the north of Scotland. His scru-toires and wardrobes were in repute up to the close of the last century ; and in the ancient art of wainscot carving he had no equal in the country. He was an intelligent man, too, as well as a superior mechanic. He was a general reader, as a little old-fashioned library in the possession of his grandson still remains to testify; and he had studied Paladio, in the antique translation of Godfrey Richards, and knew a little of Euclid. With all his general intelli-gence, however, and all his skill, he failed to discover the latent capabilities of his apprentice. Kenneth was dull and absent, and had no heart to his work; and though he seemed to understand the principles on which his master's various tools were used, and the articles of his trade con-structed, as well at least as any workman in the shop, there were none among them who used the tools so awkwardly, or constructed the articles so ill. An old botching carpen-ter who wrought in a little shop at the other end of the town was known to the boys of the place by the humorous appellation of "Spull [*i. e.* spoil] the Wood," and a lean-sided, ill-conditioned boat which he had built, as " the Wilful Murder." Kenneth came to be regarded as a sort of second "Spull the Wood," — as a fashioner of rickety tables, ill-fitted drawers, and chairs that, when sat upon, creaked like badly-tuned organs; and the boys, who were beginning to regard him as fair game, sometimes took the liberty of asking him whether he, too, was not going to build a boat? Such, in short, were his deficiencies as a mechanic, that in the third year of his apprenticeship his master advised his father to take him home with him and set him to the plough; an advice, however, on which the farmer, warned by his previous experience, sturdily refused to act.

It was remarked that Kenneth acquired more in the last year of his apprenticeship than in all the others. His skill as a workman still ranked a little below the average ability; but then it was only a little below it. He seemed, too, to enjoy more, and become less bashful and awkward. His master on one occasion took him aboard a vessel in the harbor to repair some injury which her bulwarks had sustained in a storm; and Kenneth, for the first time in his life, was introduced to the mariner's compass. The master, in after days, when his apprentice had become a great man, used to relate the circumstance with much complacency, and compare him, as he bent over the instrument in wonder and admiration, to a negro of the Kanga tribe worshipping the elephant's tooth. On the close of his apprenticeship he left this part of the country for London, accompanied by his master's eldest son, a lad of rather thoughtless disposition, but, like his father, a first-rate workman.

Kenneth soon began to experience the straits and hardships of the inferior mechanic. His companion found little difficulty in procuring employment, and none at all in retaining it when once procured. Kenneth, on the contrary, was tossed about from shop to shop, and from one establishment to another ; and for a full twelvemonth, during the half of which he was wholly unemployed, he did not work for more than a fortnight together with any one master. It would have fared worse with him than it did had it not been for his companion, Willie Sandison, who generously shared his earnings with him every time he stood in need of his assistance. In about a year after they had gone to London, however, Willie, an honest and warm-hearted, but thoughtless lad, was inveigled into a bad, disreputable marriage, and lost, in consequence, his wonted ability to assist his companion. We have seen one of Kenneth's letters to his old master, written about this time, in which he bewails Willie's mishap, and dwells gloomily on his own prospects. How these first began to brighten we are unable to say, for there occurs about this period a wide gap in his story, which all our inquiries regarding him have not enabled us to fill ; but in a second letter to his mother, now before us, which bears date 1772, just ten years after the other, there are the proofs of a surprising improvement in his circumstances and condition.

He writes in high spirits. Just before sitting down to his desk, he had heard from his old friend Willie, who had gone out to one of the colonies, where he was thriving, in spite of his wife. He had heard, too, by the same post, from his mother, who had been so kind to him during his luckless boyhood ; and the old woman was well. He had, besides, been enabled to remove from his former lodging to a fine, airy house in Duke's Court, opposite St. Martin's Church, for which he had engaged, he said, to pay a rent of forty-two pounds per annum — a very considerable sum sixty-eight years ago; and he had entered into an advantageous contract with Catherine of Russia, for furnishing all the philosophical instruments of a new college then erecting in St. Petersburg, a contract which promised to secure about two years' profitable employment to himself and seven workmen. In the ten years which had intervened between the dates of his two letters, Kenneth M'Culloch had become one of the most skilful and inventive mechanics in London, perhaps in the world. He rose gradually into affluence and celebrity, and for a considerable period before his death his gains were estimated at about a thousand a year. His story, however, illustrates rather the wisdom of nature than that of Kenneth M'Culloch. We think all the more highly of Franklin for being so excellent a printer, and of Burns for excelling all his companions in the labors of the field; nor did the skill or vigor with which they pursued their ordinary employments hinder the one from taking his place among the first philosophers and first statesmen of the age, nor prevent the other from achieving his wide-spread celebrity as at once the most original and most popular of modern poets. Be it remembered, however, that there is a narrow and limited cast of genius, unlike that of either Burns or Franklin, which, though of incalculable value in its own sphere, is of no use whatever in any other; and to precipitate it on its proper object by the pressure of external circumstances, and the general inaptitude of its possessor for other pursuits, seems to be part of the wise economy of Providence. Had Kenneth M'Culloch betaken himself to the plough, like his father and grandfather, he would have been, like them, the tacksman of Woodside, and nothing more; had he found his proper vocation in cabinet-making, he would have made tables and chairs for life, like his ingenious master Donald Sandison.

X.

THE SCOTCH MERCHANT

OF THE EIGHTEENTH CENTURY.

CHAPTER I.

Custom forms us all. Our thoughts, our morals, our most fixed
beliefs, are consequences of our place of birth. — HILL.

IT is according to the fixed economy of human affairs
that individuals should lead, and that masses should follow;
for the adorable Being who wills that the lower order of
minds should exist by myriads, and produces the higher so
rarely, has willed, also, by inevitable consequence, that the
many should be guided by the few. On the other hand, it
is not less in accordance with the dictates of His immuta-
ble justice, that the interests of the few should be subordinate to the more extended interests of the many. The
leading minds are to be regarded rather as formed for the
masses, than the masses for them. True it is, that, while
the one principle acts with all the undeviating certainty
of a natural law, the other operates partially and inter-
ruptedly, with all the doubtful efficiency of a moral one;
and hence those long catalogues of crimes committed
against the species by their natural leaders which so fill
the pages of history. We see man as the creature of des-

tiny conforming unresistingly to the one law; as a free agent, accountable for all his actions, yielding an imperfect and occasional obedience to the other. And yet his duty and his true interest, were he but wise enough to be convinced of it, are in every case the same. The following chapters, as they contain the history of a mind of the higher order, that, in doing good to others, conferred solid benefits on itself, may serve simply to illustrate this important truth. They may serve, too, to show the numerous class whose better feelings are suffered to evaporate in idle longings for some merely conceivable field of exertion, that wide spheres of usefulness may be furnished by situations comparatively unpromising. They may afford, besides, occasional glimpses of the beliefs, manners, and opinions of an age by no means remote from our own, but in many respects essentially different from it in spirit and character.

The Lowlanders of the north of Scotland were beginning, about the year 1700, gradually to recover the effects of that state of miserable depression into which they had been plunged for the greater part of the previous century. There was a slow awakening of the commercial spirit among the more enterprising class of minds, whose destiny it is to move in the van of society as the guides and pioneers of the rest. The unfortunate expedition of Darien had dissipated well-nigh the entire capital of the country only a few years before, and ruined almost all the greater merchants of the large towns. But the energies of the people, now that they were no longer borne down by the wretched despotism of the Stuarts, were not to be repressed by a single blow. Almost every seaport and larger town had its beginnings of trade. Younger sons of good family, who would have gone, only half a century before, to serve as mercenaries in the armies of the Continent, were learning to employ themselves as merchants at home. And almost every small town had its shopkeeper, who, after passing the early part of his life as a farmer or mechanic, had set himself, in the altered state of the country, to acquire the habits of his new profession, and employed his former savings in trade.

Among these last was James Forsyth, a native of the province of Moray. He had spent the first thirty years of his life as a mason and builder. His profession was a wandering one, and he had received from nature the ability of profiting by the opportunities of observation which it afforded. He had marked the gradual introduction among the people of new tastes for the various articles of foreign produce and manufacture which were beginning to flow into the kingdom, and had seen how large a proportion the profits of the trader bore — as they always do in the infancy of trade — to the amount of capital employed. Resigning, therefore, his old profession, he opened a small shop in the town of Cromarty, whose lucrative herring-fishery rendered it at this period one of the busiest little places in the north of Scotland. And as he was at once steady and enterprising, rigidly just in his dealings, and possessed of shrewd good sense, he had acquired, ere the year 1722, when his eldest son, William, the subject of the following memoir, was born to him, what at that period was deemed considerable wealth. His marriage had taken place, somewhat late in life, little more than a twelvemonth before.

William received from nature, what nature only can bestow, great force of character, and great kindliness of heart. The town of Cromarty at the time was singularly fortunate in its schoolmaster, Mr. David M'Culloch, a gentleman who terminated a long and very useful life, many years after, as the minister of a wild Highland parish in Perthshire; and William, who in infancy even had begun to manifest that restless curiosity which almost always characterizes the dawn of a superior intellect, was placed at a very early age under his care. The school — one of Knox's strongholds of the Reformation — was situated in a retired wooden corner behind the houses, with the windows, which were half-buried in the thatch, opening to the old, time-worn Castle of Cromarty. There could not be a more formidable spectre of the past than the old tower. It had been from time immemorial the seat of the hereditary sheriffs of the district, whose powers at this period still remained entire; and its tall, narrow front of blind wall, its embattled turrets and hanging bartizans, seemed associated with the tyranny and violence of more than a thousand years. But the low, mean-looking building at the foot of the hill was a masked battery raised against its authority, which was to burst open its dungeon-door, and to beat down its gallows. There is a class — the true aristocracy of nature — which have but to arise from among the people that the people may be free; and the humble old school did its part in separating its due proportion of these from the mass. Of two of the boys who sat at the same form with William Forsyth, one, the son of the town-clerk, afterwards represented the county in Parliament; and the other, of still humbler parentage, attracted, many years after, when librarian of the University of Edinburgh and Professor of Oriental Languages, the notice of the far-known Dr. Samuel Johnson.

The scheme of tuition established in our Scotch schools of this period was exactly that which had been laid down by Knox and Craig, in the Book of Discipline, rather more than a century and a half before. Times had altered, however; and, though still the best possible, perhaps, for minds of a superior order, it was no longer the best for intellects of the commoner class. The scheme drawn up by our first reformers was stamped by the liberality of men who had learned from experience that tyranny and superstition derive their chief support from ignorance. Almost all the knowledge which books could supply at the time was locked up in the learned languages. It was appointed, therefore, "that young men who 'purposed to travill in some handicraft or other profitable exercise for the good of the commonwealth, should first devote ane certain time to grammar and the Latin tongue, and ane certain time to the other tongues and the study of philosophy." But what may have been a wise and considerate act on the part of the ancestor, may degenerate into merely a foolish custom on the part of the descendant. Ere the times of Mr. M'Culloch, we had got a literature of our own; and if useful knowledge be learning, men might have become learned through an acquaintance with English reading alone. Our fathers, however, pursued the course which circumstances had rendered imperative in the days of their great-grandfathers, merely because their great-grandfathers had pursued it; and the few years which were spent in school by the poorer pupils of ordinary capacity, were absurdly frittered away in acquiring a little bad Latin and a very little worse Greek. So strange did the half-learning of our common people, derived in this way, appear to our southern neighbors, that there are writers of the last century who, in describing a Scotch footman or mechanic, rarely omit making his knowledge of the classics an essential part of the character. The barber in " Roderick Random " quotes Horace in the original; and Foote, in one of his farces, introduces a Scotch valet, who, when some one inquires of him whether he be a Latinist, indignantly exclaims, " Hoot awa, man ! a Scotchman and no understand Latin ! "

The school of Cromarty, like the other schools of the kingdom, produced its Latinists who caught fish and made shoes ; and it is not much more than twenty years since the race became finally extinct. I have heard stories of an old house-painter of the place, who, having survived most of his school-fellows and contemporaries, used to regret, among his other vanished pleasures, the pleasure he could once derive from an inexhaustible fund of Latin quotation, which the ignorance of a younger generation had rendered of little more value to him than the paper-money of an insolvent bank ; and I remember an old cabinet-maker who was in the practice, when his sight began to fail him, of carrying his Latin New Testament with him to church, as it chanced to be printed in a clearer type than any of his English ones. It is said, too, of a learned fisherman of the reign of Queen Anne, that, when employed one day among his tackle, he was accosted in Latin by the proprietor of Cromarty, who, accompanied by two gentlemen from England, was sauntering along the shore, and that, to the surprise of the strangers, he replied with considerable fluency in the same language. William Forsyth was a Latinist, like most of his school-fellows ; but the natural tone of his mind, and the extent of his information, were in keeping with the acquirement ; and while there must have been something sufficiently grotesque and incongruous, as the satirists show us, in the association of a classic literature with humble employments and very ordinary modes of thought and expression, nothing, on the other hand, could have seemed less so than that an enterprising and liberal-

minded merchant should have added to the manners and
sentiments of the gentleman the tastes and attainments of
the scholar.

CHAPTER II.

The wise and active conquer difficulties by daring to attempt them; Sloth
and Folly shiver and shrink at sight of toil and hazard, and make the
impossibility they fear. — ROWE.

WILLIAM FORSYTH in his sixteenth year quitted school,
and was placed by his father in a counting-house in London, where he formed his first acquaintance with trade.
Circumstances, however, rendered the initiatory course a
very brief one. His father, James Forsyth, died suddenly
in the following year, 1739; and, leaving London at the
request of his widowed mother, whose family now consisted
of two other sons and two daughters,—all of them, of course,
younger than himself, — he entered on his father's business
at the early age of seventeen. In one interesting instance
I have found the recollection of his short stay in London
incidentally connected with the high estimate of his character and acquirements formed by one of the shrewdest
and most extensively informed of his mercantile acquaintance. "I know," says a lady who has furnished me with
some of the materials of these chapters, " that Mr. Forsyth
must have spent some time in a London counting-house,
from often having heard my father repeat, as a remark of
the late Henry Davidson of Tulloch, that ' had the Cromarty merchant remained in the place where he received

his first introduction to business, he would have been, what no Scotchman ever was, lord mayor of London.'" I need hardly add that the remark is at least half a century old.

The town of Cromarty, at the time of Mr. Forsyth's settlement in it, was no longer the scene of busy trade which it had been twenty years before. The herring-fishery of the place, at one time the most lucrative on the eastern coast of Scotland, had totally failed, and the great bulk of the inhabitants, who had owed to it their chief means of subsistence, had fallen into abject poverty. They seemed fast sinking, too, into that first state of society in which there is scarce any division of labor. The mechanics in the town caught their own fish, raised their own corn, tanned their own leather, and wore clothes which had employed no other manufacturers than their own families and their neighbor the weaver. There was scarce any money in the district. Even the neighboring proprietors paid their tradesmen in kind; and a few bolls of malt or barley, or a few stones of flax or wool, settled the yearly account. There could not, therefore, be a worse or more hopeless scene for the shopkeeper; and had William Forsyth restricted himself to the trade of his father, he must inevitably have sunk with the sinking fortunes of the place. Young as he was, however, he had sagacity enough to perceive that Cromarty, though a bad field for the retail trader, might prove a very excellent one for the merchant. Its valuable, though at this time neglected harbor, seemed suited to render it, what it afterwards became, the key of the adjacent country. The neighboring friths, too, — those of Dingwall, Dornoch, and Beauly, which wind far into the Highlands of Ross and Sutherland, — formed so many broad pathways leading into districts which had no other roads at that period; and the towns of Tain, Dornoch, Dingwall, Campbelton, and Fortrose, with the seats of numerous proprietors, are situated on their shores. The bold and original plan of the young trader, therefore, was to render Cromarty a sort of depot for the whole; to furnish the shopkeepers of the several towns with the commodities in which they dealt, and to bring to the very doors of the proprietors the various foreign articles of comfort and luxury with which commerce could alone supply them. And, launching boldly into the speculation at a time when the whole country seemed asleep around him, he purchased a freighting-boat for the navigation of the three friths, and hired a large sloop for trading with Holland and the commercial towns of the south.

The failure of the herring trade of the place had been occasioned by the disappearance of the herrings, which, after frequenting the Frith in immense shoals for a long series of years, had totally deserted it. It is quite according to the nature of the fish, however, to resume their visits as suddenly and unexpectedly as they have broken them off, though not until after the lapse of so many seasons, perhaps, that the fishermen have ceased to watch for their appearance in their old haunts, or provide the tackle necessary for their capture; and in this way a number of years are sometimes suffered to pass, after the return of the fish, ere the old trade is re-established. To guard against any such waste of opportunity on the part of his townspeople was the first care of William Forsyth, after creating, as it were, a new and busy trade for himself; and, representing the case to the more intelligent gentlemen of the district, and some of the wealthier merchants of Inverness, he succeeded in forming them into a society for the encouragement of the herring-fishery, which provided a yearly premium of twenty marks Scots for the first barrel of herrings caught every season in the Moray Frith. The sum was small; but as money at the time was very valuable, it proved a sufficient inducement to the fishermen and trades-people of the place to fit out a few boats, about the beginning of autumn every year, to sweep over the various fish-ing-banks for the herrings ; and there were few seasons in which some one crew or other did not catch enough to entitle them to the premium. At length, however, their tackle wore out ; and Mr. Forsyth, in pursuance of his scheme, provided himself, at some little expense, with a complete drift of nets, which were carried to sea each sea-son by his boatmen, and the search kept up. His exer-tions, however, could only merit success, without securing it. The fish returned for a few seasons in considerable bodies, and several thousand barrels were caught ; but they soon deserted the Frith as entirely as before ; and more than a century elapsed from their first disappearance ere they revisited their old haunts with such regularity and in such numbers as to render the trade remunerative to either the curers or the fishermen.

Unlike the herring speculation, however, the general trade of William Forsyth was eminently successful. It was of a miscellaneous character, as became the state of a country so poor and so thinly peopled, and in which, as there was scarce any division of labor, one merchant had to perform the work of many. He supplied the proprietors with teas and wines and spiceries, with broadcloths, glass, delft-ware, Flemish tiles, and pieces of japanned cabinet-work; he furnished the blacksmith with iron from Sweden, the carpenter with tar and spars from Norway, and the farmer with flaxseed from Holland. He found, too, in other countries markets for the produce of our own. The exports of the north of Scotland at this period were mostly malt, wool, and salmon. Almost all rents were paid in kind or in labor; the proprietors retaining in their own hands a portion of their estates, termed demesnes or mains, which was cultivated mostly by their tacksmen and feuars, as part of their proper service. Each proprietor, too, had his storehouse or girnel, — a tall, narrow building, the strong-box of the time, which at the Martinmas of every year was filled from gable to gable with the grain-rents paid to him by his tenants, and the produce of his own farm. His surplus cattle found their way south, under charge of the drovers of the period; but it proved a more difficult matter to dispose to advantage of his surplus corn, mostly barley, until some one, more skilful in speculation than the others, originated the scheme of converting it into malt, and exporting it into England and Flanders. And to so great an extent was this trade carried on about the middle of the last century, that, in the town of Inverness, the English under Cumberland, in the long-remembered year of Culloden, found almost every second building a malt-barn.

The town of Cromarty suffered much at this period, in at least the severer winters, from scarcity of fuel. The mosses of the district were just exhausted; and as our proprietors had not yet betaken themselves to planting, there were no woods, except in some of the remoter recesses of the country, where the remains of some of the ancient forests were still suffered to survive. Peats were occasionally brought to the town in boats from the opposite side of the Frith; but the supply was precarious and insufficient, and the inhabitants were content at times to purchase the heath of the neighboring hill, in patches of an hundred square yards, and at times even to use for fuel the dried dung of their cattle. "A Cromarty fire" was a

term used over the country to designate a fire just gone
out; and some humorist of the period has represented a
Cromarty farmer, in a phrase which became proverbial, as
giving his daughter the key of the peat-chest, and bidding
her take out a peat and a half that she might put on a
good fire. It was the part of Mr. Forsyth to divest the
proverb of its edge, by opening up a trade with the northern ports of England, and introducing to the acquaintance
of his townspeople the "black stones" of Newcastle, which
have been used ever since as the staple fuel of the place.
To those who know how very dependent the inhabitants
are on this useful fossil, there seems an intangible sort of
strangeness in the fact that it is not yet a full century
since Mr. Forsyth's sloop entered the bay with the first
cargo of coal ever brought into it. One almost expects to
hear next of the man who first taught them to rear corn,
or to break in, from their state of original wildness, the
sheep and the cow.

Mr. Forsyth had entered upon his twenty-fourth year,
and had been rather more than six years engaged in business, when the rebellion broke out. There was an end to
all security for the time, and of course an end to trade; but
even the least busy found enough to employ them in the
perilous state of the country. Bands of marauders, the
very refuse of the Highlands, — for its better men had
gone to the south with the rebel army, — went prowling
over the Lowlands, making war with all alike, whether
Jacobites or Hanoverians, who were rich enough to be
robbed. Mr. Forsyth's sloop, in one of her coasting voyages of this period, when laden with a cargo of government
stores, was forced by stress of weather into the Dornoch
Frith, where she was seized by a party of Highlanders,
who held her for three days, in the name of the prince.

They did little else, however, than consume the master's sea-stock, and joke with the ship-boy, a young but very intelligent lad, who, for many years after, when Mr. Forsyth had himself become a ship-owner, was the master of his vessel. He was named Robertson; and as there were several of the Robertsons of Struan among the party, he was soon on very excellent terms with them. On one occasion, however, when rallying some of the Struans on their undertaking, he spoke of their leader as " the Pretender." " Beware, my boy," said an elderly Highlander, " and do not again repeat that word. There are men in the ship who, if they heard you, would perhaps take your life for it; for remember, we are not all Robertsons." Another party of the marauders took possession of the town of Cromarty for a short time, and dealt after the same manner with the stores of townspeople, whether of food or clothing, as the other had done with the stores of the shipmaster. But they were rather mischievous thieves than dangerous enemies; and except that they robbed a few of the women of their webs and yarn, and a few of the men of their shoes and bonnets, they left them no very grave cause to regret their visit.

It so chanced, however, that Mr. Forsyth was brought more seriously into contact with the rebels than any of his townsmen. The army of the prince, after the failure of the attempt on England, fell back on the Highlands; and a body of sixteen hundred king's troops, which had occupied Inverness, had retreated northwards, on their approach into the county of Sutherland. They had crossed by the Ferry of Cromarty in the boats of the town's fishermen; and these, on landing on the northern side, they had broken up to prevent the pursuit of the rebels. Scarcely had they been gone a day, however, when an agent of government, charged with a large sum of money, the arrears of their pay, arrived at Cromarty. He had reached Inverness only to find it in possession of the rebels; and after a per- ilous journey over a tract of country where almost every second man had declared for the prince, he found at Cromarty his further progress northward arrested by the Frith. In this dilemma, with the sea before him and the rebels behind, he applied to William Forsyth, and, communicating to him the nature and importance of his charge, solicited his assistance and advice. Fortunately Mr. Forsyth's boat had been on one of her coasting voyages at the time the king's troops had broken up the others, and her return was now hourly expected. Refreshments were hastily set before the half-exhausted agent; and then hurrying him to the feet of the precipices which guard the entrance of the Frith, Mr. Forsyth watched with him among the cliffs until the boat came sweeping round the nearer headland. The merchant hailed her in the passing, saw the agent and his charge safely embarked, and, after instructing the crew that they should proceed northwards, keeping as much as possible in the middle of the Frith until they had either come abreast of Sutherland or fallen in with a sloop-of-war then stationed near the mouth of the Spey, he returned home. In the middle of the following night he was roused by a party of rebels, who, after interrogating him strictly regarding the agent and his charge, and ransacking his house and shop, carried him with them a prisoner to Inverness. They soon found, however, that the treasure was irrecoverably beyond their reach, and that nothing was to be gained by the further detention of Mr. Forsyth. He was liberated, therefore, after a day and night's imprisonment, just as the rebels had learned that the army of Cumberland had reached the Spey; and he returned to Cromarty in time enough to witness from the neighboring hill the smoke of Culloden. In after-life he used sometimes to amuse his friends by a humorous detail of his sufferings in the cause of the king.

CHAPTER III.

So spake the Fiend; and with necessity
The tyrant's plea excused his devilish deeds.
MILTON.

By far the most important event of the last century to the people of Scotland was the rebellion of 1745. To use an illustration somewhat the worse for the wear, it resembled one of those violent hurricanes of the tropics which overturn trees and houses and strew the shores with wreck, but which more than compensate for the mischiefs they occasion by dissipating the deadly vapors of plague and pestilence, and restoring the community to health. Previous to its suppression the people possessed only a nominal freedom. The church for which they had done and suffered so much had now been re-established among them for nearly sixty years; and they were called, as elders, to take a part in its worship, and to deliberate in its courts. The laws, too, especially those passed since the union, recognized them as free. More depends, however, on the administration of law than on even the framing of it. The old hereditary jurisdictions still remained entire; and the meanest sheriff or baron of Scotland, after holding a court composed of only himself and his clerk, might consign the freest of his vassals to his dungeon, or hang him up at his castle-door. But the rebellion showed that more might be involved in this despotism of the chiefs and proprietors of the country than the oppression of individuals, and that the power which they possessed, through its means of calling out their vassals on their own behalf, to-day, might be employed in precipitating them against the government on the morrow. In the year 1747, therefore, hereditary jurisdictions were abolished all over Scotland, and the power of judging in matters of life and death restricted to judges appointed and paid by the crown. To decide on such matters of minor importance as are furnished by every locality, justices were appointed; and Mr. Forsyth's name was placed on the commission of the peace; a small matter, it may be thought, in the present day, but by no means an unimportant one ninety years ago, to either his townspeople or himself.

Justices of the peace had been instituted about a century and a half before. But the hereditary jurisdictions of the kingdom leaving them scarce any room for the exercise of their limited authority, the order fell into desuetude; and previous to its re-appointment, on the suppression of the rebellion, the administration of the law seems to have been divided, in at least the remoter provinces, between the hereditary judges and the church. The session records of Cromarty during the establishment of Episcopacy are still extant, and they curiously exemplify the class of offences specially cognizable by the ecclesiastical courts. They serve, too, to illustrate, in a manner sufficiently striking, the low tone of morals which obtained among the people. Our great-great-grandfathers were not a whit wiser nor better nor happier than ourselves; and our great-great-grandmothers seem to have had quite the same passions as their descendants, with rather less ability to control them. There were ladies of Cromarty, in the reign of Charles II., " maist horrible cussers," who accused one another of being " witches and witch getts, with all their folk afore them," for generations untold; gentlemen who had to " stand at the pillar " for unlading the boats of a smuggler at ten o'clock on a Sabbath night; " maist scandalous reprobates " who got drunk on Sundays, " and abused decent folk ganging till the kirk;" and " ill-conditioned royit loons who raisit disturbances and faught i' the scholars' loft" in the time of divine service. Husbands and their wives do penance in the church in this reign for their domestic quarrels; boys are whipped by the beadle for returning from a journey on the Sabbath; men are set in the *jougs* for charging elders of rather doubtful character with being drunk; boatmen are fined for crossing the ferry with passengers " during church time ; " and Presbyterian farmers are fined still more heavily for absenting themselves from church. Meanwhile, when the session was thus employed, the sheriff was amusing himself in cutting off men's ears, starving them in his dungeon, or hanging them up by the neck on his gallows. A few dark traditions, illustrative of the intolerable tyranny of the period, still survive ; and it is not yet more than nine years since a quantity of human bones, found in digging on an eminence a little above the harbor, which in the reign of Charles is said to have been a frequent scene of executions, served as an attestation to their general truth. It is said that the last person sentenced to death on the gallows-hill of Cromarty was a poor Highlander who had insulted the sheriff, and that, when in the act of mounting the ladder, he was pardoned at the request of the sheriff's lady.

There is much of interest in catching occasional glimpses

of a bygone state of society through the chance vistas of tradition. They serve to show us, in the expressive language of Scripture, " the rock whence we were hewn, and the hole of the pit whence we were dug." They serve, too, to dissipate those dreamy imaginings of the good and happiness of the past in which it seems an instinct of our nature to indulge, and enable us to correct the exaggerated estimates of that school of philosophy which sees most to admire in society the further it recedes from civilization. I am enabled to furnish the reader with one of these chance glimpses.

An old man who died about ten years ago, has told me that, when a boy, he was sent on one occasion to the manse of a neighboring parish to bring back the horse of an elderly gentleman of the place, a retired officer, who had gone to visit the minister with the intention of remaining with him for a few days. The officer was a silver-headed, erect old man, who had served as an ensign at the battle of Blenheim, and who, when he had retired on half pay about forty years after, was still a poor lieutenant. His riding days were well-nigh over; and the boy overtook him long ere he had reached the manse, and just as he was joined by Mr. Forsyth, who had come riding up by a cross-road, and then slackened bridle to keep him company. They entered into conversation. Mr. Forsyth was curious in his inquiries, the old gentleman communicative, and the boy a good listener. The old man spoke much of the allied army under Marlborough. By far the strongest man in it, he said, was a gentleman from Ross-shire, Munro of Newmore. He had seen him raise a piece of ordnance to his breast which Mackenzie of Fairburn, another proprietor of the same district, had succeeded in raising to his knee, but which no other man among more than eighty thousand could lift from off the ground. Newmore was considerably advanced in life at the time, — perhaps turned of fifty; for he had arrived at mature manhood about the middle of the reign of Charles II.; and, being a singularly daring as well as an immensely powerful man, he had signalized himself in early life in the feuds of his native district. Some of his lands bordered on those of Black Andrew Munro, the last Baron of Newtarbat, one of the most detestable wretches that ever abused the power of pit and gallows. But as at least their nominal politics were the same, and as the baron, though by far the less powerful man, was in perhaps a corresponding degree the more powerful proprietor, they had never come to an open rupture. Newmore, however, by venturing at times to screen some of the baron's vassals from his fury, — at times by taking part against him in the quarrel of some of the petty landholders, whom the tyrant never missed an occasion to oppress, — was by no means one of his favorites. All the labors of the baron's demesnes were of course performed by his vassals as part of their proper service. A late, wet harvest came on, and they were employed in cutting down his crops when their own lay rotting on the ground. It is natural that in such circumstances, they should have labored unwillingly. All their dread of the baron even, who remained among them in the fields, indulging in every caprice of a fierce and cruel temper, aggravated by irresponsible power, proved scarcely sufficient to keep them at work; and, to inspire them with deeper terror, an elderly female, who had been engaged during the night in reaping a little field of her own, and had come somewhat late in the morning, was actually stripped naked by the savage, and sent home again. In the evening he was visited by Munro of Newmore, who came, accompanied by only a single servant, to expostulate with him on an act so atrocious and disgraceful. Newmore was welcomed with a show of hospitality; the baron heard him patiently, and, calling for wine, they sat down and drank together. It was only a few weeks before, however, that one of the neighboring lairds, who had been treated with a similar show of kindness by the baron, had been stripped half naked at his table, when in a state of intoxication, and sent home with his legs tied under his horse's belly. Newmore, therefore, kept warily on his guard. He had left his horse ready saddled at the gate, and drank no more than he could master, which was quite as much, however, as would have overcome most men. One after one the baron's retainers began to drop into the room, each on a separate pretence; and, as the fifth entered, Newmore, who had seemed as if yielding to the influence of the liquor, affected to fall asleep. The retainers came clustering round him. Two seized him by the arms, and two more essayed to fasten him to his chair; when up he sprang, dashed his four assailants from him as if they had been boys of ten summers, and, raising the fifth from off the floor, hurled him headlong against the baron, who fell prostrate before the weight and momentum of so unusual a missile. In a minute after, Newmore had reached the gate, and, mounting his horse, rode away. The baron died during the night, a victim to apoplexy, induced, it is said, by the fierce and vindictive passions awakened on this occasion; and a Gaelic proverb, still current in the Highlands of Ross-shire, shows with what feelings his poor vassals must have regarded the event. Even to the present day, a Highlander will remark, when overborne by oppression, that "the same God still lives who killed Black Andrew Munro of Newtarbat."

CHAPTER IV.

Are we not brothers?
So man and man should be;
But clay and clay differs in dignity,
Whose dust is both alike.
SHAKSPEARE.

IT was no unimportant change to the people of Cromarty, which transferred them from the jurisdiction of
hereditary judges to the charge of a justice such as Mr.
Forsyth. For more than thirty years after his appointment he was the only acting magistrate in the place; and
such was the confidence of the townspeople in his judgment and integrity, that during all that time there was not
in a single instance an appeal from his decisions. In office
and character he seems to have closely resembled one of
the old landammans of the Swiss cantons. The age was a
rude one. Man is a fighting animal from very instinct, and
his second nature, custom, mightily improves the propensity; and nine tenths of the cases brought before Mr. Forsyth were cases of quarrels. With the more desperate
class of brawlers he could deal at times with proper sever-
ity. In most instances, however, a quarrel cost him a few
glasses of his best Hollands, and cost no one else anything.
The disputants were generally shown that neither of them
had been quite in the right; that one had been too hasty,
and the other too ready to take offence; that the first blow
had been decidedly a wrong, and the second unquestionably a misdemeanor; and then, after drinking one another's

health, they parted, wonderfully pleased with the decision of Mr. Forsyth, and resolved to have no more fighting till their next difference. He was much a favorite, too, with the townsboys. On one occasion, a party of them were brought before him on a charge of stealing green peas out of a field. Mr. Forsyth addressed them in his sternest manner. There was nothing, he said, which he so abhorred as the stealing of green peas; it was positively theft. He even questioned whether their parents did right in providing them with pockets. Were they again to be brought before him for a similar offence, they might depend, every one of them, on being locked up in the Tolbooth for a fortnight. Meanwhile, to keep them honest, he had resolved on sowing a field of peas himself, to which he would make them all heartily welcome. Accordingly, next season the field was sown, and there could not be a more exposed locality. Such, however, was the spirit of the little men of the place, all of whom had come to a perfect understanding of the decision, that not one pod of Mr. Forsyth's peas was carried away.

Before the close of 1752, when he completed his thirtieth year, Mr. Forsyth had succeeded in settling his two brothers in business, the one as a shopkeeper in Dingwall, the other as a merchant in Newcastle. Both gained for themselves, in their respective circles of acquaintance, the character of worthy and intelligent men; and their descendants still occupy respectable places in society. They had acquired their education and formed their habits of business under the eye of William; and now, in the autumn of this year, after he had thus honorably acquitted himself of the charge devolved upon him by the death of his father, he found himself at liberty to gratify an attachment formed several years before, by marrying a young lady of great worth and beauty, Miss Margaret Russell, a native of Morayshire. She was the daughter of Mr. Russell of Earlsmill, chamberlain to the Earl of Moray.

I shall indulge, with leave of the reader, in a brief view of the society to which Mr. Forsyth introduced his young wife. The feudal superior of the town, and proprietor of the neighboring lands, formed, of course, its natural and proper head. But the proprietor of this period, a Captain William Urquhart of Meldrum, had thrown himself so fairly beyond its pale, that on his own estate, and in his own village, there were none to court favor or friendship at his hands. He was a gentleman of good family, and had done gallant service to the Spaniards of South America against the buccaneers. He was, however, a stanch Catholic, and he had joined issue with the townspeople, headed by Mr. Forsyth, in a vexatious and expensive lawsuit, in which he had contended, as patron of the parish, for the privilege of presenting them with a useless, time-serving clergyman, a friend of his own. And so it was, that the zeal, so characteristic at the time of the people of Scotland, — a zeal for religion and the interests of the kirk, — had more than neutralized in the minds of the townspeople their scarcely less characteristic feelings of respect for the laird. His place, therefore, in the society of the town was occupied by persons of somewhat less influence than himself. There was a little circle of gentility in it, rich in blood but poor in fortune, which furnished a sort of reposing place for the old prejudices of the people in favor of high descent, of ladies who were "real ladies," and gentlemen with coats of arms. Whenever there was aught to be done or resisted, however, the whole looked up to Mr. Forsyth as their man of thought and action.

26*

At the head of this little community there was a dowager lady, the many virtues of whose character have found a warm encomiast in the judicious and sober-minded Doddridge. The good Lady Ardoch has been dead for the last seventy years, and yet her name is scarcely less familiar in the present day, to at least the more staid townspeople, than it was half a century ago. She was a daughter of the Fowlis family, one of the most ancient and honorable in Scotland; the ninth baron of Fowlis was slain fighting under the Bruce at Bannockburn. Her three brothers — men whose heroism of character and high religious principle have drawn forth the very opposite sympathies of Philip Doddridge and Sir Walter Scott — she had lost in the late rebellion. The eldest, Sir Robert Munro, the chief of his clan, died, with his youngest brother, at the battle of Falkirk; the third was shot about nine months after by an assassin, who had mistaken him for another by whom he had been deeply injured, and whose sorrow and remorse on discovering that he had unwittingly killed one of the best of his countrymen, are well described by Sir Walter in his "Tales of a Grandfather." Next in place to the good Lady Ardoch was the good Lady Scotsburn, — the widow of a Ross-shire proprietor, — who derived her descent from that Archibald, Marquis of Argyle, who acted so conspicuous a part during the troubles of the times of Charles I., and perished on the scaffold on the accession of Charles II. In excellence of character and the respect with which she was regarded, she very much resembled her contemporary Lady Ardoch. There were, besides, a family of ladies in the place, the daughters of Urquhart of Greenhill, a merchant of the times of the herring drove, and a scion of the old Urquharts of Cromarty, — and another much-respected family, the descendants of one of the old clergymen of the place, a Mr. Gordon. A few ladies more, of rather lower pretensions, whom the kindness of relatives in the south enabled to be hospitable and genteel, some on fifty pounds a year and some on thirty, and a few retired half-pay ensigns and lieutenants, one of whom, as we have seen, had fought in the wars of Marlborough, completed what was deemed the better society of the place. They had their occasional tea-parties, at which they all met; for Mr. Forsyth's trade with Holland had introduced, ere now, about eight teakettles into the place. They had, too, what was more characteristic of the age, their regular prayer-meetings; and at these — for Christianity, as the equalizing religion of free men, has ever been a breaker-down of casts and fictitious distinctions — the whole graver people of the town met. The parlor of Lady Ardoch was open once a fortnight to the poorer inhabitants of the place; and the good lady of thirty descents knelt in her silks at the same form with the good fisherwoman in her *curch* and *toy*.

It is not, however, by notices such as these that adequate notions of the changes which have taken place within the last century in the very framework of Scottish society can be conveyed to the reader. "The state of things is so fast changing in Scotland," says Dr. Johnson, in one of his letters to Boswell, " that a Scotchman can hardly realize the times of his grandfather."

Society was in a transition state at the time. The old adventitious bonds which had held it together in the past still existed; but opinion was employed in forging others of a more natural and less destructible character. Among these older ties, the pride of family — a pride which must have owed its general diffusion over Scotland to the clans and sects of the feudal system — held by far the most important place. There was scarce an individual, in at least the northern counties, whose claim to self-respect was not involved in the honor of some noble family. There ran through his humble genealogy some silver thread of high descent; some great-great-grandfather or grandmother connected him with the aristocracy of the country ; and it was his pride and honor, not that he was an independent man, but that he was in some sort a dependent gentleman. Hence that assumption of gentility on the part of the Scotch so often and so unmercifully lashed by the English satirists of the last century. Hence, too, in no small measure, the entire lack of political whiggism among the people. Under the influence of the feelings described, a great family might be compared to one of those fig-trees of the East which shoot their pendulous branches into the soil, and, deriving their stability from a thousand separate roots, defy the tornado and the hurricane. Be it remembered, too, that great families included in this way the whole of Scottish society, from its upper to its lower extreme.

Now, one of the objections to this kind of bond was the very unequal measure of justice and protection which it secured to the two grand classes which it united. It depressed the people in the one scale in the proportion in which it raised the aristocracy in the other. It did much for Juggernaut, but little for Juggernaut's worshippers. Though well-nigh as powerful at this time in the north of Scotland as it had been at any previous period, it was fast losing its influence in the southern districts. The persecutions of the former age had done much to lessen its efficacy, by setting the aristocracy, who, in most instances, held by the court politics and the court religion, in direct and hostile opposition to the people. And the growing commerce of the larger towns had done still more to lower it, by raising up from among the people that independent middle class, the creators and conservators of popular liberty, without which the population of any country can consist of only slaves and their masters. Even in the northern districts there were causes coming into operation which were eventually to annihilate the sentiment in at least its more mischievous tendencies. The state of matters in the town of Cromarty at this time, where a zealous Catholic was struggling to obtrude a minister of his own choosing on a Protestant people, furnishes no bad illustration of the nature of some of these, and of their mode of working. The absurd and mischievous law of patronage was doing in part for the Lowland districts of the north what the persecutions of the Stuarts had done for those of the south an age before, and what the large sheep-farm system, and the consequent ejection of the old occupants of the soil, has done for the Highlands an age after. And the first two were causes admirably suited to awaken a people who had derived their notions of rational liberty solely through the medium of religious belief. Their whiggism was a whiggism not of this world, but of the other; and as the privilege of preparing themselves for heaven in what they believed to be exclusively the right way was the only privilege they deemed worth while contending for, their first struggle for liberty was a struggle that their consciences might be free. The existence, too, of such men among them as Mr. Forsyth, men who had risen from their own level, had a twofold influence on the contest. They formed a sort of aristocracy of the people that served to divide the old feelings of respect which had been so long exclusively paid to the higher aristocracy; and they were enabled, through their superior intelligence, to give a weight and respectability to the popular party which it could not otherwise have possessed.

William Forsyth was singularly unfortunate in his marriage. Towards the close of the first year, when but learning fully to appreciate the comforts of a state to which so many of the better sentiments of our nature bear reference, and to estimate more completely the worth of his partner, she was suddenly removed from 'him by death, at a time when he looked with most hope for a further accession to his happiness. She died in childbed, and the fruit of her womb died with her. Her husband, during the long after-course of his life, never forgot her, and for eleven years posterior to the event he remained a widower for her sake.

CHAPTER V.

There is a certain lively gratitude which not only acquits us of the obligations we have received, but, by paying what we owe them, makes our friends indebted to us. — LA ROCHEFAUCAULD.

AMONG the school-fellows of William Forsyth there was a poor orphan boy named Hossack, a native of the landward part of the parish. He had lost both his parents when an infant, and owed his first knowledge of letters to the charity of the schoolmaster. His nearer relatives were all dead, and he was dependent for a precarious subsistence on the charity of a few distant connections, not a great deal richer than himself; among the rest, on a poor widow, a namesake of his own, who earned a scanty subsistence by

her wheel, but who had heart enough to impart a portion
of her little to the destitute scholar. The boy was studious
and thoughtful, and surpassed most of his school-fellows;
and, after passing with singular rapidity through the course
pursued at school, he succeeded in putting himself to college. The struggle was arduous and protracted. Sometimes he wrought as a common laborer, sometimes he ran
errands, sometimes he taught a school. He deemed no
honest employment too mean or too laborious, that for-
warded his scheme; and thus he at length passed through
college. His townspeople then lost sight of him for nearly
twenty years. It was understood, meanwhile, that some
nameless friend in the south had settled a comfortable an-
nuity on poor old widow Hossack, and that a Cromarty
sailor, who had been attacked by a dangerous illness when
at London, had owed his life to the gratuitous attentions
of a famous physician of the place, who had recognized
him as a townsman. No one, however, thought of the
poor scholar; and it was not until his carriage drove up
one day through the main street of the town, and stopped
at the door of William Forsyth, that he was identified with
"the great doctor" who had attended the seaman, and
with the benefactor of the poor widow. On entering the
cottage of the latter, he found her preparing gruel for supper, and was asked, with the anxiety of a gratitude that
would fain render him some return, "O, sir, will ye no tak'
brochan?" He is said to have been a truly excellent and
benevolent man, — the Abercromby of a former age; and
the ingenious and pious Moses Browne (a clergyman who,
to the disgrace of the English Church, was suffered to lan-
guish through life in a curacy of fifty pounds per annum)
thus addresses him in one of his larger poems, written im

mediately after the recovery of the author from a long and dangerous illness.

> The God I trust, with timeliest kind relief,
> Sent the beloved physician to my aid
> (Generous, humanest, affable of soul,
> Thee, dearest Hossack — oh, long known, long loved,
> Long proved; in oft-found tenderest watching cares,
> The Christian friend, the man of feeling heart);
> And in his skilful, heaven-directed hand,
> Put his best pleasing, only fee, my cure.
>
> SUNDAY THOUGHTS, PART IV.

To this gentleman Mr. Forsyth owed a very useful hint, which he did not fail to improve. They were walking together at low ebb along the extensive tract of beach which skirts, on the south, the entrance of the Frith of Cromarty. The shore everywhere in this tract presents a hard bottom of boulder stones and rolled pebbles, thickly covered with marine plants; and the doctor remarked that the brown tangled forests before them might be profitably employed in the manufacture of kelp, and, at the request of Mr. Forsyth, described the process. To the enterprising and vigorous-minded merchant the remark served to throw open a new field of exertion. He immediately engaged in the kelp trade; and, for more than forty years after, it enabled him to employ from ten to twelve persons during the summer and autumn of each year, and proved remunerative to himself.

There is a story of two of Mr. Forsyth's kelp-burners, which, as it forms a rather curious illustration of some of the wilder beliefs of the period, I shall venture on introducing to the reader. The Sutors of Cromarty were known all over the country as resorts of the hawk, the eagle, and the raven, and of all the other builders among dizzy and

inaccessible cliffs; and a gentleman of Moray, a sportsman
of the old school, having applied to a friend in this part of
the country to procure for him a pair of young hawks, of a
species prized by the falconer, Tam Polson, an unsettled,
eccentric being, remarkable chiefly for his practical jokes,
and his constant companion Jock Watson, a person of
nearly similar character, were entrusted with the commission, and a promise of five pounds Scots, no inconsiderable
sum in those days, held out to them as the reward of their
success in the execution of it. They soon discovered a
nest, but it was perched near the top of a lofty cliff, inaccessible to the climber; and there was a serious objection
against descending to it by means of a rope, seeing that
the rope could not be held securely by fewer than three or
four persons, who would naturally claim a share of the reward. It was suggested, however, by Tam, that by fasten-
ing the rope to a stake, even one person might prove sufficient to manage it when the other warped himself down;
and so, providing themselves with the stay-rope of one of
their boats, and the tether-stake of one of their cattle, —
for, like most of the townspeople, they were both boatmen
and croft-renters, — they set out for the cliff early on a
Monday morning, ere the other members of the kelp party
with whom they wrought were astir. The stake was driven
into the stiff diluvial clay on the summit of the cliff; and
Tam's companion, who was the lighter man of the two,
cautiously creeping to the edge, swung himself over, and
began to descend; but, on reaching the end of the stay-
rope, he found he was still a few feet short of the nest;
and, anxious only to secure the birds, he called on his companion to raise the stake, and fix it a little nearer the brink.
The stake was accordingly raised; but the strength of one
man being insufficient to hold it on such broken ground,

and far less than sufficient to fasten it down as before, Tam, in spite of his exertions, staggered step after step towards the edge of the precipice. " O Jock! O Jock! O Jock !" he exclaimed, straining meanwhile every nerve in an agony of exertion, " ye'll be o'er like a pock o' weet fish." " Gae a wee bittie down yet," answered the other. "Down! down! deil gae down wi' ye, for I can gae nae further," rejoined Tam ; and, throwing off the rope, — for he now stood on the uttermost brink, — a loud scream, and, after a fearful pause of half a minute, a deep hollow sound from the bottom told all the rest. " Willawins for poor Jock Watson," exclaimed Tam Polson; "win the gude five pounds wha like, they'll no be won, it seems, by either him or me."

The party of kelp-burners were proceeding this morning to the scene of their labors, through a heavy fog ; and as they reached the furnace one by one, they sat down fronting it, to rest them after their walk, and wait the coming up of the others. Tam Polson had already taken his place among the rest; and there were but two amissing, the man whose dead body now lay at the foot of the cliff, and a serious elderly person, one of his neighbors, whose company he sometimes courted. At length they were both seen as if issuing out of a dense cloud of mist.

" Yonder they come," said one of the kelp-burners ; " but gudesake ! only look how little Jock Watson looms through the fog as mickle's a giant."

" Jock Watson ! " exclaimed Polson, starting to his feet, and raising his hands to his eyes, with a wild expression of bewilderment and terror, "aye, murdered Jock Watson, as sure as death ! "

The figure shrank into the mist as he spoke, and the old man was seen approaching alone.

"What hae ye done to Jock Watson, Donald?" was the eager query put to him, on his coming up, by half a dozen voices at once.

"Ask Tam Polson there," said the old man. "I tapped at Jock's window as I passed, and found he had set out wi' Tam half an hour afore daybreak."

"Oh," said Tam, "it was poor murdered Jock Watson's ghaist we saw; it was Jock's ghaist." And so he divulged the whole story.

The British Linen Company had been established in Edinburgh about the year 1746, chiefly with a view, as the name implies, of forwarding the interests of the linen trade; and in a few years after, Mr. Forsyth, whose character as an active and successful man of business was beginning to be appreciated in more than the north of Scotland, was chosen as the Company's agent for that extensive tract of country which intervenes between the Pentland Frith and the Frith of Beauly. The linen trade was better suited at this time to the state of the country and the previously-acquired habits of the people than any other could have been. All the linens worn in Scotland, with the exception, perhaps, of some French cambrics, were of home manufacture. Every female was skilled in spinning, and every little hamlet had its weaver, who, if less a master of his profession than some of the weavers of our manufacturing towns in the present day, was as decidedly superior to our provincial weavers. A knowledge of what may be termed the higher departments of the craft was spread more equally over the country than now; and, as is always the case before the minuter subdivisions of labor take place, if less could be produced by the trade as a body, the average ability ranked higher in individuals. In establishing the linen trade, therefore, as the skill essential to carrying it on already existed, it was but necessary that motives should be held out sufficiently powerful to awaken the industry of the people; and these were furnished by Mr. Forsyth, in the form of remunerative prices for their labor. The town of Cromarty, from its central situation and excellent harbor, was chosen as the depot of the establishment. The flax was brought in vessels from Holland, prepared for the spinners in Cromarty, and then distributed by the boats of Mr. Forsyth along the shores of the Friths of Dornoch, Dingwall, and Beauly, and northwards as far as Wick and Thurso. At the commencement of the trade the distaff and spindle was in extensive use all over the north of Scotland, and the spinning-wheel only partially introduced into some of the towns; but the more primitive implement was comparatively slow and inefficient, and Mr. Forsyth, the more effectually to supplant it by the better machine, made it an express condition with all whom he employed for a second year, that at least one wheel should be introduced into every family. He, besides, hired skilful spinners to go about the country teaching its use; and so effectual were his measures that, in about ten years after the commencement of the trade, the distaff and spindle had almost entirely disappeared. There are parts of the remote Highlands, however, in which it is still in use; and the writer, when residing in a wild district of western Ross, which borders on the Atlantic, has repeatedly seen the Highland women, as they passed to and from the shore, at once bending under the weight of the creel with which they manured their lands, and ceaselessly twirling the spindle as it hung beneath the staff.

CHAPTER VI.

The less we know as to things that can be done, the less sceptical are we as to things that cannot. — COLTON.

ABOUT five years after the establishment of the linen trade, Mr. Forsyth became a shipowner; and as he had made it a rule never to provide himself from other countries with what could be produced by the workmen of his own, his first vessel, a fine large sloop, was built at Fortrose. There had been ship-builders established at Cromarty at a much earlier period. Among the designations attached to names, which we find in the older records of the place, there is none of more frequent occurrence than that of ship-carpenter. There are curious stories, too, connected with ship-launches, which serve to mark the remote period at which these must have occurred. An occasion of this kind, at a time when the knowledge of mechanics was more imperfect and much less general than at present, was always one of great uncertainty. Accidents were continually occurring; and superstition found room to mingle her mysterious horrors with the doubts and fears with which it was naturally attended. Witches and the Evil Eye were peculiarly dreaded by the carpenter on the day of a launch; and it is said of one of the early Cromarty launches that, the vessel having stopped short in the middle of her course, the master-carpenter was so irritated with a reputed witch among the spectators, to whom he attributed

27*

the accident, that he threw her down and broke her arm.
A single anecdote, though of a lighter cast, preserves the
recollection of Mr. Forsyth's ship-building at Fortrose.
The vessel was nearly finished-; and a half-witted knave,
named Tam Reid, who had the knack of tricking everybody, — even himself at times, — was despatched by Mr.
Forsyth with a bottle of turpentine to the painters. Tam,
however, who had never more than heard of wine, and
who seems to have taken it for granted that the bottle he
carried contained nothing worse, contrived to drink the
better half of it by the way, and was drugged almost to
death for his pains. When afterwards humorously charged
by Mr. Forsyth with breach of trust, and urged to confess,
truly, whether he had actually drunk the whole of the
missing turpentine, he is said to have replied, in great
wrath, that he " widna gie a'e glass o' whiskey for a' the
wine i' the warld."

Mr. Forsyth's vessels were at first employed almost exclusively in the Dutch trade; but the commerce of the
country gradually shifted its old channels, and in his latter
days they were engaged mostly in trading between the
north of Scotland and the ports of Leith, London, and
Newcastle. There are curious traditionary anecdotes of
his sailors still afloat among the people, which illustrate
the credulous and imaginative character of the age. Stories of this class may be regarded as the fossils of history;
they show the nature and place of the formation in which
they occur. The Scotch sailors of ninety years ago were
in many respects a very different sort of persons from the
sailors of the present day. They formed one of the most
religious classes of the community. There were even found-
ers of sects among them. The too famous John Gibb was
a sailor of Borrowstounness; and the worthy Scotchman

who remarked to Peter Walker that "the ill of Scotland he found everywhere, but the good of Scotland nowhere save at home," was a sailor too. Mr. Forsyth was much attached to the seamen of this old and venerable class, and a last remnant of them might be found in his vessels when they had become extinct everywhere else. On the breaking out of the revolutionary war, his sloop, the Elizabeth, was boarded when lying at anchor in one of our Highland lochs by a press-gang from a king's vessel, and the crew, who chanced to be all under hatches at the time, were summoned on deck. First appeared the ancient weather-beaten master, a person in his grand climacteric; then came Saunders M'Iver, the mate, a man who had twice sailed round the world about half a century before; then came decent Thomas Grant, who had been an elder of the kirk for more than forty years; and last of all came old, gray-headed Robert Hossack, a still older man than any of the others. "Good heavens!" exclaimed the officer who commanded the party, "here, lads, are the four sailors who manned the ark alive still." I need hardly add, that on this occasion he left all her crew to the Elizabeth.

Some of the stories of Mr. Forsyth's sailors may serve to enliven my narrative. The master of the Elizabeth, in one of his Dutch voyages, when on the eve of sailing for Scotland, had gone into a tavern with the merchant from whom he had purchased his cargo, and was shown by mistake into a room in which there lay an old woman ill of a malignant fever. The woman regarded him with a long and ghastly stare, which haunted him all the evening after; and during the night he was seized by the fever. He sent for a physician of the place. His vessel was bound for sea he said, and the crew would be wholly unable to bring her home without him. Had he no medicine potent enough to arrest the progress of the disease for about a week? The physician replied .in the affirmative, and prescribed with apparent confidence. The master quitted his bed on the strength of the prescription, and the vessel sailed for Cromarty. A storm arose, and there was not a' seaman aboard who outwrought or outwatched the master. He began to droop, however, as the weather moderated, and his strength had so failed him on reaching Cromarty, that his sailors had to carry him home in a litter. The fever had returned, and more than six weeks elapsed after his arrival ere he had so far recovered from it as to be able to leave his bed. The story is, I believe, strictly true; but in accounting, in the present day, for the main fact which it supplies, we would perhaps be inclined to attribute less than our fathers did to the skill of the physician, and more to the force of imagination and to those invigorating énergies which a sense of danger awakens.

Old Saunders M'Iver, the mate of the Elizabeth, was one of the most devout and excellent men of the place. There was in some degree, too, a sort of poetical interest attached to him, from the dangers which he had encountered and the strange sights which he had seen. He had seen smoke and flame bursting out of the sea in the far Pacific, and had twice visited those remote parts of the world which lie directly under our feet, — a fact which all his townsmen credited, for Saunders himself had said it, but which few of them could understand. In one of his long voyages, the crew with whom he sailed were massacred by some of the wild natives of the Indian Archipelago, and he alone escaped by secreting himself in the rigging, and from thence slipping unobserved into one of the boats, and then cutting her loose. But he was furnished with neither oars nor sail; and it was not until he had been tossed at the mercy of the tides and winds of the Indian Ocean for nearly a week, that he was at length picked up by a European vessel. So powerfully was he impressed on this occasion, that it is said he was never after seen to smile. He was a grave and somewhat hard-favored man, powerful in bone and muscle even after he had considerably turned his sixtieth year, and much respected for his inflexible integrity and the depth of his religious feelings. Both Saunders and his wife—a person of equal worth with himself—were especial favorites with Mr. Porteous of Kilmuir, — a minister of the same class with the Pedens, Renwicks, and Cargills of a former age, — and on one occasion, when the sacrament was held in his parish, and Saunders was absent on one of his Dutch voyages, Mrs. M'Iver was an inmate of the manse. A tremendous storm burst out in the night-time; and the poor woman lay awake, listening in utter terror to the fearful roarings of the wind, as it howled in the chimneys and shook the casements and the door. At length, when she could lie still no longer, she arose, and, creeping along the passage to the door of the minister's chamber, "O Mr. Porteous!" she said, "Mr. Porteous, do ye no hear that, and poor Saunders on his way back fra Holland! Oh, rise, rise, and ask the strong help o' your Master!" The minister accordingly rose, and entered his closet. The Elizabeth, at this critical moment, was driving onwards, through the spray and darkness, along the northern shore of the Moray Frith. The fearful skerries of Shandwick, where so many gallant vessels have perished, were close at hand, and the increasing roll of the sea showed the gradual shallowing of the water. M'Iver and his old townsman Robert Hossack stood together at the binnacle. An immense wave came rolling behind, and they had but barely time to clutch to the nearest hold when it broke over them half-mast high, sweeping spars, bulwarks, cordage, all before it in its course. It passed, but the vessel rose not. Her deck remained buried in a sheet of foam, and she seemed settling down by the head. There was a frightful pause. First, however, the bowsprit and the beams of the windlass began to emerge; next the forecastle, — the vessel seemed as if shaking herself from the load, — and then the whole deck appeared, as she went tilting over the next wave. "There are still more mercies in store for us," said M'Iver, addressing his companion; "she floats still." "O Saunders! Saunders!" exclaimed Robert, "there was surely some God's soul at work for us, or she would never have cowed yon."

There is a somewhat similar story told of two of Mr. Forsyth's boatmen.' They were brothers, and of a much lighter character than Saunders and his companion; but their mother, who was old and bed-ridden, was a person of singular piety. They had left her, when setting out on one of their Caithness voyages, in so low a state that they could scarce entertain any hope of again seeing her in life. On their return they were wrecked on the rocky coast of Tarbat, and it was with much difficulty that they succeeded in saving their lives. "O brother, lad!" said the one to the other, on reaching the shore, "our poor old mither is gone at last, or yon widna have happened us. We maun just be learning to pray for ourselves." And the inference, says the story, was correct; for the good old woman had died about half an hour before the accident occurred.

CHAPTER VII.

Soft as the memory of buried love,
Pure as the prayer which childhood wafts above,
Was she.

BYRON.

UNMARRIED men of warm affections and social habits begin often, after turning their fortieth year, to feel themselves too much alone in the world for happiness, and to look forward with more of fear than of desire to a solitary and friendless old age. William Forsyth, a man of the kindliest feelings, on completing his forty-first year was still a widower. His mother had declined into the vale of life; his two brothers had settled down, as has been already related, in distant parts of the country. There were occasional gaps, too, occurring in the circle in which he moved. Disease, decay, and accident kept up the continual draught of death; friends and familiar faces were dropping away and disappearing; and he began to find that he was growing too solitary for his own peace. The wound, however, which his affections had sustained, rather more than ten years before, had been gradually closing under the softening influence of time. The warmth of his affections and the placidity of his temper fitted him in a peculiar manner for domestic happiness; and it was his great good fortune to meet, about this period, with a lady through whom, all unwittingly on her own part, he was taught to regard himself as no longer solitary in the

present, nor devoid of hope for the future. He was happy
in his attachment, and early in 1764 she became his wife.

Miss Elizabeth Grant, daughter of the Rev. Patrick
Grant of Duthel, in Strathspey, and of Isabella Kerr of
Ruthven Manse, was born in Duthel in the year 1742, and
removed to Nigg, in Ross-shire, about twelve years after,
on the induction of her father into that parish. Her character was as little a common one as that of Mr. Forsyth
himself. Seldom indeed does nature produce a finer intellect, never a warmer or more compassionate heart. It
is rarely that the female mind educates itself. The genius
of the sex is rather fine than robust; it partakes rather of
the delicacy of the myrtle than the strength of the oak,
and care and culture seem essential to its full development. There have been instances, however, though rare,
of women working their almost unassisted way from the
lower to the higher levels of intelligence; and the history
of this lady, had she devoted her time more to the regis-
tration of her thoughts than to the duties of her station,
would have furnished one of these. She was, in the best
sense of the term, an original thinker; one of the few whose
innate vigor of mind carry them in search of truth beyond
the barriers of the conventional modes of thought. But
strong good sense, rising almost to the dignity of philosophy, a lively imagination, and a just and delicate taste,
united to very extensive knowledge and nice discernment,
though these rendered her conversation the delight of the
circle in which she moved, formed but the subordinate
excellences of her character. She was one of the truly
good, the friend of her species and of her God. A diary,
found among her papers after her death, and now in the
possession of her friends, shows that the transcript of duty
which her life afforded was carefully collated every day

with the perfect copy with which Revelation supplied her, and her every thought, word, and action, laid open to the eye of Omniscience. In the expressive language of Scripture, she was one of those " who walk with God." There was nought, however, of harshness or austerity in her religion. It formed the graceful and appropriate garb of a tender-hearted and beautiful woman of engaging manners and high talent. With this lady Mr. Forsyth enjoyed all of good and happiness that the married state can afford, for the long period of thirty-six years.

His life was a busy one; his very pleasures were all of the active kind; and yet, notwithstanding his numerous engagements, it was remarked that there were few men who contrived to find more spare time than Mr. Forsyth, or who could devote half a day more readily to the service of a friend or neighbor. But his leisure hours were hardly and fairly earned. He rose regularly, winter and summer, between five and six o'clock, lighted his office-fire, if the weather was cold, wrote out his letters for the day, and brought up his books to the latest period. Ere the family was summoned to breakfast he was generally well nigh the conclusion of his mercantile labors. The family then met for morning prayer; for, like the Cotter in Burns, Mr. Forsyth was the priest of his household, and led in their devotions morning and evening. An hour or two more spent in his office set him free for the remainder of the day from labor on his own behalf; the rest he devoted to the good of others and his own amusement. Once a month he held a regular Justice of Peace Court, in which he was occasionally assisted by some of the neighboring proprietors, whose names, like his own, were on the commission of the peace. But the age was a rude one; and differences were so frequently occurring among the people

that there were few days in which his time was not occupied from twelve till two in his honored capacity of
peace-maker for the place. The evening was more his own.
Sometimes he superintended the lading or unlading of his
vessels; sometimes he walked out into the country to visit
his humble friends in the landward part of the parish, and
see how they were getting on with their spinning. There
was not a good old man or woman within six miles of Cromarty, however depressed by poverty, that Mr. Forsyth
did not reckon among the number of his acquaintance.

Of all his humble friends, however, one of the most respected, and most frequently visited by him, was a pious,
though somewhat eccentric, old woman, who lived all
alone in a little solitary cottage beside the sea, rather more
than two miles to the west of the town, and who was
known to the people of the place as Meggie o' the Shore.
Meggie was one of the truly excellent, — a person in whom
the Durhams and Rutherfords of a former age would have
delighted. There was no doubt somewhat of harshness
in her opinions, and of credulity in her beliefs; but never
were there opinions or beliefs more conscientiously held;
and the general benevolence of her disposition served wonderfully to soften in practice all her theoretical asperities.
She was ailing and poor; and as she was advancing in
years, and her health became more broken, her little earnings — for she was one of Mr. Forsyth's spinners — were
still growing less. Meggie, however, had "come of decent
people," though their heads had all been laid low in the
churchyard long ere now; and though she was by far too
orthodox to believe, with the son of Sirach, that it "is
better to die than to beg," it was not a thing to be thought
of that she should do dishonor to the memory of the
departed by owing a single meal to the charity of the

parish. She toiled on, therefore, as she best could, content with the merest pittance, and complained to no one. Mr. Forsyth, who thoroughly understood the character, and appreciated its value, and who knew, withal, how wretchedly inadequate Meggie's earnings were to her support, contrived on one occasion to visit her early, and to stay late, in the hope of being invited to eat with her; for in her more prosperous days there were few of her visitors suffered to leave her cottage until, as she herself used to express it, they had first broken bread. At this time, however, there was no sign of the expected invitation; and it was not until Mr. Forsyth had at length risen to come away that Meggie asked him hesitatingly whether he would "no tak' some refreshment afore he went?"

"I have just been waiting to say yes," said the merchant, sitting down again. Meggie placed before him a half-cake of barley-bread and a jug of water.

"It was the feast of the promise," she said; "'thy bread shall be given thee, and thy water shall be sure.'"

The merchant saw that, in her effort to be hospitable, she had exhausted her larder; and, without remarking that the portion was rather a scanty one, partook with apparent relish of his share of the half-cake. But he took especial care from that time forward till the death of Meggie, which did not take place till about eight years after, that her feasts should not be so barely and literally feasts of the promise.

Mr. Forsyth, in the midst of his numerous engagements, found leisure for a few days every year to visit his relatives in Moray. The family of his paternal grandfather, a farmer of Elginshire, had been a numerous one; and he had an uncle settled in Elgin as a merchant and general dealer who was not a great many years older than himself. For the judgment of this gentleman Mr. Forsyth entertained the highest respect, and he rarely engaged in any new undertaking without first consulting him. Indeed, a general massiveness of intellect and force of character seemed characteristic of the family, and these qualities the well-known work of this gentleman's son, " Forsyth's Italy," serves happily to illustrate. There is perhaps no book of travels in the language in which the thoughts lie so closely, or in the perusal of which the reader, after running over the first few chapters, gives himself up so entirely to the judgment of the author. The work is now in its fourth edition; and a biographical me· moir of the writer, appended to it by his younger brother, Mr. Isaac Forsyth of Elgin, shows how well and pleasingly the latter gentleman could have written had he employed in literature those talents which have rendered him, like his father and his cousin, eminently successful in business.

When on one of his yearly visits, Mr. Forsyth inquired of his uncle whether he could not point out to him, among his juvenile acquaintance in Elgin, some steady young lad, of good parts, whom he might engage as an assistant in his business at Cromarty. Its more mechanical details, he said, were such as he himself could perhaps easily master; but then, occupying his time as they did, without employing his mind, they formed a sort of drudgery of the profession, for which he thought it might prove in the end a piece of economy to pay. His uncle acquiesced in the remark, and recommended to his notice an ingenious young lad who had just left school, after distinguishing himself by his attainments as a scholar, and who was now living unemployed with some friends at Elgin. The lad was accordingly introduced to Mr. Forsyth, who was much pleased with his appearance and the simple ingenuousness of his manners, and on his return he brought him with him to Cromarty.

Charles Grant, for so the young man was called, soon became much a favorite with Mr. Forsyth and his family, and was treated by them rather as a son than a dependant. He had a taste for reading, and Mr. Forsyth furnished him with books. He introduced him, too, to all his more intelligent and more influential friends, and was alike liberal in assisting him, as the case chanced to require, with his purse and his advice. The young man proved himself eminently worthy of the kindness he received. He possessed a mind singularly well balanced in all its faculties, moral and intellectual. He added great quickness to great perseverance; much warmth and kindliness of feeling to an unyielding rectitude of principle; and strong good sense to the poetical temperament. He remained with Mr. Forsyth for about five years, and then parted from him for some better appointment in London, which he owed to his friendship. It would be no unprofitable or uninteresting task to trace his after course; but the outlines of his history are already known to most of my readers. His extensive knowledge and very superior talents rendered his services eminently useful; his known integrity procured him respect and confidence; the goodness of his disposition endeared him to an extensive and ever-widening circle of friends. He rose gradually through a series of employments, each, in progression, more important and honorable than the one which had preceded it. He filled for many years the chair of the honorable East India Company's Court of Directors, and represented the county of Inverness in several successive parliaments; and of two of his sons, one has had the dignity of knighthood conferred upon him for his public services, and the other occupies an honorable, because well-earned, place among the British peerage. Mr. Grant continued through life to cherish the memory of his benefactor, and to show even in old age the most marked and assiduous attentions to the surviving members of his family. He procured writerships for two of his sons, John and Patrick Forsyth; and, at a time when his acquaintance extended over all the greater merchants of Europe, he used to speak of him as a man whose judgment and probity, joined to his singularly liberal views and truly generous sentiments, would have conferred honor on the magisterial chair of the first commercial city of the world. It was when residing in the family of William Forsyth that Mr. Grant first received those serious impressions of the vital importance of religion which so influenced his conduct through life, and to which he is said to have given expression, when on the verge of another world, in one of the finest hymns in the language. Need I apologize to the reader for introducing it here?

HYMN.

With years oppressed, with sorrows worn,
Dejected, harassed, sick, forlorn,
   To thee, O God! I pray;
To thee these withered hands arise;
To thee I lift these failing eyes; —
   Oh, cast me not away.

Thy mercy heard my infant prayer;
Thy love, with all a mother's care,
   Sustained my childish days;
Thy goodness watched my ripening youth,
And formed my soul to love thy truth,
   And filled my heart with praise.

O! Saviour, has thy grace declined?
Can years affect the Eternal Mind,
   Or time its love decay?
A thousand ages pass thy sight,
And all their long and weary flight
   Is gone like yesterday.

Then, even in age and grief, thy name
Shall still my languid heart inflame,
   And bow my faltering knee.
O, yet this bosom feels the fire,
This trembling hand and drooping lyre
   Have yet a strain for thee.

Yes, broken, tuneless, still, O Lord!
This voice, transported, shall record
   Thy bounty, tried so long;
Till, sinking slow, with calm decay,
Its feeble murmurs melt away
   Into seraphic song.

CHAPTER VIII.

Good is no good but if it be spend;
God giveth good for none other end.
                SPENSER.

THE year 1772 was a highly important one to the people
of Cromarty. By far the greater part of the parish is occupied by one large and very valuable property, which,
after remaining in the possession of one family for nearly
a thousand years, had passed in little more than a century
through a full half-dozen. It was purchased in the latter

part of this year by George Ross, a native of Ross-shire, who had realized an immense fortune in England as an army agent. He was one of those benefactors of the species who can sow liberally in the hope of a late harvest for others to reap; and the townspeople, even the poorest and least active, were soon made to see that they had got a neighbor who would suffer them to be idle or wretched no longer.

He found in William Forsyth a man after his own heart; one with whom to concert and advise, and who entered warmly into all his well-laid schemes for awakening the energies and developing the yet untried resources of the country. The people seemed more than half asleep around them. The mechanic spent well-nigh two thirds of his time in catching fish and cultivating his little croft; the farmer raised from his shapeless party-colored patches, of an acre or two apiece, the same sort of half-crops that had satisfied his grandfather. The only trade in the country was originated and carried on by Mr. Forsyth, and its only manufacture the linen one which he superintended. In this state of things, it was the part assigned to himself by the benevolent and patriotic Agent, now turned of seventy, to revolutionize and give a new spirit to the whole; and such was his untiring zeal and statesman-like sagacity that he fully succeeded.

One of his first gifts to the place was a large and commodious pier for the accommodation of trading vessels. He then built an extensive brewery, partly with the view to check the trade in smuggling, which prevailed at this time in the north of Scotland to an enormous extent, and partly to open a new market to the farmers for the staple grain of the country. The project succeeded; and the Agent's excellent ale supplanted in no small measure, from Aberdeen to John O'Groat's, the gins and brandies of the Continent. He then established a hempen manufactory, which has ever since employed about two hundred people within its walls, and fully twice that number without; and set on foot a trade in pork, which has paid the rents of half the widows' cottages in the country for the last forty years, and is still carried on by the traders of the place to an extent of from fifteen to twenty thousand pounds annually. He established a nail and spade manufactory; brought women from England to instruct the young girls in the art of working lace; provided houses for the poor; presented the town with a neat, substantial building, the upper part of which serves as a council-room, and the lower as a prison; and built for the accommodation of the poor Highlanders, who came thronging into the town to work on his lands or in his manufactories, a handsome Gaelic chapel. He set himself, too, to initiate his tenantry in the art of rearing wheat; and finding them wofully unwilling to become wiser on the subject, he tried the force of example, by taking an extensive farm under his own management, and conducting it on the most approved principles of modern agriculture. It is truly wonderful how much may be effected by the well-directed energies of one benevolent and vigorous mind. It is to individuals, not masses, that the species owe their advancement in the scale of civilization and rationality. George Ross was a man far advanced in life when he purchased the lands of Cromarty, and he held them for but fourteen years, for he died in 1786, at the great age of eighty-five; and yet in these few years, which might be regarded as but the fag-end of a busy life, he did more for the north of Scotland than had been accomplished by all its other proprietors put together since the death of President Forbes.

Mr. Forsyth was ever ready to second the benevolent and well-laid schemes of the Agent. He purchased shares in his hempen manufactory, — for Mr. Ross, the more widely to extend its interests, had organized a company to carry it on — and took a fine snug farm in the neighborhood of the town into his own hands, to put into practice all he had learned of the new system of farming. Agriculture was decidedly one of the most interesting studies of the period. It was still a field of experiment and discovery; new principles, little dreamed of by our ancestors, were elicited every year; and though there were hundreds of intelligent minds busy in exploring it, much remained a sort of *terra incognita* notwithstanding. Mr. Forsyth soon became a zealous and successful farmer, and spent nearly as much of his evenings in his fields as he did of his mornings in his counting-house. The farmers around him were wedded to their old prejudices, but the merchant had nothing to unlearn; and though his neighbors smiled at first to see him rearing green crops of comparatively little value from lands for which he paid a high rent, or, more inexplicable still, paying the rent and suffering the lands to lie fallow, they could not avoid being convinced at last that he was actually raising more corn than any of themselves. Though essentially a practical man, and singularly sober and judicious in all his enterprises, his theoretical speculations were frequently of a bolder character; and he had delighted in reasoning on the causes of the various phenomena with which his new study presented him. The exhaustive properties of some kinds of crop; the restorative qualities of others; the mysteries of the vegetative pabulum; its well-marked distinctness from the soil which contains it; how, after one variety of grain has appropriated its proper nourishment, and then languished for lack of sustenance, another variety continues to draw its food from the same tract, and after that, perhaps, yet another variety more ; how, at length, the productive matter is so exhausted that all is barrenness, until, after the lapse of years, it is found to have accumulated again, — all these, with the other mysteries of vegetation, furnished him with interesting subjects of thought and inquiry. One of the best and largest of his fields was situated on the edge of that extensive tract of table-land which rises immediately above the town, and commands so pleasing a prospect of the bay and the opposite shore ; and from time immemorial the footpath which skirts its lower edge, and overlooks the sea, had been a favorite promenade of the inhabitants. What, however, was merely a footpath in the early part of each season, grew broad enough for a carriage-road before autumn ; and much of Mr. Forsyth's best braird was trampled down and destroyed every year. His ploughman would fain have excluded the walkers, and hinted at the various uses of traps and spring-guns ; at any rate, he said, he was determined to *build up the slap ;* but the merchant, though he commended his zeal, negatived the proposal ; and so the *slap* was suffered to remain unbuilt. On sometimes meeting with parties of the more juvenile saunterers, he has gravely cautioned them to avoid his ploughman Donald M'Candie. Donald, he would say, was a cross-grained old man, as they all knew, and might both frighten them and hurt himself in running after them. Mr. Forsyth retained the farm until his death ; and it shows in some little degree the estimation in which he was held by the people, that his largest field, though it has repeatedly changed its tenant since then, still retains the name of Mr. Forsyth's Park.

Shortly after he had engaged with the farm, Mr. Forsyth built for himself a neat and very commodious house, which, at the time of its erection, was beyond comparison the best in the place, and planted a large and very fine garden. Both serve to show how completely this merchant of the eighteenth century had anticipated the improvements of the nineteenth. There are not loftier nor better-proportioned rooms in the place, larger windows, nor easier stairs; and his garden is such a one as would satisfy an Englishman of the present day. These are perhaps but little matters. They serve, however, to show the taste and judgment of the man.

CHAPTER IX.

'Tis not that rural sports alone invite,
But all the grateful country breathes delight;
Here blooming Health exerts her gentle reign,
And strings the sinews of the industrious swain.

GAY.

I AM not of opinion that the people of the north of Scotland are less happy in the present age than in the age or two which immediately preceded it; but I am certain they are not half so merry. We may not have less to amuse us than our fathers had; but our amusements somehow seem less hearty, and are a great deal less noisy, and, instead of interesting the entire community, are confined to insulated parties and single individuals. A whole hecatomb of wild games have been sacrificed to the genius of trade and the wars of the French Revolution. The age of holidays is clean gone by ; the practical joke has been extinct for the last fifty years ; and we have to smuggle the much amusement which we still contrive to elicit from out the eccentricities of our neighbors, as secretly as if it were the subject of a tax.

In the early and more active days of Mr. Forsyth, the national and manly exercise of golf was the favorite amusement of the gentlemen ; and Cromarty, whose links furnished a fitting scene for the sport, was the meeting-place of one of the most respectable golf-clubs in the country. Sir Charles Ross of Balnagown, Sheriff M'Leod of Geanis, Mr. Forsyth and the Lairds of Newhall, Pointzfield, and Braelanguil were among its members. Both the sheriff and Sir Charles were very powerful men, and good players. It was remarked, however, that neither of them dealt a more skilful or more vigorous blow than Mr. Forsyth, whose frame, though not much above the middle size, was singularly compact and muscular. He excelled, too, in his younger days, in all the other athletic games of the country. Few men threw a longer bowl, or pitched the stone or the bar further beyond the ordinary bound. Every meeting of the golf-players cost him a dinner and a dozen or two of his best wine ; for, invariably, when they had finished their sport for the day, they adjourned to his hospitable board, and the evening passed in mirth and jollity. Some of the anecdotes which furnished part of their laughter on these occasions still survive ; and, with the assistance of the wine, they must have served the purpose wonderfully well. All the various casks and boxes used by Mr. Forsyth in his trade were marked with his initials W. F., that he might be the better able to identify them. They were sometimes suffered so to accumulate in the outhouses of the neighboring proprietors, that they met the eye at every

turning; and at no place was this more the case than at
Pointzfield. On one occasion a swarm of Mr. Forsyth's
bees took flight in the same direction. They flew due west
along the shore, followed by a servant, and turned to the
south at the Pointzfield woods, where the pursuer lost
sight of them. In about half an hour after, however, a
swarm of bees were discovered in the proprietor's garden,
and the servant came to claim them in the name of his
master.

"On what pretence?" demanded the proprietor.

"Simply," said the man, "because my master lost a
swarm to-day, which I continued to follow to the beginning of the avenue yonder; and these cannot be other
than his."

"Nonsense," replied the proprietor. "Had they belonged
to your master they would have been marked by the W. F.,
every one of them."

Eventually, however, Mr. Forsyth got his bees; but
there were few golf-meetings at which the story was not
cited against him by way of proof that there were occasions when even he, with all his characteristic forethought,
could be as careless as other men.

It was chiefly in his capacity of magistrate, however,
that Mr. Forsyth was brought acquainted with the wilder
humors of the place. Some of the best jokes of the townsmen were exceedingly akin to felonies ; and as the injured
persons were in every case all the angrier for being laughed
at, they generally applied for redress to their magistrate.
There is a transition stage in society, — a stage between
barbarism and civilization, — in which, through one of the
unerring instincts of our nature, men employ their sense of
the ludicrous in laughing one another into propriety; and
such was the stage at which society had arrived in the

north of Scotland in at least the earlier part of Mr. Forsyth's career. Cromarty was, in consequence, a merry little place, though the merriment was much on the one side, and of a wofully selfish character. The young, like those hunting parties of Norway that band together for the purpose of ridding their forests of the bears, used in the long winter evenings to go prowling about the streets in quest of something that might be teased and laughed at; the old, though less active in the pursuit, — for they kept to their houses, — resembled the huntsmen of the same country who lie in wait for the passing animal on the tops of trees. Their passion for the ludicrous more than rivalled the Athenian rage for the new; and while each one laughed at his neighbor, he took all care to avoid being laughed at in turn.

The poor fishermen of the place, from circumstances connected with their profession, were several degrees lower in the scale of civilization than most of their neighbors. The herring-fishery had not yet taught them to speculate, nor were there Sabbath schools to impart to them the elements of learning and good manners; and though there might be, perhaps, one of fifty among them possessed of a smattering of Latin, it was well if a tithe of the remaining forty-nine had learned to read. They were, however, a simple, inoffensive race of people, whose quarrels, like their marriages — for they quarrelled often, though at a small expense — were restricted to their own class, and who, though perhaps little acquainted with the higher standards of right, had a code of foolish superstitions, which, strange as it may seem, served almost the same end. They respected an oath, in the belief that no one had ever perjured himself and thriven; regarded the murderer as exposed to the terrible visitations of his victim, and the thief as a person doomed to a *down look;* reverenced the Bible as a protection from witchcraft, and baptism as a charm against the fairies. Their simplicity, their ignorance, their superstition, laid them open to a thousand petty annoyances from the wags of the town. They had a belief, long since extinct, that if, when setting out for the fishing, one should interrogate them regarding their voyage, there was little chance of their getting on with it without meeting with some disaster; and it was a common trick with the youngsters to run down to the water's edge, just as they were betaking themselves to their oars, and shout out, "Men, men, where are you going?" They used, too, to hover about their houses after dark, and play all manner of tricks, such as blocking up their chimney with turf and stealthily filling their water-stoups with salt-water just as they were about setting on their *brochan*. One of the best jokes of the period seems almost too good to be forgotten.

The fairies were in ill repute at the time, and long before, for an ill practice of kidnapping children and annoying women in the straw; and no class of people could dread them more than fishers. But they were at length cured of their terrors by being laughed at. One evening, when all the men were setting out for sea, and all the women engaged at the water's edge in handing them their tackle or launching their boats, a party of young fellows, who had watched the opportunity, stole into their cottages, and, disfurnishing the cradles of all their little tenants, transposed the children of the entire village, leaving a child in the cradle of every mother, but taking care that it should not be her own child. They then hid themselves, amid the ruins of a deserted hovel, to wait the result. Up came the women from the shore; and, alarmed by the crying of the children and the strangeness of their voices, they went to their cradles and found a changeling in each. The

scene that followed baffles description. They shrieked and
screamed and clapped their hands; and, rushing out to
the lanes like so many mad creatures, were only unhinged
the more to find the calamity so universal. Down came the
women of the place, to make inquiries and give advices;
some recommending them to have recourse to the minister, some to procure baskets and suspend the changelings
over the fire, — some one thing, some another; but the
poor mothers were regardless of them all. They tossed
their arms and shrieked and hallooed; and the children,
who were well-nigh as ill at ease as themselves, added, by
their cries, to the confusion and the uproar. A thought
struck one of the townswomen. " I suspect, neighbors,"
she said, "that the loons are at the bottom of this. Let's
bring all the little ones into one place, and see whether
every mother cannot find her own among them." No
sooner said than done; and peace was restored in a few
minutes. Mischievous as the trick was, it had this one
effect, that the fairies were in less repute in Cromarty ever
after, and were never more charged with the stealing of
children. A popular belief is in no small danger when
those who cherished learn to laugh at it, be the laugh
raised as it may.

29*

CHAPTER X.

Blest be that spot, where cheerful guests retire
To pause from toil and trim their evening fire;
Blest that abode, where want and pain repair,
And every stranger finds a ready chair.
GOLDSMITH.

THERE were two classes of men who had no particular cause of gratitude to Mr. Forsyth. Lawyers, notwithstanding his respect for the profession, he contrived to exclude from the place, for no case of dispute or difference ever passed himself, nor was there ever an appeal from his decisions; and inn-keepers found themselves both robbed of their guests by his hospitality, and in danger of losing their licenses for the slightest irregularity that affected the morals of their neighbors. For at least the last twenty years of his life, his house, from the number of guests which his hospitality had drawn to it, often resembled a crowded inn. Did he meet with a young man of promising talent, however poor, who belonged in any degree to the aristocracy of nature, and bade fair to rise above his present level, he was sure of being invited to his table. Did he come in contact with some unfortunate aspirant who had seen better days, but who in his fall had preserved his character, he was certain of being invited too. Was there a wind-bound vessel in the port, Mr. Forsyth was sure to bring the passengers home with him. Had travellers come to visit the place, Mr. Forsyth could best tell them all what deserved their notice; and nowhere could he tell it half so well as at his own table. Never was there a man who, through the mere indulgence of the kindlier feelings of our nature, contrived to make himself more friends. The chance visitor spent perhaps a single day under his roof, and never after ceased to esteem the good and benevolent owner. His benevolence, like that of John of Calais in the old romance, extended to even the bodies of the dead; an interesting instance of which I am enabled to present to the reader.

Some time in the summer of 1773 or 1774, a pleasure-yacht, the property of that Lord Byron who immediately preceded the poet, cast anchor in the bay of Cromarty, having, according to report, a dying lady on board. A salmon-fisher of the place, named Hossack, a man of singular daring and immense personal strength, rowed his little skiff alongside in the course of the day, bringing with him two fine salmon for sale. The crew, however, seemed wild and reckless as that of a privateer or pirate; and he had no sooner touched the side, than a fellow who stood in the gangway dealt his light skiff so heavy a blow with a boat-hook that he split one of the planks. Hossack seized hold of the pole, wrenched it out of the fellow's grasp, and was in the act of raising it to strike him down, when the master of the yacht, a native of Orkney, came running to the gun-wale, and, apologizing for the offered violence, invited the fisherman aboard. He accordingly climbed the vessel's side, and disposed of his fish.

Lord Byron, a good-looking man, but rather shabbily dressed, was pacing the quarter-deck. Two proprietors of the country, who had known him in early life, and had come aboard to pay him their respects, were seated on chairs near the stern. But the party seemed an unsocial one. His lordship continued to pace the deck, regarding his visitors from time to time with an expression singularly repulsive, while the latter had the blank look of men who, expecting a kind reception, are chilled by one freezingly cold. The fisherman was told by the master, by way of explanation, that his lordship, who had been when at the soundest a reserved man, of very eccentric habits, was now unsettled in mind, and had been so from the time he had killed a gentleman in a duel; and that his madness seemed to be of a kind which, instead of changing, deepens the shades of the natural character. ·He was informed further, that the sick lady, a Miss Mudie, had expired that morning; that she was no connection whatever of his lordship, but was merely an acquaintance of the master's, and a native of Orkney, who, having gone to Inverness for the benefit of her health, and becoming worse, had taken the opportunity, in the absence of any more eligible conveyance, of returning by Lord Byron's yacht. The master, who seemed to be a plain, warm-hearted sailor, expressed much solicitude regarding the body. The unfortunate lady had been most respectable herself and most respectably connected, and was anxious that the funeral should be of a kind befitting her character and station; but then, he had scarce anything in his own power, and his lordship would listen to nothing on the subject. "Ah," replied Hossack, "but I know a gentleman who would listen to you, and do something more. I shall go ashore this moment, and tell Mr. Forsyth."

The fisherman did so, and found he had calculated aright. Mr. Forsyth sent townswomen aboard to dress the corpse, who used to astonish the children of the place for years after by their descriptions of the cabin in which it lay. The days of steamboats had not yet come on, to render such things familiar; and the idea of a room panelled with mirrors, and embossed with flowers of gold, was well suited to fill the young imagination. The body was taken ashore; and, contrary to one of the best established canons of superstition, was brought to the house of Mr. Forsyth, from which, on the following day, when he had invited inhabtants of the place to attend the funeral, it was carried to his own burying-ground, and there interred. And such was the beginning of a friendship between the benevolent merchant and the relatives of the deceased which terminated only with the life of the former. Two of his visitors, during the summer of 1795, were a Major and Mrs. Mudie from Orkney.

I may mention, in the passing, a somewhat curious circumstance connected with Lord Byron's yacht. She actually sat deep in the water at the time with a cargo of contraband goods, most of which were afterwards unloaded near Sinclair's Bay, in Caithness. Hossack, ere he parted from the master, closed a bargain with him for a considerable quantity of Hollands, and, on being brought astern to the vessel's peak on the evening she sailed from Cromarty, he found the place filled with kegs, bound together by pairs, and heavy weights attached to facilitate their sinking, in the event of their being thrown overboard. It is a curious, but, I believe, well-authenticated fact, that one of the most successful smuggling vessels of the period, on at least the eastern coast of Scotland, was a revenue-cutter provided by government for the suppression of the trade.

Besides the chance visitors entertained at the hospitable board of the merchant, there were parties of his friends and relatives who spent, almost every summer, a few weeks in his family. The two daughters of his brother, who had removed to England so long before, with the son and daughter of the other brother, who had settled in

Dingwall; the brother of his first wife, a Major Russell, with the brother and sisters of his second; his relatives from Elgin; a nephew who had married into a family of rank in England, and some of his English partners in the hempen manufactory, were among the number of his annual visitors. His parties were often such as the most fastidious would have deemed it an honor to have been permitted to join. He has repeatedly entertained at his table his old townsman Duncan Davidson, member of Parliament at the time for the shire of Cromarty, the late Lord Seaforth, Sir James Mackintosh, and his old protegé Charles Grant, with the sons of the latter, Charles and Robert. The merchant, when Mr. Grant had quitted Cromarty for London, was a powerful and active man, in the undiminished vigor of middle life. When he returned, after his long residence in India, he found him far advanced in years, indeed considerably turned of seventy, and, in at least his bodily powers, the mere wreck of his former self. And so affected was the warm-hearted director by the contrast, that, on grasping his hand, he burst into tears. Mr. Forsyth himself, however, saw nothing to regret in the change. He was still enjoying much in his friends and his family; for his affections remained warm as ever, and he had still enough of activity left to do much good. His judgment as a magistrate was still sound. He had more time, too, than before to devote to the concerns of his neighbors; for, with the coming on of old age, he had been gradually abridging his business, retaining just enough to keep up his accustomed round of occupation. Had a townsman died in any of the colonies, or in the army or navy, after saving some little money, it was the part of the merchant to recover it for the relatives of the deceased. Was the son or nephew of some of his humble neighbors.

trepanned by a recruiting party, — and there were strange arts used for the purpose fifty years ago, — the case was a difficult one indeed if Mr. Forsyth did not succeed in restoring him to his friends. He acted as a sort of general agent for the district, and in every instance acted without fee or reward. The respect in which he was held by the people was shown by the simple title by which he was on every occasion designated. They all spoke of him as "the Maister." "Is the Maister at home?" or, "Can I see the Maister?" were the queries put to his servants by the townspeople perhaps ten times a day. Masters were becoming somewhat common in the country at the time, and esquires not a great deal less so; but the "Maister" was the designation of but one gentleman only, and the people who used the term never forgot what it meant.

In all his many acts of kindness the merchant was well seconded by his wife, whose singularly compassionate disposition accorded well with his own. She had among the more deserving poor a certain number to whom she dealt a regular weekly allowance, and who were known to the townspeople as "Mrs. Forsyth's pensioners." Besides, rarely did she suffer a day to pass without the performance of some act of charity in behalf of the others who were without the pale; and when sickness or distress visited a poor family, she was sure to visit it too. Physicians were by no means so common in the country at the time as they have since become; and, that she might be the more useful, Mrs. Forsyth, shortly after her marriage, had devoted herself, like the ladies of an earlier period, to the study of medicine. Her excellent sense more than compensated for the irregularity of her training; and there were few professors of the art of healing in the district whose prescriptions were more implicitly or more successfully followed, or whose medicine-chest was oftener emptied and replenished. Mr. Forsyth was by no means a very wealthy man, — his hand had been ever too open for that, — and, besides, as money had been rapidly sinking in value during the whole course of his career as a trader, the gains of his earlier years had to be measured by a growing and therefore depreciating standard. It is a comfortable fact, however, that no man or family was ever ruined by doing good under the influence of right motives. Mr. Forsyth's little .fortune proved quite sufficient for all his charities and all his hospitality. It wore well, like the honest admiral's; and the great bulk of it, though he has been nearly forty years dead, is still in the hands of his descendants.

CHAPTER XI.

Good and evil, we know, in the field of this world grow up together almost inseparably. — MILTON.

THERE are few things more interesting, in either biography or history, than those chance tide-marks, if I may so express myself, which show us the ebbs and flows of opinion, and how very sudden its growth when it sets in on the popular side. Mr. Forsyth was extensively engaged in business when the old hereditary jurisdictions were abolished; not in compliance with any wish expressed by the people, but by an unsolicited act on the part of the government. Years passed, and he possessed entire all his earlier energies, when he witnessed from one of the

windows of his house in Cromarty the procession of a
Liberty and Equality Club. The processionists were afterwards put down by the gentlemen of the county, and
their leader, a young man of more wit than judgment, sent
to the jail of Tain ; but the merchant took no part either
for or against them. He merely remarked to one of his
friends, that there is as certainly a despotism of the people
as of their rulers, and that it is from the better and wiser,
not from the lower and more unsettled order of minds,
that society need look for whatever is suited to benefit or
adorn it. He had heard of the Dundees and Dalziels of a
former age, but he had heard also of its Jack Cades and
Massaniellos ; and after outliving the atrocities of Robes-
pierre and Danton, he found no reason to regard the
tyranny of the many with any higher respect than that
which he had all along entertained for the tyranny of the
few.

The conversation of Mr. Forsyth was rather solid than
sparkling. He was rather a wise than a witty man. Such,
however, was the character of his remarks, that it was the
shrewdest and best informed who listened to them with
most attention and respect. His powers of observation
and reflection were of no ordinary kind. His life, like old
Nestor's, was extended through two whole generations
and the greater part of the third, and this, too, in a century which witnessed more changes in the economy and
character of the people of Scotland than any three centuries which had gone before. It may not be uninteresting
to the reader rapidly to enumerate a few of the more important of these, with their mixed good and evil. A brief
summary may serve to show us that, while we should
never despair of the improvement of society on the one
hand, seeing how vast the difference which obtains be-

tween the opposite states of barbarism and civilization, there is little wisdom in indulging, on the other, in dreams of a theoretical perfection, at which it is too probable our nature cannot arrive. Few great changes take place in the economy of a country without removing some of the older evils which oppressed it; few also without introducing into it evils that are new.

It was in the latter days of Mr. Forsyth that the modern system of agriculture had begun to effect those changes in the appearance of the country and the character of the people by which the one has been so mightily improved and the other so considerably lowered. The clumsy, inefficient system which it supplanted was fraught with physical evil. There was an immense waste of labor. A large amount of the scanty produce of the country was consumed by a disproportionably numerous agricultural population; and, from the inartificial methods pursued, the harvest, in every more backward season, was thrown far into the winter; and years of scarcity, amounting almost to famine, inflicted from time to time their miseries on the poorer classes of the people. It was as impossible, too, in the nature of things, that the system should have remained unaltered after science had introduced her innumerable improvements into every other department of industry, as that night should continue in all its gloom in one of the central provinces of a country after the day had arisen in all the provinces which surrounded it. Nor could the landed interests have maintained their natural and proper place had the case been otherwise. There were but two alternatives, advance in the general rush of improvement, or a standing still to be trampled under foot. With the more enlightened mode of agriculture the large-farm system is naturally, perhaps inevitably, connected; at least, in no branch of industry do we find the efficient adoption of scientific improvement dissevered from the extensive employment of capital. And it is this system which, within the last forty years, has so materially deteriorated the character of the people. It has broken down the population of the agricultural districts into two extreme classes. It has annihilated the moral and religious race of small farmers, who in the last age were so peculiarly the glory of Scotland, and of whom the Davie Deans of the novelist, and the Cotter of Burns, may be regarded as the fitting representatives; and has given us mere gentlemen-farmers and farm-servants in their stead. The change was in every respect unavoidable; and we can only regret that its physical good should be so inevitably accompanied by what must be regarded as its moral and political evil.

It was during the long career of Mr. Forsyth, and in no small degree under his influence and example, that the various branches of trade still pursued in the north of Scotland were first originated. He witnessed the awakening of the people from the indolent stupor in which extreme poverty and an acquiescent subjection to the higher classes were deemed unavoidable consequences of their condition, to a state of comparative comfort and independence. He saw what had been deemed the luxuries of his younger days, placed, by the introduction of habits of industry, and a judicious division of labor, within the reach of almost the poorest. He saw, too, the first establishment of branch-banks in the north of Scotland, and the new life infused, through their influence, into every department of trade. They conferred a new ability of exertion on the people, by rendering their available capital equal to the resources of their trade, and gave to character a money-value which even the most profligate were compelled to recognize and respect. Each of these items of improvement, however, had its own peculiar drawback. Under the influence of the commercial spirit, neighbors have become less kind, and the people in general less hospitable. The comparative independence of the poorer classes has separated them more widely from the upper than they had ever been separated before; and mutual jealousies and heartburnings mark, in consequence, the more ameliorated condition. The number of traders and shopkeepers has become disproportionably large; and while a few succeed and make money, and a few more barely maintain their ground at an immense expense of care and exertion, there is a considerable portion of the class who have to struggle on for years, perhaps involved in a labyrinth of shifts and expedients that prove alike unfavorable to their own character and to the security of trade in general, and then end in insolvency at last. The large command of money, too, furnished at times by imprudent bank accommodation, has in some instances awakened a spirit of speculation among the people, which seems but too much akin to that of the gambler, and which has materially lowered the tone of public morals in at least the creditor and debtor relation. Bankruptcy, in consequence, is regarded with very different feelings in the present day from what it was sixty years ago. It has lost much of the old infamy which used to pass downwards from a man to his children, and is now too often looked upon as merely the natural close of an unlucky speculation, or, worse still, as a sort of speculation in itself.

There is one branch of trade, in particular, which has been suffered to increase by far too much for the weal of the country. More than two thousand pounds are squandered yearly in the town of Cromarty in spirituous liquors alone, — a larger sum than that expended in tea, sugar, coffee, soap, and candles, put together. The evil is one of enormous magnitude, and unmixed in its character; nor is there any part of the country, and, indeed, few families, in which its influence is not felt. And yet in some of the many causes which have led to it we may trace the workings of misdirected good, natural and political. A weak compassion on the part of those whose duty it is to grant or withhold the license without which intoxicating liquors cannot be sold, has more than quadrupled the necessary number of public houses. Has an honest man in the lower ranks proved unfortunate in business; has a laborer or farm-servant of good character met with some accident which incapacitates him from pursuing his ordinary labors; has a respectable, decent woman lost her husband, — all apply for the license as their last resource, and all are successful in their application. Each of their houses attracts its round of customers, who pass through the downward stages of a degradation to which the keepers themselves are equally exposed; and after they have in this way irremediably injured the character of their neighbors, their own, in at least nine cases out of ten, at last gives way; and the fatal house is shut up, to make way for another of the same class, which, after performing its work of mischief on a new circle, is to be shut up in turn. Another great cause of the intemperance of the age is connected with the clubs and societies of modern times. Many of these institutions are admirably suited to preserve a spirit of independence and self-reliance among the people exactly the reverse of that sordid spirit of pauperism which has so overlaid the energies of the sister kingdom; and there are few of them which do not lead to a general knowledge of at least the simpler practices of business, and to that spread of intelligence which naturally arises from an intercourse of mind in which each has somewhat to impart and somewhat to acquire. But they lead also, in too many instances, to the formation of intemperate habits among the leading members. There is the procession and the ball, with their necessary accompaniments; the meeting begun with business ends too often in conviviality; and there are few acquainted with such institutions who cannot assign to each its own train of victims.

Another grand cause of this gigantic evil of intemperance, — a cause which fortunately exists no longer, save in its effects, — was of a political nature. On the breaking out of the revolutionary war, almost every man in the kingdom fit to bear arms became a soldier. Every district had its embodied yeomanry or local militia, every town its volunteers. Boys who had just shot up to their full height were at once metamorphosed into heroes, and received their monthly pay; and, under an exaggerated assumption of the military character, added to an unwonted command of pocket-money, there were habits of reckless intemperance formed by thousands and tens of thousands among the people, which have now held by them for more than a quarter of a century after the original cause has been removed, and which are passing downwards, through the influence of example, to add to the amount of crime and wretchedness in other generations.

In no respect does the last age differ more from the present than in the amount of general intelligence possessed by the people. It is not yet seventy years since Burke estimated the reading public of Great Britain and Ireland at about eighty thousand. There is a single Scotch periodical of the present day that finds as many purchasers, and on the lowest estimate twice as many readers, in Scotland alone. There is a total change, too, in the sources of popular intelligence. The press has supplanted the church; the newspaper and magazine occupy the place once occupied by the Bible and the Confession of Faith. Formerly, when there were comparatively few books and no periodicals in this part of the country, there was but one way in which a man could learn to think. His mind became the subject of some serious impression. He applied earnestly to his Bible and the standards of the church; and in the contemplation of the most important of all concerns, his newly-awakened faculties received their first exercise. And hence the nature of his influence in the humble sphere in which he moved; an influence which the constitution of his church, from her admission of lay members to deliberate in her courts and to direct her discipline, tended powerfully to increase. It was not more intellectual than moral, nor moral than intellectual. He was respected not only as one of the best, but also as one of the most intelligent men in his parish, and impressed the tone of his own character on that of his contemporaries. Popular intelligence in the present age is less influential, and by far less respectable, in single individuals; and, though of a humanizing tendency in general, its moral effects are less decided. But it is all-potent in the mass of the people, and secures to them a political power which they never possessed before, and which must prove for the future their effectual guard against tyranny in the rulers; unless, indeed, they should first by their own act break down those natural barriers which protect the various classes of society, by becoming tyrants themselves. There is a medium-point beyond which liberty becomes license, and license hastens to a despotism, which may, indeed, be exercised for a short time by the many, but whose inevitable tendency it is to pass into the hands of the few.

A few of the causes which have tended to shut up to so great an extent the older sources of intelligence may be briefly enumerated. Some of them have originated *within*, and some *without* the church.

The benefits conferred on Scotland by the Presbyterian Church, during at least the two centuries which immediately succeeded the Reformation, were incalculably great. Somewhat of despotism there might, nay, must have been, in the framework of our ecclesiastical institutions. The age was inevitably despotic. The church in which the Reformers had spent the earlier portion of their lives was essentially and constitutionally so. Be it remembered, too, that the principles of true toleration have been as much the discovery of later ages as those principles on which we construct our steam-engines. But whatever the framework of the constitutions of our church, the soul which animated them was essentially that spirit " wherewith Christ maketh his people free." Nay, their very intolerance was of a kind which delighted to arm its vassals with a power before which all tyranny, civil or ecclesiastical, must eventually be overthrown. It compelled them to quit the lower levels of our nature for the higher. It demanded of them that they should be no longer immoral or illiterate. It enacted that the ignorant baron should send his children to school, that they, too, might not grow up in ignorance ; and provided that the children of the poor should be educated at the expense of the state. A strange despotism truly, which, by adding to the knowledge and the virtue of the people among whom it was established, gave them at once that taste and capacity for freedom without which men cannot be other than slaves, be the form of government under which they live what it may.

Be it remembered too, that, whatever we of the present age may think of our church, our fathers thought much of it. It was for two whole centuries the most popular of all establishments, and stamped its own character on that of the people. The law of patronage, as re-established by Oxford and Bolingbroke, first lowered its efficiency; not altogether so suddenly, but quite as surely, as these statesmen had intended. From being a guide and leader of the people, it sunk, in no small degree, into a follower and dependant on the government and the aristocracy. The old Evangelical party dwindled into a minority, and in the majority of its Church of Scotland became essentially unpopular and uninfluential. More than one half our church stood on exactly the same ground which had been occupied by the curates of half a century before ; and the pike and musket were again employed in the settlement of ministers, who professed to preach the gospel of peace. A second change for the worse took place about fifty years ago, when the modern system of agriculture was first introduced, and the rage for experimental farming seemed to pervade all classes, — ministers of the church among the rest. Many of these took large farms, and engaged in the engrossing details of business. Some were successful and made money, some were unfortunate and became bankrupt. Years of scarcity came on ; the price of grain rose beyond all precedent ; and there were thousands among the suffering poor who could look no higher in the chain of causes than to the great farmers, clerical and lay, who were thriving on their miseries. It is a fact which stands in need of no comment, that the person in the north of Scotland who first raised the price of oatmeal to three pounds per boll was a clergyman of the established church. A third change which has militated against the clergy is connected with that general revolution in manners, dress, and modes of thinking which, during the last forty years, has transferred the great bulk of our middle classes from the highest place among the people to the lowest among the aristocracy; the clergymen of our church, with their families, among the rest. And a fourth change, not less disastrous than even the worst of the others, may be traced to that recent extension of the political franchise which has had the effect of involving so many otherwise respectable ministers in the essentially irreligious turmoil of party. There is still, however, much of its original vigor in the Church of Scotland; a self-reforming energy which no radically corrupt church ever did or can possess; and her late efforts in shaking herself loose from some of the evils which have long oppressed her give earnest that her career of usefulness is not hastening to its close.

There is certainly much to employ the honest and enlightened among her members in the present age. At no time did that gulf which separates the higher from the lower classes present so perilous a breadth, at no time did it threaten the commonwealth more; and if it be not in the power of the equalizing influence of Christianity to bridge it over, there is no other power that can. It seems quite as certain that the spread of political power shall accompany the spread of intelligence, as that the heat of the sun shall accompany its light. It is quite as idle to affirm that the case should be otherwise, and that this power should not be extended to the people, as to challenge the law of gravitation, or any of the other great laws which regulate the government of the universe. The progress of mind cannot be arrested; the power which necessarily accompanies it cannot be lessened. Hence the imminent danger of those suspicions and dislikes that the opposite classes entertain each of the other, and which are in so many instances the effect of mistake and misconception. The classes are so divided that they never meet to compare notes, or to recognize in one another the same common nature. In the space which separates them, the eaves-dropper and the tale-bearer find their proper province ; and thus there are heart-burnings produced, and jealousies fostered, which even in the present age destroy the better charities of society, and which, should the evil remain uncorrected, must inevitably produce still sadder effects in the future. Hence it is, too, that the mere malignancy of opposition has become so popular, and that noisy demagogues, whose sole merit consists in their hatred of the higher classes, receive so often the support of better men than themselves. It is truly wonderful how many defects, moral and intellectual, may be covered by what Dryden happily terms the "all-atoning name of patriot," — how creatures utterly broken in character and means, pitiful little tyrants in fields and families, the very stuff out of which spies and informers are made, are supported and cheered on in their course of political agitation by sober-minded men, who would never once dream of entrusting them with their private concerns. We may look for the cause in the perilous disunion of the upper and lower classes, and the widely-diffused bitterness of feeling which that disunion occasions.

CHAPTER XII.

> Death is the crown of life:
> Were death denied, poor men would live in vain;
> Were death denied, to live would not be life.
>
> YOUNG.

MR. FORSYTH was for about forty years an elder of the church, and never was the office more conscientiously or more consistently held. It was observed, however, that, though not less orthodox in his belief than any of his brother elders, and certainly not less scrupulously strict in his morals, he was much less severe in his judgments on offenders, and less ready in sanctioning, except in extreme cases, the employment of the sterner discipline of the church. On one occasion, when distributing the poor's funds, he set apart a few shillings for a poor creature, of rather equivocal character, who had lately been visited by the displeasure of the session, and who, though in wretched poverty, felt too much ashamed at the time to come forward to claim her customary allowance.

"Hold, Mr. Forsyth," said one of the elders, a severe and rigid Presbyterian of the old school, — "hold ; the woman is a bad woman, and doesn't deserve that."

"Ah," replied the merchant, in the very vein of Hamlet, "if we get barely according to our deservings, Donald, who of us all shall escape whipping? We shall just give the poor thing these few shillings which she does not deserve, in consideration of the much we ourselves enjoy which we deserve, I am afraid, nearly as little."

"You are a wiser man than I am, Mr. Forsyth," said the elder, and sat down rebuked.

No course in life so invariably smooth and prosperous in its tenor that the consolations of religion — even regarding religion as a matter of this world alone — can be well dispensed with. There are griefs which come to all ; and the more affectionate the heart, and the greater its capacity of happiness, the more keenly are these felt. Of nine children which his wife bore to him, William Forsyth survived six. Four died in childhood; not so early, however, but that they had first engaged the affections and awakened the hopes of their parents. A fifth reached the more mature age at which the intellect begins to open, and the dispositions to show what they are eventually to become, and then fell a victim to that insidious disease which so often holds out to the last its promises of recovery, and with which hope struggles so long and so painfully, to be overborne by disappointment in the end. And a sixth, a young man of vigorous talent and kindly feelings, after obtaining a writership in India through the influence of his father's old protegé, Mr. Charles Grant, fell a victim to the climate in his twentieth year. Mr. Forsyth bore his various sorrows, not as a philosopher, but as a Christian; not as if possessed of strength enough in his own mind to bear up under each succeeding bereavement, but as one deriving comfort from conviction that the adorable Being who cared for both him and his children does not afflict his creatures willingly, and that the scene of existence which he saw closing upon them, and which was one day to close upon himself, is to be succeeded by another and a better scene, where God himself wipeth away all tears from all eyes. His only surviving son, John, the last of four, left him, as he himself had left his father more than fifty years before, for a house of business in London, which he afterwards quitted for India, on receiving an appointment there through the kindness of Mr. Grant. Mr. Forsyth accompanied him to the beach, where a boat manned by six fishermen was in waiting to carry him to a vessel in the offing. He knew too surely that he was parting from him for ever; but he bore up under the conviction until the final adieu, and then, wholly overpowered by his feelings, he burst into tears. Nor was the young man less affected. It was interesting to see the effects of this scene on the rude boatmen. They had never seen "the Maister" so affected before; and as they bent them to their oars, there was not a dry eye among them.

Age brought with it its various infirmities, and there were whole weeks in which Mr. Forsyth could no longer see his friends as usual; nor even when in better health — in at least what must often pass for health at seventy-seven — could he quit his bedroom before the middle of the day. He now experienced how surely an affectionate disposition draws to itself, by a natural sympathy, the affection of others. His wife, who was still but in middle life, and his two surviving daughters, Catherine and Isabella, were unwearied in their attentions to him, anticipating every wish, and securing to him every little comfort which his situation required, with that anxious ingenuity of affection so characteristic of the better order of female minds. His sight had so much failed him that he could no longer apply to his favorite authors as before; but one of his daughters used to sit beside him and read a few pages at a time, for his mind was less capable than formerly of pursuing, unfatigued, long trains of thought. At no previous period, however, did he relish his books more. The state of general debility which marked his decline resembled that which characterizes the first stage of convalescence in lingering disorders. If his vigor of thought was lessened, his feelings of enjoyment seemed in proportion more exquisitely keen. His temper, always smooth and placid, had softened with his advance in years, and every new act of attention or kindness which he experienced seemed too much for his feelings. He was singularly grateful; grateful to his wife and daughters, and to the friends who from time to time came to sit beside his chair and communicated to him any little piece of good news; above all, grateful to the great Being who had been caring for him all life long, and who now, amid the infirmities of old age, was still giving him so much to enjoy. In the prime of life, when his judgment was soundest and most discriminative, he had given the full assent of his vigorous understanding to those peculiar doctrines of Christianity on which its morals are founded. He had believed in Jesus Christ as the sole mediator between God and man; and the truth which had received the sanction of his understanding then, served to occupy the whole of his affections now. Christ was all with him, and himself was nothing. The reader will perhaps pardon my embodying a few simple thoughts on this important subject, which I offer with all the more diffidence that they have not come to me through the medium of any other mind.

It will be found that all the false religions, of past or of present times, which have abused the credulity or flattered the judgments of men, may be divided into two grand classes, — the natural and the artificial. The latter are exclusively the work of the human reason, prompted by those uneradicable feelings of our nature which constitute man a religious creature. The religions of Socrates and Plato, of the old philosophers in general, with perhaps the exception of the sceptics, and a few others, — of Lord Herbert of

Cherbury, Algernon Sidney, and Dr. Channing, of all the better Deists, of the Unitarians too, and the Socinians of modern times,—belong to this highly rational but unpopular and totally inefficient class. The God of these religions is a mere abstract idea; an incomprehensible essence of goodness, power, and wisdom. The understanding cannot conceive of him, except as a great First Cause,—as the incomprehensible source and originator of all things; and it is surely according to reason that he should be thus removed from that lower sphere of conception which even finite intelligences can occupy to the full. But in thus rendering him intangible to the understanding he is rendered intangible to the affections also. Who ever loved an abstract idea? or what sympathy can exist between human minds and an intelligent essence infinitely diffused? And hence the cold and barren inefficiency of artificial religions. They want the vitality of life. They want the grand principle of *motive;* for they can lay no hold on those affections to which this prime mover in all human affairs can alone address itself. They may look well in a discourse or an essay, for, like all human inventions, they may be easily understood and rationally defended; but they are totally unsuited to the nature and the wants of man.

The natural religions are of an entirely different character. They are wild and extravagant; and the enlightened reason, when unbiassed by the influences of early prejudice, rejects them as monstrous and profane. But, unlike the others, they have a strong hold on human nature, and exert a powerful control over its hopes and its fears. Men may build up an artificial religion as they build up a house, and the same age may see it begun and completed. Natural religions, on the contrary, are, like the oak and the chestnut, the slow growth of centuries;

their first beginnings are lost in the uncertainty of the fab-
ulous ages; and every addition they receive is fitted to
the credulity of the popular mind ere it can assimilate
itself to the mass. The grand cause of their popularity,
however, consists in the decidedly human character of
their gods; for it is according to the nature of man as a
religious creature that he meets with an answering nature
in Deity. The gods of the Greek and Roman were human
beings like themselves, and influenced by a merely human
favoritism. The devotion of their worshippers was but a
more reverential species of friendship; and there are perhaps few men of warm imaginations who have become
acquainted in early life with the Æneid of Virgil, or the
Telemaque of Fenelon, who are not enabled to conceive,
in part at least, how such a friendship could be entertained. The Scandinavian mythology, with the equally
barbarous mythologies of the East, however different in
other respects, agree in this main principle of popularity,
the human character of their gods. The Virgin Mother
and the many saints of the Romish Church, with its tangi-
bilities of pictures and images, form an indispensable com-
pensation for its lack of the evangelical principle; and it
is undoubtedly to the well-defined and easily-conceived
character of Mohammed that Allah owes the homage of
the unreckoned millions of the East.

Now, it is according to reason and analogy that the true
religion should be formed, if I may so express myself, on
a popular principle; that it should be adapted, with all the
fitness which constitutes the argument of design, to that
human nature which must be regarded as the production
of the common author of both. It is indispensable that
the religion which God reveals should be suited to the human nature which God has made. Artificial religions, with

all their minute rationalities, are not suited to it at all, and therefore take no hold on the popular mind; natural religions, with all their immense popularity, are not suited to improve it. It is Christianity alone which unites the popularity of the one class with the rationality, and more than the purity, of the other; that gives to the Deity, as man, his strong hold on the human affections, and restores to him, in his abstract character as the father of all, the homage of the understanding.

The change which must come to all was fast coming on William Forsyth. There was a gradual sinking of his powers, bodily and intellectual; a thorough prostration of strength and energy; and yet, amid the general wreck of the man, the affections remained entire and unbroken; and the idea that the present scene is to be succeeded by another was continually present with him. Weeks passed in which he could no longer quit his bed. On the day he died, however, he expressed a wish to be brought to a chair which stood fronting a window, and the wish was complied with. The window commands a full view of the main street of the place; but though his face was turned in that direction, his attendants could not suppose that he took note any longer of the objects before him; the eyes were open, but the sense seemed shut. The case, however, was otherwise. A poor old woman passed by, and the dying man recognized her at once. "Ah, yonder," he said, addressing one of his daughters who stood by him, "is poor old Widow Watson, whom I have not seen now for many weeks. Take a shilling for her out of my purse, and tell her it is the last she will ever get from me." And so it was; and such was the closing act of a long and singularly useful life; for his death, unaccompanied apparently by aught of suffering, took place in the course of the evening, only a few hours after. He had completed his seventy-eighth year. All the men of the place attended his funeral, and many from the neighboring country; and there were few among the assembled hundreds who crowded round his grave to catch a last glimpse of the coffin, who did not feel that they had lost a friend. He was one of nature's noblemen; and the sincere homage of the better feelings is an honor reserved exclusively to the order to which he belonged.

Mrs. Forsyth survived her husband for eight years. And after living in the continued exércise of similar virtues, she died in the full hope of the same blessed immortality, leaving all who knew her to regret her loss, though it was the poor that mourned her most. Their three surviving children proved themselves the worthy descendants of such parents. There is a time coming when families of twenty descents may be regarded as less noble, and as possessing in a much less degree the advantages of birth; for, partly, it would seem, through that often marked though inexplicable effect of the organization of matter on the faculties of mind, which transmits the same character in the same line from generation to generation, and partly, doubtless, from the influence of early example, they all inherited in no slight or equivocal degree the virtues of their father and mother. A general massiveness and force of intellect, with a nice and unbending rectitude of principle, and great benevolence of disposition, were the more marked characteristics. Catherine, the eldest of the three, was married in 1801 to her cousin Isaac Forsyth, banker, Elgin, the brother and biographer of the well-known tourist; and, after enjoying in a singular degree the affection of her husband and family, and the respect of a wide circle of acquaintance, she died in the

autumn of 1826, in her fifty-seventh year. Isabella continued to reside in her father's house at Cromarty, which
maintained in no small degree its former character, and
there cannot well be higher praise. None of Mrs. Forsyth's
old pensioners were suffered to want by her daughter;
and as they dropped off, one by one, their places were supplied by others. She was the effective and active patron-
ess, too, of every scheme of benevolence originated in the
place, whether for the benefit of the poor or of the young.
She was married in 1811 to Captain Alexander M‘Kenzie,
R. M., of the Scatwell family, and died in the spring of
1838, in her sixty-eighth year, bequeathing by will three
hundred pounds to be laid out at interest for the behalf
of three poor widows of the place. John, the youngest
of the family, quitted his father's house for India, as has
been already related, in 1792. He rose by the usual steps
of promotion as resident at various stations, became a
senior merchant, and was appointed to the important
charge of keeper of the Company's warehouse at Calcutta,
with the near prospect of being advanced to the Board of
Trade. His long residence in India, however, had been
gradually undermining a constitution originally vigorous,
and he fell a victim to the climate in 1823, in the forty-
fifth year of his age. He had married an English lady
in Calcutta, Miss Mary Ann Farmer, a few years before,
and had an only daughter by her, Mary Elizabeth Forsyth,
who now inherits her grandfather's property in Cromarty.
His character was that of the family. For the last fifteen
years of his life he regularly remitted fifty pounds annually
for the poor of Cromarty, and left them a thousand pounds
at his death. The family burying-ground fronts the parish
church. It contains a simple tablet of Portland stone,
surmounted by a vase of white marble, and bearing the

following epitaph, whose rare merit it is to be at once highly eulogistic and strictly true : —

William Forsyth, Esquire,

DIED

the 30th January, 1800, in the 78th year of his age;
A Man loved for his benevolence,
honored for his integrity, and
revered for his piety.
He was religious without gloom;
cheerful without levity;
bountiful without ostentation
Rigid in the discharge of his own duties, he was
charitable and lenient in his judgment of others.
His kindness and hospitality were unbounded;
and in him the Destitute found a Friend,
the Oppressed a Protector.

On the 7th August, 1808, aged sixty-six, died

Elizabeth,

His beloved Wife,
in obedience to whose last desire
this Tablet is inscribed to his Memory,
which she ever cherished with tender affection,
and adorned by the practice of similar virtues.
With characteristic humility
she wished that merely her Death should be recorded
on this stone;
and to those who knew her no other memorial was wanting,
nor is it necessary, even if it were possible,
to delineate to the passing stranger ·
the beauty of her deportment,
the strength of her understanding,
and the benignity of her heart;
but rather
to admonish him, from such bright examples,
that the paths of godliness and virtue lead
to happiness on earth,
and the assurance of joys beyond the grave.

Of their children, they survived PATRICK, who died at the age of 20 in the East Indies; and JAMES, ISABELLA, MARGARET, WILLIAM, and ELIZABETH, who, with their parents, were buried in this place.

VALUABLE
LITERARY AND SCIENTIFIC WORKS,

PUBLISHED BY

GOULD AND LINCOLN,

59 WASHINGTON STREET, BOSTON.

ANNUAL OF SCIENTIFIC DISCOVERY FOR 1860; or, Year-Book of Facts in Science and Art, exhibiting the most important Discoveries and Improvements in Mechanics, Useful Arts, Natural Philosophy, Chemistry, Astronomy, Meteorology, Zoology, Botany, Mineralogy, Geology, Geography, Antiquities, &c., together with a list of recent Scientific Publications; a classified list of Patents; Obituaries of eminent Scientific Men; an Index of Important Papers in Scientific Journals, Reports, &c. Edited by DAVID A. WELLS, A. M. With a Portrait of Prof. O. M. Mitchell. 12mo, cloth, $1.25.

VOLUMES OF THE SAME WORK for years 1859 to 1853 inclusive. With Portraits of Professors Agassiz, Silliman, Henry, Bache, Maury, Hitchcock, Richard M. Hoe, Profs. Jeffries Wyman, and H. D. Rogers. Nine volumes, 12mo, cloth, $1.25 per vol.

This work, issued annually, contains all important facts discovered or announced during the year.

☞ Each volume is distinct in itself, and contains *entirely new matter.*

INFLUENCE OF THE HISTORY OF SCIENCE UPON INTELLECTUAL EDUCATION. By WILLIAM WHEWELL, D. D., of Trinity College, Eng., and the alleged author of "Plurality of Worlds." 12mo, cloth, 25 cts.

THE NATURAL HISTORY OF THE HUMAN SPECIES; Its Typical Forms and Primeval Distribution. By CHARLES HAMILTON SMITH. With an Introduction containing an Abstract of the views of Blumenbach, Prichard, Bachman, Agassiz, and other writers of repute. By SAMUEL KNEELAND, Jr., M. D. With elegant Illustrations. 12mo, cloth, $1.25.

"The marks of practical good sense, careful observation, and deep research, are displayed in every page. The introductory essay of some seventy or eighty pages forms a valuable addition to the work. It comprises an abstract of the opinions advocated by the most eminent writers on this subject. The statements are made with strict impartiality, and, without a comment, left to the judgment of the reader." — *Sartain's Magazine.*

KNOWLEDGE IS POWER. A View of the Productive Forces of Modern Society, and the Results of Labor, Capital, and Skill. By CHARLES KNIGHT. With numerous Illustrations. American Edition. Revised, with Additions, by DAVID A. WELLS, Editor of the "Annual of Scientific Discovery." 12mo, cloth, $1.25.

☞ This is emphatically *a book for the people.* It contains an immense amount of important information, which everybody ought to be in possession of; and the volume should be placed in every family, and in every School and Public Library in the land. The facts and illustrations are drawn from almost every branch of skilful industry, and it is a work which the mechanic and artisan of every description will be sure to read with a RELISH. (25)

IMPORTANT WORKS.

A TREATISE ON THE COMPARATIVE ANATOMY OF THE ANIMAL KINGDOM. By Profs. C. TH. VON SIEBOLD and H. STANNIUS. Translated from the German, with Notes, Additions, &c. By WALDO I. BURNETT, M. D., Boston. One elegant octavo volume, cloth, $3.00.

This is believed to be incomparably the best and most complete work on the subject extant; and its appearance in an English dress, with the additions of the American Translator, is everywhere welcomed by men of science in this country.

UNITED STATES EXPLORING EXPEDITION; during the years 1838, 1839, 1840, 1841, 1842, under CHARLES WILKES, U. S. N. Vol. XII. MOLLUSCA AND SHELLS. By AUGUSTUS A. GOULD, M. D. Elegant quarto volume, cloth, $6.00.

THE LANDING AT CAPE ANNE; or, THE CHARTER OF THE FIRST PERMANENT COLONY ON THE TERRITORY OF THE MASSACHUSETTS COMPANY. Now discovered, and first published from the ORIGINAL MANUSCRIPT, with an inquiry into its authority, and a HISTORY OF THE COLONY, 1624—1628, Roger Conant, Governor. By J. WINGATE THORNTON. 8vo, cloth, $1.50.

☞ "A rare contribution to the early history of New England." — *Mercantile Journal.*

LAKE SUPERIOR; Its Physical Character, Vegetation, and Animals. By L. AGASSIZ and others. One volume octavo, elegantly Illustrated, cloth, $3 50.

THE HALLIG; OR, THE SHEEPFOLD IN THE WATERS. A Tale of Humble Life on the Coast of Schleswig. Translated from the German of BIERNATSKI, by Mrs. GEORGE P. MARSH. With a Biographical Sketch of the Author. 12mo, cloth, $1.00.

As a revelation of an entire new phase in human society, this work strongly reminds the reader of Miss Bremer's tales. In originality and brilliancy of imagination, it is not inferior to those;— its aim is far higher.

THE CRUISE OF THE NORTH STAR; A Narrative of the Excursion made by Mr. Vanderbilt's Party in the Steam Yacht, in her Voyage to England, Russia, Denmark, France, Spain, Italy, Malta, Turkey, Madeira, &c. By Rev. JOHN OVERTON CHOULES, D. D. With elegant Illustrations, &c. 12mo, cloth, gilt backs and sides, $1.50; cloth, gilt, $2.00; Turkey, gilt, $3.00.

PILGRIMAGE TO EGYPT; embracing a Diary of Explorations on the Nile, with Observations Illustrative of the Manners, Customs, and Institutions of the People, and of the present condition of the Antiquities and Ruins. By Hon. J. V. C. SMITH, late Mayor of the City of Boston. With numerous elegant Engravings. 12mo, cloth, $1.25.

POETICAL WORKS.

COMPLETE POETICAL WORKS OF WILLIAM COWPER; with a Life and Critical Notices of his Writings. Elegant Illustrations. 16mo, cloth, $1.00.

POETICAL WORKS OF SIR WALTER SCOTT. Life and Illustrations. 16mo, cloth, $1.00.

MILTON'S POETICAL WORKS. With a Life and elegant Illustrations. 16mo, cloth, $1.00.

☞ The above Poetical Works, by standard authors, are all of uniform size and style, printed on fine paper from clear, distinct type, with new and elegant illustrations, richly bound in full gilt, and plain.

IMPORTANT NEW WORKS.

CYCLOPÆDIA OF ANECDOTES OF LITERATURE AND THE FINE ARTS. Containing a copious and choice Selection of Anecdotes of the various forms of Literature, of the Arts, of Architecture, Engravings, Music, Poetry, Painting, and Sculpture, and of the most celebrated Literary Characters and Artists of different Countries and Ages, &c. By KAZLITT ARVINE, A. M., author of "Cyclopædia of Moral and Religious Anecdotes." With numerous Illustrations. 725 pp. octavo. Cloth, $3.00 ; sheep, $3.50 ; cloth, gilt, $4 00 ; half calf, $4.00.

This is unquestionably the choicest collection of *Anecdotes* ever published. It contains *three thousand and forty Anecdotes:* and such is the wonderful variety, that it will be found an almost inexhaustible fund of interest for every class of readers. The elaborate classification and Indexes must commend it especially to public speakers, to the various classes of *literary and scientific men, to artists, mechanics,* and *others,* as a DICTIONARY *for reference,* in relation to facts on the numberless subjects and characters introduced. There are also more than *one hundred and fifty fine Illustrations.*

THE LIFE OF JOHN MILTON, Narrated in Connection with the POLITICAL, ECCLESIASTICAL, and LITERARY HISTORY OF HIS TIME. By DAVID MASSON, M.A., Professor of English Literature, University College, London. Vol. I., embracing the period from 1608 to 1639. With Portraits, and specimens of his handwriting at different periods. Royal octavo, cloth, $0.00.

This important work will embrace three royal octavo volumes. By special arrangement with Prof. Masson, the author, G. & L. are permitted to print from advance sheets furnished them, as the authorized American publishers of this magnificent and eagerly looked for work. Volumes *two* and *three* will follow in due time : but, as each volume covers a definite period of time, and also embraces distinct topics of discussion or history, they will be published and sold independent of each other, or furnished in sets when the three volumes are completed.

THE GREYSON LETTERS. Selections from the Correspondence of R. E. H. GREYSON, Esq. Edited by HENRY ROGERS, author of "Eclipse of Faith." 12mo, cloth, $1.25.

"Mr. Greyson and Mr. Rogers are one and the same person. The whole work is from his pen, and every letter is radiant with the genius of the author. It discusses a wide range of subjects, in the most attractive manner. It abounds in the keenest wit and humor, satire and logic. It fairly entitles Mr. Rogers to rank with Sydney Smith and Charles Lamb as a wit and humorist, and with Bishop Butler as a reasoner. Mr. Rogers' name will share with those of Butler and Pascal, in the gratitude and veneration of posterity." — *London Quarterly.*

"A book not for one hour, but for all hours ; not for one mood, but for every mood ; to think over, to dream over, to laugh over." — *Boston Journal.*

"The Letters are intellectual gems, radiant with beauty, happily intermingling the grave and the gay. — *Christian Observer.*

ESSAYS IN BIOGRAPHY AND CRITICISM. By PETER BAYNE, M. A., author of "The Christian Life, Social and Individual." Arranged in two Series, or Parts. 12mo, cloth, each, $1.25.

These volumes have been prepared by the author exclusively for his American publishers, and are now published in uniform style. They include nineteen articles, viz. :
FIRST SERIES :— Thomas De Quincy. — Tennyson and his Teachers. — Mrs. Barrett Browning. — Recent Aspects of British Art. — John Ruskin. — Hugh Miller. — The Modern Novel ; Dickens, &c. — Ellis, Acton, and Currer Bell.
SECOND SERIES :— Charles Kingsley. — S. T. Coleridge. — T. B. Macaulay. — Alison. — Wellington. — Napoleon. — Plato. — Characteristics of Christian Civilization. — The Modern University. — The Pulpit and the Press. — Testimony of the Rocks : a Defence.

VISITS TO EUROPEAN CELEBRITIES. By the Rev. WILLIAM B. SPRAGUE, D. D. 12mo, cloth, $1.00 ; cloth, gilt, $1.50.

A series of graphic and life-like Personal Sketches of many of the most distinguished men and women of Europe, portrayed as the Author saw them in their own homes, and under the most advantageous circumstances. Besides these "pen and ink" sketches, the work contains the novel attraction of a *fac-simile of the signature* of each of the persons introduced.　　(28)

CHAMBERS' WORKS.

CHAMBERS' CYCLOPÆDIA OF ENGLISH LITERATURE. A
Selection of the choicest productions of English Authors, from the earliest to the present
time. Connected by a Critical and Biographical History. Forming two large imperial
octavo volumes of 700 pages each, double column letter press; with upwards of 300
elegant Illustrations. Edited by ROBERT CHAMBERS. Cloth, $5.00; sheep, $6.00; full
gilt, $7.50; half calf, $7.50; full calf, $10.00.

This work embraces about one thousand Authors, chronologically arranged, and classed as
poets, historians, dramatists, philosophers, metaphysicians, divines, etc., with choice selections
from their writings, connected by a Biographical, Historical, and Critical Narrative; thus presenting a complete view of English Literature from the earliest to the present time. Let the reader
open where he will, he cannot fail to find matter for profit and delight. The selections are gems —
infinite riches in a little room; in the language of another, "A WHOLE ENGLISH LIBRARY FUSED
DOWN INTO ONE CHEAP BOOK!"

☞ THE AMERICAN edition of this valuable work is enriched by the addition of fine steel and
mezzotint engravings of the heads of SHAKSPEARE, ADDISON, BYRON; a full-length portrait of
DR. JOHNSON; and a beautiful scenic representation of OLIVER GOLDSMITH and DR. JOHNSON.
These important and elegant additions, together with superior paper and binding, and other
improvements, render the AMERICAN far superior to the English edition.

W. H. PRESCOTT, THE HISTORIAN, says, "Readers cannot fail to profit largely by the labors
of the critic who has the talent and taste to separate what is really beautiful and worthy of their
study from what is superfluous."

"I concur in the foregoing opinion of Mr. Prescott."—EDWARD EVERETT.

"A popular work, indispensable to the library of a student of English literature."—DR. WAY-
LAND.

"We hail with peculiar pleasure the appearance of this work."—*North American Review.*

**CHAMBERS' MISCELLANY OF USEFUL AND ENTERTAIN-
ING KNOWLEDGE.** Edited by WILLIAM CHAMBERS. With elegant Illustrative Engravings. Ten volumes. Cloth, $7.50; cloth, gilt, $10.00; library sheep, $10.00.

"It would be difficult to find any miscellany superior or even equal to it. It richly deserves the
epithets 'useful and entertaining,' and I would recommend it very strongly, as extremely well
adapted to form parts of a library for the young, or of a social or circulating library in town or
country."—GEO. B. EMERSON, Esq.—*Chairman Boston School Book Committee.*

CHAMBERS' HOME BOOK; or, Pocket Miscellany, containing a Choice
Selection of Interesting and Instructive Reading, for the Old and Young. Six volumes.
16mo, cloth, $3.00; library sheep, $4.00; half calf, $6.00.

This is considered fully equal, and in some respects superior, to either of the other works of the
Chambers in interest; containing a vast fund of valuable information. It is admirably adapted to
the School or Family Library, furnishing ample variety for every class of readers.

"The Chambers are confessedly the best caterers for popular and useful reading in the world."
— *Willis' Home Journal.*

"A very entertaining, instructive, and popular work."—*N. Y. Commercial.*

"We do not know how it is possible to publish so much good reading matter at such a low
price. We speak a good word for the literary excellence of the stories in this work; we hope our
people will introduce it into all their families, in order to drive away the miserable flashy-trashy
stuff so often found in the hands of our young people of both sexes."—*Scientific American.*

"Both an entertaining and instructive work, as it is certainly a very cheap one."—*Puritan Recorder.*

"If any person wishes to read for amusement or profit, to kill time or improve it, get 'Chambers' Home Book.'"—*Chicago Times.*

**CHAMBERS' REPOSITORY OF INSTRUCTIVE AND AMUS-
ING PAPERS.** With Illustrations. A New Series, containing Original Articles.
Two volumes. 16mo, cloth, $1.75.
THE SAME WORK, two volumes in one, cloth, gilt back, $1.50. (20)

GUYOT'S WORKS.   VALUABLE MAPS.

THE EARTH AND MAN; Lectures on COMPARATIVE PHYSICAL GEOGRAPHY, in its relation to the History of Mankind. By ARNOLD GUYOT. With Illustrations. 12mo, cloth, $1.25.

Prof. LOUIS AGASSIZ, of Harvard University, says : "It will not only render the study of geography more attractive, but actually show it in its true light."

Hon. GEORGE S. HILLARD says : "The work is marked by learning, ability, and taste. His bold and comprehensive generalizations rest upon a careful foundation of facts."

"Those who have been accustomed to regard Geography as a merely descriptive branch of learning, drier than the remainder biscuit after a voyage, will be delighted to find this hitherto unattractive pursuit converted into a science, the principles of which are definite and the results conclusive." — *North American Review.*

"The grand idea of the work is happily expressed by the author, where he calls it the *geographical march of history.* Sometimes we feel as if we were studying a treatise on the exact sciences ; at others, it strikes the ear like an epic poem. Now it reads like history, and now it sounds like prophecy. It will find readers in whatever language it may be published." — *Christian Examiner.*

"The work is one of high merit, exhibiting a wide range of knowledge, great research, and a philosophical spirit of investigation." — *Silliman's Journal.*

COMPARATIVE PHYSICAL AND HISTORICAL GEOGRAPHY; or, the Study of the Earth and Inhabitants. A Series of Graduated Courses, for the use of Schools. By ARNOLD GUYOT. *In preparation.*

GUYOT'S MURAL MAPS. A series of elegant Colored Maps, projected on a large scale for the Recitation Room, consisting of a Map of the World, North and South America, Geographical Elements, &c., exhibiting the Physical Phenomena of the Globe. By Professor ARNOLD GUYOT, viz.,

> MAP OF THE WORLD, *mounted*, $10.00.
> MAP OF NORTH AMERICA, *mounted*, $9.00.
> MAP OF SOUTH AMERICA, *mounted*, $9.00.
> MAP OF GEOGRAPHICAL ELEMENTS, *mounted*, $9.00.

☞ These elegant and entirely original Mural Maps are projected on a large scale, so that when suspended in the recitation room they may be seen from any point, and the delineations without difficulty traced distinctly with the eye. They are beautifully printed in colors, and neatly mounted for use.

GEOLOGICAL MAP OF THE UNITED STATES AND BRITISH PROVINCES OF NORTH AMERICA. With an Explanatory Text, Geological Sections, and Plates of the Fossils which characterize the Formations. By JULES MARCOU. Two volumes. Octavo, cloth, $3.00.

☞ The Map is elegantly colored, and done up with linen cloth back, and folded in octavo form, with thick cloth covers.

"The most complete Geological Map of the United States which has yet appeared. It is a work which all who take an interest in the geology of the United States would wish to possess ; and we recommend it as extremely valuable, not only in a geological point of view, but as representing very fully the coal and copper regions of the country. The explanatory text presents a rapid sketch of the geological constitations of North America, and is rich in facts on the subjects. It is embellished with a number of beautiful plates of the fossils which characterize the formations, thus making, with the map, *a very complete, clear, and distinct outline of the geology of our country.*" — *Mining Magazine, N. Y.*

HALL'S GEOLOGICAL CHART; Giving an Ideal Section of the Successive Geological Formations, with an Actual Section from the Atlantic to the Pacific Oceans. By Prof. JAMES HALL, of Albany. *Mounted*, $9.00.

A KEY TO GEOLOGICAL CHART. By Prof. JAMES HALL. 18mo, 25 cts.

VALUABLE TEXT-BOOKS.

THE LECTURES OF SIR WILLIAM HAMILTON, BART., late Professor of Logic and Metaphysics, University of Edinburgh; embracing the METAPHYSICAL and LOGICAL COURSES ; with Notes, from Original Materials, and an Appendix, containing the Author's Latest Development of his New Logical Theory. Edited by Rev. HENRY LONGUEVILLE MANSEL, B. D., Prof. of Moral and Metaphysical Philosophy in Magdalen College, Oxford, and JOHN VEITCH, M. A., of Edinburgh. In two royal octavo volumes, viz.,

I. METAPHYSICAL LECTURES (*now ready*). Royal octavo, cloth.

II LOGICAL LECTURES (*in preparation*).

☞ G. & L., by a special arrangement with the family of the late Sir William Hamilton, are the Authorized American Publishers of this distinguished author's *matchless* LECTURES ON METAPHYSICS AND LOGIC, and they are permitted to print the same from advance sheets furnished them by the English publishers.

MENTAL PHILOSOPHY; Including the Intellect, the Sensibilities, and the Will. By JOSEPH HAVEN, Prof. of Intellectual and Moral Philosophy, Amherst College. Royal 12mo, cloth, embossed, $1 50.

It is believed this work will be found pre-eminently distinguished.

1. The COMPLETENESS with which it presents the whole subject. Text-books generally treat of only *one class* of faculties ; this work includes the *whole*. 2. It is strictly and thoroughly SCIENTIFIC. 3. It presents a careful analysis of the mind, as a whole. 4. The history and literature of each topic. 5. The latest results of the science. 6. The chaste, yet attractive style. 7. The remarkable condensation of thought.

Prof. PARK, of Andover, says : " It is DISTINGUISHED for its clearness of style, perspicuity of method, candor of spirit, acumen and comprehensiveness of thought."

The work, though so recently published, has met with most remarkable success ; having been already introduced into a large number of the leading colleges and schools in various parts of the country, and bids fair to take the place of every other work on the subject now before the public.

THESAURUS OF ENGLISH WORDS AND PHRASES, so classified and arranged as to facilitate the expression of ideas, and assist in literary composition. New and Improved Edition. By PETER MARK ROGET, late Secretary of the Royal Society, London, &c. Revised and edited, with a List of Foreign Words defined in English, and other additions, by BARNAS SEARS, D. D., President of Brown University. A NEW AMERICAN Edition, with ADDITIONS AND IMPROVEMENTS. 12mo, cloth, $1.50.

This edition is based on the London edition, recently issued. The first American Edition having been prepared by Dr. Sears for *strictly educational purposes*, those words and phrases properly termed " vulgar," incorporated in the original work, were omitted. These expurgated portions have, in the present edition, been *restored*, but by such an arrangement of the matter as not to interfere with the educational purposes of the American editor. Besides this, it contains important additions of words and phrases not in the English edition, making it in *all respects more full and perfect than the author's edition*. The work has already become one of standard authority, both in this country and in Great Britain.

PALEY'S NATURAL THEOLOGY. Illustrated by forty Plates, with Selections from the Notes of Dr. Paxton, and Additional Notes, Original and Selected, with a Vocabulary of Scientific Terms. Edited by JOHN WARE, M. D. Improved edition, with elegant newly engraved plates. 12mo, cloth, embossed, $1.25.

This work is very generally introduced into our best Schools and Colleges throughout the country. An entirely new and beautiful set of Illustrations has recently been procured, which, with other improvements, render it the best and most complete work of the kind extant.

VALUABLE TEXT-BOOKS.

PRINCIPLES OF ZOÖLOGY; Touching the Structure, Development, Distribution, and Natural Arrangement, of the RACES OF ANIMALS, living and extinct, with numerous Illustrations. For the use of Schools and Colleges. Part I. COMPARATIVE PHYSIOLOGY. By LOUIS AGASSIZ and AUGUSTUS A. GOULD. Revised edition, 12mo, cloth, $1.00.

"It is not a mere book, but a work — a real work in the form of a book. Zoölogy is an interesting science, and here is treated with a masterly hand. It is a work adapted to colleges and schools, and no young man should be without it." — *Scientific American.*

"This work places us in possession of information half a century in advance of all our elementary works on this subject. . . . No work of the same dimensions has ever appeared in the English language containing so much new and valuable information."— PROF. JAMES HALL, *Albany.*

"The best book of the kind in our language."— *Christian Examiner.*

PRINCIPLES OF ZOÖLOGY, PART II. Systematic Zoölogy. *In preparation.*

THE ELEMENTS OF GEOLOGY; adapted to Schools and Colleges. With numerous Illustrations. By J. R. LOOMIS, President of Lewisburg University, Pa. 12mo, cloth, 75 cts.

"It is surpassed by no work before the American public." — *M. B. Anderson, LL. D., President Rochester University.*

"This is just such a work as is needed for our schools. We see no reason why it should not take its place as a text-book in all the schools in the land." — *N. Y. Observer.*

"Admirably adapted for use as a text-book in common schools and academies."— *Congregationalist, Boston.*

ELEMENTS OF MORAL SCIENCE. By FRANCIS WAYLAND, D. D., late President of Brown University. 12mo, cloth, $1.25.

MORAL SCIENCE ABRIDGED, and adapted to the use of Schools and Academies, by the Author. Half morocco, 50 cts.

The same, CHEAP SCHOOL EDITION, boards, 25 cts.

This work is used in the Boston Schools, and is exceedingly popular as a text-book wherever it has been adopted.

ELEMENTS OF POLITICAL ECONOMY. By FRANCIS WAYLAND, D. D. 12mo, cloth, $1.25.

POLITICAL ECONOMY ABRIDGED, and adapted to the use of Schools and Academies, by the Author. Half morocco, 50 cts.

"It deserves to be introduced into every private family, and to be studied by every man who has an interest in the wealth and prosperity of his country. It is a subject little understood, even practically, by thousands, and still less understood theoretically. It is to be hoped this will form a class book, and be faithfully studied in our academies, and that it will find its way into every family library; not there to be shut up unread, but to afford rich material for thought and discussion in the family circle." — *Puritan Recorder.*

All the above Works by Dr. Wayland are used as text-books in most of the colleges and higher schools throughout the Union, and are highly approved.

☞ G. & L. keep, in addition to works published by themselves, an extensive assortment of works published by others, in all departments of trade, which they supply at publishers' prices. They invite the attention of Booksellers, Travelling Agents, Teachers, School Committees, Clergymen, and Professional men generally (to whom a liberal discount is uniformly made), to their extensive stock. Copies of Text-books for examination will be sent by mail or otherwise, to any one transmitting ONE HALF the price of the same. ☞ Orders from any part of the country promptly attended to with faithfulness and despatch. **(33)**

VALUABLE WORKS.

THE LIMITS OF RELIGIOUS THOUGHT EXAMINED. By
Henry Longueville Mansel, B. D., Prof. of Moral and Metaphysical Philosophy, Magdalen College, Oxford, Editor of Sir William Hamilton's Lectures, etc. etc. With the Copious Notes of the volume translated for the American Edition. 12mo, cloth, $1.25.

☞ This is a *masterly* production, and may be safely said to be one of the most important works of the day.

FIRST THINGS; or, The Development of Church Life. By Baron Stow, D. D. 16mo, cloth, 75 cts.

HEAVEN. By James William Kimball. With an elegant vignette title-page. 12mo, cloth, $1.00.

" The book is full of beautiful ideas, consoling hopes, and brilliant representations of human destiny, all presented in a chaste, pleasing and very readable style." — *N. Y. Chronicle.*

THE PROGRESS OF BAPTIST PRINCIPLES IN THE LAST HUNDRED YEARS. By T. F. Curtis, Professor of Theology in the Lewisburg University, Pa., and author of " Communion," &c. 12mo, cloth, $1.25.

Eminently worthy of the attention, not only of Baptists, *but of all other denominations.* In his preface the author declares that his aim has been to draw a wide distinction between *parties* and *opinions.* Hence the object of this volume is not to exhibit or defend the Baptists, *but their principles.* It is confidently pronounced the best exhibition of Baptist views and principles extant.

THOUGHTS ON THE PRESENT COLLEGIATE SYSTEM in the United States. By Francis Wayland, D. D. 16mo, cloth, 50 cents.

SACRED RHETORIC; or, Composition and Delivery of Sermons. By H. J. Ripley, D. D., Prof. in Newton Theol. Inst. To which is added, Dr. Ware's Hints on Extemporaneous Preaching. Second thousand. 12mo, cloth, 75 cts.

THE PULPIT OF THE REVOLUTION; or, The Political Sermons of the Era of 1776. With an Introduction, Biographical Sketches of the Preachers and Historical Notes, etc. By John Wingate Thornton, author of " The Landing at Cape Anne," etc. 12mo, cloth. *In press.*

THE EIGHTEEN CHRISTIAN CENTURIES. By the Rev. James White, author of " Landmarks of the History of England." 12mo, cloth. *In press.*

THE PLURALITY OF WORLDS. A New Edition. With a Supplementary Dialogue, in which the author's Reviewers are reviewed. 12mo, cloth, $1.00.

This masterly production, which has excited so much interest in this country and in Europe, will now have an increased attraction in the addition of the Supplement, in which the author's reviewers are triumphantly reviewed.

THE CAMEL; His Organization, Habits, and Uses, considered with reference to his introduction into the United States. By George P. Marsh, late U. S. Minister at Constantinople. 12mo, cloth, 63 cts.

This book treats of a subject of great interest, especially at the present time. It furnishes a more complete and reliable account of the Camel than any other in the language ; indeed, it is believed that there is no other. It is the result of long study, extensive research, and much personal observation, on the part of the author, and it has been prepared with special reference to the experiment of domesticating the Camel in this country, now going on under the auspices of the United States government. It is written in a style worthy of the distinguished author's reputation for great learning and fine scholarship.

(36)

VALUABLE WORKS

PUBLISHED BY

GOULD AND LINCOLN,

59 WASHINGTON STREET, BOSTON.

THE CHRISTIAN LIFE; SOCIAL AND INDIVIDUAL. By PETER BAYNE, M. A. 12mo, cloth, $1.25.

There is but one voice respecting this extraordinary book, — men of all denominations, in all quarters, agree in pronouncing it one of the most admirable works of the age.

MODERN ATHEISM; Under its forms of Pantheism, Materialism, Secularism, Development, and Natural Laws. By JAMES BUCHANAN, D. D., L. L. D. 12mo, cloth, $1.25.

" The work is one of the most readable and solid which we have ever perused." — *Hugh Miller in the Witness.*

NEW ENGLAND THEOCRACY. From the German of Uhden's History of the Congregationalists of New England, with an INTRODUCTION BY NEANDER. By MRS. H. C. CONANT, author of " The English Bible," etc. 12mo, cloth, $1.00.

A work of rare ability and interest, presenting the early religious and ecclesiastical history of New England, from authentic sources, with singular impartiality. The author evidently aimed throughout to do exact justice to the dominant party, and all their opponents of every name. The standpoint from which the whole subject is viewed is novel, and we have in this volume a new and most important contribution to Puritan History.

THE MISSION OF THE COMFORTER; with copious Notes. By JULIUS CHARLES HARE. With the NOTES translated for the AMERICAN EDITION. 12mo, cloth, $1.25.

THE BETTER LAND; or, The Believer's Journey and Future Home. By the Rev. A. C. THOMPSON. 12mo, cloth, 85 cts.

A most charming and instructive book for all now journeying to the " Better Land."

THE EVENING OF LIFE; or, Light and Comfort amidst the Shadows of Declining Years. By REV. JEREMIAH CHAPLIN, D. D. A new Revised, and much enlarged edition. With an elegant Frontispiece on Steel. 12mo, cloth, $1.00.

☞ A most charming and appropriate work for the aged, — large type and open page. An admirable " Gift" for the child to present the parent.

THE STATE OF THE IMPENITENT DEAD. By ALVAH HOVEY, D. D., Prof. of Christian Theology in Newton Theol. Inst. 16mo, cloth, 50 cts.

A WREATH AROUND THE CROSS; or, Scripture Truths Illustrated. By the Rev. A. MORTON BROWN, D. D. Recommendatory Preface, by JOHN ANGELL JAMES. With a beautiful Frontispiece. 16mo, cloth, 60 cts.

"' Christ, and Him crucified 'is presented in a new, striking, and matter-of-fact light. The style is simple, without being puerile, and the reasoning is of that truthful, persuasive kind that ' comes from the heart, and reaches the heart.' " — *N. Y. Observer.*

(11)

WORKS FOR CHURCH MEMBERS.

THE CHRISTIAN'S DAILY TREASURY; a Religious Exercise for every Day in the Year. By Rev. E. TEMPLE. A new and improved edition. 12mo, cloth, $1.00.

☞ A work for every Christian. It is indeed a "Treasury" of good things.

THE SCHOOL OF CHRIST; or, Christianity Viewed in its Leading Aspects. By the Rev. A. R. L. FOOTE, author of "Incidents in the Life of our Saviour," etc. 16mo, cloth, 50 cts.

THE CHRISTIAN PASTOR; His Work and the Needful Preparation. By ALVAH HOVEY, D. D., Prof. of Theology in the Newton Theol. Inst. 16mo, pp. 60; flexible cloth, 25 cents; paper covers, 12 cents.

APOLLOS; or, Directions to Persons just commencing a Religious Life. 32mo, paper covers, cheap, for distribution, per hundred, $6.00.

THE HARVEST AND THE REAPERS. Home Work for All, and how to do it. By Rev. HARVEY NEWCOMB. 16mo, cloth, 63 cts.

This work is dedicated to the converts of 1858. It shows what *may* be done, by showing what has been done. It shows how much there is NOW to be done at home. It shows HOW to do it. Every man interested in the work of saving men, every professing Christian, will find this work to be for him.

THE CHURCH-MEMBER'S MANUAL of Ecclesiastical Principles, Doctrines, and Discipline. By Rev. WILLIAM CROWELL, D. D. Introduction by H. J. RIPLEY, D. D. Second edition, revised and improved. 12mo, cloth, 75 cts.

THE CHURCH-MEMBER'S HAND-BOOK; a Plain Guide to the Doctrines and Practice of Baptist Churches. By the Rev. WILLIAM CROWELL, D. D. 18mo, cloth, 38 cts.

THE CHURCH-MEMBER'S GUIDE. By the Rev. JOHN A. JAMES. Edited by J. O. CHOULES, D. D. New edition. With Introductory Essay, by Rev. HUBBARD WINSLOW. Cloth, 33 cts.

"The spontaneous effusion of our heart, on laying the book down, was: 'May every church-member in our land possess this book, and be blessed with all the happiness which conformity to its evangelical sentiments and directions is calculated to confer.'"— *Christian Secretary.*

THE CHURCH IN EARNEST. By Rev. JOHN A. JAMES. 18mo, cloth, 40 cts.

"Its arguments and appeals are well adapted to prompt to action, and the times demand such a book. We trust it will be universally read."— *N. Y. Observer.*
"Those who have the means should purchase a number of copies of this work, and lend them to church-members, and keep them in circulation *till they are worn out!*"— *Mothers' Assistant.*

CHRISTIAN PROGRESS. A Sequel to the Anxious Inquirer. By JOHN ANGELL JAMES. 18mo, cloth, 31 cts.

☞ One of the best and most useful works of this popular author.

"It ought to be sold by hundreds of thousands, until every church-member in the land has bought, read, marked, learned, and inwardly digested a copy."— *Congregationalist.*
"So eminently is it adapted to do good, that we feel no surprise that it should make one of the publishers' excellent publications. It exhibits the whole subject of growth in grace with great simplicity and clearness."— *Puritan Recorder.*

(12)

VALUABLE NEW WORKS.

GOD REVEALED IN NATURE AND IN CHRIST; including a Refutation of the Development Theory contained in the "Vestiges of the Natural History of Creation." By Rev. JAMES B. WALKER, author of "THE PHILOSOPHY OF THE PLAN OF SALVATION." 12mo, cloth, $1.00.

PHILOSOPHY OF THE PLAN OF SALVATION; a Book for the Times. By an AMERICAN CITIZEN. With an Introductory Essay by CALVIN E. STOWE, D. D. ☞ New improved and enlarged edition. 12mo, cloth, 75 cts.

YAHVEH CHRIST; or, The Memorial Name. By ALEXANDER MACWHORTER. With an Introductory Letter by NATHANIEL W. TAYLOR, D. D., Dwight Professor in Yale Theol. Sem. 16mo, cloth, 60 cts.

SALVATION BY CHRIST. A Series of Discourses on some of the most Important Doctrines of the Gospel. By FRANCIS WAYLAND, D. D. 12mo, cloth, $1 00; cloth, gilt, $1.50.

CONTENTS. — Theoretical Atheism. — Practical Atheism. — The Moral Character of Man. — The Fall of Man. — Justification by Works Impossible. — Preparation for the Advent. — Work of the Messiah. — Justification by Faith. — Conversion. — Imitators of God. — Grieving the Spirit. — A Day in the Life of Jesus. — The Benevolence of the Gospel. — The Fall of Peter. — Character of Balaam. — Veracity. — The Church of Christ. — The Unity of the Church. — Duty of Obedience to the Civil Magistrate (three Sermons).

THE GREAT DAY OF ATONEMENT; or, Meditations and Prayers on the Last Twenty-four Hours of the Sufferings and Death of Our Lord and Saviour Jesus Christ. Translated from the German of CHARLOTTE ELIZABETH NEBELIN. Edited by MRS. COLIN MACKENZIE. Elegantly printed and bound. 16mo, cloth, 75 cts.

THE EXTENT OF THE ATONEMENT IN ITS RELATION TO GOD AND THE UNIVERSE. By Rev. THOMAS W. JENKYN, D. D., late President of Coward College, London. 12mo, cloth, $1.00.

This work was thoroughly revised by the author not long before his death, exclusively for the present publishers. It has long been a standard work, and without doubt presents the most complete discussion of the subject in the language.

"We consider this volume as setting the long and fiercely agitated question as to the extent of the Atonement completely at rest. Posterity will thank the author till the latest ages for his illustrious argument." — *New York Evangelist.*

THE SUFFERING SAVIOUR; or, Meditations on the Last Days of Christ. By FRED. W. KRUMMACHER, D. D., author of "Elijah the Tishbite." 12mo, cloth, $1.25.

" The narrative is given with thrilling vividness, and pathos, and beauty. Marking, as we proceeded, several passages for quotation, we found them in the end so numerous, that we must refer the reader to the work itself." — *News of the Churches (Scottish).*

THE IMITATION OF CHRIST. By THOMAS A KEMPIS. With an Introductory Essay, by THOMAS CHALMERS, D. D. Edited by HOWARD MALCOM, D. D. A new edition, with a LIFE OF THOMAS A KEMPIS, by Dr. C. ULLMANN, author of "Reformers before the Reformation." 12mo, cloth, 85 cts.

This may safely be pronounced the best Protestant edition extant of this ancient and celebrated work. It is reprinted from Payne's edition, collated with an ancient Latin copy. The peculiar feature of this new edition is the improved page, the elegant, large, clear type, and the NEW LIFE OF A KEMPIS, by Dr. Ullmann.

VALUABLE BIOGRAPHIES.

EXTRACTS FROM THE DIARY AND CORRESPONDENCE OF THE LATE AMOS LAWRENCE. With a brief account of some Incidents in his Life. Edited by his son, WM. R. LAWRENCE, M. D. With elegant Portraits of Amos and Abbott Lawrence, an Engraving of their Birthplace, an Autograph page of Handwriting, and a copious Index. One large octavo volume, cloth, $1.50 ; royal 12mo, cloth, $1.00

A MEMOIR OF THE LIFE AND TIMES OF ISAAC BACKUS. By ALVAH HOVEY, Professor of Ecclesiastical History in Newton Theological Institution. 12mo, cloth, $1.25.

This work gives an account of a remarkable man, and of a remarkable movement in the middle of the last century, resulting in the formation of what were called the " Separate " Churches. It supplies an important deficiency in the history of New England affairs. For every Baptist, especially, it is a necessary book.

LIFE OF JAMES MONTGOMERY. By Mrs. H. C. KNIGHT, author of " Lady Huntington and her Friends," &c. Likeness and elegant Illustrated Title-Page on steel. 12mo, cloth, $1.25.

This is an original biography, prepared from the abundant but ill-digested materials contained in the seven octavo volumes of the London edition. The Christian public in America will welcome such a memoir of a poet whose hymns and sacred melodies have been the delight of every household.

MEMOIR OF ROGER WILLIAMS, Founder of the State of Rhode Island. By Prof. WILLIAM GAMMELL, A. M. 16mo, cloth, 75 cts.

PHILIP DODDRIDGE. His Life and Labors. By JOHN STOUGHTON, D. D. With an Introductory Chapter, by Rev. JAMES G. MIALL, Author of " Footsteps of our Forefathers," &c. With beautiful Illustrated Title-page and Frontispiece. 16mo, cloth, 60 cents.

THE LIFE AND CORRESPONDENCE OF JOHN FOSTER. Edited by J. E. RYLAND, with notices of Mr. Foster, as a Preacher and a Companion. By JOHN SHEPPARD. A new edition, two volumes in one, 790 pages. 12mo, cloth, $1.25.

" In simplicity of language, in majesty of conception, his writings are unmatched." — *North British Review.*

THE LIFE OF GODFREY WILLIAM VON LEIBNITZ. By JOHN M. MACKIE, Esq. On the basis of the German work of Dr. G. K. GUHRAUER. 16mo, cloth, 75 cts

" It merits the special notice of all who are interested in the business of education, and deserves a place by the side of Brewster's Life of Newton, in all the libraries of our schools, academies, and literary institutions." — *Watchman and Reflector.*

MEMORIES OF A GRANDMOTHER. By a Lady of Massachusetts. 16mo, cloth, 50 cts.

☞ " My path lies in a valley, which I have sought to adorn with flowers. Shadows from the hills cover it ; but I make my own sunshine." — *Author's Preface.*

THE TEACHER'S LAST LESSON. A Memoir of MARTHA WHITING, late of the Charlestown Female Seminary, with Reminiscences and Suggestive Reflections. By CATHARINE N. BADGER, an Associate Teacher. With a Portrait, and an Engraving of the Seminary. 12mo, cloth, $1.00.

The subject of this Memoir was, for a quarter of a century, at the head of one of the most celebrated female seminaries in the country. During that period she educated more than *three thousand* young ladies. She was a kindred spirit to Mary Lyon.

(17)

WORKS FOR BIBLE STUDENTS.

KITTO'S POPULAR CYCLOPÆDIA OF BIBLICAL LITERA TURE. Condensed from the larger work. By the Author, JOHN KITTO, D. D. Assisted by JAMES TAYLOR, D. D., of Glasgow. With over five hundred Illustrations. One volume, octavo, 812 pp. Cloth, $3.00; sheep, $3.50; cloth, gilt, $4 00; half calf, $4.00.

A DICTIONARY OF THE BIBLE. Serving, also, as a COMMENTARY, embodying the products of the best and most recent researches in biblical literature in which the scholars of Europe and America have been engaged. The work, the result of immense labor and research, and enriched by the contributions of writers of distinguished eminence in the various departments of sacred literature, has been, by universal consent, pronounced the best work of its class extant, and the one best suited to the advanced knowledge of the present day In all the studies connected with theological science. It is not only intended for ministers and theological students, but it is also particularly adapted to parents, Sabbath-school teachers, and the great body of the religious public.

THE HISTORY OF PALESTINE, from the Patriarchal Age to the Present Time; with Chapters on the Geography and Natural History of the Country, the Customs and Institutions of the Hebrews. By JOHN KITTO, D. D. With upwards of two hundred Illustrations. 12mo, cloth, $1.25.

☞ A work admirably adapted to the Family, the Sabbath, and the week-day School Library.

ANALYTICAL CONCORDANCE TO THE HOLY SCRIP- TURES; or, the Bible presented under Distinct and Classified Heads or Topics. By JOHN EADIE, D. D., LL. D., Author of "Biblical Cyclopædia," "Ecclesiastical Cyclopædia," "Dictionary of the Bible," etc. One volume, octavo, 840 pp. Cloth, $3.00; sheep, $3.50; cloth, gilt, $4.00; half Turkey morocco, $4.00.

The object of this Concordance is to present the SCRIPTURES ENTIRE, under certain classified and exhaustive heads. It differs from an ordinary Concordance, in that its arrangement depends not on WORDS, but on SUBJECTS, and the verses *are printed in full.* Its plan does not bring it at all into competition with such limited works as those of Gaston and Warden; for they select *doctrinal* topics principally, and do not profess to comprehend as this THE ENTIRE BIBLE. The work also contains a Synoptical Table of Contents of the whole work, presenting in brief a system of biblical antiquities and theology, with a very copious and accurate index.

The value of this work to ministers and Sabbath-school teachers can hardly be over-estimated; and it needs only to be examined, to secure the approval and patronage of every Bible student.

CRUDEN'S CONDENSED CONCORDANCE. A Complete Concordance to the Holy Scriptures. By ALEXANDER CRUDEN. Revised and Re-edited by the Rev. DAVID KING, LL. D. Octavo, cloth backs, $1.25; sheep, $1.50.

The condensation of the quotations of Scripture, arranged under the most obvious heads, while it *diminishes the bulk* of the work, *greatly facilitates* the finding of any required passage.

"We have in this edition of Cruden the *best* made *better.* That is, the present is better adapted to the purposes of a Concordance, by the erasure of superfluous references, the omission of unnecessary explanations, and the contraction of quotations, &c. It is better as a manual, and is better adapted by its price to the means of many who need and ought to possess such a work, than the former large and expensive edition."—*Puritan Recorder.*

A COMMENTARY ON THE ORIGINAL TEXT OF THE ACTS OF THE APOSTLES. By HORATIO B. HACKETT, D. D., Prof. of Biblical Literature and Interpretation, in the Newton Theol. Inst. ☞ A new, revised, and enlarged edition. Royal octavo, cloth, $2.25.

☞ This most important and very popular work has been thoroughly revised; large portions entirely re-written, with the addition of *more than one hundred pages of new matter;* the result of the author's continued, laborious investigations and travels, since the publication of the first edition,